Discover the series you can'

'A high level of realism . . . the actio
fast. Like the father of the modern thriller, Fredeₐₗₑₐ
Mariani has a knack for embedding his plots in the fears
and preoccupations of their time'

Shots Magazine

'The plot was thrilling . . . but what is all the more thrilling
is the fantastic way Mariani moulds historical events into
his story'

Guardian

'Scott Mariani is an ebook powerhouse'

The Bookseller

'Hums with energy and pace . . . If you like your conspira-
cies twisty, your action bone-jarring, and your heroes
impossibly dashing, then look no further. The Ben Hope
series is exactly what you need'

Mark Dawson

'Slick, serpentine, sharp, and very, very entertaining. If you've
got a pulse, you'll love Scott Mariani; if you haven't, then
maybe you crossed Ben Hope'

Simon Toyne

'Hits thrilling, suspenseful notes . . . a rollickingly good way
to spend some time in an easy chair'

USA Today

'Mariani constructs the thriller with skill and intelligence, staging some good action scenes, and Hope is an appealing protagonist'

Kirkus Reviews

'If you haven't read any Mariani before but love fast-paced action with a historical reference, maybe this one won't be your last'

LibraryThing

'A breathtaking ride through England and Europe'

Suspense Magazine

'This is my first Scott Mariani book . . . and I totally loved it. It goes on at a good pace, and for me Ben Hope was brilliant, the ultimate decent good guy that you are rooting for'

AlwaysReading.net

'Scott Mariani writes fantastic thrillers. His series of Ben Hope books shows no sign of slowing down'

Ben Peyton, actor (*Bridget Jones's Diary, Band of Brothers, Nine Lives*)

'A really excellent series of books, and would make a wonderful television series as well!'

Breakaway Reviews

'Scott Mariani seamlessly weaves the history and action together. His descriptive passages are highly visual, and no word is superfluous. The storyline flows from beginning to end; I couldn't put it down'

Off the Shelf Books

GRAVEYARD OF EMPIRES

Scott Mariani is the author of the worldwide-acclaimed action-adventure thriller series featuring ex-SAS hero Ben Hope, which has sold millions of copies in Scott's native UK alone. His books have been described as 'James Bond meets Jason Bourne, with a historical twist'. The first Ben Hope book, The Alchemist's Secret, spent six straight weeks at #1 on Amazon's Kindle chart, and all the others have been Sunday Times bestsellers. Scott was born in Scotland, studied in Oxford and now lives and writes in a remote setting in rural west Wales. You can find out more about Scott and his work on his official website: www.scottmariani.com

By the same author:

Ben Hope series
The Alchemist's Secret
The Mozart Conspiracy
The Doomsday Prophecy
The Heretic's Treasure
The Shadow Project
The Lost Relic
The Sacred Sword
The Armada Legacy
The Nemesis Program
The Forgotten Holocaust
The Martyr's Curse
The Cassandra Sanction
Star of Africa
The Devil's Kingdom
The Babylon Idol
The Bach Manuscript
The Moscow Cipher
The Rebel's Revenge
Valley of Death
House of War
The Pretender's Gold
The Demon Club
The Pandemic Plot
The Crusader's Cross
The Silver Serpent

To find out more visit **www.scottmariani.com**

SCOTT MARIANI

GRAVEYARD

OF

EMPIRES

Harper
North

HarperNorth
Windmill Green,
Mount Street,
Manchester, M2 3NX

A division of
HarperCollins*Publishers*
1 London Bridge Street
London SE1 9GF

www.harpercollins.co.uk

HarperCollinsPublishers
Macken House, 39/40 Mayor Street Upper
Dublin1
D01 C9W8 Ireland

First published by HarperNorth in 2022

1 3 5 7 9 10 8 6 4 2

A catalogue record for this book
is available from the British Library

ISBN: 978-000-850571-4

Printed and bound in the UK using 100% renewable
electricity at CPI Group (UK) Ltd

This book is produced from independently certified FSC™ paper
to ensure responsible forest management.

For more information visit: www.harpercollins.co.uk/green

GRAVEYARD OF EMPIRES

for Sifu
Once known, forever loved, never forgotten

PROLOGUE

Afghanistan, February 1989

Rigby Cahill paused on the steep, rocky slope to catch his breath, condensation billowing in great clouds from his rasping lungs. The icy mountain wind burned his cheeks raw and his hands felt numb. Pushing sixty years of age, he wondered if maybe he was getting too old for this kind of stuff.

He and his team of Afghan diggers had climbed several hundred metres from the valley far below. The small convoy of vehicles that had brought them as far as they could up the mountainside looked like miniature models from up here. Abdul and the others halted for a moment while their boss stood panting and gasping a few moments longer. One or two of them exchanged private grins at the expense of the wealthy American guy who was paying them for this little expedition. Paying a lot of money, because this was by no means a safe place to be. The men were all carrying rifles as well as shovels and picks.

'Give me a minute, guys,' Rigby said. As he clapped his hands to get the circulation going again he gazed at the landscape around him, the same bleakly majestic scenery that had remained completely unchanged since Alexander the Great had marched his vast army though these same mountains, more than three hundred years before the birth of Christ. Even back in Alexander's day this land had already been steeped in ancient history and soaked in the blood of countless dead. So many wars had been fought, so many had cruelly perished here. But Rigby understood the truth: that it was this barren, hostile, pitiless place itself that had been the ruination of every successive invading force, no matter how powerful, that had tried to make their conquest against it.

That was an intimidating thought for an outsider like Rigby Cahill, however well intentioned, who had made it his business to travel from a faraway land to disturb Afghanistan's ancient secrets and wake up its ghosts. Hunting for lost antiquities was what he did for a living, whether it was relocating caches of stolen art from Nazi treasure trains, diving on sunken galleons off the coast of Sumatra or hacking through the South American jungle in search of Paititi, the fabled Incan City of Gold. He was no stranger to the some-times hostile and dangerous corners of the world. And yet, this place haunted him. The looming white-capped mountains seemed to be watching, as though they knew something. The eerie moaning whistle of the wind made Rigby shiver with something more than cold.

He moved on, but only a few steps before he halted again, thinking he could make out a different sound half masked behind that of the wind. A distant crackling rumble. Like an earthquake, perhaps. Or a faraway clap of thunder? Craning his neck upwards he scanned the wintry pallor of the sky, a vast great dome above them, the cold sun directly overhead reflecting dazzlingly against the snowy peaks. He couldn't see a single cloud. He glanced quizzically at Abdul, who shook his head with a knowing look and said, 'Gunfire. The Mujahideen are not far away. We must be careful.'

They trekked onwards and upwards, dislodging rocks that tumbled down the slope. Now and then the crackle of distant gunfire still reached their ears, and the atmosphere was tense among the men. With the Soviets gone, the war was technically over; but the Afghan Mujahideen warriors were still everywhere, armed to the teeth and ready for action, while the political situation in general remained extremely unstable. Trouble was liable to erupt again at any time, and Rigby was painfully aware that time, itself, was a commodity he might not have much of.

It took them another half-hour or so of climbing before they finally reached the spot. Rigby checked his map once more and looked around him, orientating himself from his memory of last time he'd visited this place. That was ten years ago, back in 1979 just before the Russian tanks and troops had flooded into Afghanistan and made a mess of his plans, forcing him to abandon his search after such a tantalisingly promising start. All this time he'd been jumping with impatience to come back here and find out whether his instincts had been right, that the tentative discovery of the gold coins pointed to the existence of something far greater. If so, he could only hope and pray that nobody else had beaten him to it the intervening years.

This was it now. The moment of truth.

The men stood in a silent circle around him as Rigby crouched down and examined the ground. There were no particular landmarks anywhere, barely a wind-torn bush, nothing but rock; but he'd pictured this spot so many times in his mind during the past ten years that it was burned deep into his memory. Yes, here was the big stone under which he'd found the hollow containing the small but sensational cache of gold Alexandrine coins. His heart had been fluttering like a butterfly on that day ten years ago, just like it was doing now.

A decade of anxiety was at an end. In all these years, his discovery had remained safe. If he was right about what might lie buried here, then it was all his for the finding!

He nodded, barely able to contain his excitement. 'This is the place,' he said to Abdul, the only one of the digger team who spoke English. 'Let's get started.'

'Right here?' Abdul said, pointing straight down at his feet.

Rigby hesitated, casting his expert eye over the ground as though it were an X-ray machine that could discern the shapes of ancient city walls buried deep under all those tons of rock and dirt. Trusting his intuition he motioned to a slight mound a few yards away. 'Let's try over there instead.' He directed them to spread out a little and dig in different parts of it, to scatter their risk of missing the right spot.

The men propped their rifles against boulders, unslung their packs, grabbed their shovels and picks and set to work. Rigby stood back and watched, but his impatience soon got the better of him and he grabbed a pick for himself and joined them. He was physically quite out of shape, as the climb had proved, but now his enthusiasm was unstoppable as he hacked and chipped breathlessly away. Gradually, they hollowed out the top of the mound and spread their efforts over the surrounding area. It was tough work and sweat stung Rigby's eyes despite the cold. The distant gunfire seemed to have died away, though he was barely even aware of it.

Just when Rigby was beginning to doubt his judgement as to where they should be digging, his pick blade hit something hard that gave a dull clang unlike the sound of a normal rock. He kept working at it, pouring sweat and puffing like an asthmatic rhinoceros, and within a few more minutes he'd uncovered what appeared to be the corner of a stone block. He got down on his knees and carefully brushed away the loose dirt. The block's straight edges were chipped and crumbled with age but beyond any doubt a manmade object. There was another one right beside it, some bits of the ancient mortar still visible.

He called to the workers and showed them what he'd discovered, and they all started digging energetically to uncover more of it. 'Careful, careful,' he kept urging them, even though none except Abdul could understand a word he said. 'These stone blocks are over two thousand years old!'

The hours dragged wearily by. Shovel load by shovel load, boulder by boulder, they stripped away the rubble of two millennia and the first tantalising outline of the ancient walls revealed itself. The temperature had dropped a couple more degrees as evening approached, and Rigby's teeth were chattering. The threatening gunfire in the distance was long gone by now, but that didn't mean that the Mujahideen warriors wouldn't be back. Many different units belonging to different factions patrolled these hills regularly, on foot, in jeeps or on horseback, bristling with weapons. These were lean, tough, battle-hardened, implacable men who'd known nothing but fighting and hardship all their lives. After years of bitter guerrilla war, with backing from their secret allies the CIA, they'd managed to defeat the might of the USSR. What enemy would they set their sights on next?

The light was beginning to fail by the time Rigby's men had unearthed the rectangular shape of a large stone slab, broad and long enough to be the floor base of a significant building. There was no longer much doubt in Rigby's mind of what they were looking at, but he still needed the final proof.

It wouldn't be long before he had it.

Through a five-inch-wide crack in the floor slab, Rigby shone a torch to see that beneath it was a hollow chamber of indeterminate size, partially collapsed. As he angled the light this way and that his heart leapt at the unmistakable glimmer of gold from within. Abdul was poised at his shoulder, peering intently through the crack and seeing what he saw. The Afghan's normally laconic expression filled with excitement.

Now, their tiredness completely forgotten, they set about widening the crack to get at what was inside. 'Gently, gently!' Rigby said over and over. 'Don't do any more damage than you have to!' Using crowbars they carefully worked at the gap until it was possible for the most slightly built of them, a fourteen-year-old boy called Safi, to slip through and drop down into the hollow space below. Rigby was worried that the chamber might collapse and bury the boy alive.

The casket was much too heavy for young Safi to bring up, so they had to lower a rope with a sling attached and haul it up through the gap, swaying and swinging precariously as it inched upwards. Rigby was hoarse from repeatedly urging caution. At last, the casket was through the gap, grabbed by eager hands that set the swinging golden oblong box carefully down on the ground. At the same moment there was a cry from inside the chamber, and for a heart-stopping instant Rigby thought something terrible must have happened to the boy. But no, Safi had found another casket!

The second casket was soon joined by a third, then a fourth, all laid out in a row. By the light of torches and lanterns Rigby knelt on the ground and used a brush to wipe away the filth of millennia to reveal the royal seal of Alexander the Great cast in gold on the side of the first casket.

This was it. The final, irrefutable proof he'd hoped to find. He bowed his head, almost weeping with emotion as thousands of years of history seemed to flash in front of him. He murmured, 'My God. We found it. We found it.'

The men were hopping from foot to foot with excitement. Rigby took out a penknife and gently, oh so gently, prised open the seal of the first casket lid. As the lid came up, he breathed in the air that had been trapped inside for some 2,300 years.

But nothing could have totally prepared him for what the casket contained. He reached in a trembling hand and came out with a fistful of glinting gold. Coins, jewellery, figurines. Magnificent objects from the time of Alexander. More, far far more, than had ever been found in one place before now.

It was unbelievable. Dizzying. He'd come here simply in the hope of uncovering the Alexandrian lost city of Zakara. This was a hundred times – no, a thousand times – beyond what he could have dreamed of. And for all they knew, there could be dozens more caskets buried inside the chamber.

By now Safi had come up from the hole and was standing behind Rigby's shoulder, Abdul at the other, staring at the loot like hungry hawks. As they all watched, Rigby opened the second casket. It was even fuller than the first. Then the third.

Rigby had tears in his eyes. He couldn't tear his gaze away.

Abdul's initial excitement seemed to have died down, and he was looking thoughtful. He muttered, 'Who does this belong to?'

'It belongs to Afghanistan,' Rigby told him. 'To your country. It'll be the finest exhibit in the state museum in Kabul.'

Abdul shook his head. He said softly, 'No.'

Rigby wasn't quite sure he'd heard right. 'What do you mean, no?'

The *clack* of a rifle bolt in the darkness. Rigby's blood froze. He turned slowly to see the muzzle of the weapon pointing in his face, held by Safi.

Abdul said, 'No. It belongs to us.'

Chapter 1

Ben Hope often reflected on all the bad things he'd done in his life. The failures, the mistakes, the disappointments, the times when he hadn't managed to achieve what he'd set out to do, or had fallen short of the rigorous standards he expected of himself. The people he'd hurt, sometimes intentionally, sometimes not. Whatever his professional track record might indicate about his character and integrity, however many personal sacrifices he'd made in the pursuit of doing good, and in spite of his history of saving lives and bringing justice to the wrongdoers of this world, there were moments when all he could see about himself was fault and weakness, and his mind was preyed on by remorse and self-blame over the path he'd taken in his life.

And yet, for all that, in his more reflective moments even he had to admit that he must have done some good things too. Because every now and then, according to the laws of fate, or karma, or whatever obscure metaphysical forces were responsible for the allocation of recompenses and just deserts, as the case may be, an unexpected reward came to him that he couldn't otherwise have deserved.

One such reward was close beside him at this moment, as the pair of them stood there alone on the empty, windswept beach, clasping hands, listening to the crash and boom of the waves breaking on the shore and watching the glimmering orange ball of the sun dip gradually over the sea.

Neither one of them spoke until the sun had finally vanished behind the horizon, the distant cloud banks like a mountain range glowing in a dramatic blaze of crimsons, golds and purples. Then the colour slowly faded, the spectacle died away and the chill of dusk began to set in.

She leaned her head against his shoulder and tenderly squeezed his hand. 'Our last sunset,' she said.

'It didn't have to be,' he replied.

'You know it did, Ben.'

Her name was Abbie Logan, and she'd been part of his life – pretty much his whole life in fact – for the last six weeks. They had met by chance in her native Australia, and then a romantic impulse (not something that often occurred in Ben's daily existence) had prompted him to invite her to come back to France with him.

Half English, half Irish on his mother's side, he had moved around a great deal in his past, both during and since his military days; but for some years now he'd been settled in a quiet corner of Normandy, a place called Le Val. Abbie had never been to Europe before, never known anywhere outside of the Northern Territory in which she'd been born and raised.

Their time together had been among the happiest that Ben could remember: showing her some of his favourite haunts, walking around the ancient woods and rolling green fields that surrounded Le Val, swimming in the sea, hiking in the hills, introducing Abbie to some of the local cuisine, and generally enjoying one another's company to the utmost. They'd managed to compress six months' worth of intense romance into as many weeks, and sometimes it had seemed to him that it could go on forever. But after a lot of heart-felt discussion, the two of them had come to the mutual acceptance that this couldn't be the love of their lives. Abbie had her own life to return to, her own direction, her roots in her beloved Northern Territory and the responsibility of running the successful air charter business she'd inherited from her late father. As much as she'd treasured every moment of her time here with Ben and would never forget it, this just wasn't her world. And so the time would soon be coming for them to part ways. One final night together, and she'd be leaving in the morning.

'I'm going to miss you, Abbie Logan,' he repeated for the hundredth time that day, wrapping his arm around her shoulders and drawing her in tight. She brushed a lock of blond hair away from her face and smiled up at him with a twinkle of those impossibly blue eyes.

'I'm going to miss you too, Ben Hope,' she replied. 'Until the next time, eh? Australia's not that far to travel, for a globe-trotting adventurer like you.'

'You just try to keep me away,' he replied.

But they both knew in their hearts that tomorrow morning would probably be the last time they would see each other. Ben ached at the thought of losing her. But what else could he do? Propose marriage? He could imagine her response: 'Why spoil a good thing, Ben?' And he'd have had to agree.

Abbie had travelled to France in unlikely style, on a private jet belonging to Ben's sister's business corporation, Steiner Industries. It wasn't exactly a typical mode of transport for Ben either, and how that situation had come about was a long story. Whatever the case, despite being a keen pilot with a passion for aircraft and a particular admiration for Ruth's sleek white Bombardier Global, Abbie had staunchly refused to be indulged in such privileged luxuries for the return trip. Early next morning he drove her the twenty kilometres from Le Val to the airport at Cherbourg, where her commercial flight was due to depart at ten. Neither of them wanted a big emotional farewell. By unspoken mutual consent no sloppy sentiments, and especially not the dreaded words 'I love you' or anything like them, were to be expressed. She gave him a tight hug, a last quick kiss, and then she was gone.

He stood outside the terminal and lit a Gauloise in the mid-morning sunshine as her plane took off. He watched it until it disappeared into the distance, then crushed out his cigarette, turned his back and walked slowly with a heavy heart to his BMW Alpina.

'Well, that's that,' he said to his German shepherd, Storm, who was waiting for him in the back of the car. The seats were all nicely matted with black, tan and golden dog hair. He thumped his tail happily and made a little whimper.

'You liked her, didn't you?' Ben asked him.

Thump, thump.

'Yeah. Me too. Between you and me, buddy, I think I liked her a little too much. Anyway, let's go home.'

The old stone house at Le Val stood on the site of an even older manor dating back to medieval times. During its history the place had been a farm, one of the many that dotted Ben's peaceful rural area. But in its modern incarnation, since Ben and his old friend Jeff Dekker had bought the property as a base for their then newly founded business, the house stood hidden from the quiet country road at the end of a long track guarded by high gates and surrounded by an impenetrable wire mesh fence that enclosed the whole sizeable acreage like a military base.

The need for such an impressive level of security was down to the nature of the work that went on there. Le Val was designated as a tactical training facility, which meant that Ben, Jeff, their associate Tuesday Fletcher and the small, hand-picked team of employees were involved in teaching some highly specialised skills to delegations of military, police, security and VIP protection personnel who travelled from all over Europe and beyond to learn from the best teachers in the business.

What made the Le Val team so uniquely qualified to pass on such expertise was, in large part, the military background of its two principal founders. Ben had spent well over a decade serving in theatres of war all over the world with 22 SAS, the British army's most elite special forces regiment, working his way up to a final rank of major before he'd quit to go freelance, locating and rescuing kidnap victims held for ransom. Jeff's career had been on the naval side, an equally long stint with the Special Boat Service, the SAS's waterborne counterpart. Between them, Ben and Jeff had a wealth of tactical experience second to none – not to mention the almost supernatural skills brought to the table by the redoubtable Tuesday Fletcher, ex-army sniper *extraordinaire*.

The training facilities at Le Val included two firing ranges, a so-called 'killing house' modelled on the one used to train SAS troopers in the finer points of close-quarter battle, an extensive cross-country area over which they practised evasion and survival techniques, a track and skid pan where defensive driving skills were sharpened up, and more besides. Almost from Day One, their teaching courses had been in such demand that there was a waiting list a mile long and the place was nearly always buzzing with activity.

All of which made the current quiet spell they were enjoying rather unusual. They didn't exactly *do* holidays at Le Val, but since Ben and Jeff had returned from Australia, where they'd been attending to some urgent family business of Jeff's, the two had each had their separate reasons for taking some time out of the normally hectic schedule. Ben's reason was Abbie, with whom he'd been so preoccupied lately; while Jeff had needed the rest period to recuperate from a broken collar bone and a nasty injury to his hand, sustained during their eventful trip away. The hand had been attended to by doctors back in Australia but caused some concern to his surgeon here in France. After two delicate operations, it was on the mend but still not fully operational, though the prognosis was optimistic.

And then to cap it all, Jeff had now come down with some kind of summer flu bug that had reduced him to a sneezing, sniffling, watery-eyed, red-nosed miserable wreck for the last several days. Jeff being Jeff, though, he had fiercely refused to surrender to his condition and go to bed like a normal person, instead confining himself to the living-room sofa where he spent his days huddled under a blanket, slurping mugs of hot lemon juice with honey and whisky (Ben's special recipe, made with an extra-generous slug of his favourite single malt scotch) and griping incessantly at the television.

Nobody would have denied that Jeff Dekker possessed a great many admirable qualities as a person, but he absolutely made for the world's most cantankerous, irritable and difficult patient. Unable to stand it any longer, Tuesday had taken advantage of the quiet spell to fly off for a week to Jamaica, where he had about a thousand brothers, sisters, cousins and assorted other relatives.

So it was a much emptier house than usual to which Ben came home on his return from the airport – all the more depressingly so, now that Abbie was gone. Empty, but not silent. As Ben walked inside the front hallway with Storm trotting happily at his heels, he could hear the sound of the TV from down the long, narrow passage. It was a rare thing for anyone at Le Val to watch television, partly because Ben didn't much care for idly goggling at a screen, and also because they were usually far too busy with more important matters.

He walked along the passage towards the living room. It sounded as though Jeff was watching the news, as he'd been doing virtually around the clock these last days. TV news was another thing Ben didn't much care for, considering that much of what the mainstream media reported was a pile of barefaced lies and propaganda. Along with the sound of the commentator, Jeff's voice could be heard raised in an indignant protest at whatever was being talked about.

Ben paused at the door, steeling himself for another round of his friend's irascible moods, then opened it and went in.

Jeff was sitting there with his mug, his blanket, and an angry scowl that softened only slightly as Ben walked into the room.

'What's up?' Ben asked.

Jeff jabbed an accusing finger at the screen. 'Oh, you should see this, mate. Things are going from bad to worse out there. Those stupid bloody bastards couldn't have made a bigger balls-up of it if they'd done it on purpose.'

Chapter 2

'I don't want to see it,' Ben said, deliberately averting his eyes from the television. But even without taking in the images on the screen he knew exactly what Jeff was talking about. Ben hadn't been so tied up with Abbie Logan these last few weeks as to be blind to what was going on in the rest of the world. Specifically, the political situation that had been rapidly, and disastrously, unfolding in a particular part of the world that Ben happened to know very well.

It was always the same tired old story. Every time a large-scale military operation stood down after months or even years of presence in a foreign country, even when the campaign had been more or less successful the withdrawal necessarily created scenes of absolute chaos, both among the bewildered civilians and even among the troops, who often had little clue what was going on. And in this particular case, the situation was far, far worse, because the campaign had been going on for a long, long time and been anything but successful.

After two decades of the most unproductive and costly war since its humiliating retreat from Vietnam some forty-five years earlier, the US army had finally withdrawn from

Afghanistan. As many had predicted, it was an inglorious ending to a largely worthless campaign. Though US leaders had been mooting the pull-out for years and had had any amount of time to prepare adequately, in the event they'd managed to botch things so badly that a large number of fellow Americans and their allies, men, women and children, had been left stranded at the mercy of the country's new rulers. And as everyone had known and feared would happen, those new rulers were the Taliban, a hardcore fundamentalist regime that had grown up out of the complex and conflicted military and political situation of recent decades. The whole damn picture was so muddied by covert CIA and other shadowy intelligence influences, secret allegiances and under-the-table political dealing that it had become an inextricable mess. Ben doubted that anyone would ever know the real, whole truth. And he certainly wasn't interested in trying to figure it out.

Looking perplexed by Ben's reaction, Jeff snatched up the TV remote and hit the mute button. 'Why don't you want to see it?' he asked in the sudden silence of the room.

'Because it's none of my affair,' Ben replied simply.

Jeff shook his head. 'Bollocks. You were there in Afghanistan, back in the day. You knew the situation on the ground better than anyone.'

'Did I? Did any of us really have a clue what we were doing there?'

'Except we risked our bloody lives, and a lot of us lost theirs.'

'True enough,' Ben said. 'Fighting a so-called war on terror that nobody could ever hope to win. And for what,

Jeff? What did we achieve, except support the official narrative that was all based on lies and deception?'

'I can't believe you really mean that,' Jeff protested. 'You of all people.'

'I do, and I'm sick of the whole thing. That's why I'm not interested in sitting there all day staring at the television. It was never really our fight and in any case it's all over now. End of story.'

'Hold on a minute—'

'I'm not getting drawn into this,' Ben said. 'Enjoy the show, but leave me out. I'm not bothered, okay?'

He and Jeff saw eye to eye on most subjects, and in all the years they'd known one another there had seldom been a disagreement. But before this discussion could turn argumentative, Ben withdrew from the room and closed the door behind him. Lingering there for just a moment before he walked away, he heard the TV volume come back on and Jeff resume his angry grumbling. Angry at Ben now, too, for his lack of interest.

Ben sighed, left his friend to it and headed back outside into the sunshine. It was a fine, warm day and he had relatively little to do. Storm had followed him from the house and was sitting there looking up at him expectantly with those golden-amber eyes full of intelligence and his jaws open in the nearest thing to a doggy smile. Ben knew what he was thinking.

'You want to go for a walk? Come on, then.'

The farmhouse was the largest of the buildings – the office, the teaching classrooms, and the converted stable block in which Jeff had his quarters – that ringed the cobbled yard. From there it was just a five-minute stroll past the rear of the firing ranges and down a wildflower-edged track that led to the woods.

As he walked, Ben felt sorry that he'd spoken sharply to Jeff. It was true that he wanted nothing to do with all this talk of Afghanistan. He was thoroughly sick of that whole part of his past.

And yet, as much as he wanted to distance himself from the whole mess, he could understand why so many people, Jeff among them, were deeply concerned about these recent political upheavals. Even to the most limited understanding of the ordinary public watching the news broadcasts, it was clear that the US military withdrawal had been a complete and unmitigated disaster. From Ben's experienced perspective as a former professional soldier it was even worse – and in fact he already knew much more about the depressing current situation in Afghanistan than he'd been willing to discuss with Jeff.

The occupying American troops had pulled out of the country so fast, ostensibly to reduce the risk of being attacked as they retreated, that they had left the Afghan security forces in chaos. With their American overseers suddenly no longer there to marshal them, corrupt officers had been reported to be stealing their men's food and wages, even their ammunition. Police and military forces had crumbled in the face of the advancing Taliban, now emboldened by the American retreat and smelling victory.

Initially the embattled Afghan government, never much more than a puppet administration for the Americans, had declared it would stand and fight to prevent the Taliban from taking over the country. Ministers had delivered all the usual sabre-rattling speeches in which they promised to hold onto their proud homeland, just as they had kept it out of the hands of the Mujahideen for three whole years after the last invading army, the Soviets, had pulled out way back in 1989. Meanwhile, the reality was that, according to leaks from inside government itself, even as they stood there making these assurances to the Afghan public, almost all of those same ministers had already made arrangements to relocate their families outside the country. So much for standing their ground.

As for the ordinary citizens, it was easy to imagine the state of terror in which they lived from day to day as the imminent likelihood of a Taliban takeover loomed large. As repressive and frequently brutal as the existing regime might already have been, such a change could only be for the far, far worse. Many still remembered the chaotic violence that had swept the country after the communist government finally collapsed in '92 and the rebels took control for the first time. It was hard to forget the image of the then Afghan president, Muhammad Najibullah, captured, castrated, murdered and then hanged from a traffic kiosk for all to see. Things would surely be even more terrible now, as the rebels thirsted for revenge for the treatment of so many of their comrades at the hands of the Americans. The Taliban's seizure of power threatened a return to the days of fundamentalist tyranny. The forced marriages of young girls to their fighters. The ritual stoning and amputations, the mass executions in sports stadiums, the flogging in the streets of any man without a beard, and the genocidal massacre of anyone who opposed them.

In the capital city of Kabul, home to most of the country's more liberal-minded citizens, many residents had consoled themselves that the Taliban's move against their city would be months away, if indeed it happened at all. The American leaders had assured them that a US military pull-out wouldn't mean the end of the United States' involvement in the running of the country, or that its people would be abandoned to their fate.

But that hope had been dashed as the Americans started pulling out wholesale and events began to roll faster that anyone could have imagined. Zaranj was the first provincial centre to fall to the aggressive Taliban advance. The very next day a second capital, Sherberghan, fell too. The day after that, three more northern cities: Sar-i-pul, Takhar and Kundruz. Scenes of panic in Kabul as crowds crushed into the airport in their mad dash to get out before it was too late. Internet and phone networks collapsed. The roads were log-jammed with traffic.

And then, the news reached them that Kandahar City had now fallen too. Meanwhile, Taliban units continued to advance at a blinding pace. They took control of Herat, then of Ghazni, just seventy miles from the capital. The US Embassy in Kabul closed its doors and diplomats began feverishly destroying classified materials, while shifting their operations to the relative safety of the airport where three thousand US troops were expected to land at any time, not to repel the incoming rebel forces but to oversee the evacuation of US citizens and their allies.

By now almost at the gates of the capital, the Taliban had stated that it had no intention of hurting the city in a bloody battle. In the event, they didn't have to. Total surrender came quickly. With barely a shot fired Afghan forces, demoralised and often leaderless, threw down their arms and let the encroaching rebels take possession of billions of dollars' worth of military equipment, weapons and vehicles that had been provided to them by the US and its allies. Towns and cities were falling everywhere, and sometimes it took no more than just a simple phone call to force their surrender. *We're coming. Get out of our way.*

In Kabul itself, police and army deserted their posts in panic, leaving the road to the capital wide open and defenceless. The chain of command was in total disarray, the city falling into anarchy as criminal gangs started looting, helping themselves not just to whatever goods they could pillage from stores but also to the well-stocked armouries of abandoned police stations. People were wild with fear, thousands making their last scramble to the airport. Jets and helicopters roared over the city. Despite the Taliban's promise of a ceasefire to allow a peaceful evacuation, the rattle of automatic gunfire could now be heard around the outskirts. Motorcades forced their way through gridlocked traffic as those VIPs and officials who hadn't already fled now made their hasty exit. One of those was the president himself, whose personal helicopters were on standby at the airport. Government staff quarrelled and even fought over who would be allowed to board the overcrowded aircraft, which being fully fuelled for the president's escape had limited passenger capacity. Finally getting off the ground, the president's chopper headed away across the mountains, flying low to avoid detection by US military aircraft, which still controlled Afghan airspace. His escape route took him first to neighbouring Uzbekistan and thence to Abu Dhabi.

The news that the president had run away was the last nail in the coffin for Kabul's frightened citizens. All pretence at stability was now officially dissolved. The Green Zone lay deserted as the last pockets of police and soldiers took off their uniforms, laid down their weapons and simply walked away. Others chose to side with the heavily armed Taliban fighters who were beginning to appear in parts of Kabul, riding motorcycles or crammed into open pickup trucks. Islamist flags were being raised everywhere and the streets resounded to taranas, Islamic chants, blaring from cell phones and ghetto blasters. Many of the fighters carried captured American weapons in place of their traditional Russian AK-47s inherited from the era of war against the Soviets.

And on it went as the purge began. No sooner had the Taliban taken control but the worst fears of many people were realised. The rest would soon be history.

But Ben didn't care.

He reached the bottom of the track where it became a narrow beaten path through the trees, and a little while later he arrived at the secluded little wooded dell that was one of his favourite spots. On his walks or jogs around the property he'd often stop here to sit for a while among the ruins of the old medieval church. Plans to restore it to its former glory had never quite come about, and the tumbledown steeple and ivied walls were pretty much as they'd ever been, nestling quietly in the leaf-dappled shade of the woods. He settled on a wall with his legs dangling comfortably in space, lit a Gauloise and listened to the birds singing in the treetops. The stillness and serenity of this place had always invited him to reflect and find solace from life's personal troubles. Sometimes it worked, but sometimes it didn't.

Not all such troubles could be so easily forgotten.

These last few happy weeks with Abbie had provided a pleasant temporary reprieve to the nagging feeling, which had been eating at him for some time before, that he was no longer satisfied with his life here, and that it might be time to move on. Now that he was deprived of the comfort of Abbie's presence by his side day and night, those restless thoughts threatened to come creeping back into his mind.

Paradoxically, it was thinking about her that had got him feeling that way again: Abbie's very decisive and straightforward sense of her own direction in life had acted like a catalyst to make him ponder where he himself was going. He felt stuck in a rut, as though he was missing out on his life's true purpose, as though his compass needle had stopped indicating north and his energies were somehow blocked and unfulfilled. What did the future hold for him? Right now, he truly couldn't muster up any clear vision of it. He only felt that something was missing. Try as he might, he couldn't shake the self-doubt from his mind.

At the same time he wondered, as he often had in the past, if all this self-reflection was good for him. It was a trait he'd always tended towards, not necessarily one he was proud of, and he'd often envied his friends Jeff and Tuesday for their uncomplicated view of life. He couldn't share his feelings with them, because he knew what their response would be. Tuesday would just smile his dazzling smile and say,

'Hey, man, you worry too much.' Jeff would probably come out with something less complimentary. And now that Abbie was gone, there was nobody to confide in except the dog.

'What do you think I should do, buddy?' he asked Storm. But Storm just cocked his head to one side and said nothing, wisely keeping his opinion to himself.

'Suit yourself,' Ben said. 'Thanks for the advice.'

Little did Ben know at that moment that something was soon set to happen which would push his personal worries to the far back of his mind for a long time to come, and perhaps for good. Because real trouble, the kind of trouble he'd been born to deal with, was lurking just around the corner. And if any reminder were needed of what his life's purpose really was, then he was about to get one.

Chapter 3

After returning from his walk, he was climbing the short flight of steps to the front door of the house and thinking about preparing a light lunch when he heard the phone ringing from the office building across the yard. Since Jeff was presumably still glued to his sick bed in front of the television and there was nobody else around, he went over to answer the call himself.

In truth the office wasn't Ben's most favourite part of Le Val, its crowded desks, swivel chairs and filing cabinets uncomfortably synonymous in his mind with the torture of filling out tax returns, poring over accounts, wrangling with insurance companies, and all of the other mind-numbing paperwork and administrative chores that regrettably went with running a business. Another reason for wanting out of it, he thought darkly to himself as he walked into the empty office, snatched up the phone and said, 'Le Val. Can I help you?'

The line was crackly, as though the call was long-distance, although in this day and age of substandard mobile communications you could never be too sure. After a moment's hesitation the unfamiliar caller's voice on the line stammered, 'Uh, w-would it be possible to speak to, uh, somebody there called Ben? I'm sorry, that's the only name I have.'

It was a man's voice, but soft in tone and short on confidence. The stranger spoke very fast with a jerky, nervy, quick-fire delivery and a nasal, twangy accent that Ben could pinpoint to the US west coast. Ben could picture him as tall and beaky, with glasses. Perhaps not the typical kind of prospective client at Le Val.

'This is Ben Hope,' he replied. 'May I ask who's calling?'

'Thank God,' replied the caller, with a sigh of relief. Ben heard him cup the phone handset and call out in a muffled voice to someone else, 'It's him. We found him!' Then collecting himself the stranger said, 'Uh, Mr Hope, my name is Linus Twigg, and I'm calling you from San Diego.'

Ben thought that was unusual, too. Not because the call was from San Diego, per se. Le Val received training course inquiries from all over the world, though never so strange and awkward. What made it particularly unusual was that the time here in France was just past midday. California being nine hours behind, it meant that this Linus Twigg had dialled his number at three a.m. This was obviously an important call for him, whoever he was.

'Uh, I hope I'm not calling at a bad time,' the stranger went on anxiously. 'Boy, you've no idea how happy I am that we got the right number. What a relief!'

The note of strain in Linus Twigg's voice was obvious. He sounded tense and emotional, almost at breaking point with nervous exhaustion. 'Pleased to hear from you, Linus,'

Ben said. 'But I'm afraid you have me at a bit of a loss. I have no idea who you are.'

'I'm so sorry. I should have said. We're all pretty rattled here. It's the middle of the night and my brain's just so frazzled I can hardly think straight.'

'Start again,' Ben said, in a calm tone to reassure him. 'Take it easy. Deep breaths, nice and slow. And then tell me exactly what this is about.'

Linus Twigg took another moment to compose himself, then making a concerted effort to talk more coherently he explained, 'Like I said, I'm calling from San Diego, from our company offices. You don't know me, but I believe you knew my boss.'

Ben was about to say, 'Did I?' when the light flooded in and he remembered that he *did* know one person in San Diego, though he'd never been there. He hadn't seen her in a long time, either. He recalled that the last time they'd spoken, not so long ago, she'd mentioned having relocated the family business from New York to San Diego. She'd sounded happy and upbeat. Ben had been able to picture her then the way he was visualising her now: the gypsy curls of raven-black hair, the intelligent dark eyes reflecting the same no-nonsense attitude as the general way she handled herself. She was maybe thirty-six or thirty-seven years old, a very capable lady and not someone to be messed with.

But this anxious-sounding call from her employee in the middle of the night told him something was terribly wrong.

Ben asked, 'Your boss is Madison? Madison Cahill?' Then before Twigg could reply, something he'd said flashed alarmingly in Ben's mind and he added, 'Hold on. Did I hear you right – what do you mean, I *knew* her? Has something happened to Madison? Is she okay?'

'That's the reason I had to call you,' Twigg said. 'We didn't know what else to do.'

'Cut to the chase, Linus. Is Madison all right?'

'No, she isn't. Well, she could be. Or she might not be. We just don't know.'

'You don't *know?*'

'No. Jesus, we're all so upset. What if . . . *what if—*'

Linus Twigg sounded desperate with anxiety and close to tears. If Ben had been with him in person, he wouldn't have known whether to sit the guy down with a stiff drink or just beat the truth out of him. He said sharply, 'Linus! What do I have to do to get you to explain what's going on?'

'I'm sorry. I'm not making any sense, am I? Here it is. It's bad news, I'm afraid. The worst. Well, maybe not the *very* worst, if you know what I mean—'

'*Linus!*'

Twigg swallowed hard with an audible gulp that sounded more like a sob, then came straight out with it.

'Madison's missing.' He was breathing fast and the words tumbled out as he explained, 'That is to say, we know where she is. Or at any rate, we think we do. I mean, more or less. But we do know for certain that she isn't where she's supposed to be, which is back here again. She should have been home by now but there's been no contact. Nothing. Not a peep. It's so awful!'

Ben hardly heard the rest of it, because an icy grip had taken hold of his heart at the sound of the word 'missing'. It was one he'd heard too many times before, and he'd had a lot more experience than most people of just what it could entail. In a tight voice he said, 'Linus. Stop babbling and tell me where you *think* she was when this happened.'

'Afghanistan,' Twigg said. 'That's where she was. Or is. At any rate, that's where she went, three weeks ago. And that's the last we saw of her.'

Ben's eyes closed. Now it was his turn to take a deep breath. He asked, 'What the hell was she doing in Afghanistan?'

'She was there on business,' Twigg replied. 'You know what we do here at Cahill Enterprises, right? I assumed . . . I thought . . .'

'You thought right, Linus,' Ben said. 'I get the picture.'

Ben had encountered some interesting and colourful characters in his life, and Madison Cahill was one of those. While other people sat in offices and attended conferences and boardroom meetings, Madison's job was travelling to the far corners of the world in search of lost treasures. Her father, the late, great Rigby Ignatius Boddington Cahill, had made a long and highly profitable career out of that slightly nebulous grey zone between being a regular archaeologist and an out-and-out fortune hunter. Whatever multi-million-dollar riches he might have raked in for himself over the years, there was no denying that he'd been responsible for the recovery of many lost wonders of history. Who could blame him if they just so happened to be extraordinarily valuable, or for charging an exorbitant finder's fee to the governments and private museums to whom he delivered the goods?

By the time Rigby died, a saddened old man in retirement in Hawaii, his business had fallen into neglect and his once-thriving New York offices had closed up. That was when Madison had decided to take up the reins and restore the family firm to its former glory. Before she'd started hunting treasures for a living, she'd hunted other things: namely, people. After a successful career as a fugitive recovery agent for the United States federal government, she'd gone independent and become what some people might have called (though she hated the term) a bounty hunter.

That was how Ben had first got to meet her, while on a job in Serbia. Their very first encounter had involved her pointing a loaded 9mm Beretta pistol at him. Which normally wouldn't have boded too well for their future relationship, not to mention Madison's own future survival – but they'd swiftly got over that initial hiccup to become friends and allies. Facing death together at the hands of a sadistic Serbian gangland kingpin called Zarko Kožul had probably done something to cement that bond.

While their association had never blossomed into anything more romantic, it had come fairly close at times and there had always been a certain chemistry between them, in one of those slow-burn relationships that never quite seemed to come off. They'd remained in contact nonetheless, and Ben liked her a lot.

And now, this had to happen.

'All right,' Ben said. 'From the beginning. Tell me everything you know.'

Chapter 4

Linus Twigg's explanation began with what Ben had already more or less inferred, which was that Madison had been on a business trip to Afghanistan, searching for an archaeological site of special historical importance, when the current crisis exploded.

'It's been our latest project,' Twigg said, the words gushing out of him. 'To rediscover the site of Zakara. You see, Mr Cahill, her father, our company founder, spent decades searching for it, but in the end the political situation there just made it impossible to carry out any kind of proper excavations. First the Russians invaded, and he had to get out in a hurry. Then ten years later the Russians left, and he went back there hoping he'd be able to carry on, but he had more problems. The region was so unsettled that soon afterwards he had to abandon his plans again, and what with one thing after another the place has been too hot to go near ever since.'

Ben listened impatiently. A potted history of old man Cahill's exploits in Afghanistan wasn't what he needed to hear right now, fascinating as it might be. 'Okay. And Madison?'

'A couple months ago she got it into her head to travel out there and take up where her father left off. She was convinced that the situation there was pretty stable, with our troops still in place and the Taliban under control. We knew about the coming pull-out, but everybody thought it would happen slowly. Well, not everybody. I warned her it wasn't safe. But you know Madison. Once she latches onto something, she won't let go. And now look what's happened, and she's stuck right in the middle of it.'

'What's Zakara?'

'It's a lost city. Incredibly ancient and terribly important. It dates back all the way to—'

'Whatever,' said Ben, for whom ancient lost cities were of little interest even at the best of times. 'More to the point, *where* is it?'

'A long way from anywhere, deep in a place called the Bamiyan Valley. There are no towns or cities anywhere nearby, nothing except maybe a few small villages.' Twigg paused. 'But that's not where she went missing, as far as we know. She was in Kabul for a couple of weeks, hooking up with some contacts there and getting things organised for the expedition out to the Zakara site.'

'So she went missing in Kabul?'

'Maybe. We don't know.'

'You keep saying you don't know.'

'That's because we truly don't.'

'Okay,' Ben said. 'She was in Kabul. Was she alone there? Did she travel with anyone else?'

'She usually goes places on her own, when it's just a scouting expedition like this was. I guess I could have gone with her, being her personal assistant. But she's got her own way of doing things, you know?'

Twigg probably didn't realise it, but his tone betrayed his intense private relief at having stayed behind in the relative safety of San Diego. He continued, 'But she wasn't on her own when she got there, because we had people in Kabul. Our main contact there was a guy called Aziz Qeyami, who was in touch with Mr Cahill over the years. He still works at the Kabul Cultural Heritage Institute.'

Ben grabbed a notepad and pen, and wrote that name down. 'Go on.'

'The plan was that he'd travel on with her to the Zakara site, with a small team of others, to check the place out before calling in specialist contractors. Anyhow, she was in regular contact with base the first couple of weeks, and it looked like they were set to head out to the site any time. Then the news broke that the whole situation had suddenly taken a turn for the worse, the troops were pulling out in a real hurry and the Taliban were advancing so fast on the city that everyone was going apeshit. We didn't hear anything from her in a couple of days, and we were starting to get worried when she called to say things were a little hairy but she was okay and had managed to get a place on a plane out of there. That would have been the last group of US citizens to be evacuated before the doors slammed shut.'

'And she wasn't on the plane.'

'We had a pretty good idea she wouldn't be. Because the very same day she was meant to leave, just hours before the flight was scheduled, we got another call from her.'

'What did she say?'

'She said there'd been a change of plan. Things were going to crap, she was cut off from reaching the airport and she was going to try to get out of the city another way.'

'Another way, meaning by road?'

'We don't know,' Twigg repeated once again. 'Her call only lasted a few seconds. Sounded like there was a lot of chaos going on close by. Could have been gunfire, and people yelling in the background. Then the line went totally dead. We tried and tried to call her back, but the cell phone networks must have gone down. Great timing.'

Ben was thinking hard, clutching his phone tight against his ear. 'So assuming she managed to get out of Kabul, where might she have gone?'

'Your guess is as good as mine,' Twigg said.

'Except it's not, is it? You must have some idea.'

Twigg sighed. 'I'm not saying this is the case. I'm not even saying it's likely. But it's possible, just possible, that she *might* have decided to try to make her way to the Zakara site.'

'With the whole country falling apart around her in a violent revolution.'

'Like I said, once Madison's got an idea in her head, wild horses couldn't drag it out of there. Who knows what could have driven her? Maybe she had some last-minute change of heart, knowing that if she got on that plane, she might not get this chance again for years. Or ever.'

'That would be insane,' Ben said. 'All the way overland through the mountains to the Bamiyan Valley, with Taliban fighters everywhere, rolling around in tanks and armoured cars, armed with billions of dollars' worth of military hardware, hunting for renegade Americans to kill. She wouldn't stand a chance.'

'You obviously don't know Madison as well as we do. She can be headstrong. To say the least. The more you push her, the harder she'll push right back at you.'

Ben considered what Twigg was saying. He tried to picture Madison travelling alone in some rental car, a western woman on her own in an extremely hostile land, trying to reach some remote spot in the mountains to carry out what seemed to him like an impossible quest. The odds were gigantic, seemingly unsurvivable. Twigg was right when he said Madison had never backed down from a challenge in her life. Headstrong wasn't the word. But there was another possibility.

'If she did take that option,' Ben said. 'If she's really that crazy, and assuming she'd have been able to get out of Kabul at all, would she have tried to make the trip alone?'

'We had the same idea,' Twigg replied. 'It occurred to us that she might have gone off with Aziz and the team, or whichever of them was able to get out of the city in one piece. You've got to bear in mind that anyone involved in preserving ancient cultural artefacts from Afghan history isn't exactly flavour of the month with the Taliban. These are the same fanatical nutjobs who went around blowing up and smashing any relic they could find, last time they seized power. They're hellbent on erasing anything that predates their own religion, which only started, like, yesterday, in the seventh century. Anyhow, we tried calling the Cultural Institute, hoping someone there might be able to offer some kind of information, or maybe a cell phone number for Aziz. At least if we knew he was with her, that would be some kind of consolation. I'm told he knows the country like the back of his hand. But no joy. Nobody seemed to know where he was, or if they did, they were too afraid to say. Soon after that, the Institute's phone line went dead too. That was eight days ago.'

'And there's nobody else you can try contacting?'

'Oh, you can try,' Twigg replied. 'You can try until you're blue in the face, but it won't get you anywhere. I must've called the US Embassy in Kabul a hundred times until it turned out the reason they weren't answering the phone was they were shut down and relocated to some makeshift new premises in Qatar. It appears that the ambassador got out on the same flight that Madison was supposed to have been on, along with all the diplomats and workers.'

'Have you called there too?' Ben asked.

'You bet I have, and every time you get through to some new staffer who doesn't have any better idea than we do what the hell's going on out there. And it's the same picture back here in the States. All anyone can tell you for sure is that any US citizen or any of our allies left stranded there now are totally on their own. Thousands of them. There's nobody left in Afghanistan to look out for their interests, and nobody's coming to help. Meanwhile there are all these terrible rumours online that the Taliban are going door to door, targeting Americans or anyone else who helped the occupying forces, slaughtering them and hanging their dead bodies out of helicopters circling the city. Like an example to what's gonna happen to any westerner they catch. It's barbaric, and it's like nobody in our so-called civilised world, including our own administration, gives a damn what's happening. And the whole time, still no word from Madison, Aziz or anyone.'

The picture was a grim one, for sure. The next question now had to be what to do about it. Ben broke into Twigg's rapid flow of words by asking, 'How did you get my number?'

'She talked about you, this guy she'd met years ago who had this seriously impressive past history doing all kinds of wild stuff. I mean, she never told us exactly what you did. I don't know if she even knew the details. But it was clear that you used to be . . . how can I put this? Used to be involved in that world. A military person. An *operator*, if that's the right word. A specialist at rescuing people, or something. I have no idea what I'm talking about. We couldn't remember your name. But we were all brainstorming to come up with some kind of idea about what to do, and it was Marsha – that's Marsha Ackerworth, our office manager – who thought to search Madison's desk for her personal address book, and there it was, listed under B for 'Ben', with no surname and this number in Europe. So we agreed we'd call you. We didn't know what else to do. And so here I am, Mr Hope. Sitting here with my colleagues in our office at three in the morning, after all these sleepless nights, praying that maybe there's one person in the world who can do something to save our friend. Please. I beg you. We're all begging you, from our hearts. Can you help us?'

Chapter 5

Linus Twigg's stark plea for help was powerful and hit Ben very hard. The impact was harder still, when to an appalled silence at the other end of the line Ben made the only reply that he could. His words hurt him most of all.

'You and your colleagues did the right thing calling me, Linus. I appreciate that you let me know what's happening. But I can't promise to be able to help. Because there frankly isn't a lot that I can do.'

When Twigg spoke again, his voice sounded faint and almost incoherent with shock and emotion. 'You were our last hope.'

'I'm sorry,' Ben said.

'But I don't understand. I thought that rescuing missing people, kidnap victims and such, was what you do for a living.'

'Used to do,' Ben said.

'But Madison said you saved all these people. Children. Women. You went in and got them out. It sounded amazing.'

'I did what I did,' Ben said. 'I'm not a hero. And I'm not a superman. I can't work miracles. The people I helped were mostly in Europe. France, Germany, Italy, Spain, Britain.

Not in exploding war zones that are almost totally inaccessible from the outside. They were taken by gangs of opportunistic crooks who hid them in cellars, attics, outhouses, and had a financial vested interest in keeping them alive. Not by whole regiments of heavily armed fanatics who have no interest in keeping their enemies alive for a single moment, and won't hesitate to butcher them on the spot. I had the advantage of surprise, and time was usually on my side. I could slip in, get the victims out and get them home. Sometimes I was able to call on contacts and connections to help me do that. That's how one man on his own can make a difference. But in Afghanistan, you'd need an army. One that's a hell of a lot bigger than all the US military combined, and a damn sight better led. You saw what happened to them.'

'You're saying it can't be done.'

Ben said, 'I know how you're feeling, hearing this. I feel the same way, believe me. But you have to be realistic. Even if a lone operator like me was able to reach the Afghan border and slip through the Taliban lines to go searching for one missing person in six hundred thousand square kilometres of mountain wilderness swarming with dedicated enemy forces; even if I was able to track her movements and find where she might have gone, there's extremely little chance I'd find her before they do. And a very real possibility that, after eight days, she's already one of the many people they've caught and murdered.'

'Oh. Christ.'

'I'm sorry. It's bad. I feel like shit telling you these things. But that's how it is. Trust me. I have seen quite a bit of action in Afghanistan and it's not a good place to be. Not when something like this happens. And this current situation looks to be worse than anything I ever experienced there.'

'Is there *nothing* we can do?' Twigg pleaded.

'Pray that she might have managed to slip out of the country,' Ben replied. 'If she'd headed southeast from Kabul, it's only a few hundred kilometres to the Pakistan border. She's tough and resourceful. If she was able to make her way to Peshawar, or maybe even to Islamabad, she'd be sure to find help there and contact us. I swear to you that I'd be on the first plane out there.'

'Pray,' Twigg said. 'That's your best advice?'

'Along with going on doing what you've already been doing,' Ben said. 'Don't stop hammering the US Embassy in Qatar. They're sure to be keeping track of all known movements of refugees out of Afghanistan. If Madison is among them, they'll have that information. Humanitarian camps are being set up in different places to harbour the flood of people who managed to get out. She could be in one of those.'

'Then why hasn't she contacted us already?'

'Stand by your phone,' Ben said. 'She might do just that, at any moment. She could be trying right now, to let you know she's okay.'

'But you don't think it's likely.'

'I didn't say it was impossible.'

'This isn't what we thought you were going to tell us. We thought—'

'I know,' Ben said. 'But I won't lie to you.'

'And we're supposed to sit here and just ride it out, fingers crossed and hope for the best? How long before we give up on her being alive? Weeks? Months? And what then? Just shrug our shoulders, put it down to "shit happens" and go on without her? How can we do that?'

Ben said nothing.

'Madison's not just our boss. She's our friend. She built this company back up after her father died, gave us our jobs. We do great things together. She looks after us. We . . . we *love* her.'

Ben went on saying nothing. Inside, his spirits sank another notch towards rock bottom.

'I wish there was some other way,' Twigg muttered disconsolately. 'Something else. I don't know. Something more.'

'If I can think of one,' Ben said, 'you'll be the first to know. I promise you.'

The call ended soon afterwards, with Twigg almost weeping and Ben not feeling much better. The icy chill of his initial reaction had turned to a boiling rage. He sat there in the empty, silent office for a long time, so stunned he could barely believe what he'd just heard. But if it was true, everything he'd told Twigg was no less so. The odds were overwhelming enough to make this an impossible situation. For all practical purposes, Madison might as well be an astronaut stranded alone on Mars, with no possibility of rescue or resupply.

Yet he'd promised he would try to think of some way he could help her. That's what he would do.

And that's what he did do. Try.

He was thinking about it as he returned to the house to break the news to Jeff about Twigg's call. But the living room was empty and the TV was turned off, because sometime during the phone conversation Jeff had finally given in to his feverish state and slunk quietly off to his quarters to crawl into bed. That's where Ben found him, fast asleep, and didn't have the heart to waken him. Jeff would only make himself sicker with pointless worry, if he knew what had happened.

Ben returned to the house, went into the kitchen to pour himself a measure of Laphroaig, and ended up downing three or four of them as he sat there thinking and unable to come up with anything useful. Some hours later he was back out at the old church in the woods with Storm peering anxiously up at his beloved master, understanding something was wrong as Ben paced up and down among the ruins, racking his brains and consumed with frustration and grief at the thought of harm coming to his friend Madison Cahill.

Was this the best he could do? Was he really going to stand idly by, surrender to resignation and let her die out there?

Did he have any choice?

Early next morning, after a sleepless night, Ben drove the Le Val Land Rover across to the nearest town of Valognes to pick up some necessary supplies. He hadn't seen Jeff since yesterday, and hadn't wanted to disturb his rest. During that time Ben had spent every single moment turning the whole situation over and over in his mind, almost to the point of madness, and coming up totally empty. Now he was hoping that getting out of the house and doing something different might help to stimulate his tormented mind and allow some brilliant, ingenious plan to suddenly pop up, fully formed and ready for action.

It didn't.

He was submerged deep in thought as he carried a box of groceries out of his usual épicerie in the main street of Valognes to the Landy parked at the kerbside and opened the tailgate to dump it in the back.

And he was still lost in his internal world, balancing what-ifs and worst-case scenarios against meagre half-baked possibilities that never went anywhere, when the two unsmiling men in dark coats seemed to materialise out of thin air and came walking purposefully up to him. Short hair. Lean, sombre faces. Serious eyes. One stayed silent while the other said tersely in a London accent, 'Major Hope?'

Chapter 6

Ben turned to look at them, returning their stony gaze. As they walked closer, Storm, who'd been curled up against the inner bulkhead of the Land Rover, shot to his feet instantly alert with his ears pricked and gave the strangers a low warning growl.

If the two men were unnerved by the dog, they didn't show it. The one who'd spoken spoke again, putting on a smile that looked incongruous on his face. 'Lovely day, isn't it?'

Ben didn't reply. It was clear they knew exactly who he was. And the way they moved, the way they held themselves, the confident air with which they approached: everything about them revealed to Ben exactly who they were, too. In that same moment he knew they must have been watching Le Val and followed him here for a particular reason. Which spoke of a high degree of organisation, and a fair level of skill to have been able to shadow him unnoticed. Ben's sixth sense in these matters had been unusually sharp even before it had been honed to a razor edge by his years of military training and experience.

And that told him, as loud and clear as though they'd read him out a list of credentials, that these two guys had been through some of the same kind of training he had. Operators, and still in the business by all accounts.

They came within four steps and halted, standing three feet apart, making a triangle with Ben as he stood very still next to his vehicle and watched them closely.

'You haven't followed me all the way to Valognes to talk about the weather,' he said, breaking his silence. 'So what do you want?'

'To take you for a little trip,' said the one who'd spoken before. The other just stared.

'Too late,' Ben said. 'Just been on one. Now my shopping's done and I'm going home.'

'You can make this easy on yourself,' the man said. 'We have instructions. We're required to carry them out.'

'I can make it easy on you, too,' Ben said. 'By pretending that I didn't see you. So turn around and walk away, while the going's good.'

The man shook his head. 'Not an option, I'm afraid.'

'Don't be like that,' said the other. 'We're not looking for trouble.'

'Tell that to the dog,' Ben replied. Storm was eyeing them unblinkingly. A low rumble was coming from deep in his chest, like distant thunder. One false move, and he was ready to fly at them.

'Nice doggie,' said the first man. 'What's his name?'

'I wouldn't get too close, if I were you.'

'Just making friends,' the man said.

'A trip to where?' Ben asked.

'London.'

'Can't say I was planning on visiting the place any time soon.'

The man shrugged. 'Not our problem. Orders.'

'Whose?'

The man pointed a finger at the sky. 'Doesn't get much higher. They're very keen to see you, Major.'

'They could have saved you a journey,' Ben said. 'I'm not interested.'

'Colonel Carstairs would be disappointed to hear that,' the man said.

That was a name Ben hadn't heard in a while, and his surprise must have shown on his face. 'Carstairs?'

'You haven't forgotten your old regimental pals, have you?' the second man said with a knowing look. 'Because they haven't forgotten you. And now they'd like to have a little chat.'

Ben certainly remembered Carstairs very well, from years ago. He must be past retirement age now, but obviously still active. He was senior SAS brass, with connections to military intelligence. Back in the day, Colonel Carstairs had been *rumoured* within the close-knit Special Forces community to be involved with a shadowy cadre called Group 13. So shrouded in mystery that even regular SAS officers like Ben had known virtually nothing about them, the unit was said to be run via the UK Foreign Office alongside others like the so-called Increment, allegedly responsible for carrying out covert, deniable missions on behalf of the Secret Intelligence Service, MI6. Those blacker-than-black ops included political assassinations, delivering secret military assistance to foreign powers, clandestine insertion and extraction of intelligence agents, and other classified missions where maximum discretion was required and to which the government could disavow all connection if compromised.

Ben had particular reasons for knowing that the whispers about Gordon Carstairs were more than just rumours. That was something he'd never told another living soul, all these years.

And now it seemed that Carstairs especially wanted to talk to him, to the extent of sending out a specialist team to pick him up. Ben thought that was interesting. He'd have bet that Tweedle-Dee and Tweedle-Dum here weren't working alone, likely part of a group of four or six. Ben knew there was no point in looking around him in the hope of spotting the others. He wouldn't see them. But they'd be there, dotted around various vantage points up and down the street and in the surrounding shops and buildings, watching.

'A little chat about what?' Ben asked.

Both men grinned. 'If they told us,' said the first one, 'they'd have to kill us.'

'Funny,' Ben said. 'I was just thinking that's what I'd have to do to make you two go away.'

The grins vanished.

The first man said, 'Correct.'

The second one said, 'Meaning, you'd have to try.'

Ben considered the situation. These two guys weren't joking around. And in any case, he had to say he was curious to know what Carstairs wanted.

'What about him?' He nodded towards Storm.

'Don't you worry, Major. We'll have someone drive your vehicle back to Le Val for you. The doggie will be fine. And Captain Dekker will be informed of your whereabouts.'

Ben paused for a long moment, then made his decision. 'Okay, boys. But I expect to be home again within a few hours.'

The men said nothing. The first one turned away from Ben and made a small gesture in the air, and moments later two black BMW saloons with tinted windows glided fast down the street and pulled up at the kerbside, one behind Ben's Land Rover and the other in front. The doors opened and the rest of the team stepped out, except for the drivers. They all had the same hard-faced look. None of them spoke as they hovered near their vehicles, all eyes on Ben. The operation was slick and unobtrusive. If any of the locals who were strolling past, going in and out of the épicerie or browsing the stalls of fruit and vegetables outside had been paying any great attention to what was going on, only the most highly astute of them might have thought there was a very discreet arrest in progress.

'Keys, please, Major?'

'Here,' Ben said, tossing them over. 'And stop calling me Major.' To the dog he said, 'It's all right, buddy. These men are going to take you home. Be on your best behaviour with them, all right?' Storm licked his master's hand, and seemed to reluctantly accept.

Two of the men got into Ben's Land Rover, while Ben was shown into the back of the rearward BMW and sat with one man either side of him. This was feeling more and more like an arrest. They'd better not push it with the tough-guy stuff, he thought, if they wanted his cooperation. He watched as the Land Rover headed off with Storm's anxious face looking out of the back window. Then the BMWs glided away from the kerb and up the street. Nobody in Ben's car said a word. He settled back in the seat, took out his cigarettes and lit one up, mostly just to annoy them. He got no reaction.

The cars drove fast out of Valognes and headed for a private airfield a few kilometres away. The route was familiar to Ben, because it was the same airfield where Jeff had earned his pilot's licence and kept the single-engine little Cessna Skyhawk that he liked to take out now and then for a joyride. Ben's escorts had flown over in something a little more robust. He wasn't completely surprised to see a sleek, compact Stratos jet sitting on the taxiway waiting for them. Someone in the front car must have radioed to say they were incoming, because the jet's engines were whining loudly and the pilots were ready to go.

Stepping out of the car Ben had a last-minute moment of hesitation; then he thought *fuck it* and strode across the tarmac to board.

It was a quiet journey, because the jet's passenger cabin was whisper-silent and his po-faced companions uttered not a single word all the way. And a short one, as they winged their way across the Channel at some 500 miles per hour. Ben sank into the plushness of the soft leather and closed his eyes. Outwardly he might have seemed asleep, but he was burning with anxiety for Madison Cahill. Every moment that went by could be the instant that a Taliban bullet went through her head – or worse, much worse, things. He should be helping her, instead of sitting on this plane surrounded by goons in suits. And yet some cloudy, undefined instinct told him that the Colonel's surprise appearance in the picture might have some role to play in all of this. Only time would tell. Whatever was up, these boys seemed in a real hurry to move things along quickly. That suited Ben just fine.

An hour later, he was in another car being whisked into central London. Tweedle-Dum and Tweedle-Dee had stayed with him, but the rest of the escort had been changed at the airport. He resisted the urge to ask where they were going, as he knew they wouldn't reply anyway.

He found out soon enough, as the cars shot down a web of backstreets and pulled through iron gates into the concrete compound at the rear of a drab, nondescript and very anonymous office building. Of course, such a meeting as he was about to have couldn't take place anywhere too conspicuous. That was Colonel Carstairs all over. As they rolled up Tweedle-Dum radioed, and moments later three more heavyset, crew-cut men came out of the building to greet them. They were certainly laying on the manpower. Ben instantly spotted the concealed firearms bulging under their suit jackets.

He was shown inside and up three floors of stairs, along a dingy corridor past various empty, disused offices and finally to a door outside which his escorts stopped. Tweedle-Dee opened the door without knocking. Behind it was a large, bare office with an internal door, an empty desk, two utilitarian chairs and a picturesque view through a dusty window pane of a brick wall. The top brass really knew how to lay these secret meetings on in style. Tweedle-Dee motioned for Ben to go in. 'Make yourself comfortable,' he said with a smirk. 'He'll be with you in a moment.'

Ben stepped into the office and the door closed behind him. Alone, he paced up and down a few times, stepped over to the window, tried the internal door and found it locked, walked back to the desk and sat down. He'd have been unhappy about being kept waiting any longer than necessary, and he wasn't. Moments later the internal door opened, and a tall man in a pinstriped suit walked into the room.

Chapter 7

Ben stood up as Carstairs came in. More to meet the man eye to eye than out of courtesy to an officer of superior rank. The colonel was in his seventies now. His hair had whitened and thinned since their last meeting. His face seemed longer and more gaunt with liver spots and pronounced bags under his eyes, and he walked with a slight stoop. He stuck out a large, bony hand and Ben took it. Carstairs might have aged shockingly but he still had a grip like a mangle.

'It's good to see you again, Benedict. Sorry to have pulled you away at such short notice. Please, take a seat.' Carstairs walked around the desk and settled his angular frame opposite him. His expression was severe and he looked tired and under pressure, but he was obviously doing everything in his limited power to appear cordial. 'I trust you're keeping well. Look fit and healthy, at any rate. Haven't changed a great deal since I saw you last.'

'I wish I could say the same about you, Colonel,' Ben could have replied, if he'd wanted to be antagonistic. Instead he said mildly, 'Let's cut to the chase. I don't suppose you brought me here for pleasantries and chit-chat. What do you want?'

'As I say, I apologise for the suddenness of this meeting. But as I'm about to reveal to you, or as much as can be revealed at the present time, we're dealing with a specific situation that has come up on us quite suddenly too. A situation in which your involvement was considered, ah, desirable.'

Ben looked at him, trying to make out what the man was thinking behind those inscrutable grey eyes. 'Desirable?'

The colonel shrugged. 'Necessary.'

'Sounds like I'm being given an order,' Ben said. 'Thing is, last time I checked, I don't work for you lot anymore.'

'Nobody ever really leaves the regiment, Major,' Carstairs said with deliberate emphasis. 'Especially not a man of your stellar qualities. You think we would have invested so heavily, both in terms of manpower and money, in forming you into the perfect fighting machine you became, just to let you go prancing merrily off into the blue any time you fancied?' He gave a dry little smile. 'Doesn't work that way. Face it, we made you. We own you. You'll be one of us until the day you die.'

Ben shook his head. 'Now I remember why you people make me so sick.' Maybe *that* was antagonistic.

'Come now, Major. What a way to talk about the unit you were so proud to serve in for all those years. Do I detect a note of resentment, hostility even?'

'You know why I had to walk away. I didn't like being asked to do certain things.'

'It's what you signed up for.'

'To be a soldier,' Ben said. 'Something I could be proud of, as a member of the best fighting force in the world. Not to be played like a pawn to carry out your illegal secret dirty deeds and hidden agendas.'

'You never were much of a team player, were you, Benedict?'

'Depends on what the game is,' Ben replied. 'I didn't have a taste for yours, that's for damn sure.'

'I remember we had this discussion before, once upon a time.'

'When you called me in for a private meeting, just like this one, and tried to recruit me into your cosy little assassination club. Yes, I remember that too. It was the last time you and I spoke.'

'You'd have been perfect material for Group 13,' the colonel said. 'A wasted opportunity.'

'For me it was a wake-up call,' Ben said. 'The day I realised I didn't want to be part of it any longer. Any of it.'

'And so you turned to the bottle instead,' the colonel sneered. 'What an ending to such an exemplary career. To leave under a cloud like that. I was disappointed in you, Benedict.'

Those were deeply unhappy memories for Ben, who had sunk to some of the lowest ebbs of his life back then. His heavy drinking, at times bordering on if not quite full-blown alcoholism then something very nearly like it, had been a throwback to the wilder period of his youth before joining the military, which on leaving SAS had then carried through into the early days of his freelance career.

He never talked about those darker times in his life, not even to his closest friend Jeff. Speaking openly about them now with Carstairs felt strange, like a confession, but also deeply cathartic.

'It was a tough decision for me to quit the regiment. I'll admit, I struggled with it. I'd given it everything I'd got. Devoted my whole life to it for thirteen years. Now I look back and I realise I have you to thank for shattering my illusions. Getting out was the best thing I ever did.'

Carstairs gave another of his sardonic little smiles and waved his hand around the room. 'And yet here you are, returned home like the prodigal son. Don't act as if you're not here by choice. A man of your talents surely wouldn't have allowed himself to be picked off the street by the likes of Kendrick and Brown if you hadn't felt even just the slightest curiosity as to what this is about. Go on, admit it. You couldn't resist, could you?'

'I'm curious,' Ben said. 'You wouldn't have gone to all this trouble unless you had a pretty serious crisis on your hands.'

Carstairs' smile melted and was replaced by a grim frown. 'You're not wrong about the gravity of the situation, I'm afraid.'

'Then why don't you get down to brass tacks and tell me?'

The colonel stood up from the desk and paced across to the window. He stood with his back to Ben, gazing through the dusty glass with the thousand-yard stare of a deeply worried man. For a player like Carstairs to be this anxious, Ben knew whatever was troubling him was even more serious than he was letting on.

Carstairs said, 'I've been asked to put together a special task force for a mission of particular importance. One that, by its nature, requires extreme delicacy in its execution and just the right kind of top-level operatives to see it through. Its codename is Operation Hydra.'

'Catchy,' Ben said.

Carstairs went on, 'After much discussion your name came high on our list of potential candidates, based on your fairly unique set of credentials and your extensive experience in that particular theatre of operations.'

Now Ben was beginning to sense that his instinct had been right: that this unexpected twist might have a role to play in serving his own purposes. Fate sometimes had a strange way of intervening to tie the loose ends together. He felt a rush of blood through his veins, though his calm expression did nothing to show it.

'I see. And what theatre of operations are we talking about?'

The colonel turned away from the window to face him. 'We want to send you back to your old hunting grounds in Afghanistan.'

Chapter 8

Carstairs looked piercingly at Ben. 'How do you feel about that, Major Hope? Are you ready to take a trip?'

The wheels were turning fast in Ben's head. Under normal circumstances he would have told Carstairs to take a hike. He wasn't an army reservist who could be recalled for service in times of war or unusual emergency. Which meant that for all the colonel's big talk about their having a hold on him for life, they technically couldn't force him to do anything he didn't want to. But in this case he was willing to make an exception, because what Carstairs was dangling in front of him was the perfect opportunity for what would otherwise have been impossible for a lone civilian, to penetrate the borders of a completely closed country. Once inside, he might have some chance of finding out what had happened to Madison Cahill.

It was a pretty tenuous proposition. Even assuming she was still alive, finding her would be needles and haystacks. But it was better to be there on the ground than helplessly pacing up and down thousands of miles away.

It didn't take long for Ben to reply. He'd already made his decision.

'I've dreamed of nothing else but to go back there,' he said.

Carstairs smiled, showing pointy grey teeth. 'I'm delighted to hear it. My superiors will be too. It was unanimously agreed you were an excellent fit for Operation Hydra. You're intimately familiar with the more remote Afghan regions as well as its urban areas. You have extensive combat experience of this enemy and understand their tactics and habits. You're fluent in Arabic as well as Dari, the official state language, and Pashto, spoken by most Taliban fighters.'

'Sounds like quite a tribute. Are you asking me to command this mission?'

'Not this time, Benedict. You'll be playing a key role but the eight-man task force will be headed by Captain Jack Buchanan. He was with B Squadron until just eight months ago, having served three years before returning to his parent unit. Promotion prospects aren't so rosy these days for officers within UKSF.'

'One of those,' said Ben, who had never been too fond of that kind of rank-climbing ambitiousness. He wasn't familiar with Buchanan. The six hundred or so men of 22 SAS were divided into four squadrons, A, B, D and G, each subdivided into four specialised troops and with its own command HQ. Ben had served with A Squadron; and in any case that was probably before Buchanan's time.

'Easy for you to say, as the youngest man in the regiment's history to make major,' Carstairs replied. 'Buchanan's an excellent soldier. Limited combat experience, but his credentials are otherwise perfect and he jumped at the chance to take on this command. Because of your time out, you come back in with the rank of trooper. I trust that isn't going to be an issue?'

'Not as far as I'm concerned. I never gave a damn about being an officer. When do I meet the team?'

'About five minutes before you'll be in the air. Speed is of the essence here and there'll be no time for proper introductions or briefings until you're on the other side ready to deploy, approximately twelve hours from now.'

'Then you'd better fill me in.'

'As far as I can. You'll have gathered that this is anything but a regular mission. We're operating strictly off the books here, even though it's been sanctioned at the very highest level.'

'I'm sure it has,' Ben said. 'By the same senior officials who'll turn their backs and deny the whole thing ever happened, if it all goes belly-up. Correct?'

Carstairs nodded. 'That's the deal. The need for secrecy is absolute. As I've already explained to Buchanan, mess this up and you're on your own. Your job will be to make sure you don't. You mustn't. You can't.' There was an edge of anxiety in his voice, as though the axe would fall on him too if the mission failed.

'I'll bear that in mind,' Ben said with a dry smile. 'And am I allowed to ask what our objective is?'

'You are,' Carstairs replied. 'And I'm authorised to give you all the information you require at present.' He paused, eyeing Ben thoughtfully. 'Before we get into that, you've been out of the game for some time. How up to date is your knowledge of the current situation in Afghanistan?'

'I like to stay reasonably abreast of things,' Ben said.

'Good. Then I needn't dwell on just how messy the situation there has become of late. As you're aware, the sudden withdrawal of US troops from the region and the ensuing Taliban takeover of the country have resulted in the most godawful chaos. Trust the Yanks to bugger it up so badly, of course. The present administration are bloody incompetents, run by a gang of wet blankets under a president who frankly ought to be in a—but I won't go on about that. In short, as a consequence of this bungled evacuation a great many people have found themselves stranded and cut off in a significantly hostile environment, to put it mildly.'

'I had heard something about it,' Ben said. 'Then Operation Hydra is a rescue mission?'

'Yes, but forget all those other poor sods. There's nothing anyone can do to help them, and they don't concern us. Instead, the focus of this task force will be on one particular individual whom we believe to be trapped behind enemy lines.'

'Believe to be?'

'The individual's exact whereabouts are uncertain at this point,' Carstairs said, sounding strangely reminiscent of the account Linus Twigg had given Ben the day earlier. 'Communications were lost some time ago. Your objective will be to penetrate deep into enemy territory, locate and extract them, making use of contacts on the ground, who will provide whatever intelligence and logistics are available. You'll be concentrating your search within Kabul to begin with, then move to the outlying areas as required. Needless to say, the capital is heavily occupied by Taliban fighters and there are multiple checkpoints on every route in and out of the city. It's not going to be a cakewalk.'

'And just who is this individual we're trying to locate?' Ben asked.

'An asset of prime importance to us. Whose safe extraction is absolutely essential, at all costs. At *all* costs,' Carstairs repeated for emphasis, peering at Ben from under his snowy eyebrows.

'Must be quite a VIP,' Ben said. 'A political asset? One of your agents who's slipped through the net of the evacuation effort?'

'For the purposes of the mission, the principal will be known by the codename "Spartan",' Carstairs replied.

'That's it?'

'That's it. Spartan's identity is on a need-to-know basis. And at this point, you don't need to know.'

Ben stared at him. 'I've been on a lot of hostage rescue missions, Colonel. I've never been asked to locate someone without knowing who they were.'

'There are reasons why it has to be that way,' Carstairs replied. 'But you won't be operating completely in the dark. The task force's efforts will be assisted and guided by a consultant, who's accompanying the mission. Until such time as Spartan is located, only he will know his identity.'

'Do *you* know his identity?' Ben asked.

Carstairs spread his hands in a gesture that said, 'If I did, I wouldn't tell you.'

'All right. This consultant, he's what, Army Intelligence?'

'A non-military operative.'

'A spook,' Ben said.

'Call it what you will. Part of your role will be to protect the consultant if things get rough. Without him, or more specifically without his knowledge, the mission fails.'

'You don't regard that as a weak spot?' Ben asked. 'He catches a bullet, gets taken by the enemy or run over by a bloody bus, and we're cooked. Putting all the eggs in one basket doesn't strike me as such a brilliant strategy.'

'You know as well as I do that no plan was ever perfect or ever will be,' Carstairs replied. 'I repeat, there are reasons.'

'How does he get in?'

'He's already there,' Carstairs said. 'He'll RV with the team when you reach our safehouse in Kabul.'

'Is he CIA? You know what I think about those guys.'

'No, he's one of ours.'

'What's his name?'

'You'll know him as Lewis Goffin.'

'What's his real name?'

'That's classified.'

'What are his credentials? Training and field experience?'

'You don't need to know that either.'

'I think I need to know if some non-combatant desk jockey ghoul from the dark corners of British Intelligence is going to get under our feet and become a liability to our team when things get hot out there,' Ben said. 'And they will, make no mistake. Anything can happen.'

'He won't get in your way.'

'And if we succeed in locating Spartan? What then?'

'Systems will be in place to extract him,' Carstairs said simply.

'Otherwise, there's no back door for the team.'

'Correct. As I said, you'll be on your own.'

Ben said nothing.

'You look unhappy, Benedict.'

'That's because I am. Your assignment stinks. Eight men deployed blind and totally unsupported on a one-way ticket into an enemy hellhole hunting for a target they can't identify, while having to babysit a dodgy MI5 character who's guarding the key information that's been withheld from them. That's not how we've ever worked before.'

'I told you this was an irregular mission,' Carstairs said. 'Are you turning it down? Well here's my private number' – handing him a plain black business card with no name on it – 'in case you change your mind. But you'd better do it pretty damn fast. Minutes count, literally.'

'To hell with that,' Ben said. 'I'm ready. Let's go.'

Chapter 9

From the anonymous office building, the same cars sped away through the city. Though as usual none of his escorts spoke a word to him, Ben quickly understood where they were headed. As anyone living in its vicinity was aware, the air base at RAF Northolt in west London had long been used by both civilian and military aircraft. Less well known was the fact that some years earlier, an SAS unit had been relocated from Hereford to a new secret base within the station, with the purpose of keeping them close by in the event of a major terror attack on the capital.

The cars whisked through security checkpoints and across the air base to an empty area where they pulled up outside an unmarked hangar much larger than its neighbours. Inside, vast and imposing inside the huge hangar, stood an A400 Atlas troop transport plane from 7 Squadron of the Joint Special Forces Aviation Wing. The four-engined monster was one of the biggest military aircraft in existence, the replacement for the venerable old Hercules aboard which Ben had flown into many theatres of operation. The Atlas was the same type of plane that the RAF had used to airlift some 17,000 people out of Kabul as part of the joint forces evacuation effort, before the gates slammed shut. It could carry more cargo a greater distance in a shorter time than its aged predecessor, with a range of over 3000 kilometres and the ability to refuel in mid-air, so this one wouldn't need to touch the ground a single time on its round trip delivering the task force to their destination.

As Ben walked into the hangar he spotted a group of men gathered by the aircraft's enormous nose landing gear. He guessed they must all have been waiting on standby pending his decision to join the mission or not. Which meant he was the last man on board. A couple of the group were obviously air crew, while the rest were dressed in casual civilian gear. A tall, athletic, dark-haired man in his mid-thirties, who had been leaning against the huge front wheel deep in discussion with one of the pilots, broke off his conversation to walk over with something of a swagger and greet Ben, smiling cordially enough. He introduced himself as Jack Buchanan, Operation Hydra's mission commander.

'Pleased to meet you, Commander.' Ben wasn't going to 'sir' anybody because he no longer considered himself part of the military. If Buchanan was taken aback by that, he didn't show it.

'Heard a lot about you,' he said.

'Probably only the repeatable bits,' Ben said.

'Come and meet the guys.'

Buchanan led Ben over to the rest of the group, and the next couple of minutes were spent on introductions. In addition to the task force commander, Bob Meadows, Pete Dixon, Will Yates, Rick Mackay and Mark Simms were all new faces to Ben, while Steve Cale, a little older than the rest, was someone he remembered from back in the day. Cale had been a perfectly capable operative – nobody who wasn't would ever make the grade to join SAS – but Ben had never liked him for his brash, loudmouthed ways.

When the brief introductions were done with, Buchanan looked at his watch and said, 'Okay, ladies and gentlemen, I suggest anyone who needs to should hit the head in short order, because it's going to be time to roll.'

None of the operatives could be allowed to carry compromising identification with them, and so before he was allowed to board the aircraft, Ben had to surrender his wallet along with anything else in his pockets, even a till receipt that could pin him to a location. Knowing that in advance, during the car journey to RAF Northolt he'd secretly slipped the colonel's business card into his cigarette pack. You never knew when such things might come in handy.

Carstairs had filled Ben in on a few more specifics before they'd parted. Back in the day an SAS unit would generally have been landed at the nerve centre of Bagram air base. The largest US military airfield in Afghanistan, it had been capable of housing over a thousand troops. Also within the ring-fenced compound had been the notorious Parwan detention centre where imprisoned Afghans had demonstrably been subjected to torture by the Americans. Afghanistan's very own Guantanamo Bay.

But those glory days of the US occupation were at an end, and now the largely abandoned base was patrolled by Taliban fighters who had suddenly found themselves in charge of the biggest militia air force in the world. Meanwhile, the Bagram base wasn't the only one that had suddenly become off-limits to allied landings. In Ben's military tours of Afghanistan he'd sometimes been landed at a smaller base in neighbouring Uzbekistan. Now that that door had been slammed shut as well, the only viable way in was by parachute drop.

'It's been a while since you last jumped out of a plane,' Carstairs had said, raising an eyebrow.

Which was true, although Ben had done a lot of crazier things since then. 'It's like riding a bicycle,' he replied. 'No problems there.'

Carstairs had explained the various methods they'd considered to land the task force in enemy territory without being detected. The ideal would have been a HALO drop, in which the parachutists would jump from over thirty thousand feet, high enough to put the aircraft out of sight of anyone on the ground, as well as beyond the effective range of surface-to-air missiles. But because they'd additionally be dropping heavy vehicles to enable the task force to travel from close to the border into Kabul, the high command had opted instead for a low-altitude drop from around 1750 feet. For that purpose they'd be using a new kind of experimental heavy drop platform for the vehicles, to cushion the jolt of a two-thousand-kilo hunk of metal hitting unforgiving rocky ground from a great height. Their total destruction on impact remained a distinct possibility; while the risk of paratroops jumping from relatively low altitude, to say nothing of the hazards of detection and/or destruction of the aircraft from the ground, wasn't insignificant either. 'But then,' the colonel had added with a cold smile, 'none of you men are strangers to taking risks.'

The pilots made their way up to the flight deck and Ben followed the rest of the task force on board via the tail hatch as the four massive turboprop engines, the most powerful ever built by a western country, started cranking noisily up for action. The old Hercules had been able to accommodate between sixty-five and ninety parachutists, plus any amount of heavy cargo. To use this even larger aircraft to transport just eight men and their kit seemed like ridiculous overkill, and was just another indicator of the unusual degree of urgency surrounding this mission. No expense was being spared to recover the mysterious 'Spartan', whoever the hell he, she or it was.

Inside the plane's cavernous hold were two American Humvees in desert camo livery, tightly strapped up inside their massive steel airdrop crates. 'We're using these instead of our own vehicles,' Buchanan said to Ben, raising his voice over the rising roar of the engines. 'Seeing as the Yanks left so many of the damn things behind in Afghanistan that they'll blend in and won't attract too much attention if we have to abandon them. The colonel's idea.'

Ben nodded. It was smart thinking on Carstairs' part. Meanwhile, everything else needed for the mission – weapons, ammunition, food, water, communications and medical gear – had been packed into supply pods that would be dropped along with the vehicles.

'The old man thinks of everything,' Buchanan said with a smirk. 'We've even got false beards.'

That might have sounded preposterous, even comical, but Ben knew it was just another example of the colonel's meticulous attention to detail. In the new normal of life in

Afghanistan, the wearing of beards was basically compulsory for all adult males, in line with the Taliban's strict interpretation of Sharia law. A clean-shaven man walking about the streets of Kabul was an instant target for beating, flogging, or much harsher punishment if he was discovered to be a westerner. Far worse still, if his captives could make him confess he was an enemy operative. The relaxed grooming standards of Special Forces personnel operating in that environment, where most or all of the guys sported bushy beards in defiance of all normal military protocol, were a necessary means of blending in. Ben had worn one for months on end during his combat tours, though his didn't grow dark enough to pass convincingly for a native. This time around, with all the will in the world there just wasn't time to let things take their natural course before going into action. And while a false beard wasn't going to fool anyone except a blind man close-up, along with the right kind of ethnic garb it could allow you to deceive the enemy from a distance. Ben had no doubt that the supply pods also contained items of clothing that would allow the task force members to blend in as much as possible with the local population.

Smart thinking all round. But then, the old man had been actively involved in these kinds of covert operations since Ben was a young boy.

'I almost forgot,' Buchanan added. 'Colonel Carstairs asked me to give you this, for old times' sake. Remembered how attached you were to these obsolete relics.' He handed Ben a small oblong aluminium box, like a camera case. Inside was a Browning Hi-Power 9mm pistol, the same make and model Ben had used with the SAS years ago, superseded now by more modern versions. A tubular silencer and a loaded magazine containing thirteen rounds of full-metal-jackets nestled in the black egg-box foam lining next to the weapon. Ben took them out, snapped in the mag, put the gun in battery, made it safe and stuck it into the natural hollow behind his right hip that the very same model pistol had moulded into his body after so many years of concealed carry. To this day, he always felt strangely naked without it there. Now he was fully dressed again, and it felt good. Hell, if one of the most efficient and reliable close-quarter combat weapons ever devised was an obsolete relic, then so was he.

'That colonel's a real sweetheart, isn't he?'

'Thought you'd be pleased,' Buchanan said.

Then the task force settled themselves into place, dwarfed like eight little Jonahs inside the belly of a gigantic whale, and within a minute the huge aircraft lurched into motion as they taxied out of the hangar and went lumbering towards the runway. Soon they were off, with that familiar old great rumbling rib-shaking roaring *whoosh* that drowned out all possibility of conversation until they were at cruising altitude and the engine note settled to a loud steady drone.

Nothing now would happen for some hours. The lull before the storm, when a great deal *would* be happening, from the instant they set boots down in enemy territory. Some of the other men exchanged the occasional shouted comment or joke, the vociferous Cale doing more than his fair share of the yakking. Ben instead spent his time catching up on lost sleep and mentally preparing himself for what was coming. Never, ever had he imagined he'd find himself once more in this situation, heading into a military operation.

Especially not one like this, a secret mission that for him contained a personal mission of far greater importance.

At some point, sooner rather than later, he knew he would have to break away from the group and go off in search of Madison. He'd have to pick the right moment to do that, and it might not be easy. The army had long ago stopped putting deserters in front of a firing squad, but nonetheless the UK Special Forces high command most likely wouldn't take too kindly to one of their hand-picked troopers going AWOL in the middle of a critical operation.

Ben was aware of it, but he didn't care. His commitment to his friend came first. He leaned back against the curvature of the fuselage, feeling its thrumming vibration against his spine, closed his eyes and went back to sleep.

Chapter 10

Hours, hours, hours.

At last, the endless monotony was broken by the pilot's announcement that they were approaching Afghan airspace. The plan was to get as deep in over the border as possible without attracting notice, and for that purpose the drop zone had been chosen in a vast, empty region of wilderness. That could have been said of much of Afghan territory. Even so, it was a risky operation. Taliban patrols could appear unexpectedly out of nowhere, with the artillery to blow them out of the sky like a wildfowler taking down a high goose.

By then the task force had donned their parachute suits and helmets and each of them had equipped himself with a C8 carbine, worn vertically on its three-point tactical sling, and ninety rounds of spare ammunition per man in case they met with resistance on the ground. Ben felt perfectly calm and absolutely ready, as though he'd been in training for this just yesterday. Nods, thumbs-up gestures and a few grins and words were exchanged among the others as they ran through a final check of their chute equipment and lined up in single file for the jump. The aircraft's tailgate yawned open to reveal the night sky and the moonlit landscape 1700 feet below.

A blast of frigid air whistled through the gaping hole. The Humvees were released first, sliding back on their angled ramps and spinning away end over end out of the tailgate, first one then the other. Five thousand kilos of armoured metal hurtling downwards through the night. Moments later, the signal came for the parachutists to follow. Ben was fourth in line. When his turn came to jump, he stepped towards the black abyss and let himself fall into the void without the least hesitation. Then it was the long, long, spiralling descent, followed by the jerk and crackle of the parachute opening. The dark ground came looming rapidly up towards him, closer and closer; then he hit and rolled as he'd done a hundred times before, and he was safely down. Three men on the ground before him, followed by the last four, their dark shapes landing with soft thuds and the canopies of their chutes settling down around them and rippling in the cold wind, the material black for minimum night visibility by any potential enemy.

Ben and the team waited for several long minutes in absolute silence, poised with their weapons at the ready and scanning the ground all around them for anything that moved, until the rumble of the aircraft had completely diminished. In the pale moonlight the seemingly infinite rocky landscape looked like the lunar surface, except for the tall mountains whose snowy upper peaks glittered in the distance.

On Buchanan's signal, the eight men quickly secured their chutes and then went jogging over the barren terrain to retrieve the dropped Humvees and kit pods. To everyone's relief, both vehicles had survived the landing intact. It was impossible to hide the drop crates. They would just have to hope that by the time the enemy found them and raised the alarm, the mission would already be accomplished.

Opening up the kit pods they transferred their gear into the vehicles. They'd been thoroughly equipped for the mission. In addition to their personal weapons, the team were provided with Claymore mines and assorted other high-explosive devices, a heavy fifty-calibre anti-materiel sniper rifle for long range shots at enemy armoured divisions, and a Stinger surface-to-air missile launcher in case they came under air attack. The heavy weapons, rockets and grenades would be stored at the Kabul safehouse while they were carrying out their covert operations within the city.

Once the kit was all stowed, the men set about changing into the loose-fitting Afghan clothing they were going to need for the mission. Ben had the same kind of traditional shalwar kameez that he'd worn undercover back in the day, and a long black cloth neck wrap that could double as a head covering. The kameez had an opening through which he could get to his concealed pistol quickly and easily, and a loose pocket in which he could store his cigarettes. He felt pretty much at home in it.

They'd been on the ground less than twenty minutes when the two-vehicle convoy set off across the barren landscape, bumping and lurching over rocks and ruts, four men to each Humvee, a dusty and uncomfortable overland journey of several hours fraught with anxiety that the Taliban could strike at any moment, in large numbers and with extremely powerful weapons.

Humvees were sometimes claimed to be bulletproof. The fact was, as their occupants knew perfectly well, nothing short of genuine tank armour was genuinely able to resist high-velocity small arms fire. If they came under serious attack from a heavily superior force, they were fish in a barrel.

Ben rode in the second vehicle with Cale, Meadows and Dixon at the wheel. Buchanan, Simmons, Mackay and Yates were leading the way. Nobody spoke. Each man settled silently into his own private thoughts. For all their training and experience, the men's nerves were raw and sharp, like a smell in the air. Riding into war, thousands of miles away from base, with no backup whatsoever and no hope of relief or rescue if things went bad. Ben was wishing he could have maintained contact with Linus Twigg in case they might have heard something from Madison.

The anticipated encounter with enemy patrols never happened. Once, the Humvees came within sight of a fast-moving column of armoured vehicles, a long way off. They killed their lights, rolled to a halt, clutched their weapons and watched tensely as the column continued on by and disappeared into the distance.

A few hours later, sometime before the first rays of dawn at a prearranged location several kilometres to the east of the Kabul city outskirts, they RV'd with Saleem, one of their contacts on the ground. Saleem and his four associates, Fathullah, Ghani, Habib and Mazdak, would have the job of sneaking the task force into the heart of the city, taking advantage of the general chaos to go rolling through the many armed checkpoints. They were posing as Taliban fighters, and they looked the part: lean, mean, hairy and suitably villainous with ammunition bandoliers criss-crossed over their chests and their assorted Russian and American automatic weapons dangling from their shoulders. They had been militia soldiers with the Northern Alliance, a coalition of Mujahideen warrior groups that were sworn opponents of the Taliban. All five men bitterly detested the new regime and were more than eager to lend their support to any effort that might do them some damage. God only knew where the colonel had dug them up from.

Come the dawn, the task force were approaching the first checkpoint. This would be the moment of truth, testing the theory that the Humvees would just blend in with all the other captured American hardware driving around Kabul. Like his four colleagues in the front vehicle, Ben was hunkered down in the back of the second with Cale, Meadows and Dixon, hidden underneath layers of stinking sackcloth while Saleem's men lounged comfortably up front, feet up on the dash, arms dangling nonchalantly from the windows, weapons propped between their knees. They were driving straight into the dragon's den and if anything went wrong at this point, the mission would certainly be oblite-rated before it had even begun. Ben's carbine was off safety and his finger was hovering close by the trigger. He exchanged glances with Meadows under the sackcloth and saw the gleam of nervous tension in the guy's eyes.

But any concerns that the Taliban guards would see through the deception – or, possibly even worse, that the ex-Northern Alliance men would cave in to the temptation of opening fire on their hated enemies – were soon dispelled as they went cruising casually through checkpoint after checkpoint, pausing to natter amicably in Pashto with the sentries and share a few jokes before rolling onwards. Meadows made eye contact again with Ben and puffed his cheeks in a sigh of relief.

'Is okay, can come out now,' said their driver, who insisted on speaking his limited English with the Special Forces men. Ben and the others emerged from their hiding place and gazed cautiously out of the Humvee's windows.

Early morning, and the city was beginning to come to life around them, their first proper glimpse of Kabul since the fall of the US occupation. It had been a fairly westernised city while the allied powers were in control, with modern, liberal mores and fashionable clothing much on display. It was immediately apparent those were all gone now, as though erased overnight by the new normality of life. From a lively cosmopolitan melting pot of diplomats, military contractors, journalists, war tourists and thriving local businesses the city had been reduced to a chaotic smoggy morass of four million frightened people living under the boot heel of extremist dictatorship. Where once you would have seen trendy young men and women sitting outside cafés talking brightly over pots of saffron tea, now, in accordance with the new rulers' hardcore interpretation of Sharia Law, women were hardly to be seen at all outdoors; while all the men now wore the traditional Afghan clothes the regime approved, not a clean-shaven face among them. Even the music was eradicated, the austere void of silence left in its absence filled by the regular several-times-a-day ululating megaphone voices calling the faithful to prayer.

And of course, everywhere you looked were the fierce enforcers of that new regime. Armoured cars and personnel carriers were a ubiquitous presence all through the capital, draped with the black-and-white banner of the Taliban and loaded with fighters sporting the masses of shiny new weaponry the Americans had so obligingly left for them. The Talib comported themselves with the triumphant air of conquering heroes, hostile eyes daring anyone to challenge them. This was their time now. Watching the citizens scurrying through the streets, bowed, downcast as they tried to go about their business as unobtrusively as possible under the steely gaze of their conquerors, Ben could sense the oppressive atmosphere of terror hanging over the city.

'Here we are, lads,' Dixon said with a chuckle. 'How's it feel being totally alone and surrounded by a hundred thousand fundamentalist crazies who want you nailed to a cross?'

'Not too much worse than a weekend at my in-laws' place,' joked Cale, and Dixon laughed. Then Meadows craned his neck towards the window, peering up as he noticed the thud of a helicopter overhead. Ben could hear it too.

'Jesus Christ,' Meadows said, pointing. 'Look at that.'

Above them, an American Blackhawk helicopter gunship was passing over the rooftops. But that wasn't what Meadows was pointing at. Clearly visible against the pale morning sky was the silhouette of the limp hanged corpse of a man swaying pendulum-like from the underside of the aircraft on the end of a rope.

Any sense of levity inside the Humvee was suddenly gone as they watched with grim faces. 'Looks like the bastards caught another one,' Dixon said.

Meadows nodded, still gazing up at the helicopter. 'Yep, anyone who spoke out against them, anyone who helped the Americans or any of their allies. They won't send the poor sods to the gulag. They'll just hunt them down and exterminate them one by one.'

It was obvious to anyone on the ground, especially to professionals who'd seen a million military choppers in action and flown in them countless times themselves, that the aircraft's flight was highly erratic. As they watched, the Blackhawk narrowly avoided fouling its rotors on a mobile phone mast, destroying itself and raining destruction onto the streets below.

'Half these guys can barely count the fingers on their own hand,' Dixon grumbled, shaking his head in disgust. 'Let alone fly a sodding helicopter. It's a wonder they even got it up in the air, the stupid numpties. How the fuck they'll get it down again is anyone's guess.'

'Whoo-hoo,' said Cale. 'Wouldn't you just love to see them crash and burn?'

Ben kept his eye on the helicopter and its grisly trophy until they disappeared from view behind some foreground buildings. Inept pilots or not, it was a stark warning to all who dared defy their new rulers. In olden days they'd have impaled the severed heads of the vanquished on the city gates as an example to all. Now they just paraded their mutilated victims across the skyline like an aerial billboard. Different times, different wars, same barbaric message. Nothing had changed in all these centuries. Nothing ever would.

He checked his weapon once more. Reminding himself what in God's name could have possessed him to want to return to this damned place.

Meadows muttered, 'Welcome to hell, boys and girls.'

Chapter 11

Ben's companions were some of the most experienced combat veterans in the business, and there wasn't one who wasn't pretty much inured to the horrors of man's inhumanity against man. Yet the spectacle of the hanging corpse was a haunting enough image to stay in the mind for a long time afterwards, and it effectively killed most of their conversation as the Humvee cut across the city.

After a convoluted journey they arrived at the safehouse, a semi-derelict apartment building in a narrow, winding and empty backstreet near an industrial zone at the far western edge of Kabul. The building opposite was some kind of warehouse, disused with a lot of broken windows and little chance of anyone inside observing their arrival. Still, for safety's sake, they donned their false beards and headgear before stepping out into the street. Ben had to take care to ensure that his blond hair was kept well out of sight. A bottle of black dye had often been among the contents of his kit bag, back in the day.

Buchanan pointed at the apartment building and signalled for Ben to come with him. Passing through a creaky iron gate and a patch of desiccated waste ground, they stalked cautiously around the side of the building until they came to the red door they'd been told about. The safehouse apartment was on the third floor. Pistols drawn they crept up a dingy stairwell and along a corridor that smelled as though something had died there recently.

At Buchanan's soft knock, the apartment door opened; and there stood the man whose real name may or may not have been Lewis Goffin. Whatever Ben's mental image of an MI5 spook might have been, this guy certainly wasn't it. And the Anglo-Saxon surname Goffin was a complete misfit as well. He was a plump olive-skinned guy in his mid or late thirties, with Mediterranean features, oily black hair and a thick black beard prematurely streaked with grey. He might have been of Greek or Cypriot origin but in the right attire he'd easily have passed for a native in Iraq, Iran or just about anywhere else in the Middle East. The perfect spy, physically at least. Goffin was wearing a traditional Afghan pakol cap and the same kind of conservative loose-fitting garb as Ben and Buchanan, and it wasn't hard to understand how he'd managed to stay safely undercover during these last weeks of the Taliban's rule over Kabul.

Ben wouldn't have known him but Buchanan, as commander, had been briefed on his description. Buchanan had also been provided with a cryptic security question to which Goffin responded with the correct password. Sometimes the most old-fashioned tricks of the spy trade were the most effective.

Leaving the two men to talk upstairs, Ben returned back down to street level to give the others the all-clear. The rest of the team got out of the Humvees and they started lugging their heavy kit up to the apartment. The larger items were dismantled along with the rest of their weaponry inside discreet black holdalls, but all the same there was the pervasive feeling that they could be observed from afar as they hurriedly brought the equipment inside the building. Once the kit had all been unloaded, Saleem and his men took off in the Humvees. Those would be hidden in a lockup garage at a different location, for future use. Meanwhile, Saleem had provided a pair of dubiously obtained commercial vans, with false plates and business logos lettered in Arabic script, to use as transport within the city.

The two-bedroomed safehouse apartment was small and dank, with a sparsely furnished living room in which the men gathered for a briefing with Goffin. Ben had never much cared for intelligence operatives and maybe he was prejudiced, but right from the start he found it difficult to like the man. Speaking with a plummy Etonian accent and sprawled casually taking up most of the living room's only sofa, Goffin was loud, opinionated and annoying. He explained that while the task force had been en route, the situation had changed. The sudden emergence of a local informer, a man Goffin called Faazel, who claimed to have knowledge of the whereabouts of Spartan, meant that the mission was now due to start immediately, that same afternoon.

Goffin gave them the address in another district of Kabul where Faazel had agreed to meet and provide his information. For a steep price, of course, but he claimed to have all the necessary funds at his disposal. 'I'll be right there with you boys,' he said with a smile that came across, at least to Ben, as a condescending kind of sneer. 'All you have to do is get me inside so I can speak with him. Should be a pretty straightforward operation. Any questions?'

Ben had been standing at the back of the room, listening in silence and finding it harder and harder to digest the vagueness of their strategy. As an officer he'd always insisted on knowing every last detail of a situation, as far as possible, before going in. The safety of his men had depended on it. But here they were, expected to function in the dark, at the whim of this supercilious intelligence goon. He had a thousand questions, but deciding to focus on the main one he asked Goffin, 'Who's Spartan?'

Goffin's smile went cold and he replied, 'That's classified. I thought that fact had already been made clear to you.'

'It has,' Buchanan said, with a warning look at Ben. 'Anyone else got a question?'

Catching and ignoring Buchanan's look, Ben pressed on, 'All the same, for practicality's sake, we should be informed. We'll soon find out anyway, if we locate him. Or her, or it, or whatever exactly the objective is.'

'*When* we find him,' Goffin said. 'There are no ifs. Failure is not an option here.'

'So it's a him,' Ben said. 'Thanks. At least now we know something.'

'You let me worry about these kinds of details, Trooper,' Goffin said icily. 'Right now, I repeat, for the second time, it's not your concern. Just do your job. Which means, do as I suggest and as your commander tells you. Do you have a problem with that?'

Ben knew that was all he'd get out of him. He relented and said nothing more. The briefing over, Goffin and Buchanan conferred quietly in one corner while Cale, Dixon and Meadows headed for the kitchen to brew coffee and rehydrate some of the MREs, meals ready to eat, from the kit. 'Shredded beef in BBQ sauce,' Cale was complaining. 'Great. I was hoping for rat stew.'

'I don't give a monkey's, pal,' Dixon grunted. 'I'm so famished I'd eat a pickled fucking camel from the feet upwards and finish off with the tail.'

'Might be able to pick one of those up at a local market,' Cale said. They bantered on like that, but Ben tuned out and went into the second bedroom where they'd piled the equipment, partly to check the bags and partly to be alone with his own thoughts.

They had just under an hour to kill before they'd be on the move again. Ben grabbed a mug of the tasteless coffee and swallowed some of the high-caloric, high-sodium offal paste that the army termed food. *Eat when you can, rest when you can*, was an old military adage. The resting part would have been welcome, but it was hard to relax whilst being treated to Goffin's loud disparaging views on the situation in Afghanistan as he spread himself out even wider on the sofa and held court to his captive audience.

'I mean, take a look around you,' he scoffed. 'Can anyone truly say this country hasn't always been an unstable shithole, right from the start? Hardly qualifies to be called a nation at all. Just a chaotic collection of disparate tribespeople speaking thirty different languages, which is three times the number of paved airfields they've ever managed to build in

86

their whole stupid country. Same as they're all as poor as shit because they've never had the wherewithal to cultivate more than a tiny fraction of their land, even though it's bigger than England and France put together. Even then the only crop they can produce worth a damn is opium. Half the population's got TB and the rest are either starving or fucked up with malaria. Anyone who makes it past age fifty is so old and decrepit they might as well be dead. What a dive,' he went on, digging deeper into his theme with a look of pure contempt on his face. 'Look what it's cost us, this half-arsed wasteland that doesn't even have any proper borders. You couldn't tell who was winning the war, because the slippery bastards could just flit in and out of the place, disappear off into fucking Pakistan whenever they pleased. And now look at them, strutting around like they own the place.'

Ben said, 'They do own the place.'

Goffin's flow was broken as though someone had kicked him up the backside. 'What did you say?'

'I said, they do own the place,' Ben repeated. 'They were handed it on a plate, and now it's theirs again for a while, whether you or I like it or not. I guess sooner or later someone will come and take it from them and then the whole thing starts again. Round and round. We're all just riding the cycle.'

'Well, listen to the big expert here,' Goffin snorted. 'Is that a fact, Mister Clever Pants?'

Ben looked him up and down. 'You know, Goffin, for a secret agent you don't half love to blabber your mouth off. All we've been hearing for the last half-hour is you. These guys are tired and they've got some actual work to do. How about you shut your pie hole for a while and let them get some rest?'

Goffin bridled and looked as if he was about to say something. Then he saw the calm, dangerous look in Ben's eyes and shut up.

The remainder of their downtime period went by in relative peace and quiet before they had to tool up and head off again. By now the two vans had turned up outside, one white and one silver, both equally battered but apparently serviceable. They bundled themselves and their personal carry weapons aboard, and set off. Ben rode in the silver van, following the lead vehicle as before, while this time Goffin joined Buchanan and the others in the first. Ben was aware of having made a real friend in the intelligence agent. And he didn't give the tiniest damn about it.

Chapter 12

Their destination lay in a district in the north of the city. To get there, once more the task force operatives had to keep out of sight in the backs of the vans while their Afghan associates did the driving. Only Goffin was able to travel up front, thanks to his appearance which allowed them to pass through the two checkpoints they encountered without any issues.

The inside of the van was as stifling as an oven. Ben and his three comrades were glad when at last they rolled to a halt and Buchanan's voice on the radio crackled, 'We're there.'

They would be going in with pistols only, for ease of concealment. Ben had the silencer threaded to the muzzle of his Browning, making the weapon feel long and cumbersome inside his waistband. With their facial disguises and head coverings in place and their firearms hidden under their shalwar kameez, the SAS men stepped out into a busy street of dirt flanked by crumbled, stained balconied buildings. Nearby was an open-air market where awning-shaded stalls displayed a bewildering array of wares, ranging from colourful fabrics to exotic herbs and spices to knock-off consumer electronics to coops filled with squawking chickens. Vendors hurried here and there with carts and barrows laden with goods. Almost every face was male, while those of the very few women to be seen were completely covered above and below the eyes. The smoke from a stall grilling meat filled the air with a charry, aromatic tang. Slow-moving pickups and motorcycles threaded their way through the throng.

The building across the street where they were due to meet Goffin's informer, Faazel, was a balconied house on three crumbling adobe-walled floors, above a stall selling melons and a tiny repair shop where two wizened guys were dismantling a motor scooter. The task force men spread out discreetly to cross the street, pausing for a few moments pretending to peruse the market stalls as a truck filled with Taliban fighters came growling slowly through the crowds. Ben noticed the way that the locals avoided making any kind of eye contact with them. Then the truck had passed on by, and the eight men led by Goffin made their way down an alley that was little more than a crack between the buildings.

A gated side entrance was unlocked. One by one they slipped through, into a small courtyard behind the building. They followed Goffin inside a doorway and up a flight of crumbling stone steps to the dim light of the first floor, yanking off the fake beards and stuffing them into their pockets as they went. There'd be no need for dissimulation during the meeting with Faazel.

The building was divided into flats, with Arabic numbers painted on their peeling doors. Goffin stopped, pointed and said softly, 'This is the one.'

'We should clear the room before you go in,' Buchanan whispered, but Goffin shook his head and replied, 'It's okay. I know him. He's cool.'

Goffin checked his watch, then knocked and opened the door. Buchanan entered first, moving cautiously with his hand on the butt of the sound-suppressed Glock pistol hidden in the folds of his kameez. Ben was through next, followed by Goffin with the rest of the team bringing up the rear.

The apartment was smaller and dingier than the safe house, and smelled strongly of mildew mixed with the smoke from the grill stall wafting in the open window. Its lone occupant was a small, wiry Afghan with the usual long black beard and baggy tunic, standing in the middle of the floor as though he'd been looking for something and not been expecting visitors. Ben noticed that he was wearing white high-top trainers. He had twitchy eyes and a nervous, suspicious expression on his face as he turned to stare at the nine men who'd just walked into the apartment.

'Faazel?' Buchanan asked in a low voice, but Goffin shook his head.

The little guy in the white trainers backed away a few steps. Ben thought he looked ready to kick up a fuss. So much for the reliable informer Goffin had been so sure of meeting here.

'Hey, it's okay, it's okay,' Goffin said in Dari, smiling and spreading his open hands to show he wasn't a threat. 'We're friends of Faazel. He said he was going to meet me here. You know where he is?'

The guy in the white trainers backed away another step, close to the far wall.

'It's cool,' Goffin said, in Pashto this time. 'My name's Yousuf. No trouble, okay? Yousuf, Faazel's cousin.'

Which didn't quite seem to account for the eight serious-faced, hard-looking foreign men Faazel's cousin had brought with him. Whatever the case, Goffin's reassurances only seemed to get the little guy more and more nervy. His right hand went behind the small of his back. Goffin held up his palms and said, 'Hey. Hey. Take it easy. Keep your hands in plain sight, okay?'

Buchanan was frowning. Ben didn't like it either. He could see what was about to unfold, several seconds before it happened.

By now the little guy was right up against the corner and could back away no further without going out of the open window to his right. He still hadn't spoken a word. His eyes were bulging and sweat was glistening on his brow. Then his right hand suddenly whipped out from behind the small of his back, clutching a chunky, shiny black US military-issue Beretta.

Ben had known. He'd even guessed what kind of pistol it was going to be. Because it went with those white high-top trainers, like peaches and cream.

The gun came out fast and swung towards them. Buchanan, standing right behind Goffin, had his Glock out even faster. Too fast, because the length of the silencer made a speed draw awkward and pulled his shot off target as he fired. The muted report of the gunshot coughed from the muzzle and a neat round nine-millimetre hole appeared in the plasterboard wall eight inches to the left of the little guy's chest. The little guy had the Beretta out at arm's length in a two-handed grip, finger on the trigger; but a fraction of a second faster than his brain could send the signal to his finger to squeeze off the shot, Ben nailed him centre-of-mass with two rounds from the silenced Browning, in such quick succession they sounded like one ragged report. The double impact jerked the little guy backwards against the wall and he slid down it, leaving an oily red smear.

Buchanan was standing there as though frozen to the spot. Ben stepped quickly over to the body, checked the pulse, found none. Stunned by the gunshots Goffin said, 'Shit.'

That was when they heard the commotion from the other side of the wall where Buchanan's bullet had struck. Raised voices, sounds of alarm and distress. For an instant Buchanan stared in horror at the hole in the plasterboard. Then bursting into action he raced from the apartment and out into the dingy corridor. Ben went after him, shouldering past Goffin and followed by the others. As he reached the corridor, Buchanan was already kicking open the door of the neighbouring apartment and bursting inside, gun in hand. Ben was right behind him, just in time to see a young teenage Afghan boy disappear out of the window. The boy made fleeting eye contact with them and then was gone.

Buchanan and Ben ran across to the window and saw the kid dropping the ten feet to a soft landing on the awning of the melon stall below, drawing an angry yell from the vendor. The boy slid to the ground and sprinted hard away after his two friends who'd already made it across the street and were disappearing into the crowds, one of them narrowly avoiding being flattened by a three-wheeler delivery scooter.

All were roughly the same age, thirteen or fourteen. The youngest was yelling loudly. Even though few people in the crowded market were paying much attention to them right at that moment, it was clear that the kids had got a clear view of the foreigners in the apartment and might raise the alarm.

Ben glanced at Buchanan and saw that his pistol was raised and aiming at the fleeing boy, about to take a shot. Ben slapped the gun down. 'Are you insane?'

'They saw us.'

Ben was about to reply when something on the floor caught his eye, and to his horror he realised that not all the kids had got away. Buchanan's missed shot had hit something after all.

The fourth young boy in the apartment had been standing close to the wall when Buchanan's stray bullet had torn through and hit him between the shoulder blades. He'd managed to stagger a couple of steps before collapsing against a threadbare sofa, behind which he was lying partially hidden. He was still alive and moving, but the blood was spilling out fast and the bullet must have nicked the aorta or perforated the heart. It was soaking his clothes almost black. His breath was coming in fast and ragged gulps of air, bright red froth foaming from the corners of his mouth.

'Oh, fuck!' yelled Meadows, seeing what Ben had seen. Ben got to the kid first, throwing himself down on his knees and rolling him over to examine the extent of the damage. It wasn't good. In seconds Ben's hands were slick and shiny with arterial blood and he knew the kid only had a few moments left to live. Meadows, the medic, wanted to step in and take over, but Ben wouldn't let him. The rest of the men stood around watching in dismay, except for Buchanan who hovered by the window looking blank. The boy's pulse felt thin and reedy and now his breathing was shallow. Then he gave a final groaning sigh and his body settled.

'He's gone, Ben,' Meadows said. 'Give it up.'

Ben passed a bloody hand over the boy's face to close his eyes. He got to his feet and looked at Buchanan, but Buchanan looked away. 'Nice work, *Commander*,' Ben said. His voice sounded strangled and thick. It was hard to get the words out. Buchanan made no reply.

'Let's get out of here,' Goffin said from the doorway.

Ben pointed at the dead boy. 'We can't just leave him like this.'

'To hell with him,' Goffin said. 'He's collateral damage. We're pulling out.'

Chapter 13

Ben looked again at Buchanan, who was supposed to be in charge of this mission, not Goffin. But right now Buchanan didn't look to be in charge of very much at all. He was staring down at his feet, his pistol hanging limp by his side. He'd screwed up badly and he knew it. Fumbled his gun in a moment of stress and fluffed a close-range shot that nobody of his skill level should have missed. That was what limited real-world combat experience could all too often do for a soldier, even a very capable one, when things got intense. Excellence on the training range was all fine and dandy. When your targets started shooting back at you for real, that was when your ability was put to the test. Buchanan should never have been given this mission, still less placed in command of it. And now this poor kid had paid for that bad choice with his life.

Outside in the street, the market crowd was still milling around largely going about its business, but now the youngsters were back. The boy who'd been last out of the window was getting an audience, pointing up at the building. People were taking notice of what he was saying, looking where the kid was pointing. A couple of them had their phones in hand. There was no telling who they could be calling. And no telling how long before this place could be swarming with Taliban fighters. Ben hated to admit it, but Goffin was right.

'Okay. Let's go.' They hurried out. Closed both apartment doors behind them, and headed fast down the stairs to the courtyard below, through the gate and into the alleyway. At its mouth Ben could see the crowd moving closer to the building, their anger gathering momentum. The direction the task force had come was totally blocked off and they have to find another way around. 'This way,' Goffin said, pointing up the alley.

They reached the far end and emerged into a warren of backstreets that radiated in all directions. The situation was highly dangerous: cut off from their transportation, their objective completely blown, with a hostile crowd that might suddenly head them off and surround them. Ironically it was Goffin who came to their rescue, calling up Saleem on the radio and delivering him a stream of directions in rapid-fire Pashto. Minutes later the vans had skirted around in a circle and came barrelling down the street. They clambered aboard and took off. Ben was glad not to be riding in the same van as Buchanan, because otherwise he might not have been able to restrain himself from knocking his head off.

Ben's anger hadn't subsided a great deal by the time they arrived back at the safehouse. Having been forced to shoot the guy in the apartment was one thing. Ben had taken down plenty of armed opponents in the past and he wouldn't have to lose sleep over this one. But the dead kid was something else. This was the first time in all Ben's operational experience that he'd been mixed up in a friendly fire incident involving a civilian bystander, and he was deeply upset by it. What the hell was he doing here, he asked himself again. He knew the answer, of course, but right now Madison Cahill seemed a very long way away.

He headed for the shower, where he spent a few minutes blasting himself with cold water to wash off the dead kid's blood and try to cool off his rage. By the time he emerged, Saleem and his guys had disappeared into the second bedroom to smoke hashish, whose acrid aroma Ben could smell in the passage. Meanwhile the rest of the team had congregated in the living room, where someone had produced a bottle of spirits and they were sharing it out in tin mess mugs. Meadows offered one to Ben, but he waved it away. He was too disgusted to even look at Buchanan. Instead he walked over to Goffin, who was slouched on his sofa looking downcast.

'Who the hell is feeding you this duff intel, Goffin?' Ben demanded. 'Your guy was supposed to be there but looks like the enemy was already onto him. For all we know they've got him by now. And you'd better hope he didn't have information about your precious Spartan, because if he did they'll have tortured it out of him.'

'How the hell do you figure they're onto him?'

'Because of the white high-top trainers the guy we shot was wearing,' Ben said. 'Have you ever bothered to take notice of the Taliban's signature choice of footwear? Not to mention the gun he nearly shot you with was US army issue. Brand new, straight out of the armourer's store, probably never been fired before. Details, Goffin. I thought they mattered to intelligence agents. So either your man Faazel is one of them, which I doubt, or they'd have laid out more of a welcome for us, or else he's got his own cover blown and the guy we shot was sniffing around his place for more clues.'

Ben could see agreement on the face of Meadows, Dixon and a couple of the others. Cale, not so much. Buchanan was looking unhappy too. Goffin shrugged. 'Yeah, well, how was I supposed to know? I'm not a fucking soothsayer.'

'Try doing your job,' Ben said. 'Now we not only have an innocent fatality on our hands, but three live witnesses who saw a bunch of western foreigners with guns in the apartment building. Doesn't look too good for your mission, does it?'

'We got out of there in time, didn't we?' Goffin countered, flushing dark. 'Nobody else saw us.'

'I'm not in the habit of depending on luck,' Ben said.

'This isn't your mission.'

'No, you're right. Because if it was, at least my guys would know who we're going around killing kids in order to find. I have a real problem with how you people are running this operation.'

Goffin stood up and jabbed a finger at Ben's chest. 'You've got a problem, all right. A hearing problem. Because I'm just not getting through to you, am I? What part of "that's above your pay grade" don't you understand?'

'I'm not getting paid to be here,' Ben replied. 'I'm here because they needed someone on board who knew what they were doing.'

'Leave it alone,' Buchanan told Ben.

Ben looked from one man to the other, and for a brief moment considered whose neck he'd most like to break first. Neither choice would probably have been such a good idea, however satisfying and well-deserved. Letting the moment pass, he turned away, snatched a set of van keys and a radio handset off the table and headed for the door.

Buchanan came after him, and stood in his way. 'And just where exactly do you think you're going?'

Ben replied, 'For a walk. Thought I might drive out into the city and see if I can find a nice park or something. There's one near the Pakistan Embassy, if memory serves me right. I fancy going for a stroll around, enjoy the feeling of grass under my feet, sit on a bench in the sunshine, read a newspaper, chill out for a while.'

'Are you crazy? We're on a fucking undercover mission here.'

'I know how that works,' Ben said. 'I was being deployed on black ops into places you've never even heard of while you were still at school, *Captain*.'

Buchanan got the hint. He shook his head. 'You can't pull rank on me. You're not a major any more. And you're not commander of this mission.'

Ben said, 'No, I'm just a guy who's decided to go for a walk. Are you going to stop me? Because you'd be picking a really, really bad moment to try that on, after your performance today. Don't even think about it.'

Ben said that with a face devoid of all expression. It made him look as hard and cold as a stone. It was a look that could chill the most confident adversary. And it was a look

100

that Jack Buchanan, for all his habitual tough-guy swagger, couldn't return. He broke eye contact and said nothing.

Ben said, 'Now step aside and let me pass.'

Buchanan hesitated a moment longer. Then with a sigh, he stepped aside and let Ben pass.

Ben said, 'Thank you.'

'Are we allowed to ask when you'll be back?' Buchanan asked sarcastically.

'You'll know when I'm back,' Ben said. 'I'll be walking in the door.'

'That's not an answer.'

'Or maybe I won't come back at all,' Ben said. 'Maybe I'm sick of your screwed-up mission and that idiot Goffin. And frankly, I'm not that interested in finding Spartan.'

'Or maybe you'll get your silly fucking head blown off,' said Cale.

'Not before you do,' Ben told him.

On his way out he passed by the second bedroom to grab a C8 carbine and an extra magazine. Saleem and his boys were quite mellow by now, and one of them offered him a toke of hashish. Then he left the apartment. He paused a moment in the empty stairwell to stick on the false beard. It fastened on with tape and was just about the stupidest piece of kit he'd ever been saddled with, but it served its purpose. He swaddled the head covering over his hair and part of his face and tied it in a knot behind his neck.

Not too convincing a disguise for anyone who might look at him twice, but in a frightened city like Kabul where the citizens scurried around with their eyes to the ground, the chances were that nobody would. Except for the Taliban, maybe, with their habit of making challenging eye contact with the conquered civilians. But Ben intended to steer clear of those guys as much as possible. He'd always had an excellent sense of direction, and by now he had a pretty good sense of where the checkpoints were, forming a route on his mental map of the city that would help avoid having to run the gauntlet. If it couldn't be avoided and things got interesting . . . well, that was what the C8 carbine was for.

He exited the building and walked out into the deserted street to where the vans were parked. The keys he'd grabbed were for the battered silver one. He got in, lit a Gauloise and took off down the street with a roar, and minutes later he was cutting east back across towards the heart of Kabul.

Ben Hope, driving through the city totally alone and surrounded by a hundred thousand fundamentalist crazies who wanted him nailed to a cross.

Chapter 14

Needless to say, Ben wasn't searching for a pleasant park where he could stroll around enjoying the feeling of grass under his feet and find a bench in the sunshine. He was headed for the offices of the Kabul Cultural Institute, where Madison's Afghan contact Aziz worked – or had worked, before he'd apparently gone missing at the same time as Madison. That was too much of a coincidence to ignore. Ben had already researched the Institute's address, back at Le Val when he was trying to figure out some kind of plan.

Now he was here, he still didn't have much of a plan. But checking the place out would be a good start.

It felt good to get away from the task force, though he knew he had maybe a couple of hours of liberty at most before he'd have to return to base. His mental map guided him along a twisty route through Kabul that, as he'd hoped, circumnavigated the numerous Taliban checkpoints. Even so, he must have passed a dozen or more of their military patrols as they cruised around the city intimidating the locals and hunting for infidels and traitors to hang, disembowel or torture to death. But Ben felt fairly safe in his van, just another anonymous vehicle out of thousands.

Safe, for the moment, leaving him to concentrate on the art of negotiating Kabul's terribly potholed roads. Drive too fast, you could end up breaking an axle. Drive too slow, you'd soon be accosted by hordes of beggars and street kids. In his dubious disguise the last thing he needed was too much attention.

Ben's destination was on a long, broad street near the centre, filled with chaotic traffic, motorcycles and scooters zipping in all directions. The air was hot and laden with fumes and dust. He passed by bazaars with their donkey carts and wagons and awnings. Ruined buildings still peppered with the scars of old bomb and battle damage. Billboards and flagpoles lining the roadside displaying the ubiquitous Taliban banner. A large mosque surrounded by a seething crowd of people, the pale sunshine gleaming on its dome and minarets; and then finally he spotted the two-storey Cultural Institute office building whose image he'd found in his online research.

As he approached the building, he saw a pair of American heavy troop transport trucks crammed with Taliban fighters halted outside, facing in opposite directions and partly blocking the road so that vehicles had to thread by in single file. At first he sensed trouble, before he realised it was just a couple of routine patrols that had stopped for a chat, happily holding up the traffic with total disdain for the city folks. He waited in line then drove slowly by, parked a hundred metres down the street and waited, watching the trucks and the fighters in his mirror. A woman was walking along the dusty roadside, clad from head to toe in her burka. As she passed by the soldiers she quickened her step, head bowed, trying to ignore their abusive tirades.

Hearts and minds. Ben had long ago learned – though he hadn't needed much teaching – to honour the ordinary people whose lives were disrupted by his military presence. These guys didn't have such scruples.

Soon afterwards, the trucks set off again and went their opposite ways; Ben flicked away his cigarette, got out of the van and started slowly walking towards the Institute building. Like the woman, he kept his head bowed towards the ground in a show of humility, averting his face from passers-by so that nobody would spot his European complexion and fake-looking beard.

Up close, the Institute offices had clearly seen much better times, looking dismal and rundown in comparison to the years-old images he'd seen. It had been a thriving place then, but now the steps and wall outside were pocked with bullet craters and the lower-floor windows were boarded up with plywood. Climbing the steps he saw that the front door was hanging open, and stepped inside the cool of a lobby entrance with what had once been a beautiful mosaic stone floor, badly cracked and chipped with tiles missing. The lobby was stripped bare of any furniture and there were empty patches on the walls where pictures had once hung. Images of relics and artefacts from Afghanistan's ancient pre-Islamic past, Ben guessed. Not something that the new regime could tolerate, in their insistence on erasing any part of the country's cultural history they considered idolatrous. Which equated to the large majority of it.

He paused, listening hard for any sign of life within the building. The place felt and sounded quite deserted, but all the same he slipped the Browning out of the folds of his kameez. To his right, a winding wooden staircase reflected the dull, dusty light streaming from a window. He made his way up to the first floor, where a row of offices lay open, chairs and desks overturned, bookcases and filing cabinets upset and their contents spilled everywhere. Had the ransackers just been smashing the place up out of spite, or were they searching for something in particular?

The second floor was just the same – or it would have been, if Ben hadn't come across the old man there. He was at least eighty, tiny and wizened and so urgently preoccupied with the task of cleaning up the debris left behind by the looters that at first he didn't notice Ben's presence there in the office doorway. The room was in such a mess that the poor old fellow clearly didn't know where to start, and he seemed close to tears with helplessness. Having pointlessly tried to arrange scattered files and piles of disordered paperwork into stacks, now he was struggling to right a tall bookcase that was much too heavy for him to manage.

Ben said in Dari, 'Salaam alaikum. Can I help you, father?'

The old man dropped the corner of the bookcase, almost crushing his feet in the process as he turned towards the doorway with fear and shock in his eyes. He took one look at Ben standing there – the baggy kameez, the dark beard, the head covering – and bolted towards another door in such panic that he tripped over a fallen chair and went tumbling. He seemed to be having difficulty getting to his feet, so Ben went over to him, grasped a skinny arm and helped him up. The old man seemed to weigh almost nothing. Ben's gesture hadn't done much to alleviate his terror, and he still backed away. At least he didn't pull out a gun.

106

Ben said, 'It's all right. I'm not one of them.' To prove the point beyond any doubt, he yanked off the fake beard and removed his head covering. He placed his right hand over his heard and nodded gently to show respect and sincerity. 'I'm sorry if I frightened you, father. Are you hurt?'

The old man looked at him very curiously for the longest time, taking in the blond hair and the blue eyes and clearly mystified by the stranger's appearance. At last he shook his head and replied in Dari, 'I'm not hurt. Who are you?'

Ben picked up the overturned chair that the old man had tripped over, set it upright and motioned for him to sit. He picked up another and sat in it himself, emphasising that he was no threat. 'I'm nobody you need to be afraid of. You have my word on it, I'm not here to hurt anyone.'

'Then why are you here?' the old man asked. 'You're not from this country, I can see that. Even though you wear Afghan clothes and try to pass yourself off as one of us. Why would you do that?'

'No, I'm from a long way away. My name's Ben. What's yours?'

'Karim.'

'Do you work here, Karim?'

Karim shrugged his narrow shoulders. 'I did. Now I'm not so sure. A poor old man like me, with nobody to look after him, who has to work until he drops dead, he is always looking for a place where he'll be well treated. They were kind to me here. I don't like to see it in such a state. You see what those filthy dogs have done? As if they haven't done enough harm already.'

Ben said, 'A man called Aziz Qeyami works here. Do you know him?'

'Aziz? Yes, of course. He's a decent and honourable man.'

'Then perhaps you know my friend too. Her name is Madison Cahill. Black hair, green eyes, slim, late thirties or thereabouts?'

Recognition showed immediately on Karim's wrinkled face. 'The American woman who was here. Yes, yes. I remember.'

Suddenly, Ben was back on the trail and he could feel the drumbeat of the chase thumping in his veins. 'When did you see her last?'

Karim shook his head and looked sad. 'Not since many days ago. She is gone. They're all gone.'

'They went together?'

'Yes, yes. Too dangerous for them here in Kabul. Your friend, and Aziz, and Ramin too.'

Ramin was a new name to Ben. 'Did they say where they were going?'

'Away from the city. To somewhere safe. That's what they said. But nowhere is safe. Things are very bad. The Taliban are killing many people. An American woman in Afghanistan, especially one so young and beautiful . . .' Karim pursed his lips and held back from saying more. 'Very bad,' he repeated.

'Please, Karim. It's important that you tell me anything you know. Anything they might have said about where they were going. I want to help keep them safe, but time is running short.'

'Who are you?'

Karim shook his head again. Ben could tell that the old man was hesitant to give away too much to a stranger, especially one who was obviously not quite above board and perhaps not to be trusted. In an extremist regime whose martial rulers were mercilessly butchering anyone who helped the hated western powers in any way, his reticence was hardly surprising. 'It will be our secret,' Ben said. 'Nobody needs to know that you and I ever met or spoke. Do you understand, Karim? I have to find her and get her out, or they will murder her. Your friends Aziz and Ramin too, and anyone else who went with her. You said yourself, nobody is safe.'

The old man looked toward the dusty window and swept an arm as though he was motioning towards the mountains. 'They are gone far away. Or I hope so for their sake, inshallah. Many have tried and failed to get out of Kabul. The Taliban are everywhere.'

'You know the name of the place?'

Karim nodded slowly. 'They are gone to find Zakara.'

The name didn't immediately mean anything to Ben. But then he remembered his conversation with Linus Twigg, and what Madison's assistant had told her about Rigby Cahill's long search for a lost city of Alexander the Great. Ben had been too worried about her to focus much on those kinds of details, but now they suddenly mattered far more.

'Zakara? In the Bamiyan Valley?' he asked, and the old man nodded again. Ben asked, 'Where exactly? Do you have anything like a GPS location, or map coordinates?'

Karim looked completely blank at the mention of GPS, but then a thought seemed to dawn on him. 'Maps, yes. The Institute has many, many maps.'

'Show me,' Ben said.

Chapter 15

By the time Ben got back to the safehouse he'd been away nearly all of the two hours he'd given himself. Folded away safely inside his kameez was the collection of ancient map prints that Karim had given him. It had taken the pair a long time to sift through all the wreckage of the offices to find the dusty old file in which they'd been catalogued away years ago, recently buried under heaps of debris. Once he had them safely in his possession, he thanked the old man for his help, promised him once again that he wouldn't breathe a word of their meeting to anyone, then hurried back to the van and raced back to base, ducking and dodging Taliban patrols all the way.

In truth, Ben almost hadn't returned to the safehouse at all. Now he had a much clearer idea of where Madison had gone and some sense of how to get there, it was all he could do to resist the urge to bail out of Operation Hydra and cut and run straight after her. It was the only real reason he'd come to this hellhole, after all; he had transport and weapons; there was little to stop him going AWOL, taking his chances, and to hell with Carstairs. The colonel had been happy enough to send eight men unsupported into a possible suicide mission with an unspecified objective. Ben owed him nothing. Let them roast him over the coals afterwards.

But another part of him simply couldn't bring himself to walk away from the others, just like that, without a word. Yes, Goffin was a pumped-up prima donna and quite possibly a liability to the success of the mission; its commander was almost certainly not up to the job, and Cale was a fool as well. But Bob Meadows was a good man, and Ben had no complaints about Dixon, Mackay, Simms or Yates either. Even fools deserved better than to be abandoned like that. If he simply failed to return to base, they'd most likely assume that he'd been stupid or unlucky enough to be caught by the enemy. In which case they'd have to hope he'd been killed outright, because few captives would have let themselves be tortured to death without giving up their comrades. Either way his loss to the mission would severely compromise the task force and weaken their morale, making them more prone to bad decisions and errors that could end up fatal to them all.

Then again, he'd said to himself as he drove away from the Institute, every hour, every minute that went by Madison could be in terrible danger – if she wasn't dead already.

Ben was sure he'd faced worse dilemmas in his life, but he couldn't remember when. He decided that his options boiled down to two choices: if he was going to quit the mission, he was going to tell Buchanan to his face. Alternatively, if they could wrap up their present business quickly enough – though it would have to be pretty damn quick – he might even be able to persuade some of the more capable team members to come with him in search of Madison. Saleem and his gang would likely come in useful, too. If they thought teaming up with Ben on this new mission gave them a chance of killing some Taliban, they'd jump at the opportunity.

Those were the conflicted thoughts swarming in his mind as he walked into the safehouse. He hadn't expected too much of a rosy reception after being away for so long, but the instant he stepped inside and saw the anxious, impatient frown on Buchanan's face, he knew that something urgent had come up during his absence.

Before Buchanan could say what, Goffin stepped in, eyeing Ben with evident dislike and looking pointedly at his watch. 'Enjoy your jolly little stroll in the park, did you?'

'Very refreshing,' Ben replied. 'I'd have brought you back an ice cream, Goffin, but I didn't know what flavour you liked.'

'So glad to hear you enjoyed yourself. Meanwhile, there's been a development. We're going to be on the move again in exactly sixteen minutes from now. If you hadn't deigned to make your appearance when you did, we were going to leave you behind. Now I suggest you get your skates on.'

'No rest for the wicked,' Cale said with a grin.

'What development?' Ben said.

Buchanan said, 'Faazel got back in touch.'

'Still in the land of the living, I see.'

'He knows they're onto him but he managed to give them the slip,' Buchanan explained. 'He's also got some fresh information on the whereabouts of Spartan. There's been a reported sighting of the target at a small town called Harafi.

We'll load the kit into the vans and proceed to the village of Ghurdak, twenty kilometres north-west of the city. That's where we'll RV with four more of Saleem's people, who'll have the Humvees ready for us to transfer into. Then onwards to Harafi to meet with Faazel, and he'll take us directly to Spartan.'

'So Spartan is there with him?' Ben asked.

'He's close by,' Goffin replied.

'And you confirmed this on the phone with Faazel?'

'He didn't phone, he texted me. But yes, we have a positive ID and a confirmed location.'

'Then why don't we just go straight to him?'

'This is how it's going to get done,' Goffin said irritably. 'The deal goes through Faazel.'

Ben asked, 'Do we have any intel on the strength of local Taliban forces at Harafi?'

'Shouldn't be a problem,' Goffin said. 'The occasional patrol passes through, but nothing heavy.'

'And Ghurdak?'

'Placc is just a sleepy little village,' Goffin said. 'We won't run into any trouble there.'

'Okay,' Ben said. 'So assuming all goes according to plan. What then?'

Buchanan replied, 'Once we have safe possession of the asset we head back west to the original DZ, where an RAF Chinook from Al Dhafra air base in Abu Dhabi will touch down to pick us up. With any luck we'll have this whole thing wrapped up in a few hours and be on our way home.'

'Halle-fucking-lujah,' Cale said in the background, but nobody was listening to him. For Ben, who'd been banking on a rapid execution of their mission as his best means of avoiding going AWOL, this turnabout was welcome news. A revised plan was spinning together in his head. The moment they had Spartan secured, he would split from the task force and make his own way with all possible speed to the Zakara site in the Bamiyan Valley. He'd have to scrap the idea of bringing Meadows, Dixon or any of the other guys along with him for backup, but he was still betting on persuading Saleem and his gang, who might also be prevailed on to call in some more of their Northern Alliance friends. That would take care of Ben's essential transportation needs, and provide useful manpower and firepower in case of a tangle with the Taliban forces. If he succeeded in finding Madison alive, Saleem's people might also offer an alternative way of getting her and himself safely out of Afghanistan, via the old escape routes through the mountains into neighbouring countries such as Uzbekistan, Tajikistan and Kyrgyzstan that the Mujahideen had used for years during their war against the Soviets.

They'd wing it, somehow. The first thing was finding her. And now that prospect seemed much closer – and all the more worrying for it.

It was on the tip of Ben's tongue to tell Buchanan his intentions, but he held back. Instead he said to Goffin, 'Let's hope your man comes through for us this time.'

'He will,' Goffin snapped. 'I trust him.'

'More than you trust us lot, apparently.' Ben said. 'Unless you're finally prepared to tell us who Golden Boy is.'

'You'll find out soon enough,' Goffin said. 'In the meantime, ignorance is bliss. If things go tits-up and you get

114

caught, at least you won't have to pretend that you don't know anything.'

'Getting caught isn't my style,' Ben said.

Goffin snorted and looked at his watch again. 'Happy to hear it. Now let's move.'

They hurriedly carted all their heavy kit down to the vans, then set off with Saleem and his friend Mazdak at the wheel and the rest of the task force concealed in the back. This time, Ben found himself riding in the front van, the white one, along with Goffin, Buchanan, Meadows, and Cale. They rolled quickly westwards through Kabul and cleared the checkpoints without incident once again thanks to the diplomatic charms of the Northern Alliance guys.

Then at last they were clear of the city, with the open plains and looming arid mountains all around, and it was safe for the hidden passengers to come out. They met little traffic on the long, dusty highway, now and then a Taliban troop convoy with trucks overflowing with gun-toting fighters and the black and white flag fluttering behind them. Once they passed a column of M1 Abrams main battle tanks and armoured cars rumbling by in the opposite direction, covered in turbaned men all clinging on to the turret and sitting astride the gun. Then the road was clear again; they passed through a couple of tiny villages, one of them apparently abandoned, roofless tumbledown houses and chickens wandering about the empty dirt streets.

Ben sat gazing out of the window and thinking about Madison. He hoped she'd made it to her father's lost city. What did she expect to find there? Ben was no archaeologist but he'd have bet that every ancient site in Afghanistan – the ones that hadn't been razed completely to the ground by the Taliban in their drive to wipe out all trace of all that predated their revered Prophet – must long since have been looted six ways from Sunday and stripped clean of anything remotely of value by enterprising locals.

That wouldn't stop her trying, of course. To risk your life for a bunch of crumbling old ruins seemed to him like a crazy thing to do. But then, apparently, a particular kind of craziness seemed to run in the blood of the Cahills. Ben couldn't entirely blame them. He'd often reflected the same thing about the Hope family, with himself as the prime example.

'Home again soon,' Meadows said next to him, breaking into his thoughts. 'Have to say I won't be sorry to get this one over and done with. I hate this bloody country.'

'It's a hard land,' Ben said. 'That's for sure. Three thousand years of constant war will tend to do that to a place. And to its people.'

'You think it will ever get better?'

Ben smiled. 'While men are in charge, I doubt it. Pretty much our greatest talent is for killing and destroying one another. It seems to be in our nature.'

'Maybe we ought to let the women have a crack at it for a change,' Meadows said.

'Someone should suggest that idea to the current rulers. I'm sure they'd be up for it.'

'Then again, maybe the women would be worse.'

'You never know,' Ben replied, thinking about Madison and her crazy ways.

Meadows grinned, then went quiet for a while. After a long pause he said in a more serious tone, 'Why are we here?'

Ben didn't understand. 'You mean, who's Spartan?'

'I mean, why were we ever here. All this fighting over nothing.'

Ben looked at him. It seemed the strangest thing for a fellow SAS soldier to come out with, even though Ben himself had been wondering the same thing for a long time.

'It was that poor kid,' Meadows said sadly. 'Watching him die like that. Makes you think, you know? About what you signed up for. What it's all about. Whether you're doing the right thing.'

Ben said, 'Yup.'

Meadows fell back into silence and didn't speak again. They'd left the highway a few kilometres back, and for the last while the road they'd been following was little more than a dust track with undulating rocky scrubland to both sides, all the way to the foot of the tall mountains in the distance. It was hard to imagine anyone being able to eke a living out of this harsh, unforgiving terrain, but here and there was a small rural holding or farmstead. They'd seen no signs of human habitation at all for a few kilometres when Goffin, up front in the passenger seat next to Saleem, pointed and said, 'Here we are, folks. Coming up on Ghurdak. Should have eyes on our Humvees any time soon. Yes, there they are.'

Goffin had been right about the place being a sleepy little village. Ghurdak wasn't quite as desolate as some of the ruined settlements they'd passed through, but nothing much stirred among the low-slung adobe houses. A wind was whistling down from the mountains, blowing up dust in the narrow dirt streets. An old, old woman was herding a line of tired-looking goats along, paying no attention to the group of men stepping out of the two vans. The Humvees were parked between a small house and an ancient dry-stone stable block, empty and waiting for them exactly as planned – but there was no sign of Saleem's associates who'd brought them here.

'This is strange,' said Saleem in Pashto, joined by Mazdak from the second van as the two of them gazed around the buildings in search of their friends. 'Where did they go?'

The old woman with the goats hurried on past. Something in her step made Ben think she was afraid. He felt a tingle in his spine. His spider-sense warning him something wasn't right. He glanced at the others. Meadows was looking apprehensive, as though he'd sensed something too. Buchanan was giving orders to start moving the kit from the vans into the Humvees.

'Never mind them,' Goffin said dismissively to Saleem. 'We're in good time to make our meeting with Faazel. That's all I care ab—'

Those were the last words ever to come out of Lewis Goffin's mouth, because in the next moment his head exploded and the blood spray spattered the windows of the van behind him.

And then it started.

Chapter 16

The bullet that took away most of Goffin's head came from a fifty-calibre rifle, fired at close range from less than a hundred metres away behind the houses. Milliseconds later, the booming report sounded over the rooftops and echoed around the mountains. But by then all hell had already broken loose and the rattle of automatic gunfire was coming in staccato bursts from all over the village.

If Ben had had time to think about it instead of ducking for cover, he'd have been remembering what Goffin had said about Faazel: the way he'd texted instead of calling, the fact that anyone could have sent that message. He'd have been thinking that Faazel was probably already dead before that; that the enemy had taken him, tortured information out of him, and that this fake rendezvous had been set up as an orchestrated ambush. And that Saleem's associates who'd brought the Humvees here to Ghurdak had already suffered a nasty death as well.

But Ben didn't have time to reflect over any of those things as the bullets were suddenly flying everywhere. The Taliban fighters had picked the perfect moment to spring their surprise attack, just as the task force were at their least prepared for it and most of their kit was still packed up in the vans, much of it not even assembled let alone combat-ready. If they hadn't been carrying their personal weapons they would have stood no chance at all against the withering enemy fire.

As it was, even so they stood very little.

It was impossible to tell how many Taliban fighters had invaded the tiny village, but it seemed like over fifty judging by the ferocity of the attack. Darting shapes of men could be seen running between the buildings, clutching assault rifles and grenade launchers. Ben had unslung his carbine and managed to get off a couple of short bursts, taking one man down and injuring another, before the ground at his feet was violently whipped into a storm of flying dirt, a line of holes punched into the bodywork of the van behind him, and he was forced to dive under the vehicle for cover.

Bob Meadows wasn't so fast to react, and his slowness cost him his life. From his prone position under the van Ben saw the bullets tear into Meadows' body, making his body jerk like St Vitus' dance before he twirled around and collapsed dead on his face in the dirt a few feet away from the van. The bullets went on shredding poor Meadows' corpse while heavy gunfire peppered the van. One tyre blew, then another; the vehicle settled lower on its suspension and for an instant Ben thought he was going to be crushed under it. He scrambled backwards in the dirt, dragging his carbine by its sling. Emerging from the other side he pulled himself up on one knee and used the van's rear quarter as cover to rattle off a couple more bursts. The butt of the carbine juddered against his shoulder and spent cartridge cases spewed from the ejector, bouncing and rolling on the ground at his feet.

The volume of the battle was ear-splitting, a constant roar of noise with guns crackling, men shouting, bullets impacting and ricocheting, here and there a shriek as one of them hit a live target, so loud you couldn't distinguish the sound of your own weapon from the many others all going off at once; total extreme concentration, no time to think, no room for hesitation or pity, kill or be killed. Ben ducked as the van's taillight exploded inches from him and showered him with plastic shards. Then he nailed the man who'd fired at him in his sights, squeezed the trigger, felt the carbine shudder in his hands, saw the man fall; instantly swivelled his muzzle to track another running figure appearing in a gap between the houses, fired again, saw that one stumble and topple over as well.

In the heat of the moment it was difficult to know what was happening to his comrades around him. Saleem and Mazdak had been standing right next to Goffin when his head had been blown off, but they were now out of sight and Ben had to assume they'd managed to race for the shelter of the stone stable block across to the left. Meanwhile Buchanan, Dixon and Cale had made a break for the corner of the low-roofed house to their right, chased by a zigzagging flurry of bullet impacts as they sprinted for cover. Buchanan made it around the corner, followed by Dixon. Cale was just a few short strides behind them when a red spray erupted from his left thigh. He tumbled over, rolled and lay flat on his belly in the dirt in the middle of the street, still gamely firing back at the enemy.

Things were getting critical now, because the limited amount of ammunition the task force had been carrying in their magazines and on their persons was fast running out and there was no question of retrieving more ordnance from the vehicles. Meanwhile the Taliban fighters, emboldened by their crushing numerical advantage, came pressing on. Their battle cry *Allahu Akbar!* could be heard shrieking wildly over the chaos of gunfire as eight, ten, a dozen men appeared from behind the buildings thirty metres up the street, bullets splatting from their American assault weapons. Seeing Cale lying there prone in the open they sprinted towards him, apparently unafraid of his return fire that took two of them down as they ran. The dust from their bullets was flying up so thick around him that he was barely visible, but Ben heard him cry out as he was hit again and again. One arm now lay useless on the ground but he kept firing one-handed. A fool, maybe, but a damn brave one.

Ben broke cover from behind the van and raced across the street, shooting as he went, grabbed Cale by the collar and started dragging him towards the corner of the house, from which Buchanan and Dixon were laying down a covering fire. Ben didn't know if he was going to make it, but he had to try. With the dead weight of Cale's body in one hand and his rattling gun in the other he felt a bullet whip past his cheek and another tear through the loose folds of his kameez. He fired back without aiming, a burst that stitched two more of the Talib across the chest and they collapsed mid-stride, falling over each other in a dead heap.

He was almost at the corner now. Buchanan and Dixon were hammering a relentless stream of firepower down the street that broke the enemy advance, killed three and sent the others into retreat.

For a heartbeat, it looked as though they could win this.

Then that changed. A grenade came whooshing from up the street and hit the white van, blasting it into flames. At almost the same moment, more enemy fire was coming from the opposite direction, from behind them, targeting the corner of the house at an angle that exposed them right out in the open. Dixon let out a grunt as though he'd been about to say something; then Ben saw the blood spouting from the side of his neck. Dixon staggered against the wall and slid to the ground, fatally wounded. Bullets thunked into his chest and face and peppered the wall around him.

Ben still had hold of Cale but Buchanan was yelling, 'He's dead!' And Ben looked down and saw the gaping red wound where Cale's heart and lungs had been blown out, shattered ribcage visible through tattered flesh. He let go of him, fired another burst this way, another that way. Saw Habib and Ghani, Saleem's guys, emerging from their cover and running to join him and Buchanan, then mowed down as a heavy machine gun down the street started up its hammering, meat-grinding slaughterhouse fire. Ben could see no sign of Saleem and Mazdak.

'This way!' Buchanan yelled. Ben's carbine was empty. He let it drop, picked up the fallen Dixon's, which still had a few rounds left, and followed Buchanan at a run along the wall of the house, where the angle of the buildings protected them from enemy fire. Running hard through a narrowing alley between the house and its neighbour. The gap at the bottom of the alley looked clear.

Then it suddenly wasn't, as more Talib appeared yelling and firing. Fifteen, twenty, a whole crowd, forcing their way up the alley straight towards them and blocking off their route. Ben and Buchanan directed a deadly blast of fire at them and several in the front rank fell, but more came running straight over the bodies of the fallen, yowling like madmen. Buchanan turned and started running back the other way. Ben stood his ground for a few seconds, firing until his carbine was emptied again and then taking out his pistol to snap off more rounds. Now there was a heap of bodies almost waist-high in the alleyway. Ben blinked blood out of his eyes from some unfelt wound, turned and ran after Buchanan.

Re-emerging into the main street, some forty yards away to his left he could see a group of three Taliban fighters were working urgently to clear a jam in the belt-fed heavy machine gun that had claimed the lives of Habib and Ghani. Their bodies lay twisted and bloody in the road. Ghani had been clutching a grenade launcher when he died. Ben had no idea where he'd got it from: maybe taken it from the body of a Talib. But now Ben quickly snatched it up, checked it was loaded and then pumped its 40mm grenade in the direction of the heavy machine gun emplacement. There was an earth-shaking explosion, flying debris and smoke. One of the houses was partially demolished, burying the HMG and two of its operators in rubble while the third staggered around in flames.

Ben threw down the launcher. No way to know how many of the task force were still alive as they raced in the direction of the vans. The enemy seemed to have fallen back for the moment, possibly to regroup before coming back even harder. The grenade-hit van was a roiling inferno belching black smoke from its open doors. The other was badly perforated with bullet holes and its windows were smashed, but it might still be drivable. If it wasn't, their one chance of escape was gone because there was no possibility of reaching the Humvees. Only one way to find out.

Buchanan tossed Ben the keys, saying, 'I'm hit. I can't drive.' Ben looked and saw the dark bloodstain soaking through his clothes from shoulder to sternum, and the way he was holding himself bent over with his teeth clenched in pain. Just then Ben heard running footsteps coming up behind him and whirled around, ready to fire. It was Saleem, bloody but apparently still all in one piece, clutching his AK-47.

Buchanan yelled, 'Let's get out of here!' For once, Ben was inclined to agree with his tactical decision. He leaped into the van, twisted the key and to his infinite relief heard the engine rasp into life. Saleem helped Buchanan inside and then piled in after him. Ben slammed the transmission into gear and floored the gas, and the van accelerated hard away, lurching over the bodies of the dead Talib that littered the street. Still driveable, all right. But how long for was another question. Because before they'd reached the end of the street the way ahead was suddenly blocked again, this time by a lumbering sandy-coloured monster.

It was what the US military called the M1117 Guardian Armoured Security Vehicle. Thirteen tons of impenetrable, unburstable, mineproof, rocketproof and unstoppable fighting machine. And it was bearing right down on them.

Chapter 17

The armoured car's turret-mounted machine gun swivelled to point straight at the oncoming vehicle and exploded into life. The light, flimsy van offered about as much protection from the devastating fifty-calibre rounds as a wet cardboard box, and if Ben hadn't swerved violently out of the gunfire's path he and his passengers would have been shredded into mincemeat. The sweeping arc of fire caught the side of the van, shearing through its roof pillars and opening up the bodywork like a can opener. The half-detached roof flapped like a sail as Ben hurtled straight for the narrow and fast-diminishing gap between the monster's armoured flank and the wall of the adobe building next to it.

From behind him Ben heard Saleem's voice indistinctly yelling something in Pashto that might have been 'You'll kill us!'

But it seemed to Ben as though someone else was already making a pretty good attempt at that. The left front wing of the van smashed through the wall, the impact throwing him and the others forward in their seats. Bits of stone block and masonry shattered what was left of the windscreen and

126

bounced harmlessly off the armoured car. The whole van tilted up sideways at a crazy angle and for an instant it seemed about to overturn – but Ben kept his foot nailed down hard to the floor, ploughed blindly onwards with the engine revs soaring and the wheels spinning, and somehow managed to keep the thing upright. Then they were through, bucking and jolting out of their seats over the rubble of the half-collapsed building. More gunfire was coming at them from different directions, bullets punching into the van's battered bodywork. Ben heard Buchanan yell something, but his words were drowned, lost in the chaotic noise, and he was more worried about the armoured car. Its gun turret was rotating around to blast them as they escaped, but as Ben glanced in his remaining mirror he saw that a chunk of rubble had wedged under the big Browning machine gun, preventing the turret from rotating all the way around.

A lucky break – but this wasn't over yet. From behind the ruined building came three Talib aiming assault rifles and a grenade launcher straight at them. Ben twisted the wheel and mercilessly rammed into the three men, rolling straight over two of them while the third was catapulted over the bonnet; a fleeting glimpse of his astonished face before he was dashed violently back down onto the road.

They kept going. More men came running after them, yelling, firing wildly, rifle bullets drilling more holes in their already badly torn-up rear. Saleem was shouting, 'Faster, faster! That way!' Leaning forwards and pointing a bloody finger. Ben swerved left and then right through more buildings. Then suddenly the last of the houses were flashing past, and they were out of the village and speeding back along the open road. The chasing gunfire was diminished to just the occasional popping crack behind them. Ben could hear something rattling loudly from under the van's bonnet and he had no idea what kind of damage had been done in there, but he kept driving the thing forwards as fast as it would go. He was having trouble seeing properly; thought it was the dust blowing in through the smashed screen – then realised that it was the blood from his head wound running into his eyes. He wiped it away, and with the movement he felt a tingling numbness in his left arm telling him it was injured too, but he didn't have much interest in that as he kept glancing in the mirror for the column of speeding trucks he fully expected to see giving chase at any moment. Nothing yet. But they'd come.

'How are we doing back there?' he shouted over the rattling engine noise.

'He is dead,' said Saleem.

Ben twisted around in his seat and saw Jack Buchanan's lifeless eyes staring straight back at him. It wasn't the first gunshot wound that had done it, as became obvious when he slumped over. He'd taken a round to the back of the head during the escape.

'I am hurt too,' Saleem said. And it was an understatement. Blood was pouring fast out of him, leaking all over the seats to mingle with the broken glass.

'I can't stop,' Ben said.

'Drive, drive. I will be okay,' Saleem replied. But he didn't sound okay. Ben drove on, coaxing every last ounce of forward momentum he could from the damaged engine. The rattle was getting worse. Still nothing in the mirror, though it couldn't last. Up ahead he spotted a smaller road branching off to the left, and took it. It was even more rutted and holed, sometimes covered by encroaching bushes, here and there blocked by boulders or completely subsided into loose dirt. The van's suspension was being pushed to the limits of its endurance.

Ben pounded relentlessly along the track, totally focused on reaching safety, keeping his mind closed to the state of his badly injured surviving passenger, and to the growing agony in his left arm. After another three kilometres with still nothing appearing in his mirror he turned off again and headed across open country. Their pursuers must have struck out along the main road from Ghurdak and it surely wouldn't be long before they realised their mistake and came doubling back to hunt for them. The M1117 armoured car could hit speeds of over 60 miles an hour. The ailing van was having increasing trouble maintaining much more than half that speed. Ben kept pushing it, but the rattle was louder than ever, the engine had started coughing and misfiring, and now there was ominous black smoke beginning to pour out from under the buckled bonnet lid.

Ben realised that Saleem had gone very quiet back there. He couldn't see him in the mirror any longer. 'Saleem?'

'I am still here,' came a feeble reply. Saleem had slumped down flat on the seat next to Buchanan's body. Ben was relieved to hear his voice.

'Hold on. You're going to be okay.'

Ben had no idea where they were now, except that they were deep in the wilderness. The arid terrain was rising steadily upwards into the foothills of the mountains that loomed all around them, as jagged as broken glass, snow on the highest peaks. Ben knew he had to find some sheltered place to stop and attend to Saleem. But even as he was thinking it, the van engine gave a last asthmatic splutter and then died completely. While it still had some momentum Ben coasted the vehicle towards a rubbly slope to the side of the track and let it go rolling and bumping down to the bottom. A rocky outcrop that looked like an ancient stone circle hid them from view of the track.

'What's happening? Why are we stopping?' asked Saleem, trying to raise himself up. His face was as pale as a corpse's and his eyes were ringed with dark circles, his body shaking with pain. The blood was everywhere, some of it Buchanan's but just as much of it his own.

'End of the road,' Ben said. 'We'll continue on foot from here.'

'I don't think I can make it,' groaned Saleem.

'You let me be the judge of that.' Ben booted open the buckled, bullet-shredded driver's door, jumped down and looked around him. The sun was slowly setting behind the mountains, gold turning to a haze of tawny orange behind the jagged peaks. The landscape was utterly empty and deathly still, not a bird, not an insect, the only sound or movement the whispering rustle of the mountain wind among the desiccated shrubs growing around the foot of the stone circle. If their pursuers were still after them, they were a long way off.

Ben opened up the side of the van, half carried the injured Saleem out and laid him gently on the ground in the shelter of the rocks with someone's Bergen propping up his head.

Much of the task force's kit had been in the van that had been blown up, but by a stroke of luck the medical supplies had been in this one.

'Thank you, my friend,' Saleem murmured.

'Don't mention it. Now let's take a look at you.' Ben wasn't as confident as he sounded, trying to reassure the gravely injured man. Any little remnant of optimism he might have felt sank to the pit of his stomach when he peeled back Saleem's blood-soaked clothing, saw the deep gunshot wound that had gone through his liver, and knew there was nothing he could do for the guy except pump him full of morphine for as long as he kept breathing. Which likely wouldn't be for very long.

'Go,' Saleem said softly. His lips were turning blue. 'Leave me here. I can't be any use to you. If they come, I will try to hold them off. Give me a gun.'

'Nonsense,' Ben told him, stabbing in a dose with an auto-injector. He had enough of them in the medical kit to euthanize a horse. Saleem could have them all, if needed. 'I'm not going anywhere without you. But there's no hurry. We got away from them. Let's sit here for a while and rest. Then you and I will carry on together.'

Ben sat down next to him in the dirt with his back against a rock. He took out his cigarettes and Zippo and lit up two, one for him, one for the dying man. They sat in silence, watching the sun disappear behind the mountains and the shadows of the standing rocks grow longer and deeper. The morphine kicked in quickly and Saleem soon looked relaxed, almost restful, eyes closed. In the fading light his blood looked almost black against the rocks.

It wasn't easy, sitting here biding your time waiting for a man to slip away. Ben spent a few minutes reflecting on the fate of Operation Hydra, now come to an end even sooner than Goffin might have hoped for. Ben thought about the irony of naming it after a mythical creature with immortal powers and many heads that would grow back double in number when cut off. In reality their operation had had only one. And now that it was well and truly sliced off, it wasn't going to grow back. He remembered what Carstairs had said: *fail and you're on your own.* No back door out of the place, every man for himself. How true the colonel's words had been. As for Spartan, whoever he was, now he was on his own too.

The darkness fell quickly, a pale moon rising. Saleem never spoke again. By the time Ben had finished his third cigarette, his silent, inert companion had drifted off to another place. Ben checked his pulse, found nothing. He looked sadly at the dead man, wishing he could bury him and Buchanan. But their remaining kit didn't include so much as a folding military shovel, even if the iron-hard ground could have been dug.

Ben considered the task ahead of him. With the mission dead, along with the men and resources he'd hoped to enlist for his own purposes, now he faced a long and dangerous journey across the Afghan wilderness with no transport, no backup, facing much worse odds than before. But that couldn't deter him from his objective of finding Madison Cahill and bringing her home. If he died trying, then so be it. Had to happen sometime.

Before the light faded completely, his first priority was to check his own wounds. He hadn't felt them at the time; then again it wasn't uncommon, in the heat of battle, for a man to sustain even quite serious damage without realising. He'd seen fingers blown off, ears sliced off and worse, with their victims perfectly unaware of it until later. Fortunately his head injury was just a small bullet graze, fairly bloody like all scalp wounds, but not even requiring a stitch. An inch lower, and it wouldn't have been so trivial. The worst he might expect was a blinding headache for a while. The bullet that had nicked his arm had gone somewhat deeper. He applied some local anaesthetic from the med kit, sutured it up and wrapped it with a field dressing. Another scar to add to the collection that laced and crisscrossed his body, each one telling its own story.

Night had fallen fully by the time he'd finished attending to himself. He couldn't risk using a torch or lighting a fire, for fear of their being spotted from a distance. Instead he groped around in the darkness as he turned his attentions to salvaging more essential supplies from the van. One of the most critical was the handheld GPS device that told him he was 144 kilometres from his objective in the Bamiyan Valley. A long way to travel, for one man alone. Each task force member had carried some MRE rations and a water canteen in his personal Bergen. There was some firelighting gear and enough two-man tents for all eight of them, though Ben would need just one for basic shelter on his long journey.

Along with the medical kit, part of their arsenal had survived as well. He still had his pistol, but he'd require something more substantial as a principal weapon. The handy, lightweight carbines were all gone and most of what was left, like the massive fifty-cal sniper rifle, the Stinger missile system and the Claymore high-explosive mines, was too heavy and cumbersome for a one-man foot expedition to carry along with all his own food, water and shelter.

But then, in the last holdall he checked, Ben found what he'd been hoping for. He'd been around guns and weapons for far too many years to get excited about them any longer. To him they were simply workman's tools, as mundane and normal as a screwdriver or a claw hammer. But there was no question that some tools were far more effective for certain tasks than others. And this one was perfect for the job he had ahead of him.

'Maximi' was the name that the Special Forces unofficially gave to the more powerful version of the old Minimi squad automatic weapon, a light machine gun that was compact enough to be carried like a rifle and gave its operator some serious firepower. The beast was belt-fed, each belt they'd been issued with holding a hundred 7.62mm rounds. Normally every man in a team would carry at least one belt for the squad machine gun in his Bergen. Ben would have to lug as much ammo as he could manage unaided. With the weapon itself, three belts draped around his shoulders like metallic yellow pythons and all the rest of his supplies loaded on his back he'd be packing as heavy a load as he'd ever carried on active duty before. But what the hell. SAS soldiers routinely tabbed long distances over all kinds of terrain with 130-odd pounds of equipment strapped to them. A few pounds more wouldn't kill him – or at least, wouldn't kill him as effectively as the enemy might.

Ben looked down at Saleem, lying there so still and peaceful he might have been sleeping. Years of unending conflict had been tough on the wildlife of these Afghan regions. All the same, he knew that there were other wild predators than humans running around these mountains. He remembered how, back in the day, he and his troop had sat listening to the eerie howling of the wolves at night. There were bears and hyenas too, and once one of his men had sworn he'd glimpsed a leopard prowling near their camp. He didn't like the idea of leaving poor Saleem lying there in the open to be eaten, so he moved his body back inside the van with Buchanan's and covered them up as best he could. Saleem's own people would have washed the body clean for admission to Heaven, wrapped him in a shroud and interred him on his right side facing towards Mecca.

Leaving the war dead behind unburied was a shitty deal at the best of times. Ben felt bad as he made his final preparations, wishing he could do more for them. That could so easily have been his body lying there in a bullet-chewed van in the middle of nowhere.

And then, he was ready. 'Okay, Madison,' he said out loud. 'Here I come.'

Chapter 18

Travelling on foot behind enemy lines is a specialised skill that SAS men train long and hard to perfect. In this instance, the whole damn country was behind enemy lines. Ben needed to move quickly, quietly and undetected, and as his own point man he'd have to remain ultra-vigilant the entire time, maintaining constant 360-degree awareness of any possible threat. Clouds drifted across the face of the moon, creating deep shadows where he felt safe and in his element. He picked his way steadily along through the darkness, always staying below the ridgelines of the hills to avoid creating a man-shaped silhouette that could be spotted a long way off.

After six hours of steady walking, high among the foothills with the forbidding presence of the mountains looming close by, Ben stopped to make his first night's camp. He'd picked his spot carefully, a textbook OP like an eagle's nest high up in the rocks with a perfect all-around field of observation and fire. Close by his tent the Maximi was set up on its pressed-steel bipod with a fresh belt loaded and ready. In SAS jargon an unexpected encounter with the enemy was called 'getting bumped'. If Ben got bumped up here, he could defend his position against a far superior force. By the time the ammo ran out there'd be a few hundred dead enemy combatants strewn all over. If they still kept coming after that, he'd fight with his knife, with rocks and stones and his bare hands if he had to. Would they get him? Probably, but they'd pay a heavy price for it.

He unpacked his first night's rations. Until he could be sure he was safe he'd be on hard routine, which meant no campfire was allowed. It was a chilly night and the warmth would have been welcome, but a fire was a beacon easily visible for miles around, while the smell of cooking could travel on the wind for long distances and alert an enemy to your presence. Whatever you ate on hard routine had to be eaten cold, sometimes raw. Survival was about sustenance. On one combat tour of Afghanistan, Ben had lived for seven straight days on powdered milk and sugar. On a couple of other occasions, a dinner of uncooked goat flesh had seemed like a Michelin five-star gourmet treat to him and his hungry men. If you needed to hunt for meat, you tried to catch your food with a snare and dispatch it with your knife, rather than risk giving your position away with gunfire.

Tonight, thanks to his supply of task force MREs, Ben had the luxury of cold beef stew, cold rice pudding and cold drinking chocolate mix: nutritious and even quite palatable once you got used to it, but a shock to the system after being used to the culinary comforts of Le Val all these years. Perhaps the soft life was getting to him, he reflected. Maybe this experience was just the thing he needed to keep his edge.

Hard routine also meant that you could leave no trace of your presence behind, which included bodily waste. If ground conditions made it difficult to bury deep, you took it with you, stashed in your Bergen. Any young trooper who'd wanted to join the SAS for the glamour and romance of it soon learned the nitty-gritty realities of their chosen way of life.

After dinner and a final observation check, Ben crawled into his tiny tent and lay there for a long while listening to the wind ruffling the canvas, his pistol ready for instant use should an unexpected visitor happen to come by. In time his eyes closed and his body relaxed, but he was never fully asleep and his senses were sharply attuned to the tiniest sound that could signal danger. The dreaming part of his mind imagined that he found Madison and a bunch of her friends partying at a luxury mansion in the mountains. She was wearing a long, black, backless, strapless evening dress and holding a crystal flute of champagne as she turned to him, standing there in his filthy bedraggled robe with his weapons and ammo belts, and demanded indignantly, 'What the hell are you doing here?' He was lost for words and dumbstruck; then when he looked at her more closely he saw that her face was a skull.

Some dreams are difficult to go back to sleep after.

He was packed up and on the move again long before the first fiery rays of dawn peeked over the crags to the east. In an ideal situation, a Special Forces unit behind enemy lines might have chosen to move only under cover of darkness and stay hidden during the daylight hours, allowing more time for rest and recuperation. But with so much distance to cover and his shockingly vivid dream still haunting him, he felt impelled to keep going as fast as he could.

On and on through the empty, mountainous wilderness, step after step, kilometre after foot-blistering kilometre, the straps of his heavy pack biting into his shoulders and his injured arm throbbing painfully. Then on some more, stopping only for the occasional drink of water. With all his senses so concentrated to the maximum for so long, sometimes his mind would begin to swim and he became worried about losing touch with reality. At a certain point he experienced the strangest sensation of being an astronaut stranded completely alone on the surface of a desolate planet, the only thing living for a million light years.

The distant rumble of trucks quickly cured him of that notion. Pinpointing the sound as coming from the northwest, he scrambled to the top of a rise and flattened himself on the ground to observe them through his binoculars. The long line of Taliban troop transporters and armoured cars was some six hundred metres away and travelling on a perpendicular course to his, from left to right along an old river valley at the base of a towering great escarpment, leaving a dust cloud that trailed like smoke behind them. Once they'd passed, he stayed low for a long time before moving on again, in case of stragglers.

For the rest of that day he saw no other living creatures, human or otherwise, apart from a pair of vultures that were pecking and tearing at the carcass of some unidentifiable animal and flapped away on huge dark wings at his approach. By the time night fell and he wearily made camp, his GPS told him that he'd covered twenty-two miles. Which wasn't bad progress, but he knew that he was going to have to try and procure some proper transportation. That would typically involve stealing a vehicle from a farm or village, which he didn't like doing for a variety of reasons – any more than he relished the much higher profile of driving around open roads. But conspicuous and risky as it might be, it was the only way he was going to have any chance of reaching his destination quickly.

And it just so happened that he'd passed a small village some kilometres back, which he'd detoured around, giving it a wide berth for fear of being spotted. He decided he'd rest for a few hours and then return to the village in the dead of night to try his luck.

Chapter 19

As planned, he rested in his tent until three in the morning, then cleared all trace of his presence there and spent the next hour silently, invisibly making his way back down the rocky slopes towards human habitation. His two-day trek had brought him up and up to high altitudes, and even though the village lay in a wide valley it was still some two thousand metres above sea level. The place was smaller than Ghurdak. Its low-roofed clay houses, ochre-coloured in the dim moonlight, were built on sandstone rises that could have been the remnants of some ancient hill fort's foundations, and maybe were. The encircling adobe wall that must have protected the villagers from tribal raiders and other enemies for a thousand years or more was mostly in ruin, and here and there the settlement had spread out beyond the original perimeter.

It was one of those outlying dwellings that Ben chose to approach rather than venture among the other more closely-clustered buildings. He moved very slowly and cautiously through the darkness, sometimes taking a full minute between steps and listening hard all the way.

The house was all in shadow. Peering over a wall into a dirt yard he saw a glimmer of moonlight reflecting dully off the body of an old pickup truck parked under a tin-roofed lean-to. Everything was basic and utilitarian in the extreme. Life was hard in a place like this. Every minute of the day would be devoted to scratching a basic subsistence out of the arid land, the way things had been done since the beginning of time. In Ben's experience people who lived that way were proud, and rightly so, but they were unimaginably poor by the lazy, cosseted standards of Joe Westerner and to even own a motor vehicle was a hell of a thing. Yet here he was, contemplating stealing it from them.

That was one of the reasons Ben didn't care much for this kind of strategy. If he'd had money, he'd have left the truck's owner a bundle of it in its place. But to do that, even to leave a token exchange like his expensive diver's watch that was probably worth a year's food, would be to leave a trace behind that might invite questions.

Another reason he disliked this whole exercise was that there were no guarantees that the risk would pay off, especially in Third World countries and even more especially in remote areas like this. You had to assume that the vehicle might be broken down, lacking fuel, sitting on flat tyres and not run for years, with a dead battery and chickens living in it. But before you could even get close enough to verify whether or not the thing was usable, you'd have to get past any number of obstacles and hazards. Any villager you might accidentally happen to run into could raise the alarm, or perhaps even grab a weapon and open fire on you.

But the biggest headache of all was dogs. Which of course was the reason why they were so popular – Ben's own place at Le Val had always been guarded by a roaming pack of German shepherds, the most acutely aware sentry ever created. As SAS soldiers knew all too well, trained attack dogs would just creep up on you without a sound and then rip into you. But any old farmyard mutt could just as easily deter an intrusion by barking its head off, even if it was tethered up.

So when a deep-throated *woof-woof-woof* started up as Ben got within ten feet of the yard wall and a man's angry voice from inside the house yelled in a dialect of Dari, 'Shut up, you stupid bastard animal' or words to that effect, he knew he'd have to abort. As the dog went on barking furiously, a light came on in a window and a bearded face peered out, Ben reluctantly slunk away into the deep shadows and started making his way back towards his camp location. Win some, lose some.

On his return journey to the camp, a thin slanting rain became an icy cold deluge that had soaked him to the skin by the time he crawled into the hastily erected shelter of his tent. It took all his willpower to resist the urge to make a fire to warm himself and dry his clothes over. The ground was too hard and stony to dig out the kind of Dakota fire pit he'd been taught to build in survival training, designed to keep the light and smoke to a minimum. Instead he lay there shivering for an hour before he gave up on the idea of sleep, struck camp for the second time that night and moved on.

All through the next day, and all through the next after that, the rain kept sheeting down. A waterproof military poncho and a decent Boonie hat might have helped keep the worst of it off, but Ben had neither. The best thing he could say about the weather was that it allowed him to refill his depleted water bottles. Like a drowned rat he plodded endlessly on, hour after numbing hour, following his course, blinking the water out of his eyes, squelching in his boots with his heavy pack chafing his shoulders. Lack of sleep and the need for a warm meal were beginning to wear him down. The small voice in his head that had started tempting him to stop and rig up a shelter grew steadily more persistent, until even he had to admit that he didn't know how much longer he could go on like this. Still nothing around him but rock, mountain and sparse, wind-beaten scrub vegetation for as far as the eye could see, not another living soul to share the empty landscape with him.

Ben thought of the many armies that had been defeated by the cruel harshness of this land. The British Empire's Afghan invasion forces of the nineteenth century had lost far more men to cold, starvation and disease than had been killed in battle. Likewise, the Soviet troops a century later had suffered terrible hardship in the pitiless Afghan wilderness, as bad as anything the Red Army had experienced during World War II. Even the toughest of men sometimes reach the limit of their endurance.

Not him, though. No damn way. He gritted his teeth, refused to cave in to weakness and soldiered doggedly on. Two hours' rest that night, then off again. Sometime before dawn the rain had stopped and a red sunrise peeped over the mountains, promising a better day. And maybe it would be, allowing him to pick up his pace. He'd covered a great distance, and kept telling himself that his destination was getting closer with every step. But he was getting weak now, and he knew it.

It was in a narrow, craggy mountain pass late that afternoon that he met the temptation that finally broke his resolve. The young curly-horned ibex goat had been rooting around in some bushes when it was startled by his approach. Ben was as surprised as it was; but then when the animal made the mistake of hesitating just a moment too long before bounding off into the rocks, he drew his pistol and shot it in the head without compunction. The rolling echo of the gunshot boomed all around the mountain pass. He was too dizzy with fatigue and hunger by now to care if anyone had heard it. If the Taliban decided to come for him now, at least he'd face them on a full stomach.

So with one cardinal rule broken, he thought *fuck it* and broke another. There was enough dead wood around to build a fire in a nook among the rocks and set up a basic spit, over which he roasted hunks of his catch. Few things had ever tasted so good, and he ate until he was full. Whatever was left over would sustain him far better than dried rations for a few more days, until he reached – or hoped to reach – Rigby Cahill's lost city of Zakara. He washed his meal down with fresh rainwater and sat back against a rock, deciding he'd rest here for an hour or two before moving on again.

Ben must have drifted off at some point as his exhaustion finally caught up with him. How long he slept he had no idea, except that evening had started to fall as he found himself suddenly jolted from a vivid and unsettling dream that was now instantly forgotten as his eyes snapped open and he sat bolt upright, as startled as the goat he'd killed earlier.

Because there was a man standing there over him.

A man draped in Afghan mountain garb, with ammo bandoliers draped crosswise around his shoulders, a turban wrapped around his head and his face partly covered by a scarf to protect against the dust and wind. There was a Kalashnikov rifle in his hands, and it was pointed right at Ben.

Chapter 20

Ben's mind was still swimming and foggy from his deep sleep. To be caught literally napping like this was something that had never happened to him before. Blinking, he threw a glance over at where his squad weapon lay propped against the rocks, too far out of reach to grab without the stranger firing first. Then Ben remembered his pistol, which he'd left resting on top of his pack to the other side of him. He instinctively darted out a hand to snatch it up.

But then he stopped.

The stranger gently shook his head as though to berate him. 'Now, now,' he said. 'Is that any way to greet an old friend?'

The stranger spoke perfect English. And now that Ben's wits were coming back to him, he saw that the man's eyes watching him with a kind of amused sparkle were the palest grey-blue in colour. Most Afghans were of Pashtun origin ethnically, with brown eyes. But more than that, even before the man spoke Ben had sensed there was something oddly familiar about him.

Ben stared, his outreached hand still hovering halfway to his pistol. Trying to place where he'd seen the stranger before.

Who was this person who'd suddenly appeared, as though out of nowhere, out here in the middle of the wilderness?

The stranger lowered his rifle, took his hand off the pistol grip and reached up to pull down his face covering and remove his turban. His features were grimed with dust and heavily bearded, but Ben couldn't have recognised him more completely if he'd seen him just yesterday. The stranger, suddenly not a stranger any longer, broke into a broad smile, and the sunlight sparkled gold and platinum off his teeth.

'Hello, Ben.'

'*Jaden?*' It seemed surreal. Maybe he was still dreaming.

Jaden Wolf laughed. 'Of all the gin joints in all the towns in all the world, eh? Well, well. This is the part where we both ask each other the same question: what the fuck are *you* doing here?'

Ben had known, worked with, and occasionally found himself up against, some of the toughest, hardest and most ruthlessly efficient killers in the world. Few of them, if any, could compare with Jaden Wolf, probably the most dangerous man Ben had ever met. Ben was also one of the few people lucky enough to be able to call him a friend.

Wolf had been a young recruit to 22 SAS when Ben was already a major. The gold and platinum teeth were the result of a nasty accident Wolf had suffered during the endurance phase of his selection test in the Brecon Beacons. The last time their paths had crossed in the middle of nowhere had been in Spain, when Wolf was on the run from a shadowy cabal who'd employed him as a professional assassin and later tried to eliminate him. That meeting had been no coincidence, because Ben had been the one they'd black-mailed into carrying out that elimination.

Then the last time Ben had seen Wolf had been at a manor house in England, when the pair had teamed up with Jeff Dekker, Tuesday Fletcher and a former SBS man called Reaper Rigby to turn the tables on the cabal and send them to hell. After that, Wolf had returned to Spain with the intention of enjoying a quiet existence as far away from trouble as he could get, making a little home for himself in some remote rural haven and learning to play the guitar. Wolf had fallen in love with the country many years earlier and he was living the dream. Ben had never expected to see him again.

And now here he was. The same old Wolf, dressed to kill and back in his natural element.

'Before you ask,' Wolf said, 'I'm not on my own. You should come and meet the guys.'

Even more confused, Ben asked, 'What guys?'

'You remember Nobby Scraggs?'

'Of course I do. Heard he left the regiment to take up security work on the oil fields in Oman.'

'Looking for an easy life. Why else would he get together with the likes of us, on a one-way ticket into a bloody death trap? Anyway, there's Nobby, and then there's Gino and Hank, Doug, Mike and Chris. He's in charge of the gang.'

'Seven men.'

'But maybe not all that magnificent,' Wolf said with a grin.

'You're going to have to explain to me what this is all about,' Ben said.

'And I will, mate, I will. But first . . .' Wolf set down his rifle, sat on a rock next to Ben's dead fire and pointed at the remains of the spit-roasted ibex. 'I'm famished, and if that tastes half as good as it smells from half a mile away, I wouldn't mind a bite.'

'Help yourself,' Ben said, still deeply mystified about what his old friend was doing here.

'Then we should really move on. Some silly bastard's been drawing all kinds of attention by lighting barbecues and letting off gunshots. Luckily it was little old me who showed up to check things out. But you never know who else might come snooping. Our Taliban friends have a lot of patrols in this area. Saw three of them yesterday.'

Ben watched as Wolf pulled out a combat knife, carved a slice of meat off the carcass and ate greedily. 'Delicious,' Wolf said, smacking his lips. 'Bit goaty, needs seasoning. But not bad at all.'

As Wolf carved himself another slice and gobbled it down, Ben quickly filled him in on the reason for his own presence here. 'Christ,' Wolf mumbled through a mouthful of meat. 'Is that Colonel Carstairs still alive? He must be ninety.' He chewed reflectively and listened as Ben went on. 'Spartan, eh? And you've no idea who the guy is?'

'None.'

'Bloody intelligence spooks. Never could stand 'em.' Wolf munched some more, then as Ben reached the end of the story he shook his head sadly. 'I remember Steve Cale. Bit of a tit, but he was all right. Bad deal. Very bad deal. We've had a few tangles with the Talib ourselves, nothing so hot. They were hard enough to deal with back in the day, when

150

all they had was a few old bangers and worn-out hardware left over from the Ruskies. Thanks to the bloody Yanks for tooling the bastards up beyond their wildest dreams with all that spanking new state-of-the-art military hardware. And there are so many of them now they're back in control. They're not just your scattered guerrilla army any more. So you came out here for a damsel in distress, did you? How romantic.'

'It's not like that.'

Wolf smiled. 'No, of course not. I'm sure she's old and fat, with eighteen kids and a wooden leg.'

'Madison's just a friend.'

'Yeah, well it sounds like your "friend" has landed herself in a spot of trouble.'

'You might say that.'

'Some people just have no sense. Or the worst luck. Hope she'll be OK. You say she's an archaeologist?'

'Kind of by default,' Ben replied. 'It wasn't her first career.'

'What was she before?'

'A bounty hunter.'

'Love it,' Wolf said. 'What charming people you know.'

'You can talk. Anyhow, Madison took the family business over from her father, Rigby Cahill. He used to travel all over the world looking for lost treasures. Spent years searching for a lost city in the Bamiyan Valley.'

Wolf raised an eyebrow. 'A lost city. No kidding. I'm seeing royal palaces, huge great columns, treasure vaults stuffed with priceless relics and chests of diamonds and rubies.'

'You always were the imaginative one,' Ben said.

'Comes to riches, I can imagine quite a bit,' Wolf replied. 'So who built this ancient lost city? The Romans? The ancient Egyptians?'

'Alexander.'

Wolf looked blank. 'Alexander who?'

'Alexander the Great,' Ben said. 'He was a Greek general. I don't think the Romans or the Egyptians ever invaded Afghanistan.'

'Smart move,' Wolf said with a chuckle. 'I'm no historian, as you can tell, but it seems to me every other bugger's tried his luck at it at one time or another, and come to rue the day they ever bothered. No wonder they call the place "the graveyard of empires".'

'True enough.'

'So this Rigby bloke, did he find his lost city?'

Ben nodded. 'Seems he did. He had to wait until the Russians were gone. But he didn't get to hang onto it for very long, because then the civil war kicked off. She came here to pick up where he left off.'

'Good luck with that,' Wolf said, spitting out a bit of gristle. 'Couldn't have picked a worse bloody time.' He looked at his watch. 'Speaking of which, we should make tracks. Come and meet the boys, and I'll fill you in on what's been happening.'

Chapter 21

After they'd finished clearing up any trace of the fire Wolf led Ben away on a different route from the one he'd taken through the labyrinth of mountain paths, sharing some of his heavy load by carrying the Maximi's ammo belts and the half-eaten carcass that would now be shared out among Wolf's mysterious companions.

The long shadows thrown by the setting sun grew darker as the light faded and the moon began to rise over the mountains. The two walked in single file a few strides apart, Ben bringing up the rear with Wolf as point man, the two of them keeping a wary eye open for any sign of an enemy patrol. Ben's weariness had magically disappeared after a good meal and a sleep. He was ready for the next phase in this strange journey – whatever the hell that might be.

After a couple of silent kilometres they clambered to the top of a nearly bare sandstone escarpment and Wolf pointed down the steep incline at the dusky valley below them, which wound between rocky crags like a canyon gorge carved out eons ago by a powerful river, now dry as dust.

'There they are,' Wolf said. Ben looked down, and in the murky shadows he saw the outline of a US military Humvee similar to the two the task force had been about to transfer into when the attack happened. He could see the shapes of four men standing near the vehicle, dressed in Afghan garb, easily mistakable for Taliban fighters from a distance in this light. They'd raised their weapons at the sight of two silhouetted figures appearing on the ridge above. Wolf signalled to them, one signalled back and they lowered their guns. Four men; Wolf had said the group totalled seven, which meant two of them must be keeping watch up on higher ground in case a patrol came by. The way they operated told Ben these were professionals. The array of automatic weapons dangling from their shoulders and stacked up by the Humvee confirmed it. He'd have expected nothing less of Wolf. But who were these men he'd teamed up with, and why?

'Look what I found,' Wolf said to them when he and Ben had reached the foot of the slope. The four robed figures walked over, peering at Ben in the semi-darkness and initially suspicious until one of them pulled off his face covering and burst out in a broad Lancashire accent, 'Christ on a bike, it's Major Hope!'

'Hello, Nobby. Just Ben these days,' Ben said. He'd always liked Scraggs, a big amiable man, about as tall and burly as the SAS would ever admit to their ranks. You could have taken him for a soft-hearted gentle giant if he hadn't been a highly trained professional warrior.

Scraggs was staring at him in disbelief as they warmly shook hands. 'A small world it is, and that's a fact. What the hell are you—?'

'Doing here?' Ben was still waiting to hear the answer to that question himself. But as he was the stranger to their camp, the onus was on him. He was about to retell the story, but instead Wolf did it for him. Scraggs and his companions listened attentively, frowning at the demise of the ill-fated SAS mission.

'I'm truly sorry to hear that, man,' the oldest in the group said to Ben, speaking for the first time in an accent that was a long way from Lancashire. He was a tall, broad-shouldered man with chiselled features and a buzz-cut as grey as his beard. He introduced himself as Chris Holt, a retired Master Sergeant previously with the US 19th Special Forces Group. 'I did five tours of Afghanistan, last one in 2004. Can't say the place has gotten any more pleasant over the years.' He motioned to the other men standing beside him. 'This here's Gino Baldacci, ex-Delta; and this is Hank Schulz, formerly of US Marine Corps Force Recon.'

All top-level operatives, all retired. Most if not all had been to Afghanistan before. Now they'd returned, apparently of their own free will, to roam about the wilderness armed up to the eyeballs.

'And you're the commanding officer?' Ben asked Holt, remembering what Wolf had told him.

'Call me team leader,' Holt replied with a dry smile. 'Only because I got on board this show before these guys. We don't do rank here. We're not exactly what you'd call an official unit.'

'So what are you?'

'We're the guys doing what the US military should be doing,' Baldacci replied with a look of disgust.

'Yeah. Thanks to an administration of worthless yellow-bellied rat-ass sleazebags in the White House, it's left up to deplorables like us to take care of business,' said Schulz.

'Mad buggers,' Nobby Scraggs added with a chuckle. 'That's what we are.'

Holt took out a radio and called up to the two unseen sentries high in the rocks. 'Mike, Doug; how's the view from up there?'

'All clear for miles,' came a crackly voice back. 'Who's the new dude?'

'Unexpected visitor,' Holt said. 'He's brought some chow with him. Come on down if you want your dinner.'

Soon afterwards they were joined by Mike Nielsen and Doug Liebowitz, who both came from similar military backgrounds to the others. With no apparent Taliban patrols in the vicinity they brewed up some evening coffee on their communal jet stove, which was running low on gas. As the red band in the western sky faded to full dark and a perfect crescent moon, sharp as a sickle blade, began its climbing arc overhead Ben shared out the remainder of his roast goat, and the eight of them sat around eating and drinking while Wolf finally explained to Ben why they were all here.

'We might not look like it,' Wolf said, 'but we're civilian volunteers. We all came over on our own coin as part of a non-governmental NEO task force, working side by side with the US military efforts to get the first wave of evacuees out of the country before the gates slammed shut.'

NEO stood for Non-combative Evacuation Operation. Which didn't at all seem to Ben like the kind of thing Jaden

Wolf would have got himself involved in. 'I thought you were living the good life in Spain.'

'I was,' Wolf replied. 'Chilling out in the sun, enjoying the local food and wine, learning to play the guitar and not having too much to do with the world. Believe me, the last thing I'd ever dreamed of doing was to get back into this game. But you couldn't ignore what was going on.'

Wolf described his rage and upset at the US leaders' apparent willingness to just walk away from so many stranded civilians, leaving them totally at the mercy of the brutal new regime. 'While the politicians and all these generals were yakking on about a controlled withdrawal, meanwhile the Taliban were killing left, right and centre. Stringing people up from choppers, cutting their heads off, slicing out tongues, sending women back to the Stone Age and pitching gays off rooftops. We thought this place was bad, last time around, but it's got a hundred times worse now. And the western media were just ignoring it.'

'Cut back a couple months before the shit hit the fan,' Holt said, 'a lot of folks could see what was coming. Veterans like us who knew the score, knew what kind of a nightmare scenario was about to land on the country, Kabul especially. A bunch of us started getting together, first on social media and then by phone and email. None of us believed that the switchover would take months or a year to happen. Anyone who's ever gone up against these guys knew they'd sweep in faster than a goddamn Blitzkrieg.'

'Right, and so we decided that something had to be done,' Wolf said. 'These bastards couldn't just be allowed to have a free hand.'

Ben was looking at his old friend and wondering at the change in him. Here was a man who, after quitting a stellar military career, had gone into business as a professional gun for hire, making stacks of cash killing whoever he was told to. His only rule had been: no women, no kids. Anyone else, you wouldn't even have seen him coming.

But Ben had always known that somewhere deep inside, Jaden Wolf's heart was as golden as those flashing custom-made teeth of his. That side of him was completely out in the open now, and combined with his warrior capability that made him an extremely effective weapon in the fight against injustice and tyranny.

'What started as just a few of us sharing our frustrations by email soon started snowballing into a bigger and bigger cooperative international effort,' Holt went on. 'We were able to make connections with some US government officials, non-governmental organisations and heads of aid charities who weren't happy with the situation either. Before we knew it, we had a list of people inside Kabul who'd be active targets of the Taliban when things got bad. A few dozen names soon turned into thousands. Meanwhile things were coming together real quick and we'd set up a forward operating base in Abu Dhabi. At that stage, our only aim was to help get as many people out as possible, while the US planes were still able to fly in and out of Kabul. But we weren't the only ones moving fast. Within a week of taking control, the Taliban had over a hundred and fifty checkpoints all through Kabul and tightening their grip more each day. We were up against the clock.'

'It's the same story for me as for all these guys,' Wolf said, nodding towards the others. 'Next thing I knew, I was one of this gang of ex-military flying out to Abu Dhabi to lend our support. From there we travelled into Kabul and started locating as many of the names on our list as we could, and getting them out before the country shut down completely. We'd be sneaking dozens at a time from safehouses all over the city and getting them to the airport any way we could. My job was to scout out new ratlines we could use to move them under the noses of the Taliban without being detected. We used ladder trucks to get people over the fence, even crawled through sewers.'

Ben asked, 'How many did you evacuate?'

'Over four thousand, within less than two weeks,' Wolf replied with a note of pride. 'A lot of whom had a pretty strong chance of dying violently if we hadn't got them out PDQ.'

'I'm amazed,' Ben said. And he wasn't kidding. The numbers were astonishing. When he'd worked as a kidnap rescue operator he'd been getting people out of trouble in ones and twos. Wolf was talking about entire planeloads of them.

That wasn't all Ben was thinking as he sat here listening to this. He was acutely aware that while all these events had been unfolding, he'd been spending his time in a state of blissful distraction with Abbie Logan. He thought about Jeff's anger at what he'd been seeing on the news, and his own lack of interest at the time. It made Ben feel ashamed that he hadn't got involved sooner. And it made him proud of his friend Jaden's selflessness and courage. He asked, 'What happened to all those people?'

'The planes flew the rescued to a humanitarian camp in UAE,' Wolf said. 'A lot of them were able to make their way home from there. A lot of others didn't have any home to go to. Aid organisations are working hard as we speak to relocate them to new and better lives elsewhere.'

'But then the gates of hell slammed shut,' Holt said. 'As everyone knew they would.'

Chapter 22

Ben said, 'Which I'm guessing is the reason you all made the jump from being non-com civilian volunteers to this,' motioning at the vehicle and the weapons that gave them all the semblance of a militia unit.

'There was nothing left for us to do in that role,' Wolf replied. 'The rest went home. Meanwhile, the seven of us got our heads together and agreed we weren't about to cut and run. Not with our work unfinished. We have the skills and the experience to make a difference, bring a little bit of the war back to the enemy while trying to help some more of the hundreds, maybe thousands, of people who're still stranded and in danger here. So we stayed behind. We knew exactly what we were getting into. We went into this eyes wide open.'

'We've been going around knocking out a few small pockets of Talib,' Holt said. 'OK, a tiny independent fighting force like ours is never gonna swing the balance of power. But at least we can give them something to think about. So far we're not doing too badly. Certainly got them all riled up. We're the reason there's all these extra patrols everywhere, buzzing around like someone poked the hornets' nest. The sons of bitches hate us, and they should. But they had it coming, for what they've done here.'

'Hate isn't the bloody word for what I think about the bastards,' said Nobby Scraggs, suddenly no longer so much the gentle giant. 'Who wouldn't feel that way about them?'

'I don't hate them,' Ben said. 'It's not my job to try to punish them. Only to help others they might hurt.'

Holt laughed bitterly. 'Yeah, well, noble sentiments apart, there's two ways of looking at that. You could just as well say that a bullet is the best way to prevent them from hurting anyone. Too many folks have been hurt already and they're only just getting started.'

Holt talked about how, as an advanced force operator back in the day, over the course of several tours to Afghanistan he had formed a close friendship with an Afghan interpreter called Maalik, who had still been working with US forces until the pull-out. As the Taliban forces swept into the city, Holt was all too aware that Maalik, and many others like him, would be a target for a horrible death. 'I knew that if they caught him,' Holt said, 'they wouldn't content themselves with putting a bullet in his head. They'd make him watch while they gang-raped his wife Fatemah in front of him and then got to work on their daughters Gita and Iman, before they gutted all three of them like fish. Then they'd burn him alive.'

'Did you get them out?' Ben asked.

Holt shook his head. 'We never found a trace of Maalik or his family. God help them. If they're alive and in hiding along with all the others who're still stuck in this place, then their best chance is to hide and pray that someone will come.'

'There's the problem,' said Schulz. 'They've got no outside help any more. It's all down to little old us.'

'How long were you planning on keeping this up?' Ben asked.

Holt smiled. 'You mean living like outlaws, just a handful of bucks between us, surviving on MREs that are five years out of date, using whatever weapons and vehicles we can steal from the enemy, trapped inside a hostile country that's virtually impossible to get out of?' He shrugged. 'As long as we can hold out, I guess. None of us is looking that far ahead.'

'Someone's got to do it,' Wolf said. 'Nobody else is lining up for the job. Might as well be us.'

'What we were born for, dude,' said Gino Baldacci, the ex-Delta guy, and he and Mike Nielsen exchanged high-fives.

'Besides,' said Nobby Scraggs, 'it's not like we've anything more useful to do back home, is it? Sat on the sofa watching the football on telly, or getting shot to bits out here trying to help folk in need? I know which I'd choose, any day of the week.'

'We're committed now,' Holt said. 'Whatever happens. This is way too important to back down from. And we've come this far, and survived. I'm going to stick it out.'

'Right to the bitter end. Last man standing,' said Nielsen.

'Got that right,' said Doug Liebowitz.

'Me too,' Wolf chimed in. 'All the way.'

'We sure could use a little more help, though,' Holt said, looking earnestly at Ben. 'A guy with your credentials, if you're half as good as Wolf says you are, would come in handy around here.'

'I'll second that,' said Scraggs. 'He saved my bacon more than once.'

'I appreciate the invitation,' Ben replied. 'But as Jaden has explained to you, I have my own plans.'

'Your friend the archaeology lady?' Holt said.

'She's the reason I'm here. I can't let her down.'

'Even if she's dead already.'

'I don't believe that,' Ben said. 'I won't. Not until I know it for sure.'

Holt sighed and puffed his cheeks. 'I hear you. And I admire your faith, man, believe me. But I can't pretend I'm not disappointed that you want to go your own way. Because where we're headed from here, it isn't going to be a picnic.'

'Where? Back to Kabul?'

'Worse,' Holt said.

'Way worse,' said Liebowitz.

'Like into the fuckin' jaws of death worse,' said Baldacci, seeming to relish the thought.

Wolf said, 'Show him, Chris.'

Holt shrugged. 'Okay, for what it's worth. We're on our own out here, so I think we can risk a little light for a couple of minutes.' He stood up from the rock he'd been sitting on and stepped towards the Humvee. From a kit bag on the front seat he took a small lantern and a map in a plastic sleeve. Setting the dim lantern on the Humvee's bonnet with a cautionary glance around the horizon he said, 'There's a Christian mission orphanage about a hundred and thirty klicks northwest of here, right up in the hills. It's been in operation for years, lasted out the Russians, even kept going through the civil war, and at the last report they had about forty kids there. Place is run by a Belgian woman called Francine Blanchet, a lay preacher who's about seventy years old and is one of your old-fashioned saints, along with her brother Patrick. In a regime that forbids the education of young girls and where Christians have to keep their faith a deadly secret out of fear of execution, she's gone on taking in little Afghan orphans and teaching them to read, write and do math. You don't need me to tell you what the Taliban would do to these kids. If they don't just shoot them dead out of hand they'll shove them into forced marriages with their fighters. Some of these girls are less than twelve years old.'

'And we can't be having that, now can we?' Scraggs said fiercely. 'Not while we're still living and breathing.'

Ben asked, 'How did you come to hear about the orphanage?'

Holt replied, 'Through a guy called Hassan Baghdadi who's one of the NEO's charitable contacts at the forward operating base in Abu. He's known Francine for years. Couldn't say enough good things about her. She's tough as a pair of old boots, won't back down from anyone. Death doesn't scare her, and you can be sure the Taliban don't scare her none either. She's always known that this shit would happen one day, but she'll hold out whatever it takes.'

Holt paused to spread the map out under the dim light. Ben got up and walked over to take a look. Wolf and the others joined them.

'This is our current location right here,' Holt said, prodding at the map. It was small-scale and highly detailed, though the area he was pointing out was bare of any place names or features. He slid his finger a few inches towards the north-west. 'And over here, a couple of days' travel across country assuming we don't run into too much resistance, is the orphanage. It's in a pretty remote location, as you can imagine it'd have to be. There's a village nearby, down in a river valley where they grow a few crops and raise some animals. Everything they need.'

'Or needed,' said Baldacci. The concerned looks on the men's faces told Ben he was missing something.

'Needed? Did something happen?'

Wolf nodded, frowning, 'You might say that. Twelve days ago, Francine Blanchet was able to make a call to our guy in Abu Dhabi. She reported that the orphanage had come under heavy bombardment from Taliban troops who'd got wind of what they were doing up there. They basically flattened the place, before they went storming into the ruins looking for survivors to kill and capture. Francine's brother Patrick died in the attack. Thankfully, as far as we know, none of the children was hurt.'

Scraggs muttered, 'Fuckers. What kind of person would shell a building full of little kids?'

'But Francine was able to make it out alive?' Ben said.

'Just in time,' Wolf replied. 'Though if the Taliban get their hands on them, they might wish they'd all been blown up instead.'

'And where are they now?'

'That's the problem,' Holt said. 'Up until three days ago we were staying in contact with our guy in Abu Dhabi via satellite phone and there'd been no further word from Francine since her call nine days earlier.'

Ben asked, 'Why up until three days ago?'

Holt replied, 'Because as of three days ago we don't have a sat phone any longer.'

'Or at least not a working one,' Wolf said. 'It took a bullet during the last little run-in we had with a patrol. Only casualty we've taken so far.'

'It can't be repaired?'

'Not without a replacement motherboard, it can't,' said Liebowitz. 'I'm pretty good at electronics. Tried switching out some components from one of our radio handsets in the hope I could bring it back to life, but no go. Kept hold of it, just in case by some freakin' miracle we manage to find the right spare parts. But until then it's toast.'

Ben nodded. 'Right. So you have no idea of what's happening with Francine Blanchet and the kids. And a lot can happen in twelve days.'

'I'm well aware of that, buddy. But right now we have to assume they're okay and hiding somewhere nearby. If they're still holding out after all this time, they're gonna be badly in need of help.'

'That's where we come in,' Wolf said.

'To rescue forty children,' Ben said, raising an eyebrow. 'The seven of you, in these vehicles, with Taliban units swarming everywhere hunting for them. I used to find missing people for a living. Just finding one could take months, not to mention the risk of extracting them from danger. But forty, all at once?'

'You saying you wouldn't have taken those odds?' Holt asked him.

'I probably would have,' Ben admitted. 'I was crazy enough to.'

'Hey, nobody said it was going to be easy,' Wolf replied, shrugging. 'If we can even find them they'll have to be fed, protected and transported out of danger right under the enemy's nose. Then we've got to find some way of relocating them to a safe new home.'

'Which doesn't exist,' Baldacci said. 'Not in this country, not any more.'

'It's a challenge,' Liebowitz said. 'Mission fuckin' impossible.'

'I love challenges,' Wolf answered with a savage grin that made him look like his namesake.

'Let's just say there are a few logistical issues to contend with,' Holt said. 'Which is why we need all the manpower we can get.'

Ben said nothing, carefully studying the map by the lantern light. He traced his finger along the route Holt had pointed out, drinking in names, places, topographical detail. That was when he realised he'd seen this map before. Or one very much like it: the print of the old map that he'd got from old Karim at the Cultural Institute in Kabul. He reached inside his kameez, pulled out the print and laid it side by side with the modern one on the Humvee's bonnet.

'What's that?' Wolf asked, peering.

Ben was too focused to reply. He'd been right. The place names weren't all the same, and the city of Zakara didn't feature at all on the modern version. But the cartographers from centuries ago had pretty much nailed it, in terms of geographical accuracy. There was no question in his mind that the two maps depicted the same region.

He looked up from the maps, already forming a new plan in his mind.

'I know that look,' Wolf said, eyeing Ben keenly. 'He's onto something.'

'Take a look at this,' Ben said, pointing again at the modern map, but in a different place from the one Holt had indicated.

'I see it,' Holt said. 'But what the hell is it? There's nothing marked on the map.'

'There is on mine,' Ben told him, tapping the print. 'It's the location of the ancient city of Zakara, where I'm headed in search of Madison, hoping she'll have made it in one piece and is still there.' He drew a line with his finger back to their present location. 'Now, you can see that my route to Zakara from here pretty much correlates with your route to the orphanage for a good part of the way, until they diverge about here.' Pointing.

Holt looked uncertain. 'Yeah, so?'

Ben said, 'So you wouldn't have to go too far out of your way to pass by the Zakara site en route.'

'You mean take a detour and slow ourselves down by going off mission?'

'Eight men can get the job done better than one,' Ben said.

'Even when that one man is Ben Hope,' Wolf added, clapping a hand on Ben's shoulder. 'Chris, I think I see what he's thinking.'

'Me too. He wants us to divert miles off our course so we can help him find his lady friend.' Holt shook his head. 'I'm sorry, buddy. I get that she matters to you, and I know you're worried about her. But these orphans are my mission priority right now.'

'They're all worth saving, Chris,' Ben said. 'Yours and mine. Each and every last one. And so here's what I propose. If I agree to help you rescue your orphans, in return you and your guys give me the backup I need to reach Madison. And if we get to Zakara and she's not there, then I won't expect you to waste more time hanging around hunting for her. We'll proceed straight to the location of the orphanage and find the kids.'

Holt said nothing. His face was working hard as he considered the choices.

'He's the best, Chris,' Wolf said. 'Without him there's only seven of us, against a million Taliban. This has got to shorten the odds.'

'Sounds like a no-lose situation to me,' said Scraggs.

Holt was silent for a few moments longer. Then his face softened and he nodded. He stuck out a hand.

'All right, buddy. You got yourself a deal.'

Chapter 23

Wolf's little fighting force and its additional new member made their camp in the dry river gorge that night, relaying one another in pairs to climb up to the higher ground to keep watch while the others rested. By dawn, with still no sighting of any patrols across a wide expanse of the horizon, they'd refuelled their vehicle, gathered up their kit, erased all trace of their camp and were ready to set off again.

The river bed wound along between the steep canyon walls until its course bent away from theirs and a rocky path led them back up onto higher ground, moving steadily north-westwards. Ben rode up front in the now slightly more crowded Humvee with Wolf at the wheel. Using a noisy motor vehicle behind enemy lines involved a lot of risk, but when there were great distances to cover the trade-off with increased visibility was sometimes considered worthwhile. Nonetheless the tension among the men was high as they constantly halted at every blind rise and before venturing into any exposed open ground to creep forward on foot to a vantage point to check the coast was clear. It was a laborious, tedious stop-start process, but it was the only way to avoid blundering straight into a surprise face-to-face encounter with the enemy.

Ben and Wolf were returning to the Humvee after about the eleventh or twelfth such stop when Ben paused, cocked his head towards the west and said, 'Hear that?'

Wolf nodded. His hearing was almost as acute as Ben's, and though nothing lived or moved anywhere across the vast rocky bowl of the landscape he, too, had picked up the sound of distant gunfire, drifting so faintly on the breeze that they'd have missed it from inside the vehicle. 'Coming from that direction. Trouble?'

'Could be,' was all Ben said. Back at the Humvee he stowed his weapon in the footwell with its ammunition belt trailing on the floor between his feet, and they carried on.

'You've no idea how glad I am that you brought this thing along,' Wolf said with a nod towards the Maximi. 'Especially all the spare belts, even if they are a bastard to lug around. We've been getting just a little too short on ammo for comfort. In fact, after that last bump we had before we found you, we're down to just a few mags per man.'

'Still nowhere near enough,' Holt said. 'We're gonna need a hell of a lot more, where we're headed.'

'Maybe we'll find a gun shop on the way where we can stock up,' Wolf joked.

'This ain't Tennessee, bro. We've as much chance of finding a Radio Shack with the parts for the sat phone.'

They drove on in silence. Hours went by. Rolling through a mountain pass now, with tall sheer crags either side from which rock slides had here and there half blocked the way ahead with huge boulders and uprooted trees. Negotiating this terrain took every ounce of concentration, and after a while Ben took over from Wolf at the wheel. The pass was curving slightly west, its looming walls forcing them a few degrees off their intended course while the road, if a never-ending rubble field could be called a road, grew steadily narrower, in places too narrow to get turned around. If a patrol were to appear up ahead, they would be blocked off with no choice but to stand and fight, almost certainly against impossible odds.

But then after a few more kilometres, the road finally emerged from the pass and the crags either side fell away to more open ground. 'Thank Christ for that,' Wolf said. 'Getting a touch claustrophobic back there.'

'Best recce the way,' Ben said, and once again they halted and climbed down from the vehicle to scout ahead a distance on foot before continuing. That was when Ben spotted the column of smoke several kilometres away to the west, climbing thick and dark into the sky from behind a dip before it was caught and dispersed by the wind.

'What's up with that, do you reckon?' asked Wolf, frowning.

'It accounts for the gunfire we heard earlier,' Ben said.

As they crouched among the rocks watching, they were joined by Holt. 'I think we should steer clear,' he told them. 'Could be a spat between rival tribes. Happens all the time in these parts, right? Not our business.'

'Or it could be there are people down there who need help,' Ben said.

'I think he's right, Chris,' Wolf said. 'I think we should check it out.'

'It'll take us even more out of our way.'

'Not by more than an hour or so,' Wolf reasoned. Holt wasn't comfortable with the idea, but he relented. 'Okay, but if things turn to dogshit it'll be on you.'

It took less than an hour to reach the source of the smoke. As they approached, Ben saw that he'd been right about people needing help. This had been no skirmish between rival tribal forces. The village, little more than a few clusters of centuries-old sandstone houses amid a gridwork of tiny narrow streets encircled by a wall, had been razed almost completely to the ground. There wasn't a man in their team who hadn't witnessed scenes like it before, but the extent of the carnage was a shocking sight. Some of the bloodied, twisted bodies that lay scattered outside the ruined village walls were those of women and the little children they'd been clutching in their arms as they fled panic-stricken from their attackers, before they were gunned down. Several houses that were still standing or only partly destroyed were still on fire, others smouldering heaps of burnt-out debris. The raiders had even slaughtered the village's livestock and blown up the well where they fetched their precious water.

Ben was the first to step through the crumbled walls and lay eyes on the even worse slaughter that had taken place inside. The village streets were littered with spent cartridge cases and ran red in places with the blood of the victims. The wails of grief and the screams of the maimed and dying were a sound you never could get used to – unless you happened to be the kind of crazed psychopath who could run amok through an innocent community, killing indis-criminately, the old and the young alike.

It was easy enough to guess who had done this. And there was little anyone could do to help these poor people. As he stood there gazing around him with an overwhelming sense of hopelessness, Ben became aware of Wolf standing at his shoulder.

'Still don't hate them, Ben?' Wolf muttered. 'Not even a little bit?'

Ben said nothing. They walked through the ravaged streets in silence. Among the dead lying about was a single Taliban fighter, slumped against a wall still clutching his brand-new American rifle. Wolf gave him a nudge with the toe of his boot, but he was definitely dead. 'Shame you can only kill them once,' Wolf said.

A few steps on, they came across a young woman sitting by the pile of blackened rubble that had been someone's home, holding a ten-year-old girl who was howling in pain and had blood all over her face from a bad gash. The woman looked alarmed as she saw Ben and Wolf, but Ben laid down his weapon and crouched beside her, telling her in Pashto that he was here to help. In a flood of words the woman explained that the child belonged to her neighbours, whose bodies were somewhere underneath all the rubble, both shot dead in front of their daughter. There was another child, a little boy. She hadn't seen him. Maybe he was dead too, she said. So many of us are dead.

Ben asked Wolf to fetch the first aid kit from the Humvee, and when it arrived he swabbed the blood away from the little girl's face, disinfected the wound and did what he could to close it up with butterfly sutures. The woman talked and wept the whole time. The child sat rigid, letting Ben do his work. As he finished attending to her, a wiry grey-haired man appeared from the smoking ruins and asked Ben if he and his companions were soldiers come to liberate them.

'I wish we could do more,' Ben told him. 'But what you see is all there are of us.' The old man nodded sadly. His name was Hamza, he said, and he was the head man of the village, or what was left of it. They were a community of tribal Shinwari people, sworn enemies of the Taliban who had in the past volunteered a young male of fighting age from every family in every village to help defeat them. The bad blood between their tribe and the country's new rulers ran deep, and the Taliban never forgot a grudge.

'They have always wanted to destroy us,' Hamza complained bitterly. 'They take money and food from us, abuse our women and force our men to fight for them. We tried to resist, but they are strong now. And this is how they repay disloyalty.' He waved around him at the ruin of his village with tears in his eyes. 'But they are even angrier than before. Because of the foreign fighters they believe have come to mount a resistance against them. That must be you,' he said, prodding at Ben with a bony finger.

Ben explained as best he could that they were only here to try to help Afghan people in trouble. 'No government sent us. We don't fight for anyone.' Hamza looked crest-fallen, but accepted the news with stoicism.

'How many were there?' asked Wolf, whose Pashto was less fluent than Ben's but still conversational. 'Many,' Hamza replied, spreading his hands. 'Forty, fifty. Perhaps even more.' Though, he admitted, he'd been hiding throughout most of the attack and hadn't seen a great deal. He was only a weak old man, not like his cousin Samiullah who had managed to kill one of them with his Martini rifle, the single enemy casualty.

'We saw the body,' Ben said. 'Where's Samiullah now?'

'They cut off his head,' Hamza replied.

When the old man had shuffled off among the ruins to attend as best he could to his surviving people, Ben and Wolf walked back to the dead Talib's corpse, relieved him of his weapon and ammunition and searched him for the other item they'd hoped they might find, and did. Ben turned on the radio handset and discovered it was tuned to a channel on which, through all the crackling and fizzing static and white noise, they could hear messages passing to and fro between what sounded like two, possibly three, roaming fighter units. Ben spent a few minutes listening in, gleaning what he could from the garbled back-and-forth chatter. 'They're active, all right. And they're not far away.'

'Could be important for us,' Wolf said. 'We need to tell Chris.'

They found Holt standing outside the village wall looking sickened and angry, restless to move on. Examining the radio from the dead fighter a thought seemed to come to him, and he turned to Liebowitz. 'Doug, this is a different model from the ones we have. Any chance you can use parts from it to fix our sat phone?'

Liebowitz shook his head. 'Sorry, bro. Has to be the same motherboard from an Iridium 9555 or you might as well try fixing it with auto spares.'

Holt said, 'Shit.' He spent a moment tuning in to the radio messages. 'What do you make of it?' he asked Ben and Wolf.

'Sounds to me like the raiding party that hit this place has split up into smaller groups,' Ben said. 'Keeping in constant contact using GPS to communicate their positions.'

'Hunting for us, you reckon?' Holt said.

'They're certainly all stirred up about something.'

'Don't you love being so much in demand,' Wolf replied.

'Except they ain't gonna find us,' Holt said with a dangerous smile. 'We're gonna find them.'

Chapter 24

They did find them, a few hours later and thirty kilometres to the north of the devastated Shinwari village. Or at any rate, one of the smaller groups into which Ben had rightly guessed the original raiding party of forty or fifty fighters had split up in order to forage over a wider area. Perched on an elevated ridge some three hundred metres away, Ben was able to count eighteen figures sitting around a camp among a ring of vehicles. He passed the binocs to Holt, who made his observation before passing them on to Wolf. 'I make it eighteen too,' Wolf said.

'There's your gun shop, brother,' Holt told him. 'These fuckers are laden with enough hardware to start another war. When they're done massacring innocent civilians, that is.'

'And all we have to do is walk down there and take it from them,' Wolf said.

'You think if we asked nicely—?' said Nobby Scraggs, watching the camp through the scope of his sniper rifle in the bushes nearby.

'Wouldn't be the same,' Wolf said.

'You don't need me to tell you, guys,' Holt said. 'None of them can be allowed to get away from us. Only takes one to run for help, and next thing we're overrun here. So no quarter, and we've no use for prisoners either.'

'Sounds okay to me,' Wolf said.

Wasting no time in case the enemy got back on the move, the eight-man team stalked invisibly down from the ridge and spread out in a curving line to engage their targets at closer range. Once they were in position their intersecting arcs of fire would leave their opponents no way out, nowhere to run and very little possibility of mounting any kind of counter-attack. For this kind of exercise, the deadly combination of speed and surprise could enable a small unit of highly trained operatives to take out a far superior force with devastating efficiency. And all eight were experts at the job. Even Ben might have had difficulty spotting his companions as they advanced stealthily into position, using every rock, dead tree and clump of bushes that could screen their approach in exactly the same way that a lioness will stalk as close as possible to a herd of grazing antelopes before unleashing the explosive energy of her attack.

The enemy didn't move. As Ben drew soundlessly closer he could hear them talking and laughing, more like a bunch of friends relaxing after a sports match than a band of raiders fresh from the slaughter of scores of innocent men, women and children. He could smell what they were smoking, too; while Taliban leaders theoretically cracked down on dope use as fundamentally against their religion, meting out all kinds of harsh punishments, many of their fighters smoked it anyway. The aroma drifted on the wind with their unsuspecting laughter. In a few moments, they wouldn't be laughing any longer.

Like the rest of the team Ben was wearing a mic and earpiece through which Holt's command to fire would come once they were all settled in position. A patch of thorny shrubs acted as the perfect cover in which he silently, discreetly set the Maximi machine gun down on its bipod, stretched out prone behind it, lined his sights up to his target and let his muscles relax and his breathing slow. 'Hope in position,' he whispered softly into his mic. 'Copy,' came the whispered reply.

The enemy were still chatting away without a care in the world. Ben thumbed off his weapon's push-button safety and waited for Holt's command. In these moments, time seemed to go by very slowly. He wondered how the rest of his companions felt about what they were about to do. For some of them, this attack might feel at least in part an act of revenge for the slaughter of the Shinwaris. Wolf had spoken very little since leaving the village, preoccupied with his own brooding thoughts; Ben sensed the rage inside him, building up in pressure like a volcano ready to blow.

For Ben himself, he saw the cold, brutal killing he was about to take part in as a necessary part of achieving his own ends, the first goal in that process being to procure enough enemy arms, ammo and supplies to see them through whatever lay ahead. He might snatch away the life of an enemy with ruthless efficiency, but he took no pleasure in gunning down a fellow human being, especially one who was a sitting target, and the aftermath of combat had always left him with a feeling of deep sadness.

As Holt's order to fire came through his earpiece there was no longer any room for such thoughts. At the exact same moment that the field of fire erupted into noise and destruction, Ben squeezed his trigger and felt the weapon judder against his shoulder like a live thing, spewing a golden arc of spent brass from its ejector, hammering its high-velocity stream of bullets into the bodies of his targets. No quarter, no hesitation, no fire wasted on the vehicles with their precious cargo of ordnance and supplies. And no chance of escape for the men in the camp.

The fighters leaped up in alarmed panic as their world exploded into chaos, but very few of them were able to deploy their weapons, let alone run for cover, before they were mowed down by the intersecting hail of gunfire. It was a textbook kill carried out by seasoned professionals. Hard, fast, methodical, absolutely efficient; and after such a long, tense build-up it was all over in seconds. By the time Holt's order to cease firing came over the radio there were eighteen dead Talibs on the ground, none of them more than two or three steps from where they'd been sitting comfortably only seconds earlier.

Ben and his seven companions waited a few moments for the last echoes of gunfire to die away, then emerged from their hidden positions and moved in on the camp, stepping over the bodies of the dead. As anticipated, the vehicles were filled with precious supplies: not only enough weaponry and crated ammunition to equip a force three times their size, but also the stores of food and water that they'd been getting worryingly low on, not to mention twelve full jerrycans of precious diesel fuel.

'To the victor belong the spoils,' Wolf said, discarding the worn-out Kalashnikov he'd been using in favour of a shiny new American M4 carbine whose previous owner had no further use for it. 'Easy come, easy go.' Along with the personal weapons taken from the dead men and a quantity of surplus ones still in their original US army crates, the rest of their haul of small arms included a heavy long-range sniper rifle, rocket launchers and even a couple of mortars.

'Good job, guys,' Holt said. 'Now let's get the hell out of here. Load as much of this stuff as you can fit into one vehicle. We'll burn the rest.'

Ben wasn't sure about the wisdom of creating a smoke plume that could be seen for miles, but he said nothing. Soon afterwards, all but one of the vehicles were blazing. The eight of them piled into their new acquisition, a six-wheel-drive US Army troop truck with a canvas top and a cargo bed crammed with supplies, and they sped away towards the south side of the ridge where they'd concealed their Humvee.

They resumed their course for Zakara with Ben at the wheel of the Humvee and Holt riding up front beside him. Holt said nothing, but Ben sensed the American was unhappy about the detour they were making from their own mission objective. Maybe he was right to be, Ben reflected. It was a depressing thought on top of the bad feelings already weighing on him after the events of the day. For the first time since setting out from Kabul, now that he was getting so much closer to his destination, he began to experience real doubts about ever finding Madison. He shut them out and focused on driving.

They covered another fifty kilometres before darkness fell and they stopped again to make camp. After a meal of spicy tinned halal meat and vegetables courtesy of the dead Talib, Ben and Wolf broke away from the rest of the group to climb a nearby hill and keep watch. Wolf was still very pensive as they sat there, bathed in the colours of the spectacular sunset. The valley they were gazing out across stretched for days' and days' drive to the hazy mountains in the far distance, not a village or a living soul anywhere between here and the horizon. At last Wolf broke his silence, saying quietly, 'This could be a beautiful place.'

'Perhaps one day it will be,' Ben replied, understanding the unspoken meaning behind his friend's words.

Wolf grunted, 'Yeah. Maybe one day the whole world will be. When all the people are gone. And something tells me we might not have to wait too long for that to happen.'

He didn't speak again for the rest of the watch. Late in the night, Ben left him to his own devices, curled up in his makeshift bed among the rocks and tried in vain to get some sleep. Tomorrow they would reach Zakara.

Chapter 25

Six hours' rest and they were away once more. This time Holt took the wheel of the Humvee, Wolf up front and Ben alone in the back with his thoughts. Holt was in a hurry, tearing aggressively onwards, maintaining their north-westerly course as closely as the rugged terrain would allow. On these non-existent roads the vehicle was lurching and pounding wildly over every boulder and rut. Ben was getting thrown about in the back, along with all their kit, but he barely noticed the rough ride. The restless anxiety that had kept him awake all night only nagged him more intensely as the hours went by. He kept seeing Madison's face in his mind, the way she'd looked that cold, damp night in Belgrade when they'd first met.

Ben remembered everything about that occasion. He'd been mixing it up outside a nightclub with some Serbian heavies who worked for the gangster he was chasing; it just so happened that Madison was after the same people. Following a brief but bloody little street battle they'd been pursued through the city in her rental car, which had suffered the same bullet-riddled fate as so many rental cars Ben had

185

ridden in over the years. Afterwards they'd retreated to a neon-lit late-night cafeteria, where they'd swapped stories and talked for hours while she smoked his cigarettes. He'd eaten a limp cheeseburger that might possibly have contained a severed human ear, though he'd been too hungry to care. She'd settled for coffee, strong and black, the way he liked it too. He could still recall the scene in perfect detail – the way she'd sat there with her elbows planted on the cafeteria table and the steaming cup in both hands, her black leather biker jacket hanging from the back of her chair with a laser-sighted Beretta nine in the pocket – the same one she'd saved his life with earlier that night. Under the jacket she'd been wearing a black T-shirt that showed her toned arms. Her hands were slim but strong. She had no rings or bracelets. She'd taken off the baseball cap she was wearing and let her thick, raven-black glossy gypsy ringlets tumble down over her shoulders. Always looking at him, always questioning, a twinkle in her eye and that way she had of raising one eyebrow, unnerving him with the impression she always knew what he was going to say before he said it. Madison had an easy manner about her that belied her sharp intelligence and the supreme self-confidence that had enabled her to shine in one of the roughest male-dominated professions going. That night in Belgrade she'd just shot three men and been through a violent high-speed car chase pursued by crooks with machine guns, but she appeared unruffled and fully in control.

Now, for the hundredth time, Ben told himself that if anyone could have made it out of Kabul and across all the miles of dangerous country to Zakara, it was Madison Cahill.

She *had* to have made it. Didn't she? He desperately needed it to be so. If he'd thought it would do him any good to pray, he'd have got down on his knees. The more he tried not to worry, the more his anxieties nibbled away at him like a shoal of hungry piranha fish. He might almost have wished for another encounter with enemy troops, just to give him something else to think about.

No such luck. All through that morning, through the hot, dusty afternoon and into early evening their little convoy seemed to be the only thing that existed in the barren wastes of Afghanistan. Wherever the remnants of the Taliban raiding party had gone, they were far, far away by now; and nor was there any sign of other patrols. Going by the GPS and Ben's old map, the Zakara site was only a few kilometres away now as another day started drawing to an end. The final leg of the journey had carried them up and up onto higher and higher ground, tracking along rocky inclines that were filled with endless hairpin bends and sometimes so steep that the vehicles growled along at a crawl in first gear and all the kit slid to the rear. The final slope was so steep that it seemed touch and go whether they'd be able to ascend it. Most civilian vehicles, especially with civilian drivers unschooled in the dark art of tackling the most extreme off-road environments on earth, wouldn't have achieved the climb, and even so it was a struggle.

At last, with the blood-red colours of sunset filling the eastern sky, they rolled to a halt at their destination. Before Holt could say, 'Well, this is it, man,' Ben was already out of the vehicle. He walked a few steps and stopped, gazing about him. The cold wind whistled in his ears. They had climbed several thousand metres to the flattened-out top of a mountain plateau with a dramatic drop below them and vast sweeping views for hundreds of kilometres around, broken only by a tall ridge rising up from the northern edge of the plateau and the massive peaks in the distance, their snowy caps pink in the sunset.

And so this was Rigby Cahill's dream, his obsession. The site of the ancient lost city of Zakara. If Ben had been a general or an emperor in those bygone times, with tens or even hundreds of thousands of men at his command, he would have considered this a perfect place to build a fortified city. Just standing here surveying this epic panorama conveyed an incredible sense of power and invincibility.

For Ben, though, it also conveyed a sense of emptiness that bordered on despair. Because there was nothing here. Nothing, and nobody. Just a few broken, crumbled remnants casting long shadows across the ground that barely even suggested anything had ever stood in this place, or that any living soul had ever set foot here, aside from the odd mountain goat.

Hearing the crunch of steps over the wind he looked around to see Wolf walking over from the vehicles, where the others were standing in a group talking in low voices and throwing glances his way.

'So much for the grand royal palaces, huge great big columns and treasure vaults filled with gold and jewels,' Wolf said, frowning in disappointment. 'Not quite what I'd imagined. You'd think a lost city would look like something a little more than a rubble field.'

'She's not here,' Ben said. 'I don't know where she is.'

'Yeah, I can see that too, mate. I don't know what to say. Looks like we came here on a wild goose chase.'

Ben had no reply. He hung his head and felt the energy leak from his body.

'Face it, Ben. There never really was much hope of finding her,' Wolf said, trying to sound consoling. 'You must have known that from the start. Right?'

Ben nodded. He sat down heavily on a rock, feeling his legs strangely weak under him.

'It's shit,' Wolf said. 'The shittiest of the shitty. I understand how you're feeling. Or at least, I think I do. But at times like this there's nothing a guy can do except move on and tell himself that there's other people out there he can help. Lots of them.'

Ben said nothing.

Wolf looked as though he wanted to say more, but couldn't find the words and just stood there, offering his friend the support and companionship of his presence if nothing else. Ben stayed silent. This was the moment he'd feared the most, and part of him must have indeed known that it was extremely likely, almost inevitable, that he'd arrive here at the end of his journey only to find a patch of empty ground. That the chances were very strong she hadn't even made it out of Kabul alive. That he'd been kidding himself all along with wishful thinking. Chasing shadows. Searching for a corpse. His dreams had told him as much, but he'd wilfully ignored them like the damn fool he was. And now here he was.

He suddenly felt very tired. Worn out to the point of collapse, as though he'd aged a hundred years in the space of two minutes and all the strength was sapped out of him. He stared at the red disc of the sun slowly dipping into the band of purple-tinged clouds across the eastern horizon. As the last rays faded, the air was already turning colder. In his low state of mind it seemed to Ben there was something ominously final about the setting of the sun, like a death, as though its light and warmth were ebbing away for the very last time and it wouldn't ever return. As though some part of him was dying along with it.

Behind them, Holt broke away from the group by the vehicles and came over to join Ben and Wolf. Wolf gave the American an unsmiling glance as if to warn him, 'Leave the guy alone.' Holt ignored it. Ben ignored him too, sitting very still on his rock with his eyes fixed on the spot where the sun had now vanished, leaving just a pale golden streak along the horizon. Holt stood there for a moment, then cleared his throat and said, 'Well, looks like your friend ain't here, buddy.'

'You noticed that, did you?' Wolf said defensively.

'I'm real sorry that's the case, though I can't say I'm surprised. So, as for our agreement—'

'I know what I said,' Ben replied, snapping back to life and turning around to glare coldly up at him. 'And I'm true to my word. You can count on that, Holt.'

Holt nodded. 'All right, then. Reckon it's maybe another eight or ten hours' journey to the orphanage. We might as well camp here tonight, get some rest and set out again at first light. Hoping we're not too late to save those poor kids.'

'We'll save them,' Ben said. 'If we can save anyone.'

'And then what?' Wolf asked quietly when Holt had gone back to rejoin the others.

'And then I'm going back to Kabul alone,' Ben said. 'Retrace my steps. Start again. And I will find her, Jaden. Even if it takes me forever. Even if I don't find her alive in the end. I will not stop.'

'And you might get yourself killed doing it,' Wolf said. 'One guy on his own, up against those kinds of crazy odds.'

'I never minded crazy odds before.'

'And lived to tell the tale. This time it could be different.'

'Maybe,' Ben replied.

'Or maybe not,' Wolf said. 'Because maybe you don't need to go it alone. You looked out for me plenty of times in the past. I'll stick with you for as long as it takes. And if things go bad, then to hell with it. I don't have anything better to do.'

Ben looked at him, knew he was being completely sincere and was deeply touched by the warmth of his friendship. 'Thanks, Jaden. It means a lot. But I can't let you do that. When this is over, you go back to Spain and get on with your life.'

'It's never over,' Wolf said. 'I spent most of my life looking out for Number One. Now it's different. Something's changed, you know? I can't go back. This is my life now.'

Ben was about to reply when he heard an indistinct cry behind him in the distance, and turned around in surprise to see four figures running across the plateau from the direction of the ridge. In the dusky light he could see that three of them were men: one slim and dark-haired, the second portly and middle-aged and the third much older again, having trouble keeping up and stumbling along with a pronounced limp.

But it wasn't the three men Ben was looking at. It was the figure in front, sprinting hard across the rocky ground, leaping over the rubble. The mountain wind blew off her cap and her black hair streamed out behind her as she ran. She called out to him again, and this time he made out her words.

'Ben? Ben Hope? Is that you? Oh my God – is that really you?'

He surged to his feet. His heart had begun to pound and his hands were shaky.

'*Madison?*'

Chapter 26

She didn't stop running until she reached him, flying past Holt and the group of astonished men and straight into Ben's arms with such force that she almost knocked him over. She buried her face into his shoulder and hugged him tightly. 'I can't believe it's you.' Then she pulled away from him, clasping his shoulders and staring into his eyes with a look of complete bewilderment. 'I'm not dreaming. It actually is you.'

Ben couldn't help but laugh out loud, those despairing emotions from moments earlier now completely washed away in a tide of bubbling happiness and relief. 'I can't quite believe it's you either.'

'When we saw you arrive we thought you were troops,' she explained in a gush of words. 'We ran and hid in our shelter back there. Then I was watching through the binoculars and I thought I must be seeing things. What on earth are you doing here?'

Keeping it as brief as possible, Ben told her about Linus Twigg's phone call; how he'd been able to take advantage of a chance opportunity to fly out to Afghanistan; how he'd learned from old Karim at the Cultural Institute that she'd escaped Kabul to go off in search of her father's Zakara site. 'There have been a couple of twists and turns along the way, but now I'm here. And here you are. It's good to see you, Madison.'

She hadn't changed a bit. Her hair was still the same raven black mane of gypsy curls, a little dusty like the old leather jacket she was wearing. Jeans and cowboy boots weren't exactly the kind of garb that would enable her to pass unnoticed in these parts. But she seemed to have made it in one piece nonetheless. She hugged him again, wrapping her arms around his neck. She kissed him twice. 'I'm so happy you're here, Ben. Hell, I've been dropping hints for years that you should come see me. Guess I had to go missing in the middle of a freakin' war zone for you to take an interest at last.' She was beaming as she said it. The last rays of the sunset glowed on her face and in her dark eyes. 'There's so much I want to tell you. I'm glad Karim is still okay. And poor Linus; he and the others must have been going nuts. I tried and tried calling them to say I was all right, but my phone died the day we were leaving Kabul. Chances of getting reception out here are about nil anyway. Are you guys able to make contact with the outside world?'

'We have a satellite phone,' Wolf said. 'With a hole in it.'

'Then I guess we're on our own, huh?'

Her three companions had caught up and were standing there uncertainly. Holt and the others had come over too, making a small crowd gathered around Madison. She asked, 'Are these your buddies?'

'We kind of bumped into one another en route.'

'So you're the ex-bounty hunter we've been hearing so much about,' Wolf said. Which perhaps wasn't the best opening line.

Madison shot him a look that could cause frostbite in midsummer. 'That would be a Federal Fugitive Recovery Special Agent. And you are?'

'Never mind him,' Ben said. 'Jaden's an old friend from way back. He's a little short on social graces.'

'Hmm,' Madison said, and eyed Wolf disparagingly for a moment before the megawatt smile came back and she turned to introduce her companions to Ben. 'This is Aziz Qeyami,' motioning at the middle-aged man. He was over-weight and out of breath, and even in the fading light Ben could see his face was flushed red from the run. 'My colleague from the Institute,' she said.

'Pleased to meet you, Aziz. Thanks for taking care of her.'

'It was she who took care of us,' Aziz chuckled, still panting.

'And this is Ramin, who worked there too. Ramin, come say hi to my friend Ben.' She beckoned over the youngest of the men. He was maybe thirty, reedy and narrow-shouldered with a mop of unruly dark hair and a somewhat confused expression. 'Hello,' he said quietly, which was apparently all they were going to get out of him for now.

'And this gentleman?' Ben asked, turning towards the eldest man. He was taller than the other two and rake-thin, with a thick head of pure white hair and a beard like Methuselah.

'No, this is Father Bugnolio,' Madison said with a warm smile. 'We met in Kabul and he hitched a ride with us.'

'Formerly of Our Lady of Divine Providence Chapel,' the old priest explained in perfect English. He reminded Ben strangely of Father Pascal, a dear old friend he had known in France, years before he'd lived there, and still missed. 'A friend of Madison's is a friend of mine,' he said, holding out a hand. His grip was strong and dry. 'I would be dead if not for her.'

'Nonsense,' Madison said. 'You don't kill that easily, Father B. Though I won't deny that things were starting to get a little hairy back there in the city. We got out by the skin of our teeth, dodging roadblocks and checkpoints. Thanks to Aziz, who knows all the backstreets better than anyone.'

Ben asked, 'How did you get here?'

'I have a jeep,' Aziz said. 'Or I did. It broke down.'

'We walked the last few miles,' Madison said. 'Hell of a climb.'

'I agree with Father Bugnolio,' Aziz said. 'We would never have made it here without her.'

Ben introduced the rest of the men. 'Did you run into Taliban units?' Holt asked Madison.

She nodded. 'Saw quite a few of them along the way. They seem to be everywhere. But we managed to stay out of sight. It was mostly pretty uneventful.'

'Actually, we were attacked,' Ramin said.

Ben asked, 'By who?'

Madison brushed it away with a dismissive gesture. 'Oh, it was nothing. Just a bunch of bandits who snuck up on our camp on the second night and tried to rob us. We saw them off easily enough.'

'Another typical Madison understatement,' said Ramin. 'There must have been a dozen of them, armed to the teeth and vicious. I've never been so terrified in my life.'

The darkness had fallen quickly as they stood there talking, and the strengthening mountain wind had a chilly bite. Madison pointed back at the ridge. 'Like I said, we're camped out at the rock shelter back there. You're all very welcome to join us. Plenty of room for twelve people. Wish I could offer you all the comforts of home, but we're running out of food and water.'

'We have enough for everyone,' Ben told her. He thought he detected a look from Holt, who obviously resented sharing their provisions with four additional mouths to feed. But Holt covered it up well, thanking Madison for letting them use their camp. 'We figured we'd stay here until first light. We'll be moving on then.'

Madison asked where, and Ben told her about the orphanage. 'You guys are seriously going to rescue forty children?' she said, cocking an eyebrow. 'What's the plan, you gonna lead them away to safety over the border like the Pied Piper?'

Wolf grinned, a glint of gold in the moonlight. 'That's the general idea.'

'God bless those poor innocents,' murmured Father Bugnolio sadly.

'We'll figure something out,' said Holt.

'Hope it works out for you,' Madison said. 'As for me, I'll be staying right here.'

Chapter 27

Ben looked at her, startled by her words. 'No chance, Madison. I came here to bring you home. First I need to help these guys take care of their business. But then I mean to finish what I set out to do.'

He could tell from her body language, the defiant set of her head, her feet braced apart and her hands planted on her hips, that it wasn't going to be easy persuading her. Same old bull-headed Madison Cahill. 'The hell you will,' she replied firmly. 'This was Dad's discovery and wild horses couldn't drag me away until I'm good and ready to leave of my own accord, thank you very much.'

'You can't stay here,' Ben protested, aware of the others all watching like hawks. 'It's not safe.'

She crossed her arms and shook her head, not budging an inch. 'Uh-uh. No way.' Then her expression softened a little and she said, 'Look, Ben, it's not that I don't appreciate what you did for me. Because believe me, it means a hell of a lot. But don't you see, if I leave now, with all that's happening I won't be able to come back for years. Maybe not ever. This was my one chance to see what Dad discovered.'

'And now you've seen it,' Ben said. 'Did you think you could live here forever? There's nothing here.'

'Not quite nothing,' Madison replied enigmatically.

'Well, you two can stand here and bicker all night if you want,' Wolf said. 'But the rest of us are going back to the camp and break out the food. I'm famished.'

'We're all hungry,' Aziz said. He laid an affectionate hand on Madison's shoulder. 'Come on. You have to eat. We can argue about this tomorrow.'

She heaved a sigh. 'All right. But I tell you I'm not going anywhere.'

They made their way to the rock shelter, carrying some of their provisions from the vehicles along with their personal weapons, just in case of unexpected visitors. Nobby Scraggs had retrieved a large cardboard box from deep in the back of the Humvee and was clutching it to his chest. It looked heavy. 'Is this where we get to find out what's in that bloody box you've been carting around with you everywhere, not letting anyone touch it?' Wolf asked him.

'Maybe,' Scraggs replied mysteriously.

The rudimentary camp site was a hollow at the foot of the escarpment ridge, well shielded from view. Madison's group had rigged up a tarpaulin awning to protect them from the worst of the wind and the torrential downpours of icy rain that could materialise with little warning and persist for days. But Ben, Wolf and the others had camped in far, far worse places in their lives. As for Madison, she looked completely at her ease out here in the wilderness, roughing it with a bunch of uncouth ex-Special Forces guys. Ben had had the privilege of knowing several exceptional women in his life, and admired them all for their independence of spirit, their resilience and inner strength. There was nothing remotely mannish about Madison Cahill, and yet she could effortlessly hold her own in the midst of the toughest, brawniest, testosterone-laden male company, just hanging with the guys as though she'd been around folks like that all her life. She laughed often and freely, didn't flinch at their crude language, nor even bat an eyelid when Nobby Scraggs emitted a trumpeting great fart and said, 'Ahhh, needed that.'

Schulz and Nielsen volunteered to take the first watch, Schulz climbing to the top of the escarpment to look east and Nielsen scanning the rest of the horizon to the west. A few minutes later they both radioed back that there were no signs of visible life anywhere for miles around. Holt said, 'In that case I guess we can afford a camp fire.'

'Luxury at last,' Wolf said.

'You don't know the half of it, mate,' said Scraggs, who was sitting on his mysterious cardboard box with his weapon across his knees, as though prepared to defend its contents with his life.

The blaze of dry brush and dead branches gathered from the lower slopes was soon crackling, and the ten of them gathered around, sitting on rocks and rolled-up sleeping bags or cross-legged on the ground, to crack open a few tins of the halal meat and vegetables salvaged from the Talibs.

'This is a veritable feast,' Ramin said, coming more to life at the sight.

'Now, Nobby, are you going to tell us what's in that sodding box,' Wolf said, 'or am I going to have to break your arms to get it off you?'

'You can try, pal,' Scraggs said with a smile as he stood up and opened the box. 'I've been saving this all the way from bloody Kabul.'

'No way!' Baldacci exclaimed when he saw what was inside. 'Dude!'

'Black market bevvies,' said Scraggs, taking out one of the dozens of beer bottles and fondling it with something like love. 'You any idea how hard they were to find? This stuff's like liquid gold in a Muslim country.'

'Here's one Muslim who will happily drink it,' said Aziz.

'And another,' said Ramin. 'To hell with the fundamentalists.'

'You've sure been keeping this under your hat, man,' said Liebowitz, delighted he hadn't volunteered for the first watch.

'Saving it for a special celebration, mate,' said Scraggs. 'We've summat to celebrate now, haven't we?' He smiled at Madison.

'Amen to that,' said the priest.

'Thanks, sweetie,' Madison said, beaming back at him.

'And I'm going to drink it,' Scraggs added, fishing around among his kit, 'out of my special jubilee mug.' He pulled it out with a flourish. The decorative mug was grandly emblazoned with a picture of the Queen.

'Please don't tell me you've been toting that pathetic piece of crap all over hell's creation,' Baldacci said with a withering look.

'Wouldn't be parted from it, pal,' Scraggs replied good-naturedly. 'Now, cheers, everyone.' He passed out the beers, went to hand one without thinking to Father Bugnolio and hesitated. 'Oh, sorry, I forgot. You don't drink, do you, being a man of the cloth and all that?'

'Father B has been keeping us morally pure all the way from Kabul,' Madison said.

Father Bugnolio smiled. 'Though in this instance I believe we can make an exception. The Bible says, "Eat thy food with gladness, and drink thy wine with a joyful heart, for God now accepteth thy works."'

'Book of Ecclesiastes,' Ben said.

'Chapter nine, verse seven,' replied Father Bugnolio. 'You know your Old Testament.'

'A throwback to a former life,' Ben said.

'And as our friend rightly says, we have something to celebrate. Therefore, I will gladly accept this kind offering,' the priest said, taking the beer. 'Thank you, my child. To your very good health, one and all.' He popped the cap like a pro, raised his bottle in a toast, took a long swig and looked as if he'd received an angelic visitation. 'Lord be praised. This is the finest meal we've had in days.'

By the flickering glow of the firelight and under the moon and stars they shared their various stories of how they'd all come to be here. Madison's was all about her father, needless to say. Ben said little about Operation Hydra, and nothing at all about its purpose. Spartan, whoever Spartan was, seemed just a faraway memory to him now. He described how he'd set out alone on foot for the first part of his journey, before his chance encounter with Wolf had brought him into contact with Holt's team.

Holt took up the baton from there, and was more forthcoming about the events that had led to the launch of the

NEO volunteer mission and their spectacular, if short-lived, run of success getting people out of Kabul. Both Madison and Father Bugnolio were full of praise for their accomplishments, while Aziz in particular was full of questions. He was deeply worried about his brother and his family, who were loyal Muslims but deeply opposed to what they regarded as the reactionary jihadist ideologies of the Taliban. The last time he'd spoken to his brother they were trying to get a place on the very last plane out; he'd heard nothing since.

'Wish I could help you there, bud,' Holt said. 'A lot of people were in the same situation.'

'I admit I was tempted to leave too, at first,' said Father Bugnolio. 'I knew about the evacuations, of course, but I resisted, feeling I should remain behind to mind my duties. What shepherd would abandon his flock to the wolves? But the chaos and violence of the ensuing persecution of Christians made me realise what little I could do, and I came to question the wisdom of my choice. Even then I was still undecided, until I was pursued through the streets by a gang of their fighters who had identified me as a Catholic priest. Perhaps if I had thought to remove my cassock before venturing outside . . .'

'That would've definitely been a smart move, mate,' said Scraggs. 'Look how we're decked out. Imagine if we were to go wandering about Kabul in British or Yank army uniform, how that'd go down.'

'Talk about a red rag to a bull, man,' Nielsen agreed.

'Anyhow,' the priest continued, 'I managed to evade them but I knew they would reappear at any moment and catch

203

me. That was when a Jeep appeared, as if by Divine inter-vention, and a voice called, 'Father! Get your behind in the car, quick!'

'Actually I might have used slightly stronger language,' Madison admitted. 'We could see he was in trouble.'

'Indeed I was. Which is why I can say with all conviction that she and her friends saved my life.'

Ramin had a slightly different story to tell. He'd worked for a while as a researcher and copywriter for the Kabul Cultural Institute, but his main focus was his activity blog-ging, in which his main – in fact his sole, he admitted – theme was to attack and denounce the Taliban and its leaders. Like many young urban Muslims he regarded himself as a liberal and a progressive, and dreaded what might happen to his country if they seized full control. He also despised them for their acts of vandalism against irreplaceable sites of historic heritage, like the giant Buddha statues harking back to Afghanistan's sixth-century past, blown to smithereens on the orders of Taliban leader Mullah Omar for being un-Islamic and idolatrous. As the takeover had become more and more imminent, Ramin had only doubled down on his scathing criticisms of the fundamentalists, posting material so inflammatory that it was sure to make him a target for punishment. It had worked perhaps better than he might have wished for. As the old order fell apart with stunning speed and the fighters came flooding into the city, Ramin found himself a marked man.

'They have lists of people they want to kill,' he complained. 'I was on one of them. *Alhamdulillah* I wasn't at home when they paid me a visit, or I would be dead now. Thrown off a tall building, my tongue sliced out, I can't bear even to imagine.' It was clear from his haunted expression that Ramin's imagination was hard at work, nonetheless.

'Maybe you shouldn't have tried so hard to piss them off,' Wolf suggested.

Ramin shrugged. 'There it is. Now what could I do? I couldn't go home again. There's an attic room at the Institute we only use for storing old books and files. I was hiding there when Madison and Aziz found me.'

'You left the door open,' Madison remarked. 'Lucky it was us.'

Ramin went on, 'And they told me they were getting out of the city. I jumped at the chance. But what a journey. I've never been so afraid.'

The conversation returned to the incident with the bandits who'd tried to raid their camp. Wolf wanted to hear the story, but Madison was being coy about it.

'She beat one of them over the head with a shovel,' Aziz said, laughing. 'And kicked another in the . . .' – glancing at the priest – 'that is to say, in the groin area.' He pointed downwards, for clarity.

'I abhor violence in all its forms,' the priest said. 'But one must confess it was a relief for the situation to be resolved in that manner. The villains beat a hasty retreat.'

'Leaving behind a neat rifle that I was happy to bring along,' Madison said, waving at the AK-47 propped up against the rocks behind her. 'Came in handy for keeping us in bush meat on the way here. I kind of forgot to swing by the grocery store as we were getting the hell out of Kabul.'

'Guns make me feel uncomfortable,' Ramin said glumly. 'I've never been around them before. Now they seem to be everywhere.'

'Better get used to it, sonny,' Wolf told him. 'And you might have to learn to use one before this is over.'

Ramin pulled an unhappy face, peering at Madison's rifle, then at Wolf's. 'It looks complicated.'

'Don't worry,' Wolf said, patting his as though it were a dog. 'I'll teach you. A child can operate one of these things.'

'And so many do, God help us,' said Father Bugnolio.

'May I?' Wolf stepped over to Madison's AK, picked it up, unloaded it and worked the action. He looked surprised, as though he hadn't expected it to function properly.

'Bolt carrier assembly was full of grit and the piston was all gunky,' Madison said nonchalantly. 'I pulled it apart, cleaned everything up and she's running like a sewing machine now.'

'Impressive,' Wolf said, putting the gun down.

'For a woman, you mean?' She laughed. 'Back where I grew up, all the kids could field strip and reassemble any rifle, shotgun or handgun you care to name in one minute flat by the time they were twelve.'

'Land of the free, home of the brave,' Baldacci said dreamily.

'I'll take a look at that M4 of yours, if you like,' she added, pointing at the carbine dangling from its sling over Wolf's shoulder.

'The SAS did teach us the basics of weapons care, but what do they know? Here, be my guest.'

Holt and the rest of the team exchanged approving looks as Madison expertly gave Wolf's carbine the once-over and returned it. 'Not bad. Though personally I never much liked the AR-15 platform, even though I do own two of them back home. They're not a rifle, they're a contraption.'

'Whoa, that's the sacred cow you're kicking there, girl,' said Baldacci.

'Can't fault them in the accuracy department, though. I can generally put ten shots on a playing card at five hundred yards. Don't know what the SAS would think about that.'

'I know what I think,' Wolf said.

'Yeah?'

'I think I'm deeply in love for the first time in my life and that you're that special one I've been waiting for. How'd you like to get married?'

Madison laughed again. 'Your friend's a charmer, isn't he?' she said to Ben.

'He has his moments.'

'Well, Mr Wolf, flattered that you asked, but I'm sorry to say that my heart already belongs to another.'

'Damn. Story of my life.'

'Somebody is an extremely lucky man,' said Father Bugnolio, looking benevolently at her.

After dinner, Schulz and Nielsen returned from their posts for some food and a pleasantly unexpected beer, and Baldacci and Liebowitz took the next watch. Ben and Madison remained by the campfire and talked into the night. Wolf and Father Bugnolio sat on rocks nearby, mostly listening. Ramin was deeply lost in his own thoughts as he gazed into the dying flames. Aziz had fallen asleep, head lolling, snoring softly. 'He gets tired,' Madison said quietly, with a worried look. 'He's not a well man, but he tries to hide it. On the climb up here I thought he was going to drop dead of a heart attack.'

'With God's blessing, he will be well,' said Father Bugnolio. 'I will pray for him. That said, without wishing to sound self-pitying, I had similar concerns for my own health as we made that arduous, interminable ascent.'

'I remember Dad telling me what a tough time he'd had of it when he came here with his guides that last time, back in '89. Their vehicles weren't up to the slope and they had to hack all the way up here on foot. Said he'd lost about ninety pounds by the time they reached the top.'

Wolf said, 'Ben told me your dad was this world-famous archaeologist.'

'Sure was that. He was my hero growing up,' Madison said. 'Mom died while I was still very young, so it was Dad who pretty much raised me on his own. How he managed to make such a great job of that while travelling all over the world and making all these incredible discoveries – well, that's just another tribute to what an amazing guy he was. I often used to go with him. Been to all kinds of remote and crazy places.'

'I liked him a lot,' Ben said. 'The one time I met him.'

'That was the very last phase of his life,' she reflected wistfully, and her gaze turned inwards for a quiet moment. 'I wish you could have known him before, Ben. He was just a shadow of what he'd once been. But he was still my dad.'

'Bless his memory,' Father Bugnolio murmured.

'Amen to that,' Ben said.

'Thanks, guys.' Madison looked down, and went quiet for a while.

'So is this your first time in Afghanistan?' Wolf asked her. 'Speaking of remote and crazy places.'

She nodded, brightening up a little. 'Yup. Been to Siberia, China, most of the Middle East, all over Europe, but never made it out this way until now. Dad had some difficulty getting into the country himself, what with all the new wars that kept breaking out every five minutes. By 1990, the door had pretty much closed. It was a huge frustration for him, being so obsessed with all things Alexandrine.' Meeting Wolf's totally blank look she added helpfully, 'That's what we say. *Alexandrine*, as in Alexander. The Great, that is.'

'Right,' Wolf said. 'You mean the Greek general guy.' As though Greek generals who'd earned themselves the sobriquet 'the Great' were ten a penny. 'We were talking about him before.'

'Yeah, that guy,' she replied, smiling. 'Oh, Dad would've talked you under the table anytime you mentioned Alexander's name. Folks who knew him soon got to avoid doing that, or he'd be at it all night. It was more than a dream for him. He ate and breathed it. His greatest goal of all, more than any of the other treasures and antiquities he spent his life searching for, was to find Alexander's lost tomb. Dragged his poor long-suffering kid daughter all over what used to be ancient Babylon, now Syria and Iraq, trying to find it. But he'd happily have settled for discovering a lost city or two. And nowhere was that a more promising prospect than the land of Bactria.'

Wolf shook his head. 'Where? Never heard of it.'

'Okay. But you must have heard of a Bactrian camel, right?'

'Think I might have eaten one once,' Wolf said, casting his mind back.

'It was a dromedary,' Ben reminded him. 'In Somalia.'

'It was some kind of camel, anyway,' Wolf replied. 'Tasted like shit, too. But as for Bactria, no idea.'

Madison said, 'Well, it so happens you're looking at it. Sitting on it. This place wasn't always called Afghanistan. You look at it now, and all you see is the hangover from the Mujahideen versus the Russians, or the Taliban and the Americans, and the talking heads on the TV and the latest social or political upheaval that's here today, gone tomorrow, but there's so much more to it than that. Right here under our asses is the stage where so many of the great dramas of ancient history took place. I'm talking epic, widescreen, cinemascope, Technicolor legends, like the biggest movie you ever saw, only ten times bigger. Where fifteen centuries of violent and bloody war and destruction like you wouldn't believe alternated with short peaceful periods when great cities appeared, empires rose up, populations exploded, trade routes thrived, fortunes were made and culture flourished, only for it all to be smashed down again as the next cycle of ruin and devastation came around, like sand castles washed away by the tide. That's the way it always went, all through the ages. And it always will.'

Chapter 28

Wolf said, 'Wow. Dramatically put. Though I will say, when it comes to violent and bloody war and destruction, there's nothing I haven't seen before.'

Madison turned to him. 'What you said about Alexander being a Greek general. In fact, he was just a little bit more than that.'

'I never did pay much attention in class,' Wolf said. 'You're the expert.'

Madison smiled. 'What I know is only a fraction of what Dad could have rattled off. Alexander was the greatest military leader of antiquity, and probably the most important player in the entire history of Afghanistan, three centuries before Christ.'

'So what was this super-important Greek doing here?'

'What all super-ambitious leaders did back then,' she replied, 'and still do today: expanding his global empire. It's a long and fascinating story. I think you'd enjoy it.'

'Uh-oh, sounds like we're about to get a history lesson,' Wolf said, grinning at Ben.

'You want one?' she asked.

'From you?' Wolf said, grinning even wider. 'Anything.'

'You might even learn something,' Ben told him.

Madison took a sip from the beer bottle she'd been nurturing since dinner. 'Let's see now. I guess the best place to start the story is in 336 BC, when Alexander inherited the throne of the Greek kingdom of Macedonia at the age of just twenty. As a boy he'd been tutored by Aristotle. He was brilliant, famously beautiful, a blond-haired blue-eyed demigod; dashing, heroic, supremely talented at the art of war and apparently incapable of fear. He always led his armies from the front, riding into battle right at the head of his men, who followed him adoringly.'

'Sounds like our very own Benedict Hope,' Wolf said. 'I could tell you stories.'

'Shut up, Jaden,' Ben muttered.

'I'll bet,' Madison said, smiling at Ben. 'Anyhow, one of Alexander's greatest conquests was his long war against the Persians, who were a mighty empire ruled at that time by King Darius III. He was called "the Great", too, as you would if you were also King of Babylon and Pharaoh of Egypt. He'd been all over, conquering left, right and centre and crowning himself ruler. But in 331 BC it was his turn to go down, when Alexander kicked his ass big-time at the battle of Gaugamela, in modern Iraq. Darius escaped, but that was the end of his reign. Now Alexander found himself the ruler of the entire Persian empire. He'd enriched himself beyond anyone's wildest dreams from its plundered treasures, and had almost limitless power over a vast kingdom. But he wanted more. So now he set his sights on the land of Bactria.'

'You wonder what drew him to such a place,' Ben said.

Madison replied, 'It's a good question. The country, if you could even call it a country at that time, was a chaotic sprawl of warring tribes and factions, highly fragmented and extremely difficult to invade because of its hostile terrain. Militarily, there wasn't a whole lot to gain from even trying. But the fact is, Alexander's interest in Bactria had a personal element to it. He was peeved that his old enemy Darius had managed to escape, even though he was beaten. And he got even more peeved when a warlord called Bessus murdered Darius and proclaimed himself "King of Kings" as Darius's natural successor.'

'Cheeky sod,' Wolf said.

'That's what Alexander thought too. He wanted that glory for himself, right? There could only be one king of kings, after all. So when Bessus fled into the hills of Bactria with his followers, Alexander decided to lead his legions after him in pursuit. The most powerful military leader of his time, or any time until then, at the head of the biggest army in the world. But as a politician he needed to frame his personal quest in grander terms for the benefit of his men. He sold them the idea that the conquest of Bactria was a noble cause, targeting the Afghan warlords who he described in much the same kinds of terms that western leaders still use nowadays – he called them a rogue regime, a band of criminals and terrorists, lawless savages of a bleak, harsh land that, more than any other, needed to be taught a lesson in civilisation. The way to do this, Alexander's way, was to crush them with overwhelming military force.'

'As you do,' Ben said. 'Sounds like pretty familiar rhetoric.'

'Nothing changes,' Madison replied. 'History just goes around in cycles. All you have to do is fill in the blanks. So in he marched with his gigantic invasion force, and promptly started conquering everything he could find and claiming it as his own. Centuries later when the British, Russians and then the Americans each in turn seized Kandahar, they were capturing a city founded by Alexander himself on his newfound territory. Its name comes from the Arabic for his own, "Iskandariya". Alexander saw it as a strategic point guarding important trade routes to the Indus Valley in the south and Kabul in the north. Now his appetite was whetted to take over the entire land. He arrived in Bagram and founded another city there, which again he named after himself: "Alexandria on the Caucasus". Its site sat undiscovered for centuries.'

'Did your dad find it?' Ben asked.

'I wish,' Madison said. 'No, it was discovered a little before his time, in 1833 by a British explorer called Charles Masson. Nowadays there's nothing much left of it, what remains mostly buried under the old US air base. Alexander used it as a staging point to go off conquering more territory, while still chasing after Bessus. Over the next few months he marched his army fifteen thousand miles all across and around the southern half of Afghanistan.'

'Can't have been a walk in the park,' Wolf said.

'That would be an understatement. In summer the army suffered from crippling heat and thirst and faced plagues of mosquitoes and flies. In winter they were hit by terrible snowstorms and ran dangerously low on provisions. You can imagine the logistical problems of keeping such a massive force supplied, consuming 255 tons of food and 150,000 gallons of water every single day. Meanwhile Bessus and his followers were waging guerrilla warfare on them, attacking Alexander's supply lines to make life even harder.'

'But I'm guessing that didn't put Alexander off,' Ben said.

'Not him, not a chance. He kept on after Bessus relentlessly, marching the army across deserts where hundreds of men died of thirst, and over the mountains and through the Khawak Pass where blizzards froze hundreds more to death. When the food ran out completely, the soldiers had to eat their own baggage animals, just like the starving British invasion force of the 1800s were forced to do. The land itself was killing them, far more effectively than their enemies could.'

'This place is a bitch, all right,' Wolf said. 'We can all attest to that.'

'Next they had to cross the Oxus River, a five-day operation made more difficult by the fact that Bessus's forces had pre-emptively burned all the boats in the region. But Bessus didn't manage to keep running for much longer. Eventually he was betrayed and brought in front of Alexander, who in his typically compassionate way had him tortured, his face hacked off, then his body torn apart between two bent trees.'

'I actually knew a guy that happened to,' Wolf commented. 'Made a hell of a—'

Ben looked at him. 'Jaden. Please.'

Madison shrugged, hacked-off faces and dismembered bodies apparently being par for the course in her world. 'So now that his personal mission against Bessus had been taken care of, you'd have thought that maybe Alexander would have called it a day and gone home to enjoy being the ruler of the biggest empire in the world. And maybe that's what he wanted, deep down – but of course that would've meant leaving this huge new territory he'd conquered vulnerable to anyone else who might think to challenge his claim on it. The main threat came from the tribal hordes of what's now Pakistan, Uzbekistan, Tajikistan and other lands beyond the mountainous borders. They had plenty of able warriors and were always looking for an opportunity to gain new footholds. With that in mind he kept marching onwards, and founded yet another new city to act as an outpost to guard the most northerly edge of his empire in central Asia.'

'Let me guess,' Wolf said. 'Another Alexandria?'

'You get the picture. This one was called Alexandria Eschate, "the furthermost Alexandria". It's not there anymore, nothing more than a few ancient foundations lying across the border in Tajikistan. But in its day it became his military base while he went on waging war against the tribes and warlords of Afghanistan. He had his hands full, because by now there was a full-scale uprising going on as the local warlords started to resent the rule being imposed on them. The revolt spread fast, and Alexander's response to it was to march his army against a number of Afghan towns and cities. He laid siege to them, smashed their resistance and massacred their whole populations down to the last man, woman and child. It was the exact same situation that happened with the British in 1879 when troops under the command of Lord Roberts were attacked, sparking off a bloody series of punitive strikes against the locals, burning and killing everything in sight.'

'Not one of our better moments,' Ben said ruefully.

'But it's another nice example of how history just keeps on repeating itself,' Madison said. 'In both cases, what had started out looking like a successful imperial campaign by an unstoppable superpower had begun to turn bad. Like the Brits, Alexander found himself beleaguered, his supply routes cut off, surrounded on all sides by a wily guerrilla force with far better local knowledge than his own, who could strike anytime, anywhere, nibble at the vulnerable edges of his army and then melt back into the safety of their hills and mountain passes where the bulk of the troops couldn't follow.'

'That'll do it,' Ben said. 'Works every time.'

Wolf nodded. 'The bigger they are, the harder they fall.'

'Except Alexander wasn't about to let that beat him so easily. He supplemented his dwindling forces with mercenary troops from Greece and Macedonia, holed up in his fort at Alexandria Eschate and got ready for a long war. The fighting got more and more brutal. But it wasn't the kind of fighting that his armies had ever been used to before. Just like the British, Russian and American invaders of the future this style of war of attrition threw them off balance and soon made their position desperate.'

'Which is when it starts to get really nasty,' Ben said.

'No kidding. As the warlords went on playing their hit-and-run games Alexander went on a full-on rampage, razing towns and cities to the ground everywhere he went, killing everyone in them, sparing nobody. While in the past he'd always treated the subjects of other parts of his empire with at least some respect for their ways and traditions, his feelings against the Afghans turned to hate and he vowed to wipe them out completely, like an act of genocide. Not all of it was about open battle – he also made full use of spies and traitors in the enemy camp. According to one ancient account, the wife of a Bactrian warlord called Spitamenes cut off her husband's head while he slept and brought it to Alexander as a peace offering.'

'Remind me never to get married after all,' Wolf said.

'Nobody would do that to you, babe,' Madison replied with a sweet smile. 'You're a pussycat next to these guys.'

'Want a bet?' Wolf said, stung by the accusation.

'Anyhow, Alexander wasn't interested in peace. He became even more cruel and obsessive, hunting down his enemies, burning and slaughtering indiscriminately. It was total war, beyond anything anyone had ever seen before. It didn't matter if the tribes were hostile or not, he massacred them anyway. Like the "friendly fire" incidents' – Madison made rabbit ears with her fingers – 'in modern times when US troops killed groups of Afghan children, and before that the campaigns of bombing villages and destroying farms and crops that the Soviets carried out in the 1980s. Russian soldiers were even ordered to slaughter horses, dogs and cats. The Soviet press labelled the Afghans as bandits, outlaws, insurgents and terrorists, just like Alexander had done, just like we did later on with our so-called war on terror.'

'This is a really depressing story,' Wolf said. 'I thought we were getting a history lesson.'

'There *is* no history,' Madison said. 'Not in the way people tend to understand it, as something that's gone and behind us. The record of the past is only there to help us understand what's happening now, and will go on happening in the future. The end result is always the same.'

'And the end result for Alexander?' Ben asked.

'It wasn't long in coming. Eventually, Afghanistan proved too much even for him. By the time he turned twenty-eight his army had been in occupation here for three years and achieved virtually nothing. He'd spent more of his life, spilled more of his own blood and lost more of his men here than anywhere else in his whole empire covering Egypt, Turkey, Syria, Iraq and Iran. It's reckoned that he massacred over 120,000 Bactrian people. While huge numbers of his soldiers had died in battle, the bulk of his losses were down to the environment itself. Mountain crossings in winter, starvation, disease took a massive toll just like they would on every invading force of the future. And like them, Afghanistan marked Alexander, as a man and as a leader. He was never the same again after this place. He was worn down and sick from repeated battle injuries, and he'd taken to drinking so heavily that he'd often be unconscious for days on end. Meanwhile his men's faith in their king had weakened. He'd been focused on Bactria for so long that his imperial domains elsewhere were crumbling.

'And so, soon afterwards, he decided to call it quits and leave Afghanistan for good. He left behind him ten thousand infantry and over three thousand cavalry, which was by far the biggest occupying force he'd ever needed to deploy in any of his territories until then. Just goes to show how, as ever, Afghanistan was the exception to the rule.'

Chapter 29

Both Ramin and Father Bugnolio had nodded off to sleep by now, and the camp fire was just a smouldering glow in the darkness. It would soon be time for the next watch. Holt and the others were huddled around in a group, quite apart from Ben, Wolf and Madison and discussing their next plans in low voices. Tomorrow would be another day, but for the moment Ben and Wolf were in another world, transported deep into the living past of a country they'd both fought in themselves but had known so little about.

'Where did Alexander go from there?' Wolf asked.

'Home to rest?' Madison replied. 'Hang up the old armour and sword, put his feet up and enjoy life with his beautiful new Afghan bride, Roxana? Oh no, not our golden boy. No matter how worn out he might have been, all he could think about was going off a-conquering again. India was his next target, a nice juicy territory he could add on to his empire. So now he marched the army through the mountains once again into Pakistan and through the Indus Valley, attacking cities and laying waste to everything in his path just like he'd done in Bactria. There were victories, and plenty of atrocities.

'But it was clear that his glory days were over. He was facing more and more rebellion among his own men, whom he could barely control any longer, while at the same time he was getting reports that the garrisons he'd left behind in Bactria were falling apart, thousands deserting their posts. His mental health was declining badly, and he suffered from depression and mania. His last journey was down the coast into Babylon, where his chickens finally came home to roost and he died at the tender age of thirty-two. Some say he was poisoned, but it's more likely he'd just worn himself out.'

Madison shrugged. 'Who knows? Maybe if he'd never come to Afghanistan at all, if he hadn't taken it upon himself to chase after Bessus for the sake of pride or whatever it was that drove him, things might have gone very differently. That's what Dad believed, that it was the land itself that killed Alexander.'

'And afterwards?' Ben asked.

'Oh, the Greeks hung around here for a while, but with Alexander gone they became more and more divided against each other, until after nearly two centuries of infighting they were eventually so weak that in about 145 BC they were driven out by nomadic invaders from the north, who plundered most of the booty that Alexander had brought with him from the conquest of Persia. From that point onwards, the place passed through so many different hands it'd make your head spin. The Parthian Empire of the first century BC gave way to the Buddhist Kushan Empire of the first century AD. They lasted a while before they were overthrown by the Sassanids in the third century. Then you've got the Kidenites, the Hephthralites, the Turk Shahi of the seventh century who brought Buddhism back, then the Hindu Shah dynasty who brought Hinduism.'

'I could never remember all this stuff,' Wolf said in amazed admiration. 'How do you do it?'

Madison sipped some more beer. 'Just a natural born genius, I guess. Or else maybe I inherited Dad's mnemonic ability for storing all kinds of useless information.' She went on, 'Next, Islam appeared in the seventh century and became dominant here for a long time, until the Mongol hordes under Genghis Khan swept through during the thirteenth century and laid waste to everything in sight. The Mongol conqueror Tamerlane was in charge in the fourteenth century, then Babur in the sixteenth. And on it goes. The Hotak Dynasty, the Durrani Empire of the eighteenth century, the Barazaki Dynasty and a whole host of temporary rulers, tribal warlords setting themselves up as emirs and governors.'

'And in the middle of all that, the British came,' Ben said.

'They sure did, in the 1830s. The most ardent imperialists of them all, playing their Great Game carving up all the territory they could snatch things didn't go so well. Of all the military campaigns in British history, their first attempt at Afghanistan was one of the most inept, incompetent and disastrous ever. Fifteen thousand troops waltzing in with more than double that number of servants, complete with brass bands, polo ponies and packs of foxhounds for the officers' entertainment, and so many supplies it took thirty thousand camels to carry them. One regiment needed two camels just to transport the officers' cigars, while another brigadier had sixty of them loaded with his personal belongings.'

'Tally ho,' Wolf said, twirling an imaginary moustache. 'I say, what, what, what? Dash it, where's Jeeves with my champagne? What a bunch of twats.'

'You might say they had it coming,' Madison said. 'In the winter of 1842 the 4,500 soldiers and 12,000 camp followers that was all that was left of their entire invasion force retreated from Kabul in a death march that only one European survived. They'd achieved literally nothing, except lead thousands of men to their deaths. Afghanistan brushed them off like insects. Thirty-five years later they came back for a second attempt, and they were a little more successful, but at such a high cost in lives that in the end it was decided the best strategy was just to leave the place alone. It just wasn't worth it.'

'Didn't stop us coming back for more later, though, did it?' Wolf said sourly. 'Silly bastards. Don't we ever learn?'

'Seems like too much to ask that we should,' Madison said. 'Time after time, whoever seizes control of this country gets their butt kicked sooner or later as someone else comes and takes it from them. A century after the Brits left for the second time, it was the Russians' turn to try their luck and wind up with their very own Vietnam, ten years of pointless warfare, fifteen thousand corpses and massive economic damage. Soon after they retreated in tatters, the Soviet Union crashed and burned. Like, whoops, there goes another one.'

'Graveyard of empires, all right,' Wolf said.

'Then came the Americans.' Madison gave a derisive snort. 'The less said about that, the better. And ours won't be the last attempt to end in spectacular failure. Dad used to say that Afghanistan was like some giant impossible mountain that nobody had ever managed to climb, or some vast desert that nobody had ever been able to cross.'

'And yet he kept trying,' Ben said.

'He was no quitter, that's for sure. When there was a challenge in front of him, he could get pretty one-track-minded about rising to it. He couldn't stand the frustration of knowing that underneath all these rocks and dirt were millennia of cultural treasures just waiting to be unearthed, but almost impossible to get to. It was one obstacle after another: first the Soviet invasion, then the civil war. It drove him crazy.'

'I'll bet that if he'd been able to get to them, the findings would've been worth a pretty penny, too,' Wolf said.

'Sure, Dad made a lot of money from his discoveries around the world. But that wasn't what really drove him. Most of the profits were funnelled straight back into the next project; and he lost millions from all those times he came away empty-handed. He wasn't interested in getting rich. The same can't be said for a lot of the other treasure hunters who explored this country in past centuries. Like Charles Masson, the British army deserter who spent years wandering all over Asia in search of valuable relics to dig up. And Sir Alexander Burns, who unearthed thousands of precious gold coins and other ancient artefacts before he was eventually hacked to bits by an angry mob.'

'How does anyone know what's buried under the ground?' Ben asked. 'I mean, where would you even start looking for it?'

'We know a lot, thanks to the efforts of archaeologists who weren't just looking to enrich themselves. By the nineteenth century scholars had already put together a pretty detailed picture of Afghanistan's lost kingdoms and treasures. Hoards of loot would sometimes be stumbled on by a farmer or a well digger. Other times, natural erosion, landslides or even earthquakes could reveal things that had been buried for centuries. Like the famous Oxus treasure found in 1877, a huge hoard of coins and jewels and other precious objects found washed up by the river.'

'So where'd it all come from?' Wolf asked.

Madison replied, 'Some experts have reckoned that a lot of it was treasure Alexander was carrying with him on his campaigns. Armies needed ready cash to pay for all kinds of expenses, and moreover he'd just come away massively enriched from the plunder of his victory against the Persians. The army's baggage trains consisted of thousands of pack animals. When they died of heat, cold, thirst, or got eaten by starving soldiers, there was no way to carry those loads on foot, especially when you were already loaded up with armour and weaponry. I'm sure a lot of soldiers filled their pockets with smaller items, but what could you do with a heavy casket full of gold coins and ingots? There'd have been no choice but to abandon them.

'Other times,' she went on, 'the treasures might have come from the reserves of ancient cities, scattered by generations of pillagers over the years. Like happened in 1946, when some frontier guards came across what became known as the Qunduz Hoard, a cache of all kinds of valuable items. The next year, a much bigger treasure turned up at Mir Zahah, on an old caravan route in the mountain borderlands between Afghanistan and Pakistan, in the same area where al-Qaeda based their operations later on.'

225

'So they can just turn up anywhere,' Wolf marvelled. 'I should have packed a shovel.'

'Then in the sixties and seventies there was a whole rash of discoveries. At a place called Balkh in 1966, a lucky farmer found yet another precious stash of gold coins and jewels. Another find came from a place called Tillya Tepe, which appropriately means "the golden mound", where a site of ancient tombs yielded up twenty thousand coins and artefacts, a mixture of Persian, Greek and Roman items. Kind of like the geological layers in a rock formation, that shows how one settlement was often built on top of the remains of another through time, dating back all the way back. Cities just like the one that once existed right here in this very spot.'

Madison waved her arm in the direction of the rubble field barely recognisable as ancient ruins, as though she could see the mighty walls and columns still standing there under the same moonlight that was flashing in her eyes as she talked. It was hard not to be infected by her enthusiasm.

'Dad's studies had convinced him that there was one Alexandrian lost city that had yet to be unearthed. No verified written records have survived to prove his theory, but he was completely certain about its existence. The ancient fortress city of Zakara.'

Chapter 30

Ben asked, 'So how old is Zakara?'

'Dad reckoned Alexander founded it in 330 BC, the year before Alexandria Eschate was established. That would make sense geographically, in terms of his travels. It stands right on the old Silk Road route network that connected ancient Afghanistan to China and India in the east, Persia in the west, and to the cities of ancient Uzbekistan to the north. That made it a very important point on the map. Though like so many other very important points, it got wiped off by the ravages of time, war and changes of rule over the centuries.'

Ben thought for a moment. 'But if Alexander always named the cities he founded after himself – Alexandria this and Alexandria that – then why not this one too? What makes Zakara the exception to the rule?'

'Great question,' Madison said, undeterred. 'And like a million other great questions in archaeology, nobody knows the answer. It could well have been named after him, once upon a time. The name Dad called it by, Zakara, dates back even further, to the Bronze Age Indus Valley civilisation.'

'They died out in around 1000 BC, didn't they?' Ben asked.

Madison looked surprised.

'I know a little bit about it,' he said. 'Long story.'

'That's right. In their heyday they were spread over a huge territory all over Asia. Then bit by bit, for no apparent reason, their civilisation just crumbled into pieces and they disappeared altogether. Another historical mystery. But we do know that Zakara was one of their cities. Before that it may even have belonged to the Helmand Culture, back in the dim and distant days of around 3000 BC.'

'But where's the evidence that Alexander ever built a new city on top of the old?' Ben replied. 'You said yourself that there aren't any written records to prove it.'

If Ben was sounding somewhat sceptical, it was for a deliberate reason. It wasn't that he personally cared one way or another whether Alexander the Great had ever set foot up here on the plateau, or whether Rigby Cahill's theory was right. But the more he listened to Madison's passionate account, the more he understood how hard it was going to be to drag her away from this place when morning came and it was time to move on. If somehow he could undermine her conviction with questioning and logic, he might have a higher chance of persuading her.

'I never said there were no written records,' Madison fired back, as rock-solid confident of her ground as before. 'I said there were no *verified* written records. See, historians are still slowly piecing together the details of the past, as we go on uncovering fresh evidence. It's the world's biggest detective job. It takes time, and a lot of what we've dug up still hasn't been catalogued, much less fitted into any kind of bigger picture that the experts can officially agree on. Sometimes bits of key evidence get stashed away half-forgotten and gathering dust in storerooms and archives without having been fully examined, so nobody makes the connection. The same way that priceless old master paintings occasionally pop up in someone's attic, or a lost music manuscript composed by Bach turns up folded between the pages of an old book. Fluke discoveries happen all the time. Which means that there are always gaps in our knowledge. Those can take years, decades, centuries to fill. Or never.'

Ben smiled. He should have known better than to try to argue with her. 'Okay,' he said. 'So you're saying that your father made a connection that nobody else had before.'

'I wasn't kidding when I told you that Dad could be obsessive. He spent three weeks sifting through heaps of unsorted artefacts in a back room at the state museum in Kabul in the fall of 1978. That was when he found it.'

'Found what?'

'A small, damaged but still decipherable piece of stone tablet that showed, or at least suggested, that Alexander had established a fort up here on the site of the original Zakara.'

'But no actual evidence of a new city being founded.'

'No, that evidence had to wait a few months to be discovered, until Dad was able to mount an expedition here with a crew of local guides and diggers.'

'What did he find?' Wolf asked, with a predatory twinkle in his eyes.

'In a hollow in the rocks, buried a couple of feet below the ground, a small hoard of Alexandrine coins and other gold artefacts from the period. It wasn't all he might have hoped for, but it was enough incentive to keep digging. If only it had worked out that way.'

'Why didn't he?'

Madison replied, 'Because a freak blizzard suddenly hit them just as they were preparing to set up a base camp. It lasted a whole day and a night, pinning them in a tent and half-burying them in a foot of snow. One of his Afghan guides suffered serious frostbite, and another almost died of hypothermia. Dad had to abort the dig to rush them away to a hospital.'

'Is there one?' Wolf asked.

'Not for a few hundred miles. By the time they got there it was touch and go whether the hypothermic guy would pull through, but thankfully he did. Dad flew home to the States and a month went by before he could return. He spent that time setting up plans and getting all the contacts in place for a major new excavation that he'd have funded out of his own pocket. If he was right, it was set to become the find of the century. Then, just as he was finally ready to come back and continue the dig . . . well, you might be able to guess what happened next. This was late December, 1979.'

'The Soviet invasion,' Ben said.

'When the Russian tanks rolled into Kabul, all his plans were totally blown to pieces. Suddenly, after years of relative stability, Afghanistan was an active war zone again, the hills full of Soviet troops shooting it out with the guerrillas, and it was impossible for him to even enter the country, let alone mount an archaeological dig.'

'I'd have been climbing the walls,' Wolf said.

'In this business you soon learn to roll with the setbacks,' Madison said. 'Dad knew there was no point in driving himself crazy over it, and he had plenty of other projects to keep him busy. Still, the war dragged on for much longer than anyone had expected. For nearly ten years Dad bided his time while the Russians slugged it out with the Mujahideen. Then in February 1989, the magic moment came. Almost the same day as the troops pulled out, he was in like Flynn and getting together his expedition team. His head guide was a local man called Abdul. Soon afterwards, they reached Zakara. Nothing had changed, not a stone moved since the last time he'd been there. Which meant the place had stayed safe from looters all those years and whatever might be under the ground would still be untouched. This time he got the men to dig in a slightly different spot. What instinct told him to look there, I'll never know. He always had amazing intuition for finding buried objects.'

'And did it turn out he'd been right?' asked Wolf, totally drawn in. Ben was just listening intently.

'You damn well bet it did,' Madison replied. 'After hours of hard digging they unearthed a rectangular stone slab that Dad realised was the floor base of a large building. Not just any old building, like a house. That would have been amazing enough, but what they found was stunning. It was the remains of a palace treasury. Underneath the slab was a buried chamber, partly collapsed, but still accessible through a crack in the stonework that one of the team, a fourteen-year-old kid called Safi, was skinny enough to be lowered down into.'

'You're killing me with the suspense,' Wolf said. 'What did they find?'

'Caskets,' she said. 'Caskets so heavy with treasure, it took three men to haul them up by rope. Inside was the biggest haul of golden artefacts from the time of Alexander that anyone had ever discovered. Along with all the ingots and statues and rings and bracelets, an estimated half a million gold coins. And to top it all, each casket was marked with the royal seal of Alexander himself. It was the proof of everything Dad had believed in. There really had been an Alexandrine city here.'

'Unbelievable,' Wolf said. But Ben had picked up on something in her wording, and asked, 'Why estimated? Didn't anyone count them?'

'Because,' she replied with a sigh, 'no sooner had Dad made his discovery, but things went south yet again. This is Afghanistan. Things so often do.'

'What happened?

'What happened was that next thing he knew, he had a gun in his face. When Abdul and his team had realised the size of the find, enough gold to make millionaires out of all of them, they went nuts. Dad couldn't do a thing to stop them taking it for themselves. The rule of law had totally broken down in the wake of the Russians leaving, so it wasn't like he could call the local cops. In fact that might made things even worse, when they started joining in the fun of filling their pockets with all they could grab. He had no choice but to stand back and watch as what could have been one of the most valuable discoveries in modern archaeological history was pillaged and scattered to the four winds.'

Chapter 31

Wolf asked, 'So why didn't he press ahead with his excavation project anyway? If he really thought there was a whole lost city under here?'

Madison replied, 'He planned on doing exactly that. Dad wasn't someone you could deter that easily. But then, that same month, the Afghan Civil War kicked off, with the Soviets supporting the Afghan government from a distance on one side, and the Mujahideen backed by the US and the Saudis on the other. In a flash, the whole nightmare had started up all over.'

'History repeating itself once again,' Ben said.

'And once again Dad had to get the hell out of there, and watch helplessly as things went from bad to worse. When the Mujahideen finally won that fight, they all just started on each other and things dragged on for years, right up until 2001. At which point, the Americans invaded and it was the start of our own Afghan war. Air strikes, troops everywhere, battles erupting, a total debacle.'

'Tell us about it,' Wolf said dourly. 'Our guys spent the next twenty years spilling their guts out to hang on to this place. And for what?'

'By then, Dad felt he was getting a little too old for all that crap. His health wasn't so great anymore, he'd slowed down a little and scaled back his operations, thinking about retirement. He never came back to Afghanistan. And until his dying day, he always regretted his unfinished business here.' Madison paused, looking sad. 'But the irony is, even if Dad had succeeded in excavating Alexandria Zakara and filled the state museum in Kabul with all kinds of amazing treasures, it would all most likely have been lost again soon afterwards. Before the civil war, the museum had managed to hang onto a huge collection of ancient artefacts dating back to the Bronze Age. The fighting in the city got so bad that most of the museum staff had to get out, while a few brave curators who stayed behind risked their lives transferring the bulk of the artefacts to a bank vault in the city to protect them from what was coming. They were right, because in 1993 and then again in 1997 the museum was hit by rocket attacks and nearly all the exhibits it still had left, sculptures, vases, glassware, frescoes, and important collections of Bactrian coins, vanished at the hands of Taliban looters.'

Ben was pretty familiar with the propensity of groups like the Taliban and al-Qaeda for trading in stolen antiquities – the same stolen antiquities they pretended to despise as being against the tenets of their faith – in order to raise large amounts of easy cash for buying weapons. And just occasionally, for their own personal gain. He asked, 'What about the stuff hidden in the vault?'

Madison shook her head. 'That's the tragedy. When the Americans threw out the Taliban and things were looking like they were stabilising again, those rescued pieces were all returned to the museum. Now the tables have turned and the Taliban are stronger than ever, it's almost certain they'll be destroyed or sold off too.'

'This damn country,' Wolf said. 'It's like a jinx.'

Ben said, 'Madison, I understand why this place is like a magnet for people in your line of work. I get what drives them to be so passionate about it. Your father was a tough and determined man. But even he had the sense to bail out when things became too difficult. If anything they're even worse now, and they're not going to improve any time soon. So what in God's name possessed you to take such a stupid risk and put yourself in harm's way like that?'

Her face hardened and a defensive glint came into her eye. 'When I took over the business after his death, I always knew I'd want to come out to Zakara and finish what he started. My way of honouring his legacy. And it seemed like a good time to do it. Everyone knew the US was going to be pulling out eventually. Our leaders talked about it for years. But we all thought the Afghan government would be able to handle things on their own and the country would stay pretty stable for a long time to come. I was naive, but I wasn't the only one. What happened, nobody saw coming.'

'She's right, Ben,' Wolf said. 'Give her a break.'

'So that's when I hooked up with Aziz and Ramin again. We spent months planning, everything was looking great. Then I'm hardly in Kabul a week before we heard the news that things were getting bad. Even then, a lot of people didn't believe it until the last minute. Soon afterwards, the panic started. It got so insane, so fast.'

'You could still have got out,' Ben said.

'Maybe I could,' she replied hotly, 'but I chose to stay because I know what those fanatical sons of bitches will do. They hadn't been in power five minutes before they were already partnering up with the Chinese government. Who of course are ready to jump in to grab whatever they can, offering financial incentives in return for a free pass at exploiting Afghanistan's massive, almost totally untapped mineral resources. It's one of the world's biggest reserves of copper, cobalt, lithium and more. A trillion-dollar goldmine that China now will have a monopoly on. You see the environmental damage they've already done in places like the Congo, Mozambique, Sierra Leone, Ecuador. These mountains are full of copper, Ben. What with the Taliban intent on destroying every last remaining piece of this country's non-Islamic past and their new buddies rolling in with the mining machinery, there won't be anything left. Three thousand years of history, up in smoke.'

'And you think you can stop it?' Ben asked her. 'You plan on being here with that rifle in your hands to bar the road to them, a year from now, or two, or three?'

'Of course not.' Madison's tone was rising and her back was stiffening like a cobra ready to strike. 'But I figure if I can save some of what's buried under the ruins of Zakara, it's got to be worth it.'

'Worth getting killed over,' Ben said. 'Or dying of starvation up here. Look around you. You think your friends will be content to tough it out with you in the wilderness, scratching around the rocks for bare scraps to survive on?' He motioned towards the sleeping figures. 'Aziz isn't well, you said so yourself. Ramin isn't someone you'd bring

236

on a camping trip, let alone this. And what about Father Bugnolio?'

'I'm a fairly resourceful gal,' she shot back at him. 'I can go it alone, if needs be.'

'Even if there's still a load of treasure waiting to be found, how do you plan on getting it out of here?'

'Huh. Says the guy who thinks he can snatch a truckload of orphanage children right out from under the noses of the Taliban fighters.'

'We'll work something out,' Ben said, his turn to get defensive now.

'And so will I, goddamnit,' she replied. 'I always do. The first step was to get here. And I managed that okay, didn't I?'

Ben stared at her. 'You're crazy. I always knew you were crazy, but I had no idea how batshit insane you really are.'

'Now, children,' Wolf said, raising his palms. 'Let's not fight.'

Madison looked about to fire back another angry retort, but then she softened and gave a lopsided smile. 'Okay, I admit I might have bitten off a little more than I could chew. But now I've got the great Ben Hope here to help me. That means anything's possible, right?'

'And me,' Wolf said, prodding his chest with his thumb.

'You too, honey. The redoubtable Mr Wolf.'

Wolf seemed to like being called 'honey'.

Ben shook his head. 'Don't kid yourself, Madison. If you think I'm interested in hanging around here playing treasure hunt, think again. I told you I'd come to Afghanistan to get you out.'

'And I told you—'

'I know. But that's not happening. You're coming with me.'

'Kicking and screaming under your arm, huh?'

'If necessary,' he replied. 'Now, you followed your father's footsteps this far. You're going to have to imitate his example one more time, and forget about this stuff until it's safe to come back here again one day.'

'Come back to what, though?'

While they'd been talking, Holt and Scraggs had switched over from Baldacci and Liebowitz to take the next watch. As before, there'd been no word from either of them since, their radio silence signalling that all was clear and the group could rest easy in the knowledge they were the only people for a great many miles in any direction. It was deep in the night now. The stars were bright, not twinkling, as hard and cold as planets. A feeling of absolute emptiness hung over the mountains, no sound of a living creature anywhere, nothing apart from the plaintive moan of the wind that had been slowly rising for the last hour and the rustle of the scrubby bushes that grew sparsely among the rocks.

But then the silence was suddenly broken by the fizz and crackle of the radio, cutting off Ben just as he was about to make a reply to Madison. Wolf made a grab for the radio handset, but Ben got to it first. At the same time, Nielsen, Baldacci and the others were snatching up theirs, suddenly all galvanised and wide awake.

Holt's voice came over the handset in an urgent whisper.

'Hey, boys and girls, I hate to interrupt your night's rest. But it looks like we're about to have company. Got a fast moving convoy of vehicles approaching from the south-east, about eight miles off, and they're heading right for us.'

Chapter 32

They quickly doused what was left of the camp fire. Those who had weapons gathered them up, while Ben and Wolf hurried away from the camp and scrambled to the brow of the flat-topped ridge where Holt had been on watch. From up here he'd been able to observe a great wide stretch of the horizon, under the vastness of the inky black sky.

Madison was close behind as Ben and Wolf reached Holt. They lay low among the rocks and bushes, watching in silence through their binoculars as the distant tail of lights gradually approached through the mountain valley below. Still a long, long way off. Holt's range estimate of about eight miles seemed accurate enough. But that distance was closing every second. Through a pause in the rising wind Ben momentarily caught the faraway grumble of diesel engines.

'Taliban patrol?' Wolf said, watching them as though he wanted to eat them. 'Why am I not surprised. This is getting to be a habit.'

Ben counted eleven vehicles, almost certainly military trucks judging by their shape. Assuming each one could be carrying upwards of ten or a dozen men – and further assuming they were armed fighters and unlikely to be friendly – that amounted to a considerable force. Far more than their little group could handle, if it came to a confrontation.

'Hard to be certain from this range,' Ben replied. 'But we can't afford to assume it isn't. And it won't be long before they get here. I'd give it about twenty-five minutes, allowing for the terrain.'

'I'd say that's optimistic, buddy,' Holt said. 'Twenty, max.'

'If they can make it up the slope in those trucks,' Wolf said. 'They might skirt around the foot of the mountain and keep moving on.'

'I doubt that,' Holt replied. 'They look like they mean business, whoever they are.'

'Are they looking for us?' Madison asked, the binoculars pressed to her eyes, steadily tracking the approaching lights. 'How'd they know we were here?'

'We can stick around and ask them that ourselves,' Holt said. 'Or we can get the hell out of here before they turn up.'

'We could hide,' Madison said.

'You want to take that chance, lady?' Holt replied tersely. 'There could be a hundred fighters down there. They find your camp, they'll know we were here and they'll spread out everywhere hunting for us.'

The wind was rising rapidly as they spoke, and now there were dark clouds scudding ominously across the sky from the north and drawing a black curtain over the moon and stars. Some heavy weather was rolling in, one of those unpredictable Afghan mountain storms that had once pinned Ben and Wolf's SAS unit down for three straight days. But the weather was the least of their concerns. Now, as the four of them went on intently watching the convoy, the line of lights appeared to come to a halt.

'Why are they stopping?' Madison wondered out loud.

Ben had been asking himself the same thing. Carefully scanning the dark valley with his powerful binoculars he made out the reason. 'They've found Aziz's Jeep.' Almost as soon as he'd said it, they were moving on again, still heading straight for the watchers.

'I don't like it,' Wolf said. 'I don't like it at all. I'd say it's time to make tracks, people. And fast.'

'Ben?' Madison asked, glancing at him.

'You know what I think,' Ben replied. 'It was never safe here. And it just became a lot less so.' He lowered his binocs and turned to look back at her. Her eyes were wide and questioning in the moonlight. He could see the mixed emotions there: anxiety, disappointment, hope, defiance. 'I know how you feel, Madison,' he said, more softly. 'But Chris and Jaden are right. Please don't make this difficult.'

'We got about eighteen minutes, people,' Holt said. 'How about we keep on debating this until this whole mountain is covered in enemy fighters?'

Madison said nothing but her whole body radiated extreme frustration. She went back to watching the lights for a moment. Then put down her binocs and heaved a painfully reluctant sigh. 'Okay. Screw it. Let's roll.'

They retreated from the brow of the ridge, keeping low, and hurried back down to the camp to rejoin the others and report what they'd seen. Aziz and Father Bugnolio took the news grimly, but Ramin was ready to panic. 'We can't stay here,' he moaned frantic with agitation. 'They'll slaughter us all.'

'We're going,' Madison said in a tight voice. 'But there's something I need to do first.'

'You'd better make it damn quick, lady, whatever it is,' Holt said, looking at his watch. The sound of the approaching convoy was clearly audible now over the roar of the wind. The first splashes of cold rain began to spatter the rocks. Baldacci, Liebowitz and Nielsen were already at work loading their kit back into the vehicles while the others pulled down the makeshift tarp shelter and set about erasing all trace of the camp, as best they could. Madison looked again at Ben, anxiety in her eyes too. He knew her too well to think she was overly worried about her own safety. It was her companions she was concerned about. And something else, too.

'Will you help me?' she asked. 'Over here.'

Before Ben could answer, she took off at a sprint towards the ruins. He followed her as she ran ahead of him in the darkness. The rain was falling harder now, driven by the wind that had risen to a howl. He lost sight of her for a moment, looking about him in confusion; then there she was, crouching among the rubble beside a row of worn, uneven stone blocks that he realised was the edge of the large rectangular slab she'd talked about earlier, the foundation of the ruined building where her father had made his discovery. As he hurried over to her, he saw the long fissure in the stone slab, just wide enough for a person of light build to squeeze through, and the two coils of rope on the ground next to her. Her hair was soaked and falling into her eyes. She brushed it away and busily set about tying the end of one of the ropes around her slender waist, knotting it tight.

'Madison,' he protested over the noise of the wind, 'we don't have time for this.'

'Then shut up and help me,' she said. 'We can't let those sons of bitches have it.'

'Have what?'

'Remember you said, "there's nothing here" and I told you "not quite nothing"?'

'Yes, and I didn't know what you were talking about then either.'

'Found it two days ago. One they missed. It was half buried where the ground had subsided. Grab this.' She tossed him the loose end of the rope she'd tied around herself, then pointed at the crack in the slab. 'I'm going to lower myself down there,' she explained quickly. 'Then you throw down that other rope there, and I'll tie it on. Then you haul me up. Okay?'

Ben was beginning to understand what she was up to, but that didn't make him feel any better about it. 'Forget it, Madison. They'll be here in less than fifteen minutes.'

'Then quit yakking and let's do this, goddamnit.' And before he could stop her, she slipped down through the crack and disappeared. It wasn't a long way down. He felt the tension on the rope slacken as she hit the bottom. Then heard her muffled voice calling up to him, barely audible over the wind, 'Okay, now toss down the end of the other rope!'

Moments later, she'd attached the second rope and was yelling for him to pull her up. She re-emerged through the crack, her hair and clothes covered in dust that the lashing rain quickly washed into grey mud. 'I got it! Now let's get it out of there.'

At that moment Wolf came running up. 'We're good to go,' he said urgently. Then his stare turned into a frown of consternation. 'Uh, excuse me for asking, but what the hell are you two doing exactly?'

There wasn't time to explain. 'Give us a hand,' Ben said. Wolf shrugged, and gamely grabbed hold of the second rope. The three of them heaved. Down below their feet something dragged, seemed to catch for a moment and then started moving again. Whatever it was, it was surprisingly heavy, making the rope twanging taut. With a lot of grunting and straining they hauled it inch by inch up to the surface, and as the mysterious object appeared at the mouth of the fissure Ben saw it was some kind of metal box. No – a casket, battered and worn with age, its carvings and inscriptions clogged by dirt.

'Help me get it out,' Madison said, and they crouched by the fissure to manhandle the immensely heavy casket through it, gasping as they set it down on the ground. Madison was grinning with pleasure.

'What's inside this thing, lead bars?' Wolf asked, rubbing his chafed hands.

'Oh, you know, the usual stuff. Bunch of gold and jewels and shit like that,' Madison replied nonchalantly.

Wolf's eyes opened wide. 'Are there more of them down there?'

'Who knows?' she answered, directing an acid look Ben's way. 'Apparently we don't have time to find out.'

'No, we don't,' Ben said. The lights of the convoy were visible over the edge of the plateau, and the rumble of their engines and crunch of their tyres and the grinding of stone on metal could be heard over the wind as they struggled up the slope. They'd be here sooner than he'd anticipated and there wasn't a moment to lose.

The three of them carried their prize back to the waiting vehicles, soaked to the skin, stumbling over rocks, straining every muscle and sinew in their wrists and arms to get the massive weight to safety. The others were all aboard by now – Holt at the wheel of the big truck with Scraggs, Father Bugnolio, Ramin and Aziz, while Baldacci and the others had jumped into the Humvee. Holt glowered at them with impatience bordering on hatred as they reached the truck. Nobby Scraggs jumped out and helped them load the casket in the back. 'Jesus wept, what is this?'

'Just a little memento of this place,' Madison replied, hopping nimbly up onto the cargo bed after it and slamming the tailgate shut behind her.

'That's sorted. Now let's get the flock out of here,' Wolf said.

They'd lost a lot of time, and what little they had left was running out fast. In less than two minutes the convoy would have reached the top of the plateau and this whole place would be alive with enemy fighters – because Ben no longer had any doubt who their unexpected visitors were.

And with that escape route blocked, there was only one other way off the plateau, one they had no choice but to take *now*, immediately, and without drawing the least attention to themselves. That was a dizzying slope strewn thick with boulders and deeply scarred by millennia of landslides, steeper than the steepest black run. Only a certifiable lunatic would have attempted to take a heavy vehicle laden with passengers and equipment over the edge of that suicidal drop, in the dark, with no lights.

Ben knew just the man for the job. More precisely, he knew two men. He motioned to Wolf, who grinned in understanding and hurried back to the Humvee to take the wheel. Ben clambered into the front of the truck, shoving Holt out of the way.

'I'll drive.'

Chapter 33

Seconds counted, the timing was everything, and it was going to be a hell of a close-run thing. Ben buckled himself into the driver's seat. The key was in the ignition but he didn't touch it. No engines, no lights. The enemy might not be crazy enough to follow them where they were going, but they could still pour enough firepower down the mountain-side after the escaping vehicles to shred them to pieces before they reached the bottom – if indeed they had any chance of reaching the bottom in one piece anyway.

It was lucky that the vehicles were parked on a slight downward incline, so that Ben only had to release the hand-brake for the truck to start freewheeling in neutral. The wheels began to turn slowly at first, then faster as they gained momentum on the slope. Ben could see almost nothing through the windscreen with the thick rain flooding down the glass, and just as little in his rear-view mirror, but he knew that Wolf would be right behind him.

Faster, faster. There was no turning back now, even if they'd wanted to. Driving almost blind, Ben felt the nose of the truck tip suddenly downward as the angle of the slope sharpened dramatically, like going over the edge of a water-fall. He yelled, 'Hang on tight, everyone. Here we go.'

And then they were in freefall, rolling wildly down the slope, hammering violently over ruts and boulders, the steering wheel like a living thing desperate to tear itself out of Ben's hands as he struggled to keep the truck straight. With all the truck's three-ton weight on its front wheels the slightest skid would almost certainly cause them to veer sideways and go into a fatal roll, killing them all just as surely as if they'd stayed behind to fight. He heard a shrill cry from the rear. Poor Ramin was definitely not cut out for this kind of thing.

Down and down they went, a racing heartbeat away from losing control. Ben was almost completely out of his seat, just the seatbelt preventing him from sprawling over the steering wheel or diving headlong towards the windscreen. In the mayhem he barely heard Madison shouting at Ramin to help her hold onto the casket, or Father Bugnolio yelling, 'God help us!' Holt was grimly holding on, one hand on the door handle and the other bracing himself against the dash, barely able to keep from plunging forward. All Ben could see out of the rain-flooded screen were craggy rocks, rocks and more rocks flashing up towards them as the truck went on bucking like a mad bronco down the impossible slope. There was no time to think. His heart was in his mouth and several times he was certain he could feel the rear end of the truck about to flip right over and start tumbling. All he could do was fight the steering and hope that Father Bugnolio's prayers might have some influence with whoever was listening up there.

The descent lasted only a few seconds, but sheer terror has a cruel way of making those kinds of moments, however transient, drag out for ever. Minutes, hours, seemed to have passed by the time the truck hit the last rut on the slope with a shuddering, teeth-jarring crash and their insane downwards angle levelled out at last.

'We made it!' Madison yelled triumphantly, pumping a fist in the air and high-fiving Father Bugnolio, who just looked confused. Ramin still hadn't opened his eyes.

And the others had made it too. Glancing in the mirror Ben was relieved to see the Humvee still coasting along behind over the levelling ground; a glimpse of Wolf's golden grin behind the wheel. He'd probably enjoyed that.

Made it, but only just in the nick of time. A flood of lights far above them lit up the rainy night sky as the enemy convoy gathered on the plateau. Even if they'd been able to spot the escaping vehicles through the lashing rainstorm, as Ben had rightly guessed it was doubtful they'd attempt to follow them. If they wanted to give chase they'd have to double back the way they'd come and then skirt around the foot of the mountain, losing several minutes and a great deal of ground.

Right down in the valley now, with no power to the wheels the truck was rolling gently to a halt. Ben kept the lights off but started the engine and they quickly picked up speed again, lurching like drunken crabs over the uneven terrain, the wipers working full speed to bat away the pounding rain. Having opened his eyes at last and realised they weren't all dead, Ramin was almost weeping with relief. Aziz sat ashen-faced next to him, clutching his heart. Madison was grinning from ear to ear while Holt and Scraggs were just staring at Ben as though he'd lost his mind. 'Don't ever do anything like that again,' Holt said.

'Didn't they teach you off-road driving in the US army?' Ben replied with a shrug.

Wolf's voice came over the radio. 'That was awesome. Can we go back up for another run?' That Wolf.

Now all they had to do was put as much physical distance between themselves and a hundred or more enemy fighters, in the hope they could build on their head start and give them the slip. Ben pushed on hard, with Wolf right behind him. The lights on the plateau slowly faded out of sight. Within minutes the rain slackened to a drizzle and then petered out altogether, the storm ended as suddenly as it had begun. The fuel gauge was dipping into the red zone but Ben kept his foot down and the miles kept passing. Nobody said much, now that the initial adrenalin rush of their escape gave way to the anxious knowledge that this wasn't over yet. Danger still lay behind them and more, much more, was waiting for them at the end of their journey.

Hours went by. Madison fell asleep with her hands still clasped around her precious casket. Ben found his Gauloises in his pocket, a little crushed and soggy but still serviceable, and lit up. Holt was using a small pencil torch to study a map. Scraggs was contentedly nursing the last of his beer bottles. As the first rays of dawn were burning like battle flames behind the mountains, they paused to look back, and saw nothing but empty horizon in their wake.

'I think we can break for coffee,' Holt said, which was the most agreeable thing Ben had heard him say in a while.

Holt seemed to have got over his foul mood from earlier. They radioed Wolf in the Humvee, and the two vehicles slowed to a halt and everyone climbed out, stretching aching limbs and rubbing their bruises from the descent down the mountain, the awoken sleepers yawning. The red dawn's glow on the endless empty landscape around them, devoid of any kind of plant or animal life whatsoever, made it seem as though they were explorers on Mars.

'I knew you'd get us out of there,' Madison said with a beaming smile at Ben as the coffee started bubbling over the jet stove. 'My hero.' She bent towards him and kissed him tenderly.

'Don't talk rubbish,' Ben would have replied, but he was too stunned by the kiss to speak.

'Hey, where's my kiss?' Wolf said indignantly. 'I'm a hero too, you know.'

'Of course you are, Wolfie,' she said. 'Come here, then.' Wolf stepped towards her like a man in a trance, received a noisy smacker on his cheek and turned as bright scarlet as the rising sun.

Ben and Scraggs looked at one another. '*Wolfie?*' Scraggs said.

Coffee among the rocks, a tactical refuel from their jerry-cans, and everyone seemed upbeat despite the fact that the jet stove had now completely run out of gas. But after a few minutes, Ben felt that uncomfortable tingle in his spine, his innate spider-sense telling him that something was wrong.

'What is it?' Madison asked as he snatched his binoculars and left her side.

'Probably nothing,' he replied. Or so he hoped. At the foot of a nearby rise, a cluster of large boulders had piled up probably eons ago to form a natural staircase. He bounded up them to a better vantage point, raised the binocs to his eyes.

And saw that his spider-sense had been right again.

The moment he spotted it, he knew that the dust plume far away on the horizon to the south-east was being made by the enemy truck convoy in pursuit. It was several miles off, but all the same their presence was an unsettling sight.

'Persistent bastards, aren't they?' said a voice at his side. Ben hadn't heard anyone climb up the rocks. Only Jaden Wolf could sneak up on him like that. Wolf's expression was as hard and keen as a hunting predator. His battle face. He took the binocs from Ben and studied the faraway dust plume. 'You ever disturb a wasps' nest?'

'Something's got them all worked up, that's for sure,' Ben said. 'And they're not giving up easily.'

'I suppose this is our payback for wiping out their pals. How the hell did they track us this far?'

Ben was considering the alternative possibility that something worse might have happened. That was, whether someone could have got to old Karim at the institute and made him reveal Madison's whereabouts to them. If word had got out about the American woman who had managed to slip out of the city, aided by two Afghan men officially considered as suspect and even traitorous, evading a number of patrols on their way across country, it might well have occurred to some Taliban higher-up that the American would make a fine trophy hostage for them, with big ransoms to be extracted from back home – while at the same time making an example of her collaborators. He hoped nothing bad had happened to the old guy. He decided not to say anything to Madison, Aziz or Ramin about it.

'We should move on,' he said to Wolf.

Some of the group took the news better than others as they quickly got underway again, but nobody was quite ready to panic yet, and even Ramin settled down after Madison assured him that everything would be okay. Holt took the wheel from Ben and Baldacci relieved Wolf in the Humvee.

For the next few hours they made steady progress heading due north-west. By midday their pursuers seemed to have receded further behind the horizon. Come late afternoon, they stopped once again to clamber up a hillside for another observation and could see no trace of the dust plume anywhere.

'Looks like we gave them the slip,' Holt said with grim satisfaction, narrowing his eyes against the rays of the slowly dipping sun.

'Maybe,' Ben replied. 'For now, anyway.'

'We got bigger fish to fry, buddy. Let's move on. Four more hours and we'll stop and make camp.'

By the time they did that, their journey had taken them back up onto higher ground. Their resting place for the night was a shady arched hollow, almost a cave, carved out smooth by some prehistoric river at the foot of a gigantic rock formation that reminded Ben of those he'd seen in Australia. Confident that they'd managed to put a large distance between themselves and their pursuers, who might by now have given up the chase, they dug out a simple but effective pit fire and ate another meal from their now dwindling supply of tinned food. Holt spread out the map he'd been studying on and off all day, and told the group that by his calculation they'd reach the location of the orphanage sometime tomorrow afternoon.

'Come what may,' Liebowitz said.

'Will there be fighting?' Ramin asked nervously.

'Whatever we find when we get there,' Holt said, 'we're committed now. We're seeing it through to the end. Ramin, Aziz, Madison, Father B, you guys want to split, you're welcome to make that choice and good luck to you.'

'I'm staying with Ben,' Madison said, and clutched Ben's arm.

'And I'm staying with Madison,' said Aziz.

'Amen to that,' Father Bugnolio chimed in. Ramin didn't seem so enthusiastic, but he was outvoted and said nothing.

After dark, everyone found a place to sleep among the rocks. Ben was tired, and drifting off the moment he put his head down. It was three in the morning when he felt a touch and was instantly alert, the Browning Hi-Power in his hand.

'Shh. Relax, it's only me,' said her warm voice in the darkness. He could dimly make out the gleam of her eyes, very close by.

'What's wrong?' he asked.

'Nothing,' she whispered, a smile in her voice. 'I was cold. Couldn't sleep. Do you mind?'

'Not at all,' he whispered back, though he wasn't sure what he was agreeing to as she slipped under his blanket and pressed herself up beside him with her hand on his chest.

'Ben?' she murmured.

'Hmm?'

'I never really thanked you for what you did. Probably seem ungrateful, I guess, but I'm not good at expressing gratitude. It's a fault. I'm working on it.'

'What did I do?'

'What kind of dumbass question is that? Coming to save me, that's what. Nobody else in the world would have done something like that for me.'

'Except Rigby.'

'But he's gone now. Which means you're the most special thing I have left.'

He replied softly, 'You don't know me, Madison. I'm not that special.'

'Yes, you are,' she murmured, and he felt the warm sweetness of her breath on his face as she moved closer still.

Then she went rigid. 'Did you hear that?'

He had heard it, and he was sitting bolt upright reaching for the pistol again. It wasn't the rumble of distant thunder. It was the unmistakable crackle of automatic gunfire, some way off, but not *that* far off. He tensed. There it was again.

Instants later, everyone was wide awake and the group had gathered together with their guns at hand.

'Reckon it's them again?' Baldacci said.

'But if it's not for us, who's it for?' Nielsen asked.

'It's an attack on another village,' said Liebowitz. 'Like before.'

Ben didn't agree. As another faraway *takatakatakataka* string of shots sounded in reply to the last one, he said, 'No, listen. That's answering fire.'

Wolf nodded. 'Ben's right. It's two groups. A gun battle going on.'

'Between who and who?' Aziz asked anxiously.

Holt said, 'Could be rival militia groups at each other's throats, or some tribal attack against a Taliban patrol. Maybe our guys, maybe another. Who gives a damn? If the assholes want to wipe one another out, fine by me.'

While they huddled around debating the issue, Nobby Scraggs had been scrolling through multiple radio channels on the off-chance of finding something. Their conversation hushed as the fizzing, distorted sound of voices suddenly crackled from his handset. 'Bingo.'

They listened. Wolf said, 'Holy shit.'

Because the snatches of urgent radio dialogue they could clearly make out weren't being spoken in Dari, Pashto or any other Afghan language any of the astonished group had ever heard. The voices were speaking English, and with British accents. Their crackly exchanges were half drowned out with the staccato rattle of small arms, tinny-sounding over the speaker. After a delay of a second or so, the real-life sound was reaching their ears, faraway but very distinct.

There could be no doubt what was happening. Two separate units of unknown but obviously British combatants were communicating on the radio channel, one of them cut off from the other and taking heavy fire.

'It's our lads,' Scraggs said, incredulous and blinking.

'What the fuck's going on?' said Holt, equally bewildered. 'It can't be. We're alone out here. Hell, we're alone in this whole goddamn country.'

'Or we thought we were,' Ben said.

Chapter 34

It was quickly agreed that Ben, Wolf, Holt, Scraggs and Baldacci would take the Humvee to locate and investigate the scene of the gun battle while the rest of the men stayed behind to guard the camp. The hardest part was persuading Madison to remain there too. She wasn't happy about it.

Moments later, with Ben at the wheel, they were racing off in the direction of the sound – or as directly towards it as the wildness of the undulating landscape would allow, with impassable drops, rockfalls, gorges and crevasses blocking their way at every turn, making it physically impossible to travel as the crow flies. The moon was bright enough to travel with no lights and they were moving upwind, so that with any luck their approach wouldn't be detected. Judging from what they could hear, the incident was taking place no more than about quarter of a mile away, but the winding roundabout route Ben was forced to take, stopping frequently to listen and adjust their course, was frustratingly longer. Ben was afraid that the fighting might suddenly come to a stop, one side or the other having won, and they wouldn't find them.

'What the hell's going on, Ben?' Wolf asked tensely beside him in the dark, jolting cab.

Ben was just as baffled as the rest. Except for Operation Hydra, the last British army unit was supposed to have been pulled out of Afghanistan long ago, before the American troop withdrawal. Had Carstairs been playing some double game? He replied, 'I don't know, Jaden, but with any luck we're about to find out.'

And they soon did. The rattle of automatic weapons much closer now, and sharp in the night air, Ben halted the Humvee at the bottom of a steep rise. The sounds were coming from beyond the ridge, carried up by the wind from the sharply sloping river gorge down below. Grabbing their kit, all five of them jumped silently from the vehicle. Communicating with signals they crept to the top of the rise and flattened themselves out among the rocks, peering cautiously over the edge into the moonlit gorge below. The rocks made long, inky-black shadows that obscured the deeper nooks and crevices down there, but with their powerful light-gathering binoculars they could see almost everything that was happening.

'Well I'll be damned,' Holt muttered.

Sure enough, as baffling and unexpected as it was, their guess had been right. Some two hundred yards away in the twisting, dry river bed at the bottom of the gorge, a small unit of combatants in what appeared to be a rag-tag mixture of British multi-terrain pattern combat uniform and native desert garb were pinned down behind rocky cover by a much superior force of robed and mostly turbaned fighters spread out on the opposite slope above them. Dark figures flitted among the crags as the Taliban fighters steadily encroached on their opponents' position, with the clear aim of working their way down into the gorge and encircling them before moving in for a final, decisive assault. Here and there the strobing yellow-white muzzle flash of automatic weapons appeared from the shadows, spewing bullets at anything that moved in a random cacophony of gunfire.

From what Ben could make out, the attackers numbered about twenty or thirty. Far less numerous than the convoy of enemy troops that had driven their own group away from the plateau the night before. It seemed to him that they must have split up into smaller groups since then as they pursued their elusive prey – and that it was while searching for them that this portion of their force had stumbled on this unexpected new enemy out here in the wilderness.

As for the much smaller British unit pinned down below, it was clear at a glance even at this range and in poor light that they weren't faring too well in the exchange. Ben could see movement, but his sharp eyes had also made out the inert shapes of what were unmistakably two bodies slumped among the rocks. He counted two – no, three – men still in the game. But their return fire had become thinner and more sporadic. They were obviously running dangerously low on ammunition. In just a few more minutes, the Taliban fighters would have worn them down to their last rounds and would be moving in for the kill. Then it would be down to knives and bayonets, a desperate last-ditch resistance from which there were unlikely to be any survivors. Ben had seen the grisly aftermath of those bloody guerrilla encounters before. Before his time, the Mujahideen fighters had been infamous for the cruel way they'd hacked up and dismembered captured Russian soldiers.

But that wasn't happening here, because now the badly outnumbered unit had got some unexpected help. As they were about to learn.

Ben and Wolf quickly set up the Maximi, its long coiling ammo belt ready for action. The perfect tool for laying down a barrage of heavy covering fire at medium-short range like this, with a spotter using binoculars to direct the high-velocity 7.62mm tracer rounds to their deadliest effect. Meanwhile Baldacci had the fifty-cal sniper rifle captured from their previous engagement up on its bipod and was snuggling in behind it, next to Scraggs and Holt with their trusty M4 carbines and grenade launchers and a whole crate-load of 40mm grenades.

Things were about to get interesting.

'Mark your targets and fire at will, gentlemen,' said Holt.

'Music to my bloody ears,' Wolf muttered, but his words were barely out before Ben squeezed the trigger. Instant bedlam as the Maximi jumped into life, directing its deafening gunfire across the valley in a sustained stream, spewing empty brass and split links all over the rocks at Ben's elbow. His old unit had often joked that if the major was ever killed in action, they'd find his body buried in a big pile of spent cartridge cases. The pile was a reality, but he wasn't ready to meet his maker just yet.

The arcing tracer fire cut its devastating swathe across the enemy position, slicing and dicing as it went. He saw a dark figure stagger, throw up his weapon and crumple to the ground; then another; then another. To Ben's right, the crashing single shots of Baldacci's rifle and the rat-tat of the M4s were a huge, sense-numbing, ear-splitting symphony of chaos and confusion. Holt rattled off most of a thirty-round magazine and then started pumping incendiary grenades, lighting up the night with a rain of fire and explosions that cleared out the nooks and crannies where more of the Taliban fighters were hiding.

The sudden, ferocious onslaught from on high had a stunning effect on the enemy, who after a disorganised defence lasting no more than about ninety seconds broke from their positions – those who still could break from them – and beat a retreat down the valley, rattling off an inaccurate return fire as they went. One or two shots ricocheted near Ben and Wolf's position; soon the shooting stopped altogether. Then they were gone, but not before eighteen of them were lying dead among the rocks.

'That ought to do it,' Wolf said in the deafened silence.

The attack might have been thwarted but the fighters would be back, and in far greater numbers if they were still within radio range of the rest of their people. 'Come on,' Ben said, grabbing the Maximi and first on his feet without waiting for Holt to give the green light. With Wolf right behind him he led the way down towards where the three surviving British soldiers were emerging from their cover. They peered uncertainly upwards and shouldered their rifles as the unexpected visitors scrambled down the rocks towards them. In their confusion they might easily have started shooting off whatever ammo they had left. Ben waved and called out in a loud, clear voice for them to hold their fire, and they hesitantly lowered their weapons.

261

But as Ben made his way down the loose slope, he could see that something wasn't quite right with the soldiers. Of course it was a shocking and nerve-shredding experience to be pinned under enemy fire with every likelihood of getting killed. Even more so when two of your comrades were already down. But that still didn't account for the way the soldiers seemed to be staggering unsteadily about. They didn't move like injured men. It was something else.

Reaching the bottom of the gorge he held up his weapon to show he wasn't a threat. He greeted the nearest of the soldiers, a tall thin trooper in British army combat trousers and a dirty, torn Afghan kameez, with his name, rank and former unit, because how could you begin to describe the unofficial status of their loose-knit bunch of maverick warriors? The mention of 22 SAS was always an effective calling card. But this time it barely seemed to have much effect, as though the soldiers were too stunned or confused to understand him.

'What the hell are you people doing here?' Ben asked.

'Apart from getting shot at,' Wolf said, joining them. 'Thought you boys might like a little help. But hey, don't all thank us at once.'

The tall thin trooper wavered on his feet and seemed to be trying to say something. Ben could see he wasn't going to get much out of this guy. 'Who's the officer in charge here?' he asked.

One of the others pointed weakly at the dark shapes of the bodies on the ground, and croaked in reply, 'Lieutenant Draper. He's dead.'

'We can see that,' Wolf said.

'And who are you, soldier?' Ben asked the one who'd pointed. But before he could get a reply, the tall thin one swayed right over on his feet, his knees gave way under him and he collapsed. Ben caught him before he could beat his brains out on a rock, and lowered him gently to the ground. Turning to the other two, he could see they weren't far off fainting either.

'Ben, these guys are sick,' Wolf said, stepping back from them with a look of suspicion. 'Some kind of fever or something. Could be infectious.'

But Ben sensed it wasn't that either. His feeling was confirmed a moment later when the soldier who'd pointed out Lieutenant Draper croaked, 'We're not sick. We haven't eaten in over a week.'

Holt and the others had joined them by now. Scraggs was calling back to the camp to say all was well and they'd radio back soon. 'These poor sons of bitches are starving to death,' Baldacci said.

'Well, they've got two less mouths to feed now, I guess,' Holt replied.

The soldier's name was Colvin, Corporal Liam Colvin. In the gasping, breathless voice of someone very close to the brink of total physical collapse, he explained that their five-man detachment had been sent out from the main unit – or what was left of their main unit – to hunt for something to eat when the Taliban fighters had appeared out of nowhere and opened fire on them.

Ben said to Colvin, 'We heard you talking over the radio. You were lucky we were in the area. Where are the rest of your men?'

'Base,' Colvin replied, too shattered to say more. He raised a feeble arm and pointed along the winding dry river gorge, in the opposite direction to the one the Taliban fighters had fled in.

'Why didn't they come out to support you when you came under fire?' Wolf demanded.

'No ammo,' Colvin gasped, steadying himself against a rock. 'W-we had the last of it.' He seemed to have run out of energy to speak another word. His companion, who hadn't spoken at all, seemed even less capable of offering any more information.

'Can you walk?' Ben asked.

Colvin's eyes fluttered open and shut. He nodded weakly. 'We'll try.'

'Then take us to your base,' Ben said.

Chapter 35

The remainder of the British unit were camped out less than quarter of a mile away from the scene of the gunfight, but it took Ben's group a long time to get there. First they had to help, virtually carry, Colvin and his two exhausted comrades up the steep bank of the gorge to the Humvee, as they were in no fit state to lead the way to the camp on foot. Then came the task of moving the bodies of Lieutenant Draper and Sergeant Flynn. You didn't leave the dead behind unless there were no other choice.

Once aboard the Humvee, the survivors were so weak with hunger that they could barely tell the way. Wolf tried to radio the main unit to warn them of their arrival, but without success. 'Their batteries must've died or something,' he muttered.

'Let's hope the guy was right about them having run out of ammo,' Scraggs said. 'Last thing we need now is to get plugged by our own boys.'

Dawn was still a couple of hours away by the time they reached the camp. Dark clouds had gathered over the face of the moon and it felt as though more bad weather was rolling in. The British unit had been sheltering in the semi-ruin of an ancient temple dug into the side of a hill near another dried-out river.

What had once been a tall, impressive entrance was crumbling, but the remainder of its walls and part of its roof were still mostly intact after all these centuries. Noticing the pitted, time-worn carvings in the stonework, Ben guessed the ruin must date back to Afghanistan's long lost Buddhist era, having somehow managed to escape the attention of the cultural vandals who would happily tear it down or blow it to pieces. Sometime in its more recent history it must have come close to suffering a similar fate, judging by the old missile craters in the rocks nearby and the rusty Russian tank shell casings that still littered the ground. An archaeologist's dream. Madison would tear his head off if she found out he'd made her miss out on seeing it.

'Who's there?' called a feeble voice from the darkness as Ben and the group approached the temple's entrance. 'Don't come any closer!'

'We're British and American aid volunteers,' Ben called back. 'Ex-SAS and US Special Forces. Got some of your people here, but your Lieutenant is dead.'

After a long pause, figures appeared from the shadows. It soon became apparent that even if the rest of the unit had possessed much in the way of ammunition, they were hardly strong enough to use it. As Ben and the others entered the ruined building they found a half a dozen men huddled around the faint light of a dying gas lantern, so weak with hunger that they could barely stand up. Only four or five were still able to help Holt, Wolf and the others bring the survivors and the casualties in from the Humvee, while Ben asked for the unit commander. There were a lot of questions to be answered.

'I'm in command here,' one of the men replied, wearily introducing himself as Captain Warner. 'It seems we owe you a debt of gratitude, whoever you are.'

'And some explanations,' Ben said. 'I wasn't aware that there were any other British servicemen left in this country.'

'Nor was I,' Warner said, eyeing Ben inquisitively in the dim light. Ben gave him a brief, pared-down account of the SAS Operation Hydra, but without getting into the specifics of its failed objective.

'Another bloody mess,' Warner said. 'It's been a disaster from the start.'

'We have food and ammo,' Ben said. 'More than enough to share around. I'm sorry about your men. We'll do what we can for you. But first, tell me what you're doing here.'

'Come and sit down before I collapse,' Warner sighed, leading him to the shadowy corner of a small chamber. The remains of a stone altar where the temple's Buddhist occupants might once have knelt and prayed now served as a makeshift bench covered in sleeping bags. The young captain slumped on it with a groan, as spent and depleted as the rest of his men.

It was too dark inside the chamber to make out much of his features, but Ben had the strangest feeling of recognition. Warner was fairly tall, around Ben's height, sandy-haired as far as Ben could tell, and appeared to be around twenty-six or twenty-seven, around the younger end of the spectrum for his rank, but definitely far too youthful to be anyone

Ben had ever served with. Perhaps a relative of someone he'd known, Ben thought – though he had no recollection of a Warner among his past army comrades.

He let it go, because there was so much more he wanted to know. But the strange feeling of déjà vu kept haunting him. Even Warner's voice, his slurred exhaustion doing little to mask the received pronunciation and speech mannerisms of a public school education, sounded oddly familiar.

Sitting there slumped wearily in the darkness Warner explained what their unit was doing here in Afghanistan. They belonged to the Pathfinder Platoon, part of the 16th Air Assault Brigade, a unit Ben knew very well. The Pathfinders operated as a slightly less elite adjunct to Special Forces, though their training regime was almost every bit as tough. They played key roles in reconnaissance and scouting operations, skilled at air insertion and penetrating deep behind enemy lines. Like the SAS and its sister regiment, Jeff Dekker's old unit the SBS, the Pathfinders often found themselves deployed on operations of a more shadowy, less official nature.

And as Ben now learned, this was one of those.

Warner and his twenty-man unit had been dropped into Afghanistan almost a month earlier, on a mission to help subvert the burgeoning alliance between its new rulers the Taliban and the Chinese government: an alliance that was deeply concerning to the suits in Whitehall and generally considered a potential disaster both politically and militarily, with regard to any future attempt to resecure the country from what they had hoped was just a temporary state of affairs. Warner explained that given the sensitive nature of the operation, they'd been working along with an MI6 agent.

'Where is he now?' Ben asked, thinking of Goffin. These damn spooks were everywhere.

'Dead,' Warner replied. 'Along with another seven of us. No, nine now,' he corrected himself with a haunted look. 'Jesus Christ. Bobby Draper was a good friend of mine.'

'How were you supposed to mess things up with the Chinese?'

'By staging a false flag attack,' Warner said. 'Or that was the plan, at any rate. Staunton – he was the MI6 chap – was helping us liaise with a tribal militia group whose purpose was to carry out a strike against Chinese officials on a scouting trip for mineral resources. Our job was to escort Staunton into the mountains to meet with the tribal leaders and negotiate a deal with them.'

Warner shrugged resignedly. 'It was simple enough, really. All it took was to persuade them to pose as Taliban fighters, which they could have done pretty convincingly, for a price of course. That was Staunton's area. Then with our support, we'd have set up an ambush and popped off a couple of their ministry people, scared the wits out of the rest, and caused a shitstorm of bad relations between Afghanistan and China that the Whitehall boffins then thought they could exploit for their own purposes. The usual bullshit political game, you know how it goes. But it never got that far, or anywhere close.'

'What went wrong?' Ben asked.

'Everything, mate,' Warner replied, the word 'mate' striking a false and somehow condescending note when uttered in that public schoolboy accent. 'We were on our way to hook up with the militiamen when we got bumped by a real Taliban patrol. Staunton got it in the head, and so did Jenkins and Hunt. Next thing we were in a running chase over a hundred miles of bloody wilderness, all our supplies shot to pieces, communications gone except for a couple of lousy radios one of which has now packed up completely, ammo dwindled away to almost nothing, stranded in the middle of nowhere with no way of getting out, and zero contact with the outside world. One truck was totalled and the other ran out of fuel, so we had to continue on foot. We've been surviving out here for weeks, slowly dying of starvation and just praying we wouldn't run into any more patrols, because God knows we're not in a fit state to tackle them. It was a miracle we found this place to shelter in. Then tonight happened.' Warner stared into space for a moment, then slapped his head angrily. 'I should have fucking gone with them. Bobby persuaded me not to.'

'You might have been killed too,' Ben said. 'But you weren't. You're here, and alive. You get to do your job, lead your people out of this and home safe.'

'Easy to say,' Warner burst out, almost close to tears. 'Get them out how? Where from? The whole place is sealed off tighter than a trout's arsehole, as dear old granddad used to say.' He went on bitterly, 'I wish I'd never accepted this mission. People advised me not to, you know. But I wouldn't listen, fool that I am. Now men are dead and it's my fault.'

Which seemed to Ben a strange outburst, coming from a Pathfinders captain. In his long and very positive past experience these were tough, steely-eyed professionals who didn't generally wear their heart on their sleeve, still less open up their innermost feelings to a total stranger. Maybe the stress and the hunger had got to Warner. Or maybe the platoon didn't recruit its officers as selectively as it used to, which seemed doubtful.

Ben still couldn't shake off the peculiar sense that he knew this guy from somewhere. It was bugging him. And though he disliked displays of self-pitying emotion in a fighting man as much as he disapproved of sneaky intel-led false flag attacks on civilian targets, he felt a genuine pity for Warner's predicament. Reaching for his last few Gauloises, he leaned across to offer him one. 'Smoke?'

'They'd kill me if they knew,' Warner replied, 'but yeah, thanks.' He took the cigarette and Ben, wondering who 'they' were, clanged open his old Zippo and held it out. The familiar, comforting orange flame cast a soft flickering light over Warner's face as he bent towards Ben to light up. It was the first time Ben had seen his features in anything more than semi-darkness; and that was when the full force of recognition hit him like a slap. He was so stunned that he forgot the burning lighter still in his hand, and his own unlit cigarette in the other.

Ben's mind was suddenly whirling as all the unanswered questions and enigmas that had been eating at him since he'd landed in this hellhole country were made crystal clear.

He knew now. And he could sense, from the sly gleam in Warner's eyes, that Warner knew he knew.

'I know you,' Ben said. 'You're—'

'All right, all right. It had to come out sometime,' Warner said irritably, sucking smoke. 'Warner isn't my actual name.

It's a cover, to hide my identity for the sake of the official records. Some bureaucrat came up with it. Their decision, not mine. I don't even like it.' He sighed. 'You can't possibly understand what it's like to have to have *everything* done for you, *everything* decided for you. Half the time I feel like I'm living someone else's life.'

'What do I call you?'

'You can call me Richard. That's what people know me as. Most people, that is. The *ordinary* folks.' He made quote marks with his fingers, the orange tip of his cigarette bobbing in the darkness. 'Or call me Rick, Ricky, whatever you want. I really don't give a damn. Except Dick. I don't like to be called Dick.'

'You're Spartan,' Ben said, shaking his head in amazement. '*You're* Spartan.'

And in fact, the unhappy, troubled young man sitting with Ben in that shadowy, bullet-pocked ruin four thousand miles from home was a little more than that.

Chapter 36

Ben couldn't have been more wrong if he'd tried. All this time he'd been wondering what the Taliban patrols swarming all over the mountains were so worked up about, the answer had been staring him right in the face but he couldn't see it. They weren't scouring the wilderness in search of Holt and Wolf's motley band of freelance warriors. And they weren't searching for the errant American woman who'd slipped out of Kabul with her companions, either.

Instead, all along they'd been looking for *this* guy. For Spartan, the mystery man whose real name had been such a closely guarded secret by the instigators of Operation Hydra – and yet whose identity had somehow, thanks to some internal leak, betrayal or intel slip-up, managed to become known to the opposition. The magic ticket that had allowed Ben to enter Afghanistan wasn't just the highest priority of the British government spooks. He was the enemy's Number One target, and for a very good reason.

For once, the logic of officialdom was so clear and under-standable that all Ben could do was smile and shake his head. Who could blame the Whitehall suits for falling over themselves to scramble together a top-secret mission to locate and extract the errant Prince Richard, the youngest of his royal generation, fourth in line to the British throne? A mission so extremely hush-hush that it had to be entrusted to the likes of Colonel Carstairs, his shadowy Group 13 associates and their man in Kabul, Lewis Goffin.

They must have been in a complete panic, Ben reflected. And they were damn right to be. If allowed to fall into the Taliban's hands, the young prince would be the most valuable and most sought-after hostage in the history of modern warfare. There was no limit to the sensational amount of international media publicity that his capture would generate. And there was nothing, literally nothing, that his delighted captors couldn't demand in exchange for his safe return. Whitehall would gladly turn over half the UK treasury in ransom, along with a signed treaty promising that the Brits and their allies would forthwith and forever give up any designs on reclaiming Afghanistan for themselves. Maybe they'd give the Taliban the keys to Buckingham Palace while they were at it. And that would be just for starters.

All these thoughts whirled through Ben's head in an instant, while the young prince formerly known as Captain Warner frowned at him in the darkness. 'What's "Spartan"?' the prince asked, quite innocently. Stuck out here totally incommunicado these last several weeks, he hadn't known a thing about it.

'You must have imagined there would be a bit of a flap going on behind the scenes, with you missing in action,' Ben said. He'd recovered from his initial surprise now, leaning his back against the wall to light his cigarette. 'Spartan was your codename, the sole objective of Operation Hydra. You're the reason I'm here.' He might have added, 'And you're the reason why Jack Buchanan, Bob Meadows, Pete Dixon, Will Yates, Rick Mackay, Mark Simms, Steve Cale and several of their loyal Afghan backup team are lying dead in the dirt between here and Kabul.'

But the prince had other things on his mind anyhow. '"Spartan",' he muttered. 'Bloody stupid name. Like "Warner". You'd think they might try and come up with something more inventive and interesting.'

'They certainly pulled out all the stops to keep it quiet, that's for sure,' Ben said. 'Not that I follow current affairs much, but even I would've heard about it if news of your disappearance had been allowed to get out.'

The prince gave a cynical grunt. 'What do you expect? They probably wouldn't have been too bothered otherwise, if I'd been just another serviceman MIA. But I suppose it's nice knowing that someone cares.' He paused, thinking. 'Huh. You know the real irony of it all? That I used every bit of influence I had to get this mission. I fought them every step of the way. Threatened to quit my role, renounce my status, walk away from the whole bloody family circus if they didn't let me.'

'Why should it matter so much to you?'

The prince stared at him for a moment. 'Why? Because I wanted to be someone like you guys,' he answered with surprising frankness. 'They wouldn't let me into the SAS, because of who I was, no matter if I passed selection or not. Can you believe that bullshit? But I wouldn't give up. I bullied and blackmailed my way into the Pathfinders because I had to prove myself. To show them I wasn't just some pretty cosseted little media darling born with a diamond-studded silver spoon in his gob. I argued, why shouldn't I be allowed to? My family have always been in action. Grandfather was covered in medals for his service in World War Two. My uncle flew helicopter combat missions in the Falklands War. Even my twat of an elder brother was allowed to piss about in jets in Afghanistan with 16 Air Assault Brigade, even if he didn't actually do much. So why not me? What was wrong with *me?* He was getting agitated now, thumping his chest with his fist.

'Maybe they thought you didn't have it in you,' Ben said calmly, looking at him. 'Maybe they were afraid you might screw things up and cause a big royal embarrassment, so to speak.'

'Hah! And maybe they were fucking right in the end. Is that what you're saying?'

'I don't have an opinion,' Ben said. 'When I do, I promise you'll be the first to know.'

'Well, thank you for your candour,' the prince muttered bitterly. 'I await your judgement with bated breath.'

'The question is,' Ben said, 'what am I supposed to do with you now?'

'Nothing,' the prince replied. 'Nothing you can do. We're all stuck in the same boat, mate.' There was that "mate" again, the young royal's self-conscious attempt to relate to his commoner underlings. It was already beginning to grate on Ben after a couple of repetitions. There had better not be a third.

Ben was about to reply when a third figure appeared silently in the semi-darkness of the temple chamber. There was just enough light to flash a golden glimmer from Wolf's teeth as he said, 'There you are. I was looking for you.'

'This is my friend and associate Jaden Wolf,' Ben said. 'Jaden, this is Captain Warner.'

Wolf nodded at him. 'Captain.'

'What the hell, why don't you tell him?' the prince said. 'He'll find out the truth soon enough anyway, come daylight when he sees me.'

'Find out what?' Wolf asked.

'Fair enough,' Ben said. 'Jaden, our friend the captain is slightly better known to the world as Prince Richard. It appears he's managed to drop off the radar of HM Forces, making him the reason for all this fuss.'

Jaden Wolf was quite possibly the most unflappable person Ben had ever known. He didn't disappoint now. 'Oh, right,' he said with barely a blink. 'Well, there you go. Richard the Lionheart, eh?'

'Oh for God's sake, not that old chestnut again,' the prince complained. 'Do you honestly think I haven't heard it before?'

Wolf shot him a careless grin, then his face became more serious. 'Anyhow, Ben, your Princeliness, excuse me for butting into your conversation, but we'd better get moving. Nielsen and Baldacci just reported from their lookout posts that there's some troop movement to the south, heading our way fast. Looks like our sweet little pals might be coming back, with about a million of their friends.'

Chapter 37

'We can hold this place, dude,' Baldacci was insisting as he and Holt argued outside.

'Sure, like Travis, Bowie and Crockett held the Alamo,' Holt replied. 'It's a freakin' death-trap and I'm not waiting around to get my lily-white ass drilled full of holes. We're out of here, right now.'

Which was another of those rare moments when Ben found himself in agreement with him. And there wasn't a lot of time to get moving, certainly not enough to bury the dead before the team piled into the Humvee along with the captain and his ten half-starved and weary soldiers, some of them so weak with hunger that they had to be virtually carried aboard. A vehicle designed to transport fewer than a dozen personnel in something less than comfort was crammed so tight with bodies there was barely enough space to pack the platoon's empty weapons and the remnants of what kit they'd been able to carry on their death march through the mountains.

'Get ready for a hell of a rough ride, people,' Wolf said, jumping into the front passenger seat.

Then they were off again, leaving the ruins of the temple behind and roaring off into the night. Ben was back at the wheel, navigating the dark wilderness with no lights and only the pale glow of the moon through the heavy, dark clouds to go by. From higher ground they could see the lights of the troop convoy like a long spangled snake curving its way across the rocky valley far to their rear, falling steadily further away with every minute Ben kept his foot to the floor, every jolt over the brutal terrain bringing more groans and moans of complaint from the jostled, crushed passengers. The enemy was always one step behind. And Ben meant to keep it that way – preferably two or three. But the presence of perhaps hundreds of Taliban fighters in the area now meant that their base camp was no longer a safe refuge, either. The moment they reached it, the now significantly more numerous group would have to be on the move again, travelling hard and fast in the hope they didn't encounter more enemy troops. Though they were still free for the moment, it felt as though a ring of steel was slowly, inexorably closing around them.

Ben was acutely aware of the prince behind him in the back of the Humvee. In all the hurry to evacuate the temple, he and Wolf were the only members of their group to have learned the real identity of 'Captain Warner'. He wondered what the reaction would be when the others found out. Driving on through the darkness he reached again for his cigarettes. Only three were left now. He wasn't a superstitious man, but in his grim state of mind it seemed like a bad omen. *What happens when the last one's gone?* he thought to himself.

One way or another, that time was coming, and he'd find out the answer.

Within an hour, the Humvee crunched to a halt at the camp and was met by a crowd of anxious faces. Wolf had already radioed ahead to say they were en route, and to get ready to pack up and go.

'Who are all these people?' Madison asked, staring at the strangers as they came limping and stumbling out of the vehicle.

'Lord, they are in a terrible state,' said Father Bugnolio. 'We cannot possibly expect these poor souls to travel any further, in their condition.'

'They'll just have to lump it,' Wolf told him. 'Or else I'll shoot them myself. That's kinder than what the Taliban will do, if they catch up with them.'

'God protect and preserve us from evil,' the priest muttered.

'Who needs him?' Wolf laughed. 'Not when you've got Ben Hope watching your back.'

Time mattered, but so did getting some nourishment into the starving soldiers before they started dropping dead on the spot. A large portion of the remaining food and water supplies was urgently dished out to the Pathfinders, who ate and drank ravenously, gathered in a circle to sit or squat among the rocks. Those who had mess tins set about doggedly emptying them, others having to content themselves with eating out of a can, using a knife or their fingers. Little was said in between bites, partly because they were too intent on replenishing their depleted systems as quickly as they could gulp it down, and partly because they were all too morose about their dead comrades left behind at the temple ruin.

The first rays of dawn were slowly creeping up behind the craggy peaks in the east, but it was still dark and still nobody in Ben's group had twigged the identity of their unusual new guest. In any case 'Captain Warner' tended to keep his face averted, like someone bashful about their appearance. He sat with his fellow Pathfinders, keeping themselves to themselves, bent over their food under the disapproving eye of Holt and a couple of the others, who were visibly annoyed about having to share their dwindling rations with these newcomers.

'Look on the bright side,' Wolf said to Holt. 'A few more guys might come in handy, where we're going.'

'Sure would,' Holt replied laconically, 'if the raggedy-ass suckers didn't look like a bunch of extras from a goddamn zombie movie.'

'You wouldn't look so hot yourself, if you hadn't eaten for weeks,' Wolf said.

'Tell you what, though,' Holt said, jerking his chin in the direction of the Pathfinders' commander. 'That captain of theirs sure looks familiar.'

'You think?' Wolf said nonchalantly.

'Yeah, pretty sure I've seen him before. Damned if I know where, though.'

'Not me,' Wolf said. To change the subject he nodded up at the high ground behind the camp where they were taking turns as lookout. 'I'll post watch.'

Holt nodded anxiously. 'Out of here in thirty, max. Be ready. And keep your eyes peeled in case they've already found us.'

'Copy that, chief.' Wolf snatched up his M4 and went bounding up the rocks, vanishing in the darkness.

So far the prince's secret was safe, but as the red dawn began to lighten the darkness, it wouldn't remain so for long. Nobby Scraggs, overseeing the feeding of the newcomers, had already noticed the strange, self-conscious glances that were passing between the Pathfinders when he found out the reason for them. Doing a startled double-take at their commander Nobby suddenly went rigid with shock and amazement. He clamped his jaws shut to stifle the expletive that almost burst out of them, and too stunned to think what else to do he ran over to tell Baldacci and Nielsen, who happened to be close by.

The news spread very quickly from there. Holt and the others were fairly surprised to hear they had a royal prince in their midst. 'Dammit, I knew there was something about that guy,' Holt kept saying. He was even more surprised to learn that Ben and Wolf had already been in on the secret. Baldacci insisted that he'd known all along too, just didn't think it was worth mentioning. But the strongest reaction to the news was that of Nobby Scraggs, the proud royalist. To the profound embarrassment of his comrades, not to mention of the prince himself, he did everything but prostrate himself on the ground at the feet of the exalted personage, and finally had to be dragged away after trying to get an autograph on his jubilee mug.

Nobby's wild enthusiasm wasn't shared by all. 'I don't see much royal-looking about the dude,' Baldacci said, emphasising his point by spitting on the ground. 'Who gives a rat's ass about any of them, anyhow?'

'I have no problem with the old dame,' said Nielsen, 'I mean, respect to her and all. She's been through a lot of shit and handled herself with style. But they have a serious problem keeping their younger generation in line, man. What a bunch of misfits.'

'I'd give'm all an ass-whupping,' Baldacci growled. 'Starting with this one right here.'

'That I'd like to see,' Nielsen chuckled.

'Maybe you will, buddy. Maybe you will.'

But not all the Americans were so disparaging. 'So that's a prince,' Madison said to Ben, eyeing him from a distance. They were sitting together by the truck, gulping a hurried coffee before it was time to get moving again. 'I've never met one before. Met the president once. It's not the same.'

'You aren't going to start carrying on like Nobby, I hope,' Ben muttered. 'Clutching at the guy's trousers and trying to kiss the royal ring.' Nobby was now banished to the other side of the camp, on pain of physical violence if he misbehaved again.

'I never do that on a first date,' Madison replied. 'Though I gotta say, he's not bad looking in the flesh. Is there a lady prince?'

'A what?' Ben blinked, confused for an instant before he understood. 'I don't really know. I don't think so.'

'He looks so sad and lonely,' she said. 'Think I'll go and say hi. Relax, I'm just curious to meet him, that's all. I told you, my heart belongs to another.'

Ben did remember her saying that, although her particular behaviour with him last night, before they'd been interrupted by the sounds of gunfire, had made him wonder about it.

Unless his imagination had been playing tricks on him, she hadn't been acting quite like a woman with a special someone waiting for her back home. The memory of it was lingering strangely in his thoughts.

'Please, Madison, leave the bloke alone.' But before Ben could stop her, she was up on her feet and striding over towards the Pathfinders with a swagger in her step that made him think, *Uh-oh.*

Ben might not have been the only one thinking it. The prince looked up as she planted herself confidently in front of him with a bright smile, her hands on her hips and her black hair streaming in the wind. None of the Pathfinders had laid eyes on a woman for weeks on end, not that they were in any state to have any notions of flirting with this one. Madison bent down, stuck out her hand and said in a voice that carried all across the camp, 'Hey, Prince, how ya doin? Sorry about your buddies back there. I'm Madison, by the way. Welcome to the gang. We're all crazy here, you should know.'

The prince was slightly thrown for a moment, gaping at her speechlessly. Then gathering his wits and casting off his mournful expression for a moment, he took her hand and flashed her one of those famously charming smiles that had graced the front page of every tabloid and celebrity magazine in the world at one time or other, if somewhat more haggard. He replied, 'Oh, don't worry, I'm perfectly used to being surrounded by crazy people.'

Ben was spared having to hear any more of Madison's conversation with the prince, because Holt came over, frowning at his watch and looking unhappy. 'We should've been out of here ten minutes ago. You got any more waifs and strays you want to bring along for the ride before we get moving?'

'Not unless more turn up,' Ben replied, meeting his eye.

Holt jerked a thumb back towards the Pathfinders, then aimed a finger at Ben like a pistol. 'You're responsible for him. We clear on that? This wasn't part of our deal, for my guys to play nanny to some pretty-boy princeling who shouldn't have been placed in command of a catering corps, let alone a special recon unit. As for his troopers, they don't look a whole lot of use to us, you ask me.'

'Give them a break,' Ben said. 'They've lost a lot of their people.'

'Yeah, well, get in line,' Holt replied not too sympathetically. 'Soldiers die. It's an occupational hazard. Meanwhile, I have a job to finish. And I mean to finish it. We're not done yet, not by a long shot.'

'Don't sweat it,' Ben said. 'A deal's a deal, Chris. I'll make sure he doesn't get in your way.'

Holt nodded. 'Okay, then we understand each other.' He looked around to where Madison was still talking to the prince and his men. 'Your lady friend seems to be getting on well with him, anyhow.'

'Hmm,' Ben replied.

Holt turned back to Ben and gave a rare smile. 'Tell you what, buddy. We ever get out of this shithole alive and you manage to get that sonofabitch home to his family in one piece, they'll probably give you a freakin' knighthood.'

Chapter 38

For all of that day, as much of the horizon as could be seen remained clear of any sighting of the enemy. The Humvee and the truck, now carrying the extra eleven passengers in the back, went on hacking north-westwards towards their destination. Neither Ben, nor Wolf, nor Holt and the others, had any clear idea of what might be waiting for them there. They didn't know whether it was their final destination, or whether there would be others lying beyond. They didn't know what the future held in store for any of them. All they knew was that the safety and lives of more innocent people were on the line and in danger if they didn't complete their task.

And in any case, there was nowhere else for them to go.

Wolf and Scraggs took turns driving the truck while Ben and Holt shared wheel duty in the Humvee. Madison spent most of her time gazing out of the dusty window, saying little. In the back, crammed between boxes of kit and Madison's treasure chest, Father Bugnolio had given up trying to read his Bible with all the lurching and rocking about. Aziz was sleeping, not looking particularly well, and as usual Ramin was in a brown study, consumed by his anxious thoughts.

Ben was deep in troubled reflections of his own, when he wasn't concentrating on pushing the Humvee over some of the most challenging off-road terrain he'd ever had to negotiate, or glancing in the mirror for signs of the dreaded dust plume in their wake telling them the pursuers were back. The strange sense of doom that had preoccupied him the night before now seemed to grow more intense in his mind, brought to the forefront of his thoughts by the hypnotic rumble of the engine and the endless emptiness of the landscape. So much of his life had been spent sitting on troop planes, in helicopters, in trucks and vehicles just like this one, thousands of miles away from home; interminable hours, days, weeks on end totally immersed in the immediate, stark, sometimes terrifying, nearly always extremely risky, reality of whatever task happened to be at hand. And yet all through that time there had always been the sense that this environment in which he found himself wasn't all that existed – that the outside world was still there, waiting for his return, if he survived long enough to go back to his life.

Now was different. The metaphorical ring of steel he'd imagined slowly coiling around him last night as they'd made their escape from the temple seemed to be closing in steadily more tightly all the time, making him feel increasingly trapped, hemmed inside an inescapable claustrophobic space from which all the air was being sucked and all the conceivable channels for escape had been systematically blocked off one by one. With each new day in this barren, unforgiving no-man's land, the world he'd known before – Le Val, his friends, his beloved dogs, the fields and the trees, the ivied ruins of the ancient church in the woods, the nearby ocean, all the favourite old haunts where he loved to spend time, the whole life he'd made for himself in that beautiful place – seemed further and further away, receding to a tiny point in the rear-view mirror of his mind, until he was afraid it might just shrink away altogether and disappear, as though it had never been more than a dream.

He'd never experienced a feeling quite like it until now, and it unsettled him to his core. He understood what it was. For the first time in his life, he was truly, deeply afraid, almost to the point of conviction, that he wasn't getting out of here. It wasn't his own mortality that frightened him. It was the thought of what it might mean for the person sitting close by, the person who was depending on him for her safe return home. The person he was beginning to realise he cared about much more deeply than he'd thought.

As if on cue, the sound of her voice broke into his worrying reflections, jerking him back to the present moment.

'How long do we have?' she was saying, leaning close and speaking loud to be heard over the engine noise and the crash and rattle of the suspension. Ben had been so lost in thought that his mind was stupid and blank for a moment, like someone woken from a deep sleep. 'How long do we have before what?' he replied ominously.

'Before we get there, dummy,' she replied, nudging him with her fist. 'Where we're going, or had you forgotten? Where this Christian mission is, or was. What's it called, anyway?'

'Why do you want to know?' Ben asked. In fact he was playing for time, unable to remember its name.

'Because I like knowing things,' she said.

'It's called Gurghazar,' Holt replied for him.

'"Gurghazar"?'Madison repeated.

'That's what it's called on the map,' Holt said. He spelled it, 'G-u-r-g-h-a-z-a-r,' saying 'zee' for 'zed' in the American way.

Madison sounded incredulous. 'No way. You're kidding. Gurghazar?'

Ben asked her, 'Why the surprise? You know the place?'

'Of course not,' she replied testily. 'Like I told you, I've never been to this country in my life before. I'm beginning to think that once would've been enough.'

'So what's the big deal with Gurghazar?'

'I don't know the place,' she explained patiently, or as patiently as it was possible for anyone to sound raising their voice to a near-shout while being violently jostled up and down and from side to side in a truck travelling far too fast for the off-road conditions. 'But Dad did. He talked about it a lot. It was another of his many obsessions when it came to the history of ancient Bactria.'

'What's so special about it?' Holt said, in a surly tone. 'You talking about the orphanage?'

'No, I never heard of that before either,' she shot back. The hardness in her eyes when she talked to Holt made it clear she didn't like him much.

Holt said, 'Far as I know, apart from some tiny backwater village, the orphanage is the only thing there.'

Madison shook her head. 'If it's not been there for thousands of years, Dad wouldn't have taken any interest in it. I'm talking about the fabled caves nearby where Alexander's men were said to have been forced to shelter in the terrible winter while they were pursuing Bessus through the mountains.'

'Here we go with the history crap again,' Holt said. Maybe he didn't like Madison much either.

'That's right, the history crap that put about ten million bucks' worth of gold and jewels into the back of this bone-shaking piece of junk you call transport, in case it slipped your mind,' she snapped at Holt. Then for Ben's benefit she added, in a softer tone, 'Nobody's ever been able to find the exact location of the caves. Dad speculated that the sheltering army might have left some mark behind. Like graffiti. Imagine that: "Demetrius was here". What a find. Or who knows, it could be something more substantial.'

'We're not going there for the sake of archaeology, lady,' Holt told her. 'I couldn't be less interested in that bullshit. There are real people out there who need our help.'

Madison froze him with a look that could make a man's nose turn black and drop off from twenty paces away. 'Hey, no problem. Let me know if you assholes need any assistance with that, okay? Because here's a real person who might be of some use to you, if it comes to it.'

From the back, Father B said, 'Bless you, my child.' The moral weight of God's Divine benediction seemed to settle the argument, because Holt said no more. Ben fell silent too, and went on driving.

The path of the burning sun traced its slow, steady arc across the dome of the pale sky as the hours went by. Nothing else changed, except the gradual morphing of the landscape as the endless miles rolled on. They crossed a zone the breadth of a medium-sized English county where the rocky ground gave way to desert sand and the terrain levelled out into rolling arid hills and dunes, the faraway peaks growing hazy in the distance. Nothing seemed to live here at all, with not enough moisture in the ground to sustain even the coarsest, hardiest scrub vegetation. Here and there, sand-storms had filled in deep crevasses, into which a heavy vehicle could lurch without warning and get badly stuck. The Humvee was generally able to roll over them, with a combination of skill and momentum, but the much larger, weightier truck, even with its rugged six-wheel drive transmission, was out of its depth in this terrain. The first time it happened, with Wolf driving, it took them almost an hour to dig the wheels out of the sand and get the truck moving again with the help of recovery tracks and a tow rope attached to the Humvee. The second time, this time with Nobby at the wheel, a jagged rock hidden under the loose sand blew out a front tyre, causing another delay while they struggled to change the half-buried wheel with no firm footing for a trolley jack. Back in motion again, all eyes were on the fuel gauges, with the contents of their spare jerrycans getting dangerously low. It was another reminder of the many ways this place could kill you. Even modern-day armies still had to worry about feeding the baggage train beasts. If they got stuck out here in this arid emptiness, they'd all be dead within a couple of days.

Now the terrain changed again, their route taking them up and up from the low-lying desert region onto higher ground that rose so sharply upward that the gaining altitude made their ears pop and crackle. From here they faced having to cross an expanse of escarpment and mountain where constricting rocky passes offered the only way through. Twice they found themselves unable to go any further and forced to turn back in search of a usable route that didn't detour too widely from their course, adding long miles and hours to their journey. Just when they thought they'd found a relatively easy passage through the crags that loomed either side of them, they lumbered through a tight gap between two enormous rocks to find the ground to one side had sheared off completely during some long-ago landslide or earthquake, leaving a vertiginous two-hundred-foot chasm into a rubble-littered valley way below to their right, a more than vertical granite wall looming high overhead to their left and the only avenue between the two a twisting, rutted boulder-strewn ledge forming a path that at its broadest was only a couple of inches wider than the wheelbases of the vehicles.

By the time they realised their potentially fatal mistake, it was already too late to turn back. Where a narrower Land Rover would have got through without too much worry, the massively squat, crablike Humvee was so wide that its outer wheels pattered and scrabbled dangerously close to the edge of the drop, an experience that was made even more disquieting by the sidewise cant of the path that sometimes tipped them over at an alarming angle, so that the passengers on the right could peer straight down from their windows at the valley floor two hundred feet below, a sight guaranteed to make the bravest soul recoil with a shudder. The truck was a foot wider still, and in the narrower stretches its three outer tyres were overhanging the brink by more than half their width, dislodging little avalanches of loose dirt and stone as its huge wheels rolled along.

One tiny slip, the minutest error of judgement on the part of either driver, or a weak section of ground that might give away under their combined seven-plus tons, and either or both vehicles wouldn't stop tumbling through space until they and their occupants were pulverised on the rocks far below.

Madison sat with her eyes tightly closed, both fists clutching the frame rails of her seat as though that could stop her falling to her death if the vehicle went over. Ramin hunched rigid and ghostlike, too terrified to speak or even breathe, while Aziz silently clutched his heart and Father B murmured prayers without much conviction in the back. Holt stretched out in his seat and tried to look bored, but his face was pale and a muscle in his jaw twitched with tension. When he thought the others were too distracted to see, he quickly wiped the perspiration from his brow.

After twenty minutes of constant dread, Ben's shirt was sticking to his back in a cold sweat. After nearly an hour, punctuated with more heart-stopping, bowel-loosening moments of super-concentrated fear than he cared to count, even his normally calm composure in moments of extreme stress had abandoned him and he felt dizzy and nauseous. From the cautious way the truck was inching along the edge of the cliff behind them, scraping its paintwork to bare metal against the wall to its left, the wing mirror on that side bent right off, the famously unflappable Jaden Wolf didn't seem to be handling the strain much more comfortably.

At last, Ben was able to relax his knotted muscles and say to Madison, 'You can open your eyes now.' When she did, breathing a loud sigh of relief, she saw that the path had begun to broaden out again, snaking its way more gently down the side of the cliff to the relative safety of the valley below.

'Well, that was interesting,' she said in a strangled voice. She touched his arm. 'You got us through, Ben. Saved our skins again.'

Ben shook his head. 'Don't thank me. Only an idiot would have led us along that road.'

'You shouldn't talk about yourself that way,' she said, irritated by his self-deprecating words. 'You had no choice. You took your chance and went for it, and you came through just like you always do. *That's* who you are. The same old Ben Hope we know and—' She hesitated, interrupting herself as though she'd been about to say something else but changed it as it was still in her mouth. '—and remember,' she finished.

'I appreciate the vote of confidence,' he said. 'Didn't feel that way back there, I'll confess.'

'Hell, that was nothing,' Holt said. 'I've led my guys through tighter squeezes plenty of times, back in the day.'

'Oh, I'll bet you have,' Madison said, giving him the evil eye. 'Bet you handled yourself like a real man, too.'

The descent from the mountain pass carried them down several thousand feet in as many seconds. Once upon a time a mighty river, fed by snow melt from the tall peaks before its course must have been diverted by landslides and seismic shifts over the course of history, had carved a smooth, rounded channel through the rocks, like a twisting bobsleigh run which they followed for a few miles until they finally climbed up onto a broad, flat plateau. Beyond that, they were happy to see that the terrain was clear and empty, with no obvious hazards in sight for miles.

'We've managed to stay more or less true to our course,' Ben said as they pulled over to rest a few minutes and check the compass and the map. 'Judging by the amount of distance we've covered, I'd say we can't be more than a couple of hours from our destination. Should get there before dark, anyhow.'

'Nothing but plain sailing between us and the caves of Gurghazar,' Madison said brightly.

'Let's not start patting ourselves on the back just yet,' Holt said. He swept an arm in a circle. 'This whole area crawls with more than just Taliban patrols. The local tribal militia groups are just as liable to be hostile, seeing as we're driving around in castoff US army vehicles. From a distance they could easily mistake us for Talibs. And even though most of them have been at war with each other for as long as anyone can remember, there's nobody they hate more than those mofos.'

'But most of the militia tribesmen still use horses and outdated weapons,' Ramin said, looking as anxious as ever. 'That's what I've read, anyhow, in one of the articles I edited for the institute. They're hardly likely to attack us, are they?'

'I wouldn't be too sure about that,' Ben replied, another of those rare occasions when he had to agree with Holt. 'These are some of the toughest and bravest warriors in the world, not to mention they're brilliant cavalrymen. They learned from elders who cut their teeth riding into battle against Russian tank battalions when they were still in their teens. They're afraid of nothing and nobody, and certainly not of us. We'll have to watch out for them.'

But a couple of hours later, Ben's estimate of their remaining distance from their destination having turned out almost exactly right, they'd seen no more sign of fierce horse-mounted Afghan tribal warriors galloping, yowling like banshees, over the plains towards them than they had of Taliban patrol convoys. In fact, there was no sign of anything alive stirring anywhere all around the points of the compass as the two dusty, battered vehicles cleared the top of a rise and, through the haze of early evening, they sighted the village quarter of a mile away on the far bank of a glittering river. Perched on the hillside some way above were the buildings of the Christian mission and orphanage. Further to the west in the background, lit blood red by the rays of the sunset, stood a tall sandstone escarpment that stretched for miles, north to south, the site of the fabled caves that Rigby Cahill had dreamed in vain for so many years of exploring.

'Gurghazar,' Madison breathed, her eyes burning with excitement as she shielded them from the glare of the setting sun with her hand. 'We found it.'

'Let's see what else we find,' Ben said.

Chapter 39

Ben and Madison climbed up onto the roof of the Humvee to get a better view of the place through their binoculars before they ventured any closer. From this distance the village looked pretty much like any other typical rural hinterlands settlement of its kind, a rambling cluster of thirty or forty primitive flat-roofed adobe houses and outbuildings, some of them dug partly into the rising slope above the river bank, the whole circled by a low drystone wall. A couple of animal corrals stood a short distance away from the perimeter, but nothing was moving within them and they appeared to be disused.

'Looks awful quiet,' Madison said, scanning the houses. 'I can't see a soul anywhere.'

Ben had been thinking the same thing. The village appeared totally abandoned, as empty as the pens that had housed its livestock. The reason for that was clear enough, and it had to do with what had happened to the orphanage. Even from far off and in fading light the silhouettes of its broken down walls and collapsed roof were plainly visible through his powerful binocs. But the thing he'd been most concerned about seeing was enemy troop movement, and there was no sign of that.

'The coast's clear,' he called down to Holt. 'Let's move in.'

This side of the river the bank sloped gently down to the water, thick with reeds and bushes. The water was about thirty yards across, its soft ripples catching the red light of the sunset. 'Looks shallow enough to ford,' Ben said. 'All the same, better be sure.' He jumped out, trotted down the bank and waded into the cold, clear water.

'Look out for crocodiles,' Madison called anxiously from the Humvee. Ben had not long ago returned from Australia where he'd learned all about crocodiles, specifically not to get anywhere near the damn things. But Afghanistan's deadly predators were more of the two-legged variety. 'Crocodiles, honestly,' he muttered. He waded out to the middle of the river where the water was no more than waist-deep, turned back towards the shore and clambered dripping into the driver's seat. The truck followed the Humvee across the river, and soon they were rolling up the far bank towards the village.

Drawing closer, their first impressions seemed to be confirmed that the villagers had abandoned their homes and fled. Maybe they'd return and maybe they wouldn't; right now, for Ben and the others, the shelled buildings further up the hill were the main priority. A narrow dirt road, not much more than a track, skirted past the village and led up the parched, rocky slope towards the orphanage.

Up close, the devastation there looked much worse. A chilly wind was blowing down from the escarpment and whistled through the desolate, fire-blackened ruins. They'd already known what to expect, from the report Holt had been given by Hassan, his man in Abu Dhabi. Even so, the extent of the damage was terrible to see, knowing that hundreds of children might have been inside the building at the time of the attack.

Everyone climbed out of the vehicles, the prince and his men emerging last from the back of the truck and gathering in a silent crowd.

'The fuckers certainly did a number on this place, didn't they?' Nobby Scraggs muttered, scowling at the wrecked buildings. They had never been grand, that was for sure. But they had provided a secure and stable home for generations of kids for whom life had been unkind until Francine Blanchet and her brother Patrick took them into their loving care. It was sad to see them now.

'Nothing we haven't seen before,' Wolf said.

Father Bugnolio shivered and crossed himself, muttering, 'I fear the worst has happened here.'

'We know they made it to safety,' Ben reminded him. 'Francine Blanchet was in contact with Chris's contacts after it happened. Only her brother was killed.'

But the priest shook his head dolefully, far from reassured. 'Where is safe in this terrible place? God help them. And us,' he added.

'I don't like it here,' Ramin said, looking around him at the deepening shadows as the sun sank over the escarpment. 'Where are we going to camp?'

'Quit bitching, Ramin,' Madison snapped at him. 'We've made it this far.'

'She's right,' Aziz said softly, placing a hand on his colleague's tense shoulder. 'Everything will be fine, you'll see.'

But from all the grim faces it was clear that nobody shared Aziz's optimism, genuine or not. To Ben, it felt like a reprise of the moment they'd arrived at Zakara and found nothing but emptiness and desolation there. This time around, it seemed pretty damned unlikely that Francine and her forty orphans were going to suddenly come running out from the ruins to greet them. He was getting a sinking feeling deep in his gut that told him they'd come here for nothing.

The hard, stony ground was littered with shell casings and bits of machine gun belt linkage. Picking up a spent cartridge, Ben saw the bottlenecked case was still untarnished and quite fresh. Meanwhile Wolf had moved off down the hill and was squatting down to carefully examine the many crisscrossed vehicle tracks in the dirt while there was still enough light to make them out. In the SAS, Wolf had been the best tracker Ben had ever worked with, able to read a bent blade of grass or a dislodged pebble like a guidebook.

'How many troops were here, Jaden?' Ben called over to him.

Wolf stood up and dusted his hands as he walked back up the hill to join them, his eyes narrowed against the sun. 'Hard to say. Tracks have been blown over by the wind. A lot, that's for sure.'

'Let's hope they don't come back in a hurry,' Madison said.

'If they do, we'll be ready for 'em,' Baldacci said with a nasty leer, and patted his M4.

'But not before we get our job done,' Holt said, repeating his mantra. 'That's what we came here to do, find these kids.'

'Amen to that,' said Nielsen.

'If they're still here,' said Liebowitz. 'Gotta say, guys, if it was me, I wouldn't have hung around this godforsaken place. I'll be surprised if we find anything more than a coupla gecko lizards and rat snakes living in these rocks.'

'We'll find them,' Holt said. 'We have to.' Those last words sounded as though he needed to convince himself, too.

'And what if we don't, man?' Liebowitz asked him. 'I mean, I always believed we would. You know that, right? But now we're here . . .' His voice trailed off.

Holt made no reply, and turned toward the truck. Ben could see the strain playing on the man, and felt pity for him. Holt had put all his hopes and energy into this rescue mission. The thought of it coming to nothing must be especially tough for him to bear.

Ben found himself wondering what inner demons were tormenting the American. Ben knew all about inner demons, from personal experience. At one time, his own guilty feelings over his lost sister had been the driving factor behind his relentless quest to travel the world saving as many kidnapped children as he could. Those kinds of motivations could drive a man to the most extreme lengths to do what he thought was the right thing. They could also lead a man straight to hell. Ben had come close to ending up there himself. Maybe Chris Holt already was.

'We'll worry about that if and when it happens,' Ben said to Liebowitz. 'For now, there's not much we can do before morning. I suggest we find a building that still has three walls and a roof on it, set up camp for the night and get some kip. Tomorrow could be a long day.'

Chapter 40

One end of what had once been a dormitory still had enough intact, uncharred roof timbers to provide shelter for twenty-three huddled bodies. The few blankets and sleeping bags they had were shared out as democratically as possible, and they made themselves as comfortable as they could.

Meanwhile, twenty-three mouths needed to be fed and watered. Wolf gathered bits of burnt timber to use as charcoal while Ben built a fire in the remains of a clay chimney at the roofless end of the building, over which to reheat what they had left to eat. Even on meagre rations, the evening meal polished off every scrap of their remaining provisions.

'That's the last of it,' Wolf said, doling out the final portion, which happened to be for the prince. He and his fellow Pathfinders were staying quiet, but looking a little healthier than they had back at their temple hideout. Handing him his mess tin Wolf said, 'I'm afraid we weren't able to offer you cucumber sandwiches and champagne, your Royal Excellency. Maybe I'll pop out to Fortnum's tomorrow for a hamper or two.'

'Leave it out, pal,' one of the prince's men muttered, giving Wolf a challenging look that he quickly averted when Wolf turned his way with killer eyes.

'I'm sorry, did you say something?' Wolf asked.

'No, nothing.'

Wolf's hard expression melted into a golden grin. 'My mistake. Enjoy your meal, fellas. I don't know where the next one's coming from.'

There were moans and muttering from the men, especially among the Americans, who resented the drain on their provisions even more bitterly now they were gone. The most vociferous of all was Hank Schulz, a man more in love with his belly than the usual ex-marine. Ben had previously noticed him sneaking the odd extra helping for himself, when he thought nobody was looking. Now he was taking the loss of their food supplies very badly, putting on a show of clutching at his stomach and complaining to anyone who would listen that he was so hungry he could eat the north end of a skunk moving south, and other variations on that theme.

Ben stepped outside, wandered around the ruins and paused by a shell-destroyed wall to gaze eastwards across the dark hills. From up here the village was pitch black against the surrounding landscape and the faintly moonlit glimmer of the river. The night was perfectly still, apart from the soft moan of the wind. He'd been standing there for a while, lost in his thoughts, when he became aware of the light footsteps coming up behind him. His body tensed at the sound purely out of instinct, and he'd have whirled around with his pistol in his hand if not for the scent of her that wafted on the air.

She came and stood close by, gazing the same direction he was. The breeze caught her hair, and glancing at her for a moment it struck him how beautiful she looked in this wild place, as though she was part of it.

'What a glorious night,' she murmured. 'It's almost peaceful here. You wouldn't think you could find much serenity in a place that's seen so much blood and war.'

'That it has,' he said. 'And there'll be more before it's over.'

'You think this country will ever be free of suffering?'

'You could ask Father B to put that question to God, in his prayers,' Ben said. 'Only He knows the answer for sure. Personally, I have my doubts.' Then, not wanting to sound too negative, he added, 'Then again, it's not all bad. You found your father's caves, after all.'

'Screw the damn caves,' she said, shaking her head with a sudden flash of bitterness in her voice. 'When I saw these ruins and thought about all those poor little kids, it really brought the truth home to me. Maybe Holt's right. Who gives a goddamn about archaeology at a time like this? What the hell was I thinking, gallivanting off on my own in the middle of a war zone in search of a bunch of stupid old relics?'

'Your dad would have done the same thing.'

She nodded. 'But he wouldn't have put everyone at risk for it, the way I did.' She turned to him, and for the first time he could see the doubt and fear in her eyes. She asked earnestly, 'Do you think we'll ever make it home again, Ben?'

'Whatever happens,' he said, 'we'll face it together.'

'That's no kind of answer.'

'It's the only one I can give you.'

She slipped a hand into his and pressed closer to him, her head against his shoulder. 'I'm so damn sorry you risked yourself for my worthless ass,' she said, 'and I'm even sorrier if I went and got us both killed for it. But I'm glad you're with me. If that makes any sense.'

Ben replied, 'I wouldn't have it any other way. And nobody's going to get killed. You least of all.'

'You say that, but it's not what you're thinking, Ben.'

'You can tell what I'm thinking?'

'Some things,' she replied. 'Not everything.'

They stood for a while longer, neither speaking, still hand in hand, each of them listening to the plaintive murmur of the wind. He sensed she wanted to say more to him, but felt uncomfortable doing it. That made him uncomfortable too, because he was aware of a strong desire to wrap his arm around her shoulders, draw her even closer and kiss her. He couldn't help but feel that would be betraying Abbie Logan. Even though he knew that Abbie was in the past now and there was nothing to betray, and she'd laugh at him for thinking it.

With an effort, he put both himself and Madison out of their misery by saying, 'We should go back inside and get some sleep.'

'Yeah,' she sighed, reluctant. 'We should.' She squeezed his hand, then let it go, and they walked back in silence to rejoin the others. The mood was sombre. In one corner Aziz and Ramin were talking low, almost a whisper. Father Bugnolio was reading his Bible in the dying firelight. Wolf and Baldacci were quietly cleaning and oiling the gleaming black weapon components that they'd field stripped and laid out on a blanket. Holt and Nielsen were off somewhere in the night, taking the first watch.

Every muscle in Ben's body was aching after the long journey here, and he felt low in spirits and incredibly tired as he found a dark corner of the building away from the rest to sleep in for a few hours until he took over the watch from Holt. Madison settled close by, wrapping herself up in a sleeping bag.

Despite his fatigue Ben took a long time to drift off. He lay awake long after she'd fallen asleep. A shaft of moon-glow shining through the partly ruined roof cast a milky pool across her. Gently, delicately, he reached out to brush away a jet-black gypsy lock of hair that had fallen over her face. His fingertips lingered there for just a moment, caressing the peach softness of her cheek as lightly as a butterfly.

Glad you're with me.

Ben rolled over and went to sleep.

He was up a couple of hours later to take the next watch, careful not to wake Madison as he stepped over her sleeping body. He and Wolf met outside, spoke briefly and then split up to go to their respective observation points. Ben saw no sign of movement anywhere across the vast horizon for the next few hours. So far, it looked as though their pursuers had lost track of them.

So then why did he keep getting that uncomfortable feeling, inside the part of his mind that housed his trusty sixth sense, that something bad was just around the corner? It felt like being inside the eye of the storm. One minute everything seems peaceful and tranquil and you think you can let down your guard a little. The next, all hell breaks loose and you're right back in the thick of it again.

'You're just being paranoid,' he told himself, and went back to watching.

At first light, he and Wolf left the camp and made their way on foot down to the village. Neither man had slept much, and Wolf looked as drawn as Ben felt. 'Maddie not coming with us?' Wolf asked casually as they crunched down the loose slope.

Ben looked at him. 'She's still sleeping.'

'Oh,' Wolf said, with a knowing twinkle. 'Thought you two had disappeared off somewhere for a long time last night. That is to say, long enough.'

'You can get that out of your head. She's just a friend.'

Wolf chuckled. 'You tell her that. I don't think she'd agree with you. Come to think of it,' he reflected, 'I'm not so sure you agree with you either, deep down.'

'What are you talking about?'

'Oh, come on, Ben. It's pretty obvious what's going on between you two.'

Irritated, Ben was about to ask his friend what was so bloody obvious when, glancing down, he saw a brownish-green scorpion appear from under a rock dislodged by their passing and scuttle over his boot. He kicked it away and it vanished among the scrubby bushes.

'I found one of those things in my kit this morning,' Wolf said, eyeing where it had gone. 'You know what they call them? The deathstalker. One tiny sting, and you're as stiff as a board in five minutes flat.'

'Just another reason for travelling to Afghanistan,' Ben said.

As they reached the village the first streaks of dawn were creeping up into the eastern sky, bathing the adobe houses and narrow dirt streets in a purplish light. The place was as still and silent as a ghost town. The one living presence they hadn't noticed when they'd passed by yesterday, and to which they were alerted now by a soft bleating *mehhhehhh* coming from beyond the broken-down village wall, was the small herd of shaggy brown, black and white goats that must have been the former occupants of the corral nearby. The animals hadn't strayed far, staying close to water and foraging among the slightly lusher vegetation growing near the riverbank.

'Well if anything can survive up here,' Wolf said, 'it's them. Until a snow leopard comes down from the mountains looking for his dinner.'

'Or a wolf,' Ben said, and Wolf smiled.

They entered the village and explored the empty alleyways. Coming to a low-roofed adobe house whose door was lying half ajar, Ben knocked on it and pushed it tentatively open, calling out in Pashto, 'Hello? Anybody here?' The answering silence was no surprise. These people were gone, run and hidden when the troops launched their attack on the orphanage in the fear that the village would be next. Maybe they'd come back; maybe they never would.

'Certainly left in a hurry, didn't they?' Wolf said, pointing at a trestle table where three abandoned dishes still contained the remains of some clay-baked bread. 'One thing about the tribal militiamen, they might be no angels but they have respect for the local villagers. They depend on them for supplies, and trade with them. But the Taliban don't give a shit. One day they might come marching in demanding that the women cook for them and wash their clothes. The next, they might just decide to kill everybody.'

He picked up a piece of bread, inspected it for weevils and took a bite out of it. 'A little on the stale side. I wouldn't recommend this to anyone who didn't have metal teeth.'

'That rules out the normal folks.'

'Thanks,' Wolf said, swallowing.

'Speaking of eating,' Ben said, 'that's something we're going to have to take care of, and soon. Got a lot more mouths to feed now.'

'Those goats back there,' Wolf said. 'Enough to keep us all going a while. Roast goat again. How yummy.'

'We're lucky we don't have to eat it raw,' Ben reminded him.

'Brings back so many fond memories,' Wolf chuckled, rolling his eyes. 'Not sure if our royal guest will appreciate such comforts, though. I don't reckon they're often on the menu at Buck Palace.'

'The trick will be catching them,' Ben said. Wolf nodded, thinking the same thing he was. The sound of a gunshot would travel for miles and alert anyone in the vicinity, friend or foe, to their presence here.

'You ever tried to outrun a goat?' Wolf said. 'Keeps you fit, that's for sure.'

'There are other ways,' Ben replied. On the trestle table was a large, well-worn knife the villagers had been using to cut up their bread. He picked it up, then stepped over to a corner where a long-handled broomstick stood propped against the wall. With the head knocked off, the broom made a decent spear shaft. He started hunting around for something to lash the knife handle to it.

'Gone native at last, I see,' Wolf said. 'Getting in touch with the old ancestral spirit. Nice.'

'Whatever works,' Ben replied, finding a strip of cured goat leather that someone had been fashioning into a belt. 'This'll do.'

'Well, Tarzan, I'll leave you to it. Got to pee.' Wolf disappeared, as Ben got on making his makeshift spear. When Wolf returned a couple of minutes later, he was looking pleased with himself. 'I found something better,' he said, showing Ben.

Wolf's discovery was an old wooden recurve bow, battered and weathered but still with plenty of spring in it and a fairly fresh bowstring fitted. Its former owner had obviously used it a good deal and taken care of it. The arrows in the goat leather quiver were homemade too, carefully fitted with flights cut from something like vulture feathers and sharp steel tips fashioned out of razor blades. It was a crude but deadly tool.

'You any good with one of these?' Wolf asked him. 'They're the one projectile weapon I can't shoot for shit.'

'Been a while,' Ben replied. He'd once, briefly, been involved with a medal-winning lady archer. Another romance that hadn't ended well, but he'd learned a lot from watching how she handled a bow and arrow.

'You kill 'em and I'll dress 'em,' Wolf said. 'Then whatever else happens out here, at least we won't starve to death.

Not for a couple of days, anyway. Unless we get shot to bits first.'

'That's what I like so much about you,' Ben told him. 'That eternal optimism.'

'My best feature.'

They left the house and wandered back out of the village, Ben armed with the bow with an arrow fitted and the quiver over his shoulder, Wolf carrying the spear just in case. 'My mouth's watering already,' Wolf said.

The sound of bleating led them towards some thorny bushes a few yards beyond the village perimeter. On the humans' approach a young brown nanny goat was startled out from the cover of the bushes and broke into a run. Ben took aim at the moving target, drew the bowstring back all the way and let go. The arrow whistled through the air, passed three inches over the running animal's shoulder and embedded itself with a vibrating *thonk* into one of the wooden posts of the livestock corral.

'Fine shot,' Wolf commented. Ben swore and quickly plucked a second arrow from his quiver. The frightened goat had gone ploughing deep into another, denser, thicket of bushes, while the rest had scattered in four directions and were rapidly disappearing out of effective range. He'd worry about them later. He moved towards the bushes, drawing the bow again, this time determined not to miss.

Something rustled. He stepped closer, searching for his target, ready to let the arrow fly. The goat was in there, just a few feet away. He could see its brown hide through the foliage, moving slightly. He took a breath and drew the bowstring until the ball of his thumb touched his cheekbone. This was it. The killing shot. And food for the hungry.

But then, with a shock, Ben lowered the bow and released the tension from the string.

Because his target, cowering terrified inside the bushes and looking up at him with huge eyes, wasn't a goat. It was a young child.

Chapter 41

The girl was about eleven or twelve years old, and she knew exactly how close she'd just come to being skewered with an arrow. Her shocked face was streaked with tears and dirt, and her long jet-black hair was all awry. She was wrapped in a dusty robe the same shade of brown as the goat, which now burst out from the far side of the clump of bushes, fixed its hunters with a slit-pupilled look of indignation and ran off to join its companions.

Ben laid down the bow, Wolf dropped his spear and carbine, and they hurried over to the young girl before she could scramble to her feet and escape from them. But as Ben waded into the bushes he saw that she couldn't run off in any case, because her slender little left ankle was all swollen and obviously quite badly sprained. She shrank away from him with a whimper of fear and pain.

'It's all right,' he said to her, speaking Pashto in a soft, reassuring tone. 'We're your friends. We won't hurt you. My name's Ben. What's yours?'

It was hard to overcome the child's fear of these two towering strangers, but as she began to understand they weren't going to kill her, she began to open up a little. Her name was Safiya, and she said she'd come down to the village before dawn to gather some water. She pointed down the slope towards the river, where the pole and two buckets she'd been carrying were lying by the bank. Clutching her sore ankle, she explained how she'd slipped on a wet rock and hurt herself. Then, seeing two men with guns descending the hill towards the village, she'd been afraid and managed to crawl up the river bank as far as the bushes, to hide from them.

'She must be one of the villagers,' Wolf said to Ben. Then switching to Pashto, which he spoke as fluently as Ben did, he pointed at the houses and asked her, 'Safiya, do you live here with your mum and dad?' The girl stared at him in confusion for a moment, then shook her head.

'Where did you come from this morning?' Ben asked her. She raised a skinny little arm from the folds of her robe and pointed, not at the village but up the hill in the direction he and Wolf had come. Ben shook his head and was about to say, 'No, you can't have come from there,' when he realised what she was telling them.

'She doesn't live with her mum and dad,' Ben said to Wolf in English. 'She doesn't have any. She's one of the orphans.'

Turning back to the girl and speaking again in her own language he asked, 'Do you know a lady called Francine Blanchet?'

Safiya's doe eyes opened wide in surprise and she nodded, all the fear vanishing from her face at the mention of the name. 'Mère Blanchet,' she replied, pronouncing it the French way. 'She's our teacher. She looks after us.'

'And where is Mère Blanchet now?' Ben asked. Without hesitation the girl raised her arm again and pointed in the same direction as before, up the hill towards the orphanage. Which made no sense. But then Ben suddenly understood that she wasn't pointing *at* the orphanage, but beyond it, in the direction of the escarpment to the west. That was when everything Madison had been telling him came back in a flash.

'The caves,' he said to Wolf. 'They're hiding up in the caves.'

'Well, I'll be damned,' Wolf muttered. 'They were there the whole time, right under our noses.'

Trying to keep his voice calm in case he frightened her, Ben said, 'Tell me, Safiya. Are all the other children there? Is everyone okay?'

Yes, she replied in a tiny voice, but they were very hungry and thirsty, and terribly scared. Mère Blanchet was too old to walk such a long way, with her stick, so she had been sending the older girls down in turn to fetch water and whatever food they could find in the village. They'd brought back all they could but there was nothing left to eat, and they could only carry a little water at a time. As she talked, tears welled up in her eyes and she began to cry. 'I did my best to fetch the water. I didn't want to let Mère Blanchet down. But my ankle hurts so much. Is it broken?'

'Let me take a look at it,' Ben said. 'No, I think you've just given it a nasty twist,' he reassured her after a careful, extremely gentle examination. 'It'll be all right in a day or two, if you rest it.'

'But what about the water?' she asked anxiously. 'Who's going to fetch the water now?'

'Don't you worry about that, baby doll,' Wolf said. 'You and your friends will soon have all the water you need. And food, too. We'll take care of all of you, we promise.' He wiped a tear from his eye. He could be a real softy at times, that Wolf.

The goats all but forgotten now, they hurried back up to the orphanage with Ben carrying Safiya in his arms. As they walked through the scorched, devastated buildings of what had been her home and sanctuary, the child began to cry again. The sound brought Madison and Father Bugnolio rushing out to meet them.

'Look what we found,' Wolf announced. 'You're not going to believe this, folks.'

'Oh, the poor dear child!'

'Hey there, sweetie pie. Where did you come from?'

Inside, the sight of so many more big men with guns was intimidating to little Safiya and she went very quiet, having to be coaxed into speaking to anyone. They laid her down on a soft nest of blankets and Madison sat with her, holding her hand and murmuring soft words that the child might not have been able to understand, but which soon soothed away her fear. Father B was a reassuring presence, hovering nearby with a saintly look of benevolence. Ben fetched a first-aid kit from the Humvee and hurried back to administer a couple of painkillers they had left and get to work binding up the little girl's ankle. 'Safiya, these are my friends, Madison and Father Bugnolio,' he told her as she stoically held out her leg for him to wrap the dressing. 'They're going to help me to look after you.'

'Is the lady your wife?' she asked, with the direct innocence of a child.

'No, she's not my wife,' he replied.

'And the man, is he a priest?' she asked, darting a look at Father B.

'Yes, he is.'

'He looks a hundred years old.'

Father Bugnolio cleared his throat. 'Thank you, my child. I do speak Pashto, as it happens.'

Ben smiled. Then sensing another presence behind him, he looked around and saw that the prince had joined them.

'I'm good with kids,' the prince whispered. 'Is there anything I can do?'

'Just be your charming self,' Madison told him.

'And this is my friend Richard,' Ben said to Safiya, laying a hand on his shoulder. The prince sat by her and clasped her other hand with what looked like real tenderness. 'Hello, little lady. Don't you worry about a thing, now. You're going to be okay.'

While they were attending to the child, Holt, Scraggs and the others gathered around Wolf to hear his report on their exploratory recce of the village. 'What about food?' Schulz kept asking urgently, too famished to care about anything much else. 'Did you find anything to eat down there?'

'There are some goats running loose nearby,' Wolf told him. 'They're domesticated, so they won't go far. We'll go back later and harvest a couple, okay?'

'Why not now? We're fuckin' dying here, dude.'

'Because we have more important things to deal with, Hank,' Wolf said in a smooth but dangerous voice.

It wasn't long before little Safiya was persuaded to guide them up to the cave where she'd been hiding with Mère

317

Blanchet and the other children. They didn't yet know if the Humvee would make it over the terrain, so it was decided that they'd make the hike on foot. The child rode piggy-back on Ben's shoulders as, together with Madison, Wolf, Holt and Baldacci, they set off up the hillside. Father Bugnolio insisted on coming too, and to his credit, so did the prince. There were no smart quips from Wolf this time. He was as hard-faced and serious as he'd been back in his days as a hired assassin.

It was a twenty-minute trek up the barren hillside, winding up and up through the rocks until the cliff face of the escarpment loomed high overhead. Without Safiya's directions they might never have found the entrance to the cave, just a narrow fissure at the foot of the cliff that they had to squeeze through one at a time but which opened up after a few yards into a much larger chamber. 'That way,' Safiya said in Pashto, her little voice echoing against the rock walls. Ben went first, the child ducking her head to avoid the low ceiling, her arms wrapped around Ben's neck. Madison followed second in line, and Wolf brought up the rear.

'It's a real warren in here,' Wolf muttered as they wound their way deeper and deeper by torchlight. One twisting shaft branched off into another, then another, a veritable underground maze dating back to the mists of prehistory, carved out by successive ice age after ice age, lying almost completely undiscovered until now. Their beams were yellowing as the batteries faded, but they could still see enough to make out the weird rock formations, stalagmites and stalactites around them.

'This is amazing,' Madison murmured, gazing around her. Her own torch was fading badly, casting a dim trembling pool over the walls. 'I'll bet these poor kids are the first people to have set foot in here for a million years.'

Then she stopped dead in her tracks and stared at something in the deep, dark shadows that Ben had walked past without noticing. She made a strange gulping sound.

Sensing something was wrong, Ben paused and looked back over his shoulder. 'Madison, what is it?'

In a tremulous voice she said, 'Ben, would you pass me your torch, please? This one's on its way out.'

He handed her his own, which was only slightly brighter, and she pointed the beam into the deep recess in the rock wall where she'd been staring. Suddenly he was able to see what had caught her attention.

Madison was transfixed. 'Scratch what I said about a million years. More like twenty-three hundred, to be precise.'

Chapter 42

The skeleton was little more than a heap of spindly dry bones, gnawed at in places by rats. Ben had seen plenty of human skeletal remains before. But he'd never seen any that were still clad in the bronze armour their owner had been wearing when he met his death millennia ago, three centuries before the birth of Christ.

In life he must have been a mighty warrior, standing well over six foot tall in all his splendour. The great bronze helm, still sporting some of its bright red plumes, had its visor open so that the bare skull peered out from inside, appearing to be grinning at them. The soldier's heroic muscled cuirass was still attached to his ribcage by ancient decayed leather straps, the ones the rats hadn't eaten. The fingers of one bony hand still clutched the hilt of his leaf-bladed bronze sword, and from his other arm, dragged down to the cave floor by its weight, hung a magnificent circular battle shield embossed with the motif of a bull's head. The ornate greaves that had protected his legs from ankle to knee had collapsed the gnawed remains of his fibulas and tibias. There was nothing much left of the leather sandals the soldier would have worn on his long, weary march through these mountains of ancient Bactria.

'Oh, him,' Safiya said nonchalantly, close to Ben's ear. 'We have to walk past him all the time. He's horrible, but you get used to it. Tell your friend she shouldn't be afraid. He won't do anything.'

'It's unbelievable,' Madison gasped. 'So the legend's true. Alexander's men really did take shelter in the caves of Gurghazar. Oh, if only Dad could have been here to see this.'

She took a step closer to the skeleton, shining the torch as she reached out with the other hand to gently stroke the bronze cuirass. But the remains were so fragile that even a slight disturbance was enough to make the skull sag from its bony shoulders. The helmet visor snapped shut and an enormous bristly spider that had been nesting there came darting out and ran across Madison's hand before she snatched it away with a yelp. 'Yikes!'

'Dude's seen better days,' said Baldacci, chortling.

Ben noticed the diamond-shaped hole that had been punched through the Greek's breastplate by some long, pointed weapon, probably a spear blade. 'Looks like someone must've had an argument.'

'Fighting over the last scrap of camel meat, most likely,' Wolf muttered.

Holt gave a derisive snort, as though he'd seen it all a thousand times before. 'That's great. Totally fascinating, I'm sure. Shall we move on now?'

Madison could barely tear herself away, enormous bristly spiders and all. 'I've got to take him with me.'

'That'd be tomb robbing, wouldn't it?' Ben said.

'Salvaging precious historical artefacts isn't tomb robbing.' Madison was her father's daughter, all right.

'Anyhow, it's too much stuff to carry. We'll come back for him if we get the chance.'

Reluctantly, very reluctantly, she agreed, handed Ben back his torch, and they pressed deeper into the tunnels. 'We're almost there,' Safiya piped excitedly. 'Wait until Mère Blanchet sees what I've brought her.'

Around a couple more twists, and Safiya cried out, 'Mère Blanchet! Mère Blanchet! I'm back!'

The sound of raised voices from deeper inside the cave echoed towards them. A moment later, the dim glow of a candle lantern appeared from the shadows up ahead. The figure holding the lantern raised it up to see better, and Ben saw a small, wiry white woman with silver hair, peering at them in the flickering light. She was wearing a long plain robe that looked almost like a nun's tunic. 'Safiya? I was so worried about you!' she called out in Pashto. Then she stiffened, seeing the torch beams and blinking from the dazzle. 'Safiya, what's happening? Who are these people?'

Ben began to speak, wanting to assure her they were no threat, but she backed away a step and in a strong authoritative voice shouted, 'Stop! Who are you?' Something metallic glinted in her hand. A small, old-fashioned but still perfectly lethal revolver the woman had whipped out of her tunic and was pointing straight at Ben's stomach.

'No, Mère Blanchet,' Safiya protested. 'These are my new friends and they've come to rescue us!'

'My name is Hope, Madame Blanchet,' Ben said to the woman, speaking English to show he wasn't one of the men who'd destroyed her orphanage. 'Please, lower your weapon. We want to help you. All of you.'

Little faces were peeking out from behind the woman's. A voice squeaked out, 'Safiya!' Safiya called back to her friends, 'Bashira! Gulnaz!'

Francine Blanchet hesitated, then let the gun down, but only a little. 'Well, Mr Hope,' she replied in perfect English with a strong remnant of a French accent. 'Whoever you are, you're very aptly named. And equally lucky that I didn't shoot you. Now please oblige me by telling me exactly what you and these people are doing here.'

Father Bugnolio laid a hand on Ben's shoulder and stepped forward to introduce himself. 'Sister, in God's name I give you my word that we come in peace. We found this poor child hurt by the river, and have tended to her minor injury. We come to offer you protection, sustenance and, God willing, rescue.'

Father B's words had their effect, winning enough of Francine Blanchet's trust that she put the revolver away. Now that the tension was relieved the children came running out from behind her skirts, greeting their friend with laughter and tears of happiness. For all their excitement at seeing Safiya again they looked thin and pale from lack of food.

Ben handed the child to Francine Blanchet, who took her in her arms with surprising strength. 'Bless you for taking care of her. And I apologise for the manner of my welcome,' she said with a smile. 'But one never knows who might coming knocking on one's door these days. Please, please, come inside, all of you.'

She led them a little way further along the craggy passage and through an inverted V-shaped cleft into a wide, high-ceilinged grotto where more candle lanterns flickered in the darkness. More children were gathered inside the grotto, children everywhere. Ben tried to do a rough head-count, but it was immediately obvious there were far more of them than the forty they'd expected, at least half as many again. Some of the kids swarmed around Safiya as Francine set her down on a blanket; others were hiding in the shadows, the braver or more curious ones coming closer to peer at these strange visitors. They seemed especially fascinated by Madison, possibly the only western woman they'd ever known apart from Mère Blanchet.

'Welcome to our humble home,' Francine said. 'It isn't quite what we have been used to these many years past, but we are safe here, for the moment, if He so chooses. Now, please, sit with me. Yes, Gulnaz, what is it?' – speaking kindly to the small girl who was tugging at her sleeve. She bent down and listened as the child whispered in her ear, darting sidelong glances at Madison.

'She wants to thank you for helping her friend, and she also wishes to know if all western ladies are as beautiful as you are,' Francine told her.

Madison laughed. 'Tell her nobody in my country is as lovely as she and all her friends are.' She stroked the girl's hair. 'Gulnaz, that's a pretty name. What does it mean?'

'It means as cute as a flower,' Francine said.

'I never saw a flower half as cute,' Madison replied, smiling.

The child whispered again into Francine's ear. 'And she also wants to know if you have seen Vida.'

324

'Who's Vida?'

'Her doll. She's extremely attached to her, but we lost her when we had to leave our home. Now, child,' she said, gently urging Gulnaz away. 'Go back and be with the others. The grown-ups have a lot of talking to do.'

They did, and Ben was happy to let Holt do a lot of it. Francine listened attentively as he explained what had brought him and his group to Afghanistan, and described their efforts to get as many people out of Kabul as possible before the iron curtain had clamped down. He told her how Hassan Baghdadi, their mutual contact in Abu Dhabi, had first alerted their aid organisation to the existence of her orphanage and the troubles that had descended on them. 'Our condolences for your late brother.'

'Thank you. He was a wonderful human being. As is dear Hassan, bless his soul. And so, all of you belong to this organisation?' she asked, looking with some confusion at Madison and Father Bugnolio. 'And you as well, young man?' she asked the prince. If she even faintly recognised his famous face in this unlikely setting, she didn't show it. The truth was, she'd been living out here in the middle of nowhere for so long, sequestered from the rest of the world, that she probably had no knowledge whatsoever of what went on in the elevated social circles of some island nation halfway across the globe.

'Our group has picked up a few new members along the way,' Ben said. 'Myself included. Madison and Father Bugnolio here are refugees from Kabul, along with two more of their friends. We're a bit of a motley bunch but we're ready to do whatever we can to help you and the children.'

'You are extremely welcome,' she replied. 'We would certainly be grateful for some food and water. The few provisions we were able to salvage from the mission are completely gone, and the children are badly in need. For my own part, an old woman like me can live virtually on fresh air, but they're young and growing.'

'We have vehicles,' Ben said. 'We can use them to fetch a lot more water from the river than a child can carry in two buckets. As for food, there's enough fresh meat walking around down there to keep everyone alive, for a while at least. Beyond that, we're going to have to figure out a plan to move you all away to safety.'

'I'm not sure there is such a place any longer,' she said with a sad smile. 'Not in Afghanistan.'

'I was thinking of somewhere else,' Ben said.

'To evacuate us all to another country? My dear young friend, you're talking about the impossible. There are sixty-four children here, aged between seven and thirteen. How on earth can it be done?'

'We can only try,' Ben said.

'Are you in contact with the outside?' Francine asked. It was a very pertinent question, because as Ben knew perfectly well, the prospect of organising such a large-scale escape over the border without some kind of outside connections was extremely poor.

Holt shook his head. 'I'm sorry to say we were, but then our sat phone was damaged.'

She nodded. 'Ah, yes. Modern technology is a wonderful thing, until it stops working. I, too, have a sat phone. That's how I was able to call dear Hassan and put out the call for help that God has now answered. But one of the girls knocked it by accident and it fell quite hard against a rock, and now it seems to be broken. I have been carrying it around with me in the hopes that it would start working again. To no avail, sadly.' She reached into the folds of her tunic and took the phone out to show them. 'Quite dead, you see? Something must be broken inside.'

At the sight of it, Holt went bolt rigid with amazement, his eyebrows flew up and his jaw dropped open. 'Holy motherfucking shit!' he burst out.

Some of the kids obviously understood a few words of English; their stunned looks quickly gave way to tittering delight. Both Francine and Father Bugnolio turned on Holt with heavy frowns of disapproval. 'Please!' Francine hissed, furious. 'Such language to use in front of the children! Where do you think you are, in a sewer?'

'I'm sorry,' Holt stammered, turning scarlet and pointing at the phone in her hands. 'It's just that that's an Iridium 9555. The same model that we have.'

'And so?' she said icily.

Ben remembered Liebowitz saying that if by some miracle they could find a spare motherboard for their Iridium, he might be able to get it up and running again. This might be the miracle they'd been waiting for.

Holt explained, 'And so it's possible one of my guys back down the hillside could switch out the parts and put together a working phone.'

Francine shrugged, still not quite ready to forgive him. 'Well, that sounds promising. Take it, by all means. But let us hear no more of these disgraceful vulgar profanities, if you please.'

It was a quietly excited, if thoroughly chastised and penitent, Chris Holt who soon afterwards accompanied Ben, Wolf and Baldacci back the way they'd come through the cave, leaving Madison, Father Bugnolio and the prince with Francine and the children. 'This could really save our asses,' Holt said, clutching the sat phone as they emerged from the cave mouth and started hurrying down the rocky slope. 'If we can find a way to make it as far west as the Iranian border, there are people I might be able to get to meet us there. Then south and across the Persian Gulf into UAE, and we'd be home and dry.'

'But how the hell are we supposed to carry them all?' Wolf said. 'Forty, we might have been able to manage in the truck. But sixty-four? Plus the rest of us, it comes to well over eighty people to transport.'

Ben had been thinking the same, and there were too many ifs and mights in Holt's plan for his liking, but he forced himself to stay focused on the immediate situation. 'We'll cross that bridge when we come to it. In the meantime, Jaden, you and I will drive the Humvee back to the village, take care of the water supply and see about bagging a few of those goats.'

'Let's hope you can fire an arrow straight this time,' Wolf said.

'Maybe you'd like to try your luck, Robin Hood,' Ben said.

'I told you I'm no good with one of tho—'

But Wolf never finished his sentence, because he was cut short by the staccato reports of automatic gunfire that came echoing up the hillside and rolled all around the valley below, sharp and clear in the still air.

Chapter 43

They froze as the sound of gunfire paused for an instant, then crackled back into action, single shots interspersed with short bursts. On such a clear day as this, across open hills and plains, the high-decibel reports of a supersonic assault rifle round could carry an enormous distance. But these were coming from not far off.

'Jesus Christ, we're under attack,' Baldacci yelled, instinctively unslinging his weapon and flicking off the safety.

'No, it's not for us,' Ben said. 'It's coming from down by the river.'

'Who the hell's doing all that shooting?' demanded Holt.

Wolf's face tightened. He groaned. 'Shit. It's Hank. I told him about the goats. He's been prattling on and on about how starving he is. The stupid bloody fool must have gone down there to bag one.'

'And sent a telegram to anyone within five miles that we're here,' Holt growled, livid with anger. 'I swear, when I get hold of that moron I'll wring his neck.'

'What's done is done,' Ben said. 'Let's keep moving.'

The firing seemed to have stopped, at least for the moment. They continued hurriedly down the hillside and reached the orphanage to find that the Humvee was gone. Moments later they discovered that, sure enough, Hank Schulz had taken it down to the village for his impromptu hunting spree. 'I couldn't stop him,' Nielsen protested to a furious Holt. 'The guy was out of his mind with hunger. I thought he was gonna shoot *me* if I got in his way.'

'Who goes hunting with a full-auto carbine?' Wolf said, shaking his head in disgust.

'A fucking meathead, that's who,' Baldacci replied. 'If Chris doesn't tear the asshole to pieces, I will.'

While they were waiting for Schulz to return, Holt showed Liebowitz Francine Blanchet's Iridium sat phone. Liebowitz stared at it as though it was a lump of kryptonite. 'Where the fuck did you get this?'

'It doesn't work. But can we use it to fix ours?'

Liebowitz grabbed their own non-functioning phone from his kit and laid the two side by side. They were exactly identical apart from the extra scuff marks on the casing on Francine's handset where it had been dropped, and the bullet hole that had drilled through theirs and killed it dead. Ben and Wolf watched as Liebowitz whipped out a tiny screwdriver and set to work removing both casings to expose the electronic innards, which he scrutinised carefully, peering from one phone to the other.

'Well?' Holt asked impatiently.

Liebowitz looked up at him with a grin. 'Yup. Looks like the motherboard on their phone is totally intact. No promises, but if I can't cannibalise all the parts we need and get this sucker working, I'm Tweetie Bird. Might take me a while, though. Without a proper soldering iron I'm gonna have to improvise something.'

'Take this,' Wolf said, handing Liebowitz the slim stiletto dagger he carried in his boot. 'You can heat the blade over a flame. It's crude, but I fixed a Clansman radio that way once.'

'I'll give it a go,' Liebowitz said.

Holt slapped him on the shoulder. 'Get it done, buddy.'

It was a few minutes later, when Liebowitz was getting deep into the guts of the dismantled phones, that they heard the rumble of the Humvee rolling up outside. 'Right,' Holt said. 'That sonofabitch is gonna get it in the neck now.'

They marched outside to be greeted by the sight of Schulz, bloodied from his hunt, dragging the carcass of a goat from the back of the vehicle. Another one lay on the load bed, one hoof hanging limp and dripping red over the edge. A blood pool was already forming on the ground and it was clear he'd gone way over the top, shooting the poor creatures almost to bits. His rifle was propped up on the Humvee's passenger seat. 'You guys gonna give me a hand, or do I have to do all the work around here?' he called to them, scowling angrily.

Holt stalked over to Schulz with clenched fists and murder in his eyes. Schulz realised too late what was coming, and the hard punch to his jaw knocked him backwards off his feet.

'You stupid prick! What's the matter with you?' Holt raged at him.

But Schulz was every bit as capable a fighter as Holt and half a decade younger, and he came up again like a steel spring with blood trickling from the corner of his mouth and a black Ka-bar combat knife in his hand. 'I'll stick you for that, you motherfucker.'

Wolf moved in to stop things getting ugly, but Ben moved faster. In three steps he was on Schulz, sidestepped the blade that sliced the air towards him, trapped the man's wrist and twisted the weapon out of his grip and dumped him hard on the ground with his face in the dirt and his arm bent up tight behind his back, half an inch from breaking.

'Kick him in the nuts,' Baldacci shouted.

'There's been enough damage done for one day,' Ben said calmly. 'Don't you think, Hank?' He laid on a little extra pressure on the twisted arm. Now it was just a quarter of an inch from breaking.

'Arrghh. Yes,' came Schulz's muffled reply from the dirt.

Ben said, 'You're an idiot, Hank. You know that, don't you?'

'Yes.'

'Let me hear you say so.'

'I'm an idiot,' Schulz said.

'What kind of idiot are you?'

'A total fucking idiot!' Baldacci yelled.

'I'm a total fucking idiot,' Schulz muttered indistinctly through his mouthful of grit and dust.

'Are you going to behave yourself from now on?' Ben asked.

'Yes.'

'Good for you,' Ben said. 'Because if you ever do anything to compromise the safety of this group again, rest assured I will break you into tiny pieces and leave you for the vultures. Got that?'

'Got it.'

Ben released him. The humiliated Schulz rose groaning to his feet, rubbing his arm and his bruised jaw. 'Leave it,' Ben warned Holt, who looked like he was ready to have another go at Schulz. 'We have other things to do. First off, let's form a butchery detail to prepare these goats for cooking. Hank, seeing as you killed them, you can get to work skinning and gutting them. Get a couple of the Pathfinders to help you.' Turning to Baldacci: 'Gino, we'll need to find some dry sticks and more charcoal to build a really hot fire for soldering the phone components. We're also going to make a pit big enough to roast these goats in. That's going to produce a lot of smoke and attractive smells for our friends who might be looking for us out there, so I suggest we post an extra two men on high ground to keep their eyes peeled for incoming enemy elements.'

'And you, what are you going to do?' Holt asked, plainly displeased at being handed out orders.

Ben looked at him. 'For starters, Jaden and I will head back down to the village and see if we can't do a more discreet job of bringing home the bacon. Although it hardly seems to matter now.'

Wolf had clambered up on part of the ruined wall, anxiously scanning the horizon from the wide open plains in the north to the mountains in the south for any sign of movement, and seeing nothing. 'You think there's anyone out there who could've heard?' he asked Ben.

'If they did, we might be seeing them in a few hours,' Ben replied. 'No use crying about it. But it means we've got a lot to do in that time.'

That was an understatement. Those next few hours were frantically busy as they crammed as much activity as they could into what might, thanks to Schulz's folly, be a fast-shrinking time window. While Liebowitz struggled to resurrect their sat phone, surrounded by bits of circuitry and the tip of the stiletto blade glowing red hot in the fire, Ben and Wolf took the Humvee back down to the village where they retrieved the bow and arrow from where they'd left it earlier. Getting the hang of it now, Ben quickly and efficiently added four more of the wandering goats to the menu for the many extra mouths they now had to feed. At this rate their fresh meat supply wouldn't last long, but they'd worry about that later.

Next they refilled every empty twenty-five-litre water jerrycan they had from the clear, sparkling river, and carried their load back up the orphanage to drop off the goat carcasses before they continued up the hill as close as they could get to the foot of the escarpment. Then came the long, weary job of lugging all the water to the cave, where Madison, Father Bugnolio, Francine and the prince, along with sixty eager children, joined in the task of carrying it inside to the grotto.

Still no sign of any movement anywhere on the horizon.

'Maybe it was a false alarm,' Wolf said to Ben, as they stood at the foot of the cliff scanning with their binoculars. 'We've got no real reason to suppose there's anyone out there within hearing range.'

'I didn't think you believed in leaving things to chance,' Ben said.

'I don't.'

'Neither do I. I think either way, it'd be best if we weren't at the orphanage any longer, if and when someone does turn up.'

'You mean, relocate the base camp here to the caves?'

Ben nodded, surveying the lie of the land with a well-practised eye. 'We have a much wider field of observation from up here, and if it comes to making a stand we're much better defended on the high ground. It's a strong position tactically. I propose keeping a double watch from now on, four sentries, changing every two hours. The vehicles will have to be concealed as best we can. Some of the Pathfinders are recovered enough now to be put to work building a rock wall and gathering all the bits of dead tree and brush they can find to make a hide. From a hundred yards away, they should be pretty hard to spot.'

'Roger that,' Wolf said. 'Makes sense to me. So are we to assume that Holt's not in command of this unit any more? You always did rise to the top when things looked set to warm up.'

Ben made no reply to that. 'Come on. We've got more work to do.'

Chapter 44

Back down at the orphanage, Ben put his plan to the rest of the men. He'd expected some resistance from Holt, but the American seemed too downcast to protest the idea of relocating their base to the caves. The reason for his glum mood was explained when he broke the news that Liebowitz had run into more problems with the repair of the sat phone.

'The damage was worse than we thought. He's got a bunch of fine soldering work to do, and it's touch and go whether we can fix it after all. Best case scenario, it's gonna take him a few more hours.'

Not all the news was bad. By now Hank Schulz and the two of the prince's men who'd been assigned to the job of butchering the goats had managed to reduce the first pair of carcasses to a glistening red heap of fine cuts ready for the skewer. In an ideal world you might have wanted to hang them up for a while for tenderness – but this was far from an ideal world, and a great many empty bellies were waiting to be filled.

While the meat was sizzling on skewers over the freshly dug fire pit, giving off a mouth-watering aroma and driving the embittered Schulz almost to the point of madness, they started moving all their kit and weaponry up to their new base. When at last the meat was ready, it was rationed out into thinly sliced strips so that everyone would get a share, and Ramin and Aziz helped Ben carry it up to be distributed among the children.

The hungry kids came flooding from the cave mouth into the sunshine to grab their portions, which some carried excitedly back inside and others ate outside, sitting on rocks and munching away with expressions of sheer delight.

Sometimes Ben had to remind himself that this wasn't all some kind of strange dream. He'd started his journey from Kabul as one man alone. Now, in a blindingly short succession of events that seemed to have crept up on him out of nowhere, he suddenly found himself taking charge of the responsibility for the lives of more than eighty people. And he was going to have to find a way out of this for all of them.

His thoughts were interrupted by the sight of Madison and Father Bugnolio emerging from the cave. 'There he is,' Father Bugnolio said. 'Come and eat,' Madison said. 'We've hardly seen you these last few hours.'

'I'll eat when everyone else has eaten,' he replied. 'That way I know there was enough to go around.'

'Bless you,' says Father B. 'Jesus said, "Let the children be fed first".'

'Mark 7:27,' Ben said.

'You're pretty good with those Bible references,' Madison said. 'Maybe you missed your true vocation.'

'Maybe I did. Where's Richard?'

'Last I saw, he was taking food to Safiya. Her ankle's better but she's still resting. That prince isn't such a bad guy, you know. He's gentle and kind of sweet.'

'Just the attributes needed to rule a country,' Ben said.

'You guys should go easier on him.'

Ben looked over at the group of children sitting outside the cave entrance enjoying their food, almost twenty of them. 'I think they should go back inside. They're too visible out here.'

'They need to get a little bit of sunshine on their bodies,' Madison said. 'Can't be cooped up inside a dank, dark cave the whole time.'

'It's not safe out here.'

'You worry too much.'

Soon afterwards Holt and Baldacci came up in the Humvee, bringing the last of the supplies from below with Nielsen following in the heavy truck. The Pathfinders had finished building the rock and branch hide, and now they were able to tuck the two vehicles away out of sight. Ben and Holt were satisfying themselves that they were well enough hidden when Wolf trotted over to say they'd found another, slightly smaller, grotto adjoining the main one that would serve to house the men. It even had a natural chimney of sorts that would funnel smoke pretty much unseen up through a deep crack in the rock. Wolf grinned. 'We've put Hank to work digging a latrine.'

'How long do you think we can stay here?' Holt asked when Wolf had gone off to help Baldacci lug gear into their new quarters.

'Not long,' Ben said. 'I reckon we need to hunker down for the rest of the day, maybe twenty-four hours at most, until we know for sure the coast's clear. Then I think we should harvest the rest of the livestock down there, top up our water and get rolling. If we jettison all our non-essential kit, prune the ordnance down to personal weapons and a ration of ammo for each man, we might be able to cram all the kids into the truck.'

'They'll be like sardines in there,' Holt said.

'It's only for about a thousand miles of wilderness, with no safe roads and troop patrols at every turn,' Ben said. 'When you got into this, Chris, you must have thought about what would be involved in getting out.'

'We hadn't bargained on having to transport so many,' Holt said. 'What about the Pathfinders?'

'They'll have to ride on the roof, the ones we can't fit into the Humvee.'

'Too darn many,' Holt said, shaking his head. 'It's impossible.'

'It might be. But I've done impossible things before, and I'm still here.'

'Whatever you say, man,' Holt muttered. He seemed about to go trudging off to join the others, then paused and looked as though there was something he wanted to say but was hesitant to come out with it. 'Hey, you know, thanks. We couldn't have done this without you, I guess.'

'It's you these kids have to thank, Chris,' Ben said. 'This whole thing was your idea.'

Holt nodded. 'I . . . I had a daughter once, you know?'

Ben nodded and said nothing, sensing what was coming.

'She died,' Holt said. 'I . . . always . . .' But it was too painful for him to continue. He blinked and shook his head.

'What was her name?' Ben asked softly.

'Mary-Ann. She was everything to Sue and me.'

'I'm sure she was,' Ben said. 'I'm sorry, Chris.'

Holt looked deeply embarrassed. 'Just wanted to say, that's all,' he mumbled, and walked off.

Alone again, Ben spent a few moments scanning the horizon. Still nothing. Then he headed back to the cool shadows of the cave, where he found Madison consoling little Gulnaz. The child was weeping bitterly in her arms.

Ben asked, 'What's the matter with her? Is she unwell? Still hungry?'

'No, she's eaten like a horse and she's fine. But she's still heartbroken about Vida. One of the older girls told her we might have to leave here soon, and she can't bear the thought of leaving her behind.'

'Her doll?'

Madison nodded. 'Francine told me that the doll was the last present her mother gave the poor kid before she died. They've been inseparable ever since, and losing Vida is like losing her mom all over again. Some of the older girls went back down to the ruins to search for her, but they haven't been able to find her.'

'It's a shame,' Ben said. He remembered a time when all his family had had left of his lost sister was her favourite teddy bear. His mother hadn't let go of that tear-soaked bear for years afterwards.

'Can't we go back and try?' Madison asked. 'One last time?'

'I don't know, Madison. It might not be a prudent thing to do, under the circumstances. The doll could be anywhere, buried under a ton of rubble and wreckage.'

'But *look* at her, Ben,' Madison said, tenderly stroking the little girl's back as she pressed her face into her shoulder, racked with tears. 'Did you ever see a poor little kid so miserable? You've been hacking up and down that hillside all day. What's one more trip? Just think how happy she'd be, if she could have her Vida back.'

'I'd have to go on foot,' he said, relenting after a pause. 'And it'd have to be a quick search.'

Madison brightened. 'Quicker if you've got help. I'll come too. We both will.'

'Absolutely not. She has to stay here.'

'But she knows better than we do what Vida looks like. What if we brought back the wrong thing?'

'I don't like it,' Ben said. He could feel his resolve beginning to crack completely under the pressure that only Madison Cahill seemed able to put on him.

'But you'll do it to please her, won't you? And me.'

There was no argument against that. Soon afterwards they were back outside and returning once more down the slope, Ben carrying Madison's AK-47 and his pistol tucked in his belt, Madison clutching the little girl's hand as she scrambled nimbly over the rocks like a baby chamois.

The fire pit near the ruins had been covered over with loose stone and the bloody remains of the butchered goats carefully hidden. The girl's tears were all dried up now as she led them through the shattered buildings to where she'd remembered she might have dropped Vida. She explained to Ben in a flood of rapid-fire Pashto how it had all happened so fast, with Mère Blanchet trying to get them out before the bad men came. In all the confusion she'd suddenly realised she didn't have Vida any more, but then it was too late to go back for her and Mère Blanchet grabbed her arm and wouldn't let go, saying 'Come on! We have to hurry!'

The doll wasn't where Gulnaz thought it was. They hunted all around for fifteen minutes, to no avail. Ben hated having to do it, but he was on the verge of declaring an end to the search when Madison let out a cry and pointed to a tiny rag foot sticking out from under a piece of collapsed wall. Ben laid down the AK and heaved the broken blocks away – and there was Vida, dusty and bedraggled, a little scorched, but otherwise unharmed. The child hugged her beloved doll to her chest with a squeal of happiness.

That was when Ben caught a fleeting movement out of the corner of his eye, and turned to see a figure running away from the ruins. A small figure; for an illogical instant he thought it was one of the other orphans, having followed them down the hill. But then he realised it was a young boy, no more than about twelve, dressed in baggy trousers and an oversized green jacket that billowed in the wind as he belted away for all he was worth.

There was no point in running after him – he had too much of a head start and he was moving too fast. But a bullet could catch him. Ben snatched up the AK, brought it to his shoulder and trained his sights on the rapidly diminishing figure. Weighing up in his mind and in his heart the brutal decision that, on the face of it, would have been the right tactical choice to make.

But he couldn't bring himself to squeeze the trigger. He lowered the weapon and watched with a sigh as the boy scampered away into the distance and disappeared over the brow of a low ridge.

'What the heck was that?' Madison asked.

'That was a scout,' Ben replied. 'They've found us.'

Chapter 45

'He must have already been hiding in the ruins when we turned up,' Ben said. 'We didn't see him until it was too late to catch him.'

A small crowd of people had gathered in a dimly lantern-lit circle within the secondary grotto to discuss the news that Ben and Madison had reported back on their hurried return. She was sitting by him, staying very close at his side and backing up every word he said. Ramin and Aziz were seated opposite, and it was hard to tell which of the pair looked more fraught with worry at this troubling new development. Mère Blanchet had joined them as well, but because of the seriousness of their discussion, none of the children had been allowed to attend. The other absentees were Schulz, who was on watch duty along with three of the Pathfinders (and had in any case been sulkily keeping himself to himself since the incident with the goats), and Liebowitz, who was still hard at work trying to fix the sat phone. He was so concentrated on repairing all those minute solder connections in the light of a fading torch that it had been decided to leave him to it.

Baldacci was frowning as he sat cradling his M4 across his knees, one foot twitching up and down with nervous agitation. 'If this kid was hiding there as you guys appeared, he must've seen you coming down the hill, right? Maybe even watched you come out of the cave.'

Ben couldn't disagree. 'Correct. And if that's the case, then he knows where we are.'

'And he'll have run straight back to report that information to his people,' Baldacci said.

Wolf, sitting to Baldacci's left, turned and gave him a defensive stare. 'Yeah, and what were Ben and Maddie supposed to have done to prevent that?'

'I know what I'd have done,' Baldacci replied darkly, and patted the M4.

'I'll bet you would,' Wolf said with a tinge of disgust. 'Then what does that make you?' Even during his long stint as a professional assassin, Wolf had worked by an unbreakable golden rule. No women, no kids.

'Just saying,' Baldacci said.

'People like you make me sick,' Madison snapped at him. 'Tell me, smartass, what kind of a world is it where *not* shooting a twelve-year-old kid in the back is the wrong thing to do?'

'Maybe not your world, lady,' Baldacci said. 'Taking care of business ain't always nice.'

Ben had been brooding over the incident since their hurried return to the caves. Maybe he should have pulled the trigger. Others would have done it, not just Gino Baldacci. Some soldiers he'd known had been forced into similar situations, acted on them and spent the rest of their lives tortured by remorse. Ben had always been thankful that in all his years of service he'd never had to face such a tough decision. His luck had held out until now; and it was painful weighing up the outcome of his choice. On the one hand, if he'd killed the boy, then whoever sent him would have got suspicious when he didn't return; but by the same token there would have been no witness to report back where their quarry were hiding.

He had to believe he'd done the right thing by letting the kid run. But at what cost?

'I've been through every possible radio channel they might be using,' Wolf said. 'Zilch. Nada. Not so much as a budgie fart. If they're close by, they're keeping absolute comms silence in order to sneak up on us by surprise.'

'Or else they're not there at all,' Holt said. 'We could be jumping the gun here. Why assume this young boy was any kind of scout? Could have been just some local kid, foraging about.'

'Then where'd he come from, mate?' Nobby Scraggs asked Holt. 'If there was another village anywhere within miles of this place, surely we'd have seen some sign of it on the way here.'

'There are still nomadic tribes, the Kochi people,' Ramin said, breaking his anxious silence. 'They've always stayed neutral and don't get involved in political divisions, moving from place to place, living in tents, carrying on the same traditional life they've lived for centuries. This boy could belong to one of them.' Turning to Ben and Madison, he added, 'And just because he ran from you, doesn't have to mean he was spying. He could have been drawn to the ruins out of curiosity, and you scared him. So, maybe this whole thing has a perfectly innocent explanation and we're getting ourselves worried over nothing.'

'Wishful thinking, bro,' Baldacci muttered, shaking his head.

Ben looked kindly at Ramin, sorry to have to burst his optimism. 'I wish I could say you were right. But a kid from a travelling community of Kochi nomads would be highly unlikely to venture very far from his people alone. And if he did he'd have been carrying a few basic essentials with him for the journey. A water canteen, a knapsack, maybe some kind of battered old rifle like a lot of them carry. This kid had none of that. Plus the Kochi people tend to be very colourful and make all their own clothes. They don't generally run around wearing US military fatigues. I'm pretty sure this kid was. An ACU combat jacket a few sizes too big for him.'

'Sounds like a boy soldier to me,' Scraggs agreed. 'God knows we've seen enough of the poor little suckers, all over the bloody world.'

'Then I guess you're probably right,' Holt said resignedly. 'Which means the rest of them won't be far behind.'

'But why would they bother with us?' Aziz asked, looking perplexed. 'They have already destroyed the orphanage, and far as they're concerned their work here is done. It makes no sense that they would come back.'

'Don't you get it? They're not interested in the orphans, not any more,' Baldacci explained impatiently. He jabbed an accusing finger in the direction of the prince, who was sitting across the circle from him and had so far not spoken a word. 'They're looking for *him*. Our very own "Captain Warner" here. Who knows how the word got out who he really is, but it must have. They've got their spies everywhere, and for all we know some of our own spooks have been feeding intel to the wrong people.'

'I don't understand,' Francine said, peering confusedly at the handsome young officer she'd assumed was just another member of the group. 'What does he mean, "who he really is"?'

'He's kind of a special case,' Madison whispered to her.

Colvin, the Pathfinder corporal, sitting next to his captain, replied to Baldacci, 'You don't know that.'

'Only way this works, my friend,' Baldacci said. 'He's been the magnet drawing them all along. They probably think that's what our outfit came here for too, sent in like the SAS boys who managed to get themselves rubbed out trying to rescue his royal ass. They found the temple hideout and the two dead guys, and they've been tracking us ever since, split up into small units to cover as much ground as they could. Now thanks to good ol' Hank they know exactly where we are. And they're comin' for us, make no mistake.'

Francine said, '*Royal?*'

'Now you're in on the secret,' Madison said to her. 'Welcome to the club.'

'It appears I was the last person in Afghanistan to know,' Francine said, cocking an eyebrow and gazing at the prince in a whole new light. 'A duke? An earl?'

'Oh, he's the real deal, honey,' Madison said. 'A bona fide future king.'

The future king sat frowning and biting his lip. 'I never asked for special treatment,' he complained in a whining tone, 'let alone for anyone to risk themselves on my account. I don't want any more responsibility than what comes with being an army officer. I'm done with being a prince. I don't want it any more.'

'Not your call to make,' Ben told him.

'Yes, it is. I resign. Hear me? You're all witnesses to my formal abdication, effective immediately.'

'Go tell that to the Taliban,' Ben said. 'I'm sure they'll accept their misunderstanding and walk away.'

'This is ridiculous! I can't help what family I happen to belong to!'

'But you're here,' Wolf said to him. 'That's all that matters. And soon they'll be here too. All of the scattered units that were out there hunting for us will converge together and they'll turn up in force.'

'How many will there be?' asked Father Bugnolio.

'Hard to say,' Ben replied. 'Could be a hundred, could be five hundred, or more. A prize catch like Richard is a powerful motivator for them. They're not about to let him slip through their net.'

'Prize catch? Net? You make me sound like some kind of bloody fish,' the prince said resentfully.

'A whopping great king salmon is what you are,' Wolf told him. 'Whether you like it or not.'

'Which leaves us with the next big question,' Holt said. 'What the hell do we do now?'

'Get the heck out of here,' the prince answered. 'As fast as we can. Right now, instead of sitting here waiting for them like sitting ducks.'

'Fine,' Wolf said. 'Then all the advance lookouts that have been quietly creeping into position in those hills across there ever since their scout reported back to them will be able to watch us pile into our vehicles and hit the road. That's if there *was* a road instead of just a rocky wilderness, and if we could squeeze everyone into our two trucks without being totally overloaded. They'll head us off before we've gone a mile. And trust me, you won't like what happens next.'

Baldacci drew his index finger across his throat with an evil leer that looked even more sinister in the dim light of the lantern.

'That's just what they'll do to the rest of us,' Wolf went on. 'You, your Eminence, they'll be sure to take alive, so they can cart you straight back to Kabul and the nearest TV studio where you'll appear in front of the world's media, battered to a bloody pulp and not so pretty any more, in what will be the biggest news story since 9-11.'

'Jaden's right,' Ben said. 'I wouldn't recommend that strategy much.'

'Then what can we do?' the prince asked, sounding almost desperate.

'The only thing we can do,' Ben replied evenly. 'This is where we'll make our stand. Whatever comes, we'll face it. Together.'

Baldacci's face spread into a broad grin. 'Now you're talking. Death or fuckin' glory, people. Love it.'

Francine shot him a frosty look and snapped, 'Your language is as foul as your friend's, young man,' indicating Holt.

'Yeah, mate, watch your effing language with ladies present,' said Scraggs.

Baldacci gave him the finger. 'Eat me.'

'But that's insane,' Ramin protested to Ben. 'There are just a handful of us. We can't defend ourselves against hundreds of heavily armed troops.'

'It is what it is,' Ben said. 'No choice. That's our only play.'

'We'd have been a lot worse off if we'd stayed at the orphanage,' Wolf explained to the fraught Ramin. 'Up here, we have a certain tactical advantage. We're built like a castle, secure from the rear and with a steep wide-open killing ground to the front that the enemy will have to cross to reach us. These caves are deep enough to be pretty bomb-proof, so the children can shelter there safely. Then if we did get overrun, we can fall back inside.'

'If we are so forced to do, will they not follow?' said Father Bugnolio.

'Of course they will,' Wolf told him. 'And we'll be waiting for them in the tunnels.'

Ramin sank his ashen face into his hands and let out a low groan of despair. 'I can't believe this is happening. I don't want to fight. I can't fight.'

'It might not come to that,' Ben said.

'But if it does,' Wolf told Ramin, 'then believe me, you'll do whatever it takes to survive. Because you're a human being, and that's what we've been doing for millions of years.'

'I won't survive,' Ramin muttered, completely sincere. 'I'll be killed. I know it.'

'If that's what you believe,' Ben replied, 'then that's what's likely to happen. A positive mental attitude is the best weapon you have, in battle.'

'Easy for you to say. You're all professional soldiers.'

'And impervious to fear or pain,' Baldacci said. 'Bullets just bounce off us. Fire can't burn us and sharpened steel gets blunted against our flesh.'

Aziz slowly nodded. He pressed the flat of his hand to his chest. 'I am not a well man. I'm old and weak, but let it not be said that I backed away from my enemies. Give me a gun and I will fight.'

'My dear fellow, if you think *you're* old,' Father Bugnolio said in amazement, 'what does that make an ancient grey-beard like me, with legs like sticks and fading eyesight? But I shall know no fear. For the Lord your God is the One who goes with you to fight for you against your enemies to give you victory.'

'Amen to that,' said Holt. 'If that's how it has to be, then so be it.'

None of which seemed to offer much consolation to Ramin. 'Stay close to me, Ramin,' Madison said to him tenderly. 'I'll look after you, okay?'

Ramin nodded sullenly.

'And you, Francine,' Ben said, turning to her, 'you stay close to the children.'

Francine shook her head and looked resolute. 'A tigress does not cower in the back of the lair with her cubs, but stands guard at the entrance to ward off danger. I'll stand and fight with the rest of you.'

'Very well,' Ben replied, seeing there was no possibility of dissuading her. 'Can you handle a gun?'

'I have my brother's rifle,' she said tersely. 'I know what to do with it.'

'Madison?'

She looked at him, jutting her chin. 'Hey, you know I can handle myself okay. If you're suggesting that I should butt out of this and leave everyone else to do the work—'

'I wouldn't even dream of it,' Ben said. 'Jaden?'

'All set,' Wolf said. 'We've enough hardware to go around, locked, loaded and ready to rock'n'roll.'

'Chris?'

'I said we were committed, whatever happens,' Holt replied. 'I meant what I said.'

'Richard?'

The prince shrugged resignedly. 'This will be my first big action,' he admitted. 'If you say we're better off drawing our battle lines up here than trying to retreat, then who am I to argue? So be it. Let's give it everything we've got.'

'Right on, Prince,' Baldacci said. 'That's the best thing I've heard you say yet.'

Ben said, 'Good enough. All right then, people. Here's what we're going to d—'

But he never finished telling them. Because just then, two things happened.

The first was that Doug Liebowitz came running in, radiant with excitement and clutching the reassembled sat phone. 'I think I've fixed it!' he announced brightly. 'No satellite connection in here, but I reckon it'll work.' His face fell at the sight of all the grim expressions turning towards him. Until this moment he'd had no idea what was going on. 'W-what?' he stammered.

Then, before anyone had time to speak, the second thing happened. Which was that the radio suddenly began to fizz and splurt, and the voice of Hank Schultz came out of the speaker, tinny and crackly but distinctly heard by everyone inside the grotto.

'Uh, guys, looks we got some activity to the north-west. A *lot* of activity. I'd say it's our Taliban buddies again, for sure.'

Ben snatched up the radio, thumbed the talk button and said, 'Copy that, Hank. How many are there?'

The crackly reply came back a moment later, 'Looks like, uh, all of 'em.'

Chapter 46

They hurried outside, blinking after the darkness of the cave and shielding their eyes in the late afternoon sun. The sight that greeted them in the valley below was no surprise. From the high ground at the foot of the escarpment they watched the Taliban troops came rolling in over the ridge, from the direction in which their scout had run off.

It wasn't just Schulz who had been right in his reckoning. Ben's own fears, voiced by Wolf, were confirmed. The dispersed enemy units that had been hunting them across the wilderness all this time had now come together en masse. Through his binoculars Ben was able to count eight heavy troop trucks and no fewer than three Guardian armoured cars. Two of those massive fighting vehicles were identical to the single one Ben and his Operation Hydra team had faced in Ghurdak, which had been formidable enough on its own. The third was even worse news, because as Ben could clearly see even from this distance, it was one of the US military's more heavily armed variants, fitted with a larger weapons turret mounting a low-pressure 90mm cannon: in effect, a small tank on wheels rather than tracks.

'Oh, what jolly fun,' Wolf commented, observing through his own glasses. 'They've brought all their new little toys to play with.'

Then it got even better, because scanning back towards the ridge Ben could make out that the three monsters and the long line of troop trucks were joined by a large number of the Taliban's more traditional, pre-arms bonanza, technical pickup trucks mounted with heavy-calibre machine guns and rocket launchers. On and on they came, appearing over the crest of the ridge in an apparently never-ending procession, until finally the last one was in sight and Ben could count fifteen in total. Four or five men to a pickup, plus eight times maybe twenty four soldiers per truck, plus the crews of the Guardians, added up roughly to a fighting force of some two hundred and seventy-five men. Meaning that Ben and his group were outnumbered more than ten to one; and that was by no means taking into account the enemy's vastly superior firepower.

'That's a lot of heavy artillery,' Holt said.

Baldacci let out a snorting, devil-may-care laugh. 'And all especially just for us. Makes you feel kinda warm and gooey inside, don't it?'

'We've seen worse odds,' muttered Scraggs. Then added under his breath, 'Though I'm fucked if I can remember when.'

'It's no less than we expected,' Ben said. Then why had his mouth suddenly gone dry and his heartbeat stepped up a notch?

As they watched, the long line of vehicles came rolling over the plain, on a course parallel with the river, until it swept around in a curve past the abandoned village and up the hillside towards the escarpment. It was obvious that they knew exactly what their objective was. Halfway up the slope, about level with the ruins of the orphanage several hundred yards from the foot of the escarpment, they dispersed into a spread-out battle formation and rolled to a halt.

The fanciest of the technicals, a muscular black off-roader with jacked-up suspension, light bars and a heavy machine gun mounted behind its cab, positioned itself in front of the line. Ben fine-focused his binocs and could see a tall, lean man standing on the pickup bed by the rear machine-gun emplacement. His beard was long and black, like the robes he was wearing, and a black turban covered his head. He held himself proudly, like the commander Ben guessed he was.

Now the commander pulled a radio handset from his robe and held it to his ear. The enemy might have been keeping strict radio silence on their approach, but they had clearly been listening in and knew what channel to use. The commander's voice came crackling over the speaker, speaking excellent English.

'My name is Muhammad Omar Nabi. Let me speak to your officer in command.'

'Mine is Hope,' Ben replied, keying his talk button. 'You can talk to me, if you want to discuss the terms of your surrender. Otherwise, don't waste your breath.'

Nabi laughed, a rasping creaky sound over the radio. 'You are funny, Hope. But soon you will not be making jokes. You have only one chance to avoid being slaughtered like dogs. That is to hand over your Spartan to us.'

Spartan. The intel had obviously been every bit as compromised as they'd anticipated. Not entirely unexpected, but it came as a shock nonetheless. Ben covered up his dismay and said, 'You're barking up the wrong tree there, my friend. There is no Spartan here. Just a few members of a volunteer non-combatant aid organisation. Wondering to what we owe the honour of such a large and impressive turnout. We're no threat to anyone.'

'I am not a man who plays games,' said Nabi. 'We know who you are. And we know *he* is with you. You have only two choices. Resist and you will die. Hand him to us, and we will let you live.'

'Live, meaning what?' Ben asked him. 'Let us walk away and starve to death out here?'

'Or remain hiding like rats in your hole,' said Nabi. 'Why should I care? As long as I have what I came here for.'

'And you'd give me your word on that?' Ben asked. He could see the horror on the faces of his companions as he said it, especially the prince's.

Muhammad Omar Nabi replied, 'My word of honour. Will you agree to our terms?'

'Tell him to go stick that machine gun up his own heathen ass,' Baldacci said.

Ben could appreciate that sentiment but put his response in slightly more diplomatic terms. 'I have a problem agreeing to that, Muhammad. I know how little your word of honour counts for you when you give it to a kafir infidel like me. Deception in war was permitted to you by your prophet. I don't play that game but I do understand the rules.'

Ben took his finger off the radio's talk button to give his enemy a chance to reply. Nabi remained silent, so Ben went on: 'But even if I could trust what you say, Muhammad, I'm afraid I'm not in the habit of giving up my men to the enemy. You're just going to have to come and get him. Better go easy, though. You don't want your prize hostage to get hurt.'

A slight pause; then Nabi said nonchalantly, 'Oh, rest assured, if I cannot have him alive, I will be content to bring back his head. For the entertainment of your western public. That is how it will be, Mashallah.'

Hearing that, the prince turned a shade paler.

Ben replied, 'You get too close, Muhammad, then maybe I'll just blow his head off myself. In which case you end up with nothing. No prize, no glory, and let's see how your superiors feel about you coming home empty-handed and on your knees, begging for mercy that you won't get.'

If Nabi was stung by those words, he hid it well. 'You lie, Hope. But I see you have made your choice.'

'It was made from the start,' Ben said. 'So be it, and let the best man win.' The negotiation, such as it had been, was over. He turned off the radio, and turned to the others. 'Everyone take cover. It's about to begin.'

Chapter 47

'I'm not running and hiding from anyone,' Wolf said.

'Me neither, dammit,' said Madison.

Ben looked at her. 'Do we have to have that conversation again? I really need you to be inside the cave to help us carry out the gear.'

She seemed about to argue, but then pulled a sour face at him and hurried back inside, leaving them to crouch among the rocks and keep a close eye on the enemy's movements. It was a race now as to who could get ready to open fire first. Their opponents looked intent on launching their initial attack with the heaviest artillery they had, the 90mm cannon. As it roared back into life, came rumbling forward of the formation and the big gun started to rotate upwards to aim up the hillside, the team were moving fast to set up the Maximi, the fifty-calanti-materiel rifle and the mortars. Ben and Scraggs started prepping the fat, stubby little artillery pieces for action while Liebowitz hunkered down behind the sniper rifle. Wolf clipped a fresh ammo belt into the Maximi's breech. By now a breathless Schulz and the Pathfinders on watch had come hurrying back from their observation posts to join the rest of them, as everyone else spread out among the rocks with their carbines, faces tense, fingers on triggers.

Muhammad Omar Nabi's command to fire echoed faintly in the valley before it was utterly obliterated by the massive report of the cannon. The big gun recoiled violently as the missile spat from its muzzle, making the whole thirteen tons rock back on its suspension. The 90mm shell was actually visible as its dark shape streaked up into the air and arced towards them in a curved trajectory. It reached its target in about half a second and slammed into the face of the escarpment with a massive impact. Ben, Wolf and the others ducked their heads down low and shielded their faces from the choking cloud of dust and the shower of stone fragments that rained down on them.

'That was a little high,' Holt said, managing a grin of bravado.

'Sighting shot,' Wolf replied. 'Next one will be bang on target.'

'Let's give them something to think about in the meantime,' Ben said.

He hadn't fired a mortar in years. Now seemed like a good time to get his hand back in. He dropped a rocket into the upward-pointing tube, moved clear and felt the blast as off it went, sailing up in a high arc before it reached the apex of its sharply curved trajectory and came dropping down like a stone towards the enemy positions. To Ben's satisfaction and drawing a whoop of fierce pleasure out of Nobby Scraggs, it landed in a direct hit on one of the technicals somewhere to the right of the Taliban commander's pickup. The vehicle instantly erupted in a fireball as it was hurled up off its wheels and turned over in mid-air. A burning figure was thrown clear of the explosion, managed to scramble to his feet and made it a few lurching steps before Wolf nailed him in the sights of the Maximi and cut him down with a burst of 7.62.

'It was the humane thing to do,' Wolf muttered.

'Screw these bastards,' Liebowitz said, fixing his own target with the big fifty-calibre rifle. Its enormous carrot-sized conical bullets couldn't hope to defeat thick plated tank armour, but they could slice through a normal vehicle like a hot knife through butter at a thousand metres and more. He fired a shot that found its mark almost before it had come hurtling out of the rifle's muzzle brake at over 3000 feet per second, ruptured the fuel tank on another of the technicals and blew it apart almost as authoritatively as Ben's mortar round.

Liebowitz worked the bolt and was scanning the killing ground for another target when, a heartbeat later, the next blast from the armoured car tank turret let rip and its missile came whooshing in. Ben barely had time to yell, 'Incoming!' and lie prone shielding his face, before it struck just a few feet above the mouth of the cave, with an impact even more devastating than the first, rocking the ground under them and resonating through the solid mass of the whole escarpment. Fire and smoke rolled over them, searing heat and more thick, choking dust that powdered their hair white.

'A little closer that ti—' Wolf started saying. Before the last word was out of his mouth Ben heard a loud *crack* and an ominous rumble from above. He twisted his head upwards just in time to see the avalanche of rocks coming down on them. The tremor from the missile strike had caused an overhanging ledge high above them on the face of the escarpment to fracture off and then calve sheer away, shattering into pieces as it came tumbling down the rock face.

The men below scrambled to get out of its path just in time – except for Liebowitz, who wasn't quick enough. The huge, spinning, bouncing boulders, some of them as big as a family hatchback, came down right on top of him, burying him under stone and dirt five feet deep. As the dust cleared Ben and Wolf ran to dig him out, joined by the prince; but the sight of the bloody, torn arm jutting out from under a massive lump of rock told them there was little point in trying to save him.

That first exchange had only been the opening salvo. Now the battle began for real, everyone firing off their weapons as fast as they could work them, a huge uninterrupted noise filling the air, so thick and so loud that it seemed to snatch the breath from their lungs. Glancing down the hillside with bullets smacking off the rocks all around him, Ben saw the two conventional armoured cars rolling closer up the slope to deploy their heavy machine guns at shorter range, supported by the technicals all hammering away with their own automatic weaponry. He got another mortar round off, then another in quick succession. The first did shocking carnage to a group of soldiers as they leaped down from their troop truck to run for cover. The second exploded harmlessly at the front of one of the armoured cars.

In the midst of the chaos, Ben was sharply aware that the big 90mm cannon was staying oddly silent. He knew that

Muhammad Omar Nabi could easily order the gunners to keep blasting away at the escarpment until the cave entrance was totally sealed off, entombing everyone inside, and everything around it was pummelled to destruction, not a single man left alive. A worrying enough scenario, but Ben didn't think that it would happen, because his instinct told him that the Taliban commander was bluffing. The tank was just for show and intimidation; it was simply too much gun to deploy when you were trying to capture such a prize hostage alive and in one piece.

And so, Ben was pretty sure this fight would be decided the hard way, mano a mano, by small arms combat. The foot soldiers who had managed to race from the trucks under cover without getting mown down by the relentless fire coming down the hillside were now threading their way up the slope from rock to rock, shooting as they came, a withering counterfire that made it almost suicidal to stick your head above the rubble to shoot back. One bullet passed very near to Ben's left ear, then another almost grazed the right side of his ribs – he felt the shock as it went by – and he looked down to see the hole in his baggy tunic. Close one. With barely a moment's hesitation he let off another mortar, watched its flight and felt a surge of triumph as it exploded just a few feet in front of Nabi's vehicle, making the commander jump to safety.

Ben's good feeling was short-lived as Nobby Scraggs, who'd been crouched close by avidly tearing open a fresh crate of mortar rounds, suddenly keeled over backwards, clutching at his chest, his face twisted in pain. Ben crawled across to him on his hands and knees. 'Nobby!'

'I'm okay,' Scraggs muttered. 'I'm okay.' But when battle-wounded soldiers said that, they were often anything but okay. Ben tore open his tunic and saw where the bullet had struck, scouring his chest quite deeply. There was a lot of blood but the damage was all muscle tissue, no deep penetration, no major vessels ruptured and no ribs broken as far as Ben could tell. 'Lie still,' he told him, shoving him behind the safety of the rocks.

'Let me fight, mate,' Scraggs rasped, struggling to get up. Ben pushed him back down, gently but firmly. 'Don't move. You're going to be okay.' Scraggs nodded and closed his eyes.

Ben wiped Scraggs' blood from his hands and returned to his mortars. A few yards away, Wolf was still churning up the scenery with the Maximi. But as the armoured cars and infantry elements crept closer up the hillside, Ben realised they must have picked up on Wolf's muzzle flash and targeted his position, directing focused heavy fire his way. Wolf didn't give a damn. He kept hammering relentlessly, his arms shaking like a motorway worker's pounding concrete with a pneumatic drill, empty cases showering in a heap beside him. Ben was afraid that if Wolf didn't duck under cover, a bullet would catch him sooner rather than later.

He yelled, 'Jaden! Down!' But Wolf either was on too much of a roll to be paying attention, or he simply couldn't hear anything above the constant ear-splitting roar of the Maximi.

Now one of the armoured cars seemed to have stopped firing from its main heavy machine gun, as though something had malfunctioned or it was out of ammo. The turret hatch flew open and a turbaned figure appeared head and shoulders out of it, going to man the 7.62 light machine gun that was his secondary armament. He opened fire on Wolf, and Ben's fear was realised as a well-aimed storm of bullets kicked up a cloud of dust around Wolf's position.

There was a loud *clack* as a round struck the Maximi, followed almost simultaneously by a yell. Wolf's fire suddenly stopped. Ben saw him slump over. He yelled out his friend's name again. 'Jaden!'

No reply from Wolf. He wasn't moving.

Chapter 48

The turret's light machine gun was still laying down so much fire on Wolf's position that there was no way Ben could run to his friend's aid. Heart thudding with anxiety, he angled his hot mortar and dropped another rocket into the smoking tube. The projectile soared up, arced over and down, and by a combination of extreme luck and great skill landed directly into the armoured car's open hatch.

An exploding mortar bomb within a confined steel capsule was virtually sure to kill or at least severely disable anyone inside. Fire erupted from the hatch. The gunner's head and arms were separated in the blast and his weapon instantly fell silent. The armoured car lumbered to a halt, burning fiercely and belching smoke.

Fearing the worst for Wolf, Ben raced over to where he was lying slumped behind the overturned Maximi and got there at the same instant as Holt, who'd seen Wolf get hit and come running. A bleeding gash had torn Wolf's forehead from a piece of his weapon's bipod that got blown away by the bullet strike and caught him on the head, but otherwise he was unhurt and only momentarily stunned.

Ben folded up the remaining bipod leg, rested the Maximi's smoking hot barrel in a cleft between two rocks and directed a sustained blast of fire at another technical that had dared to come racing up the hillside in a wild attempt to make it all the way to the top. The technical's windscreen dissolved in a bullet-shattered opaque mess, spattered red from the driver's blood, and the vehicle crashed into a boulder and rolled back down the hill, tumbling over and over and flattening three foot soldiers on its way down.

That was when Ben happened to glance across to his left and saw to his horror that Madison, against his wishes, hadn't stayed long in the relative safety of the cave. Nor had Francine Blanchet. The two women had managed to get themselves wedged behind reasonable cover a few metres from the edge of the hillside, where they were taking turns shooting at the enemy fighters working their way up the slope. Francine was well practised with the battered old Russian SKS that had once belonged to her brother, though she was so tiny that she looked like a child with the big semi-automatic rifle's wooden stock clenched against her shoulder, its snappy recoil making her whole body quake. One running figure collapsed on his face as he tried to scurry from rock to rock forty metres away. Another instantly appeared to take his place, firing wildly as he came. Francine kept her calm as bullets ricocheted all around her, took careful aim, and next thing the fighter was crumpling to the ground, clutching at his blown-open thigh.

Then Francine had to pull back to reload, and Madison took over with her AK, targeting a group of five fighters hunkered down behind the wreck of the overturned technical, all shooting continuously. Madison's return fire stitched a ragged line of holes up the side of the vehicle until it found its mark and one of them went tumbling back with a short scream. Now she'd found her aiming point she loosed off another burst that silenced two more of them, and the last two fell into retreat along with dozens of their comrades driven back by the determined fire coming from all along the foot of the escarpment.

But not for long, because just as the tide of the battle seemed to be turning in the defenders' favour, the attackers were hellbent on coming back strong. Now the second of the three armoured cars had succeeded in making it almost to the top of the hillside, across to the southern end of the escarpment where the incline was a little gentler. The southern end was also where Ben had instructed the Pathfinders to build the rock and branch hide for the Humvee and truck. He sprinted back towards his mortar position in the hope of deflecting its attack, but too late: the armoured car's grenade launchers and heavy machine gun opened up, destroying the Humvee and riddling the truck with bullets before its weapons swivelled across to blast a line of craters in the face of the escarpment, threatening to cause another rock slide like the one that had buried Liebowitz.

Pinned under cover for the moment, Ben could only watch as the armoured car kept rumbling closer. But then its driver, revving hard, overconfidently ventured onto a part of the slope where the incline was much steeper. The vehicle tilted back on itself a degree further than its centre of gravity would allow, and slowly toppled over backwards with a crash to lie there helplessly capsized like an overturned turtle, trapping the men inside.

Two monsters down. Ben heard cheering from behind him. Then he saw Hank Schulz appear as if out of nowhere, leap up on a rock and start firing at its exposed underbelly like a man demented. To no avail, because the thing was clad underneath by thick armoured plates to protect from landmine blasts, and Schulz should have known that. But before the man came to his senses to realise he was just wasting his fire, a sniper's bullet from the distant ruins of the orphanage took away the left side of his skull in a pink mist and he fell dead among the rocks.

The defenders' casualties were beginning to mount up. To the other side of where Schulz had been killed, Ben could see the inert, bloody bodies of two of the Pathfinders, tattered to pieces by the gunfire from the armoured car. He looked urgently around for the prince, then spotted him firing away from behind the cover of another large rock, though it wasn't clear what he was shooting at, or to what kind of effect.

Despite their losses they were taking their toll on the enemy, who in addition to the many foot soldiers lying dead across the killing ground had now lost seven of their technicals and were down to just the tank-mounted armoured car. But Muhammad Omar Nabi wasn't about to let his men slacken the pace of their assault. They probably had just as much to fear from their commander's wrath if they failed to take their objective. Now they redoubled their attack and came swarming up the hillside, jumping over their fallen comrades and howling at the top of their lungs. The combined gunfire of dozens of automatic weapons swept the crest of the slope, cutting down Nielsen and another of the prince's men. Ben snatched up Nielsen's fallen weapon and rattled it empty, tossed it away and drew his pistol, squeezing off shot after shot until it was empty too.

There was no choice but to retreat. Ben yelled, 'Fall back!' and the remaining defenders – Holt, Baldacci, Madison and Francine, the prince and his last few Pathfinders – abandoned their cover and ran for the cave. Ben and Wolf each grabbed one of the injured Scraggs's arms and dragged him bodily inside the entrance.

Not a moment too soon, because seconds later the attacking foot soldiers had reached the top of the hill, peppering the cave mouth with their relentless gunfire. Their battle cry 'Allahu Akbar!' echoed through the tunnels as they swarmed inside the narrow entrance one or two at a time.

But that was their undoing, because tactically the very worst mistake an assaulting force could make was to let themselves be funnelled into a narrow field of fire with no way out. Now they suddenly faced a deadly counter-attack directed from the shadowy nooks and crannies of the cave that Ben and the others had had plenty of time to reconnoitre. Before they knew what was happening, the fighters were being cut to pieces and their bodies were piling up in the narrow tunnel. Yet they kept on coming, screaming like madmen, and Ben, Wolf and Holt, the vanguard of the resistance, were pressed back towards the grotto.

There was no way, none at all, they were going to let the attackers reach the children. The fighting inside the closed space became vicious and desperate. With no room to manoeuvre a rifle or carbine, they used their knives. Slash, stab, chop; a furious exchange with no quarter given or expected. Ben felt a cold steel blade split the flesh of his shoulder and drove his own hard into the throat of the man who'd sliced him. That man went down with a bloody gurgle. Another right behind him, coming up with a wicked curved dagger that flashed in the semi-darkness. Ben dodged the cut, broke the man's wrist, head-butted another, floored yet another with a savage kick to the knee and crushed his throat. A smooth, flowing sequence of brutal, almost instinctual, violence that he'd spent much of his life perfecting. For an instant he found himself cut off from Wolf and Holt and surrounded by hostile bearded faces whose eyes gleamed with hate in the murky light. A pistol shot sounded deafeningly close by and the bullet ricocheted off the cave wall. Then suddenly in the confusion he sensed a new presence at his side, and something long and bronze-coloured gleamed in what little light penetrated the tunnel as it swung towards the bodies of his assailants. The chopping sound of steel biting into flesh; a scream; then the attackers were being driven back again towards the cave mouth – and there was Madison beside him, clutching the sword she'd taken from the skeleton of the ancient Greek warrior, swinging ferociously left and right with all her strength and energy.

Then Wolf, Holt and Baldacci were with him too, and they chased the retreating invaders back into the wider section of the tunnel where Ben, snatching up a fallen pistol, was able to shoot down three of the ones brave enough, or foolish enough, to try to stand and fight.

Now the cave mouth was clear, except for the bodies that lay strewn all over the rocky ground. The sudden silence in the aftermath was deafening as they stood there breathing hard, jangling from the intoxicating adrenalin rush of close quarter combat.

'We did it!' Madison yelled. 'We beat them back!'

'Maybe for the moment,' Ben said. His new pistol was a US-issue M9 Beretta. About a dozen rounds in the mag. Good enough. He jammed it in his belt.

'Ben, you're bleeding.'

'It's nothing,' he replied. He barely felt the pain.

Her hair was as wild as her eyes and there was blood on her face, but it wasn't her own. The bronze sword in her hand was bent out of shape from the fierce blows she'd dealt out. 'Came in handy,' she said.

'That's the second time you've saved my life,' Ben told her.

'I'll settle for a cold beer in repayment, when we get out of this.'

'It's a date.'

They peered cautiously out of the cave entrance and watched as the enemy, still numerous despite the many dead they'd left behind, fled down the hillside followed by what-ever vehicles were still operational. The foot of the escarpment was a scene of devastation, littered with debris and bodies. Across to the north side, the Humvee was on fire. It was impossible to tell how much damage the truck might have sustained.

The firing had stopped for the moment. In the lull, Ben, Wolf and the others dragged sixteen corpses out of the cave mouth and dumped them unceremoniously in a heap outside. Ben went to retrieve his Maximi, abandoned in the rush to the cave and left untouched during the attack.

Crouching low behind the rocks at the top of the rise he trained his binoculars down the hill, where the enemy, gathered in a large crowd several hundred yards away beyond the ruins of the orphanage, seemed to be organising themselves for something.

'What are they doing down there?' asked Wolf, and Ben passed him the binocs to take a look for himself. He replied, 'I don't know, but I have a strong feeling that this isn't over yet.'

And Ben was right.

Chapter 49

It soon became apparent that Mohammad Omar Nabi, seeing his men in danger of being humiliatingly defeated by this far smaller opposition force, had decided on a new strategy. Ben had thought earlier on that the man was bluffing when he'd deployed his biggest gun. Now, as the sole remaining armoured car with its oversized turret and protruding 90mm cannon barrel came rumbling back up the hill on its huge wheels, Ben was no longer so sure that the Taliban commander wasn't intent on pummelling the escarpment and the cave entrance to destruction after all.

The suspicion became a certainty when the vehicle halted two hundred yards away and the cannon sounded off with a blast like the crack of doom.

'Uh-oh,' Wolf muttered as the blurred black shape of the missile came hurtling up the hillside and they ducked for cover.

The projectile struck with far greater accuracy than before, exploding violently an uncomfortably short distance over their heads and smashing a vast crater in the rock face above the mouth of the cave. Hundreds of tons of sheet rock came crashing down in a spectacular avalanche and the two men, caught out in the open, had to scramble desperately out of its path to avoid being buried under several feet of rubble.

The dust billowed like smoke around them, powdering them chalky white from head to toe, filling their eyes and making them cough and splutter. As a gust of wind dispersed the great drifting cloud that veiled the whole escarpment, Ben saw with a shock that the cave entrance was now partially blocked. Another well-placed blast like that could see it completely sealed off, with the kids still inside.

Worse, a huge section of rock further up the looming cliff face had been badly loosened and was teetering on the brink of coming down on top of the rest. Ben and Wolf both knew in that moment that they would have to evacuate the cave – and fast, before those inside were buried in there forever.

'Here they come again,' Wolf growled. And so it was, too, because Mohammed Omar Nabi had ordered a second full-on assault. Within moments the hillside was alive once again with the chatter of gunfire. Bullets whizzed overhead and pinged off the rocks all around them.

'Cover me while I get the others out of there!' Ben yelled, and Wolf threw himself behind the Maximi with a look of loathing while Ben ran back to the cave entrance and started feverishly clearing away the lighter boulders to widen the blocked exit. Madison was the first to come clambering through, her black hair sprinkled white with dust making her look much older. 'The kids!' she screamed over the noise of Wolf's gunfire. 'We have to get those kids out!'

Wolf was pounding away savagely with the Maximi, scoring fresh hits on the remaining technicals and sending enemy fighters running about like ants. All too soon, though, his ammo belt was running short, with no more in the crate; and within a few more moments the final yard was reduced to a scattering of broken linkages and fired cases. Wolf grabbed up a fallen M4 with barely a moment's pause and continued popping off more rounds to deadly effect. But there were so many fighters down there that it seemed the more you took down, the more kept coming back at you like an irrepressible tidal wave gaining constantly on the hillside.

Blinking dust and sweat out of his eyes, Ben looked down and saw the tank climbing the slope towards them. After its deadly opening salvo the cannon had fallen silent. *Why weren't they firing?* The answer quickly became clear as the turret hatch opened and one of the crew poked his head out, wildly waving his arms and yelling at two more of his comrades who came running up. It looked as though they were having some kind of problem with the big gun. Unlike these guys, the US army troops to whom such pieces of equipment had been issued originally would have been expertly trained in clearing shell casing jams, fixing stuck ejectors or any of the other technical difficulties of operating a thirteen-ton killing machine.

The lucky delay would buy Ben and his companions a little bit of time to help get the children out of the dangerously unstable cave before these lunatics could seal their fate forever. But where could they evacuate the children to? Ben looked urgently around for an answer, then saw it.

Twenty metres from what used to be their entrance, the tumbled rocks had formed a freshly heaped stone wall. One enormous piece of the broken-off ledge had come to a rest upright like a monument, against which others had piled to make a tall barricade with a gap like a natural gateway through which they could escape to shelter behind the protection of the rocks.

It was their only chance. Ben pointed and yelled, 'That way!' Francine and Father Bugnolio had managed to scramble out of the half collapsed cave mouth. As Wolf kept up his steady fire down the hill, joined now by Holt and Baldacci as well as the prince and his men, Ben and Madison raced to help the children clamber out of the hole while Francine and Father B herded them urgently through the gap and behind the barricade, helped by Ramin and Aziz. Scraggs had had to be carried out of the cave and was unable to do anything but watch helplessly from the sidelines.

One by one, in what seemed like a never-ending stream, the children came wriggling out of the hole and into Ben's or Madison's arms. They were plastered with dust and some were crying. 'How many is that?' Ben yelled. A bullet splatted off the rocks close by. He didn't as much as flinch.

'I think that's all of them,' Madison yelled back, having kept a mental tally of each child as they got her out. 'Is it?'

But it wasn't quite all. Still to be brought out was little Gulnaz, clutching her beloved doll Vida as she hesitated just inside the gap, too afraid to come outside with all the terrible noise going on. 'Come on, baby,' Madison called to her through the hole. 'Please, you have to hurry.'

As Madison spoke, there was an ominous grinding scrape of rock. Loose stones came slithering down from the cratered escarpment and something shifted, the cave mouth narrowing perceptibly. Any moment, the entire thing was going to collapse.

'Gulnaz, come on!' Ben urged the frightened child in her own language, but all he got was a wide-eyed stare of terror from inside. He put his arm through the gap to grab her, but she backed away. And the hole was now too small for him to scramble through to fetch her out bodily.

'We can't hold these bastards off for much longer,' Wolf called across from the firing line. 'Ammo's running awful short.' His M4 was empty. Holt tossed him another thirty-round magazine. Wolf slammed the fresh mag into his receiver and set about emptying it as fast as he could in the direction of the swarming enemy troops.

And still the child refused to come out of the narrowing cave entrance. 'Ben, do something!' Madison screamed. As though one man could hold up thousands of tons of solid rock, like the mythological Titan Atlas supporting the weight of the world on his shoulders. Ben grabbed an M4 carbine from the dead hand of one of the Taliban fighters and jammed it vertically into the hole in an attempt to shore it up. But it wouldn't take the strain for long. The massive pressure bearing down from above was already bending the weapon like a toothpick.

'Come on, little one,' Ben coaxed the child, trying to hide the mounting urgency in his voice. 'It's okay. You'll be quite safe.' Her bright little eyes still just stared back at him, filled with confusion and mistrust. The grinding of shifting rock was growing louder, louder. The gun was buckling into the shape of a banana. It wasn't going to hold. It was going to give way and bend right in half under the weight.

Whatever made the child suddenly change her mind, Ben could only thank God for. She gripped his hand through the hole, and he hauled her out and clenched her tight just as the whole lot came crashing down and the cave entrance was completely sealed off. Ben and Madison rushed her to the barricade, yelling for the others to follow.

They fell back and made it to shelter just as the renewed enemy attack reached the top of the hill once again. With bullets cracking off the rock wall behind him Ben handed poor, terrified Gulnaz into the waiting arms of Francine and asked, 'Was she definitely the last?' To his huge relief Francine nodded and replied, 'Yes, they're all here.' She clasped Ben's hand with a look of the most sincere gratitude he had ever seen in anyone's eyes, but her next words were drowned by more gunfire as Holt and Baldacci ducked around the edge of the rock gateway to let off long, chattering twin bursts at the fighters working their way along the foot of the escarpment towards them. Holt yelled, 'Get those kids further back!'

It was a desperate position now. Almost a lost cause, with so many of the advantages they'd started out with whittled away one by one. Muhammad Omar Nabi, joining his troops at the rubble-strewn foot of the escarpment, must have been smiling to himself with victory so close. And he'd have been right to, because there was very little to stop him now. The shooting had paused again, but it wouldn't be for long as the enemy massed a short distance away on the other side of the barricade, mustering their forces for the final assault.

Inside the fragile shelter of the barricade, the defenders herded the children into the hollow of a little kind of dell, as far away from harm as they could get. Not nearly far enough, though.

'In the name of God,' said Father Bugnolio, 'I cannot allow this to happen.' Francine stood at his side, clutching her rifle, utterly resolute. 'Nor shall I. I will die before I see any of them harmed.'

'Then we will die together, my dear, dear lady,' the priest said, and put an arm tenderly around her shoulders.

'Stop talking like that! I can't stand it!' wailed Ramin, beside himself with fear and panic. Madison tried to reassure him. Aziz was sitting on a rock, grey and ill-looking. Nobby Scraggs was too badly hurt to do much of anything, but he'd insisted on being propped up with a carbine and spare magazine in his lap, where he fully intended to guard the children with his last breath.

'This is the one, Jaden,' Ben said to Wolf as they did their last weapons check. There were so many discarded guns lying around that Ben had had his pick, opting for a light-weight carbine in addition to his pistol.

'I love it when the odds get nasty,' Wolf said with a predatory gleam in his eye.

'Best of luck.'

Wolf grinned. 'See you on the other side, Ben.'

That was when Ben heard the familiar ominous rumbling of a powerful Perkins diesel engine and jumped up on a rock to see the armoured tank car approaching. They'd managed to get it the rest of the way up the hillside and now the beast was clambering over the rubble towards the barricade. The hairy face protruding from the open gun turret was cracked open in a big smile of triumph. Which told Ben they'd managed to fix their problem with the 90mm cannon, too. Just one or two blasts from that thing would blow the barricade to smithereens, breaching their defences for the rest of the troops to come flooding through. Foot soldiers were running alongside the tank, weapons ready for what would surely be the decisive push.

Ashen faced and wide-eyed, the prince muttered, 'Oh my God. This is the end. We're finished.'

'Hey, remember that thing I said about Richard the Lionheart?' Wolf replied. 'I was wrong. I take it back. I should have called you Richard the Chickenheart.'

The prince shook his head, as though an idea had come to him. He gripped Ben's arm. 'Listen to me. There's still time.'

'Time for what?'

'For me to talk to their commander. I can do a deal with them. My position gives me a lot of bargaining power.'

Wolf said, 'Your position gives you bugger all, your Royal Holiness. Especially when they've stuck your distinguished head on a spike and paraded it in front of the whole world. That'll sell a few newspapers, and no mistake.'

'That's not how things work,' the prince said, flushing. 'They're businesspeople, at the end of the day. Everything's open to negotiation.'

Wolf smiled at him, not unkindly. 'Oh, have you a thing or two to learn, boy.'

Ben slammed a full magazine into an M4 and tossed the weapon to the prince. 'You were born into a line of kings, Richard. Do yourself a favour and try to act like one. Now, enough talk. They'll be here in a minute, so let's get this done.'

Prince Richard stood there dumbly holding the rifle. Ben reached for his crumpled Gauloises pack. Just the one left. Now was the time. There would very likely never be another. He drew it out, flipped open his Zippo and slowly lit it. If this was going to be his last ever cigarette, he meant to savour the moment.

He was about to throw away the crumpled pack when he noticed the plain black business card inside, the one that Carstairs had given him. He'd forgotten it was even there until now.

Ben crumpled the pack in his fist with the card still inside, and tossed it away into the rocks.

'Showtime,' Wolf said.

And then the final attack began.

Chapter 50

The massed enemy forces advanced towards the barricade. Children were crying. Father Bugnolio shook hands with Francine, then spat in his palms and picked up a rifle. Ben flicked away his half-smoked cigarette and shouldered his weapon. Madison was to one side of him, the prince to the other. 'Stand firm,' Ben said to Richard. 'Make every shot count.'

The prince nodded. Something had changed in his eyes, and a kind of serenity had come into his expression. 'I'm not afraid any longer,' he said in a quiet, steady voice.

Wolf took up a kneeling position with his carbine trained on the gap in the barricade. Holt and Baldacci were close by the wall, ready to intercept whatever and whoever came through the opening.

But Muhammad Omar Nabi was no longer taking any chances, even if it meant having to content himself with taking away a dead prince. He ordered the 90mm cannon to fire.

At this close range, the screeching blast was simultaneous with the missile's impact against the barricade wall. An explosion of flame and shrapnel and flying rock, killing Holt and Baldacci who had been standing too close to the wall to have any chance of escaping the blast.

A second's stunned silence, apart from the high-pitched singing in half-deafened ears. And now the enemy soldiers came pouring through the breach. The first rank ran into a wall of gunfire and fell back momentarily before more and more flooded through the smashed barricade. This was it. It would be a fight to the last round, and then knives out, for those still standing by then.

Everything around Ben seemed to be happening in slow motion and he felt almost peaceful. War was his element, totally familiar to him in every way, and it seemed perfectly natural to him that he should meet his end this way.

But through the all-pervading, sense-numbing, blood-pumping din of battle came another sound that was decidedly *un*familiar to him. Catching a glimpse of Wolf's startled expression, it was clear that he had heard it too.

The clatter of iron-shod hooves on rock. Lots of them. And it was coming from somewhere above him. Ben glanced up, in the same direction Wolf was now gaping with a look of incredulity. What he saw made him think he must be hallucinating.

Down the half-collapsed face of the escarpment came a spectacle Ben had never dreamed of seeing in his life, let alone at this moment. It was a cavalry charge, some forty or fifty riders all clad in colourful Afghan tribal garb, leaning back in the saddle and firing automatic weapons one-handed as they spurred their horses down the steep paths of rock and rubble carved out by the shell bombardment. At their head rode a man who was obviously their commander, astride a magnificent long-maned white stallion with his reins in his teeth and a pistol in each hand.

They came cascading down on the astonished Taliban fighters, many of whom stopped shooting and stood there dumbstruck as they were either trampled under the thundering hooves or able to scatter in panic out of the path of the charge. Two riders leaped into mid-air from their mounts as they reached the foot of the slope, landed as nimbly as acrobats on the armoured car's open turret, and in the blink of an eye the bearded face that had been smiling before now screamed in agony as their curved daggers sliced his throat and punched into his body. They hurled his bloody corpse from the turret and he slithered to the ground where a big wheel rolled over him. Then they were diving into the open hatch, and over the sound of gunfire came more hideous screams as the knife work inside the vehicle was carried out with brutal efficiency. While the tank crew was being dispatched, the forty or fifty horses had all reached the foot of the escarpment and were quickly riding down the Taliban fighters.

It had seemed like a much longer time than the actual one or two seconds Ben had needed to get over his initial stunned shock and realise what was happening. This large unit of tribal militia had been drawn by the sound of the battle and decided to seize this opportunity to wipe out some of their most hated enemies.

Ben had long ago stopped believing in miracles. Maybe it was time to rethink that one.

'Come on!' he yelled, and together with Wolf, Madison, the prince and the last few Pathfinders, they ran to join in the close-packed fighting that milled all over the foot of the escarpment. Now the combat reached its peak of violence. Ben's carbine was soon empty and he drew the pistol, engaging his targets with all the speed and precision he'd been trained for. Madison had rattled her AK dry and snatched an SA80 bullpup rifle from the clawed bloody hand of the Pathfinder soldier who'd been shot dead right next to her. She was firing left and right, standing her ground with her feet planted apart, her hair blowing wild in the wind and a look of warrior ferocity on her face that could make any man fall in love with her, if there'd been time to spare her a glance in the midst of the mayhem. Meanwhile Wolf was doing what Wolf did best, carving a path of dead men in what was left of the enemy ranks.

Right in the middle of the melee, Ben found himself suddenly face to face with the tribal commander, now dismounted from his white stallion and fighting on foot with the rest of his people. He was a ruggedly handsome man in his mid-fifties, with a greying black beard and a hooked nose. He smiled at Ben, a smile that quickly dropped as Ben raised his pistol and pointed it right at him. Then Ben swivelled the weapon four inches to the right and fired past the commander, taking down the man in the long black robe and black turban who'd been about to kill him.

Only when the body hit the ground did Ben realise that the man he'd shot was Muhammad Omar Nabi. Recognising him right away, the tribal commander spat on the corpse, drew a long curved scimitar from the folds of his colourful tunic and sliced off Nabi's head in a single blow.

When the rest of the Taliban fighters saw their leader's decapitated body lying sprawled on the ground, their fighting spirit was suddenly and totally deflated. Some of them threw down their weapons, dropped to their knees and surrendered to the tribesmen, only to be summarily executed with a bullet or have their heads cut off. The rest fled for their lives, to the sound of jeers and yells of triumph from the victors. Some shots sounded and several of the escaping fighters were cut down as they ran, until their leader, still clutching his bloodied scimitar, ordered them in a huge roaring voice to cease firing.

'Let the cowards run back to their leaders and tell them what happened here today, so that they may never dare to return to these hills again!' There was more shouting and cheering, chants of 'Khan Zada! Khan Zada!' Some pointed their weapons into the air and rattled off bursts of gunfire in tribute to their leader and his triumph.

It was over. But it had been a bloody battle, one of the bloodiest Ben had ever known. Horses and men lay dead everywhere. The tribesmen had dragged the armoured car crew out of their vehicle. One was horribly wounded but still alive, and he screamed for mercy as they threw him down and beheaded him.

Ben spotted Madison and Wolf in the crowd, still very much alive, and his heart filled with relief. He turned towards the tribal commander. Up close, the roguish, piratical look about the man was belied by the sharp gleam of intelligence in his eye, and a warmth of expression that seemed to hint at a thoughtful nature.

Speaking in Pashto he said, 'My name is Hope, Benedict Hope.'

'I am Khan Zada,' the man replied, and with a broad sweep of his arm he added, 'These are my lands. For a thousand years my tribe have lived in and ruled this territory, for as far as the eagle can fly in a day in any direction.'

'We're honoured to be humble visitors to your domain,' Ben said, with a deferential nod. 'And even more grateful to you for your intervention here today.'

Khan Zada seemed pleased. 'Benedict,' he said, mulling over the name. 'In your language it means "blessed", does it not?'

'Something like that,' Ben said.

'Allah be praised.'

'And yours means a very great man,' Ben said. 'If I'm not mistaken.'

Now the tribal commander seemed even more pleased. 'You are the leader of your people?'

'The command fell to me,' Ben says. 'Otherwise I'm just a common civilian.'

'But you are clearly a great warrior. You saved my life, my friend. For that, it is I who must thank you.'

Ben replied, 'Then as a friend, with the deepest respect, Khan Zada, I must beg you to stop your men executing the prisoners.'

'It is our time-honoured custom,' Khan Zada said casually. 'However,' he added after a moment's careful consideration, 'a man who saves another's life becomes his blood kin, like a brother. And I will grant my brother's wish.'

Turning to his men, he boomed out the order for them to spare the remaining prisoners. 'Let them scurry away like the sons of diseased sewer rats that they are, and hide their faces forever in shame.' He turned back to Ben with a beaming smile. 'There, brother. It is done.'

'I thank you again, Khan Zada,' Ben said, shaking his strong hand. 'It's you who saved my life. All our lives. You couldn't have come at a better time. But where on earth did you come from?'

Khan Zada's smile became even broader. 'My people know these hills better than anyone,' he explained. 'Far better than the best of these Taliban vermin, who mostly grew up as worthless street filth in the city slums and could not survive one month out here in the open ground. There is a small pass that leads up the north face of the escarpment, hidden from view to those who are unaware of its existence. We heard the sounds of battle from a great way off, and rode faster than the wind to get here in time. These devils have visited my lands before, murdering innocent people and destroying all in their path. It was time that they were taught a lesson.'

He prodded Muhammad Omar Nabi's headless body with his foot, looking down at it with contempt. 'I am the one called a warlord. But these mangy dogs are the true bringers of blood and suffering in my country.'

Ben said, 'I think some of my kind have brought a lot of that as well, in the past. And your own, Khan. None of us is clean of guilt.'

Khan Zada nodded sagely and gazed at Ben with his strangely penetrating eyes. 'Then let us look to the future, when perhaps one day, inshallah, peace will return to this unhappy place.'

'I wish it with all my heart,' Ben replied sincerely, and they shook hands again. 'Now if you'll allow me, I have to see to my people.'

Chapter 51

A people sadly very much reduced. Out of the original group Ben had joined, only Wolf and Nobby Scraggs had survived. Prince Richard was the last man standing among his Pathfinders, who had fallen one by one in that last fierce round of fighting. Aziz and Ramin had managed to come through completely unscathed, the latter still dazed and finding it hard to believe he was still here.

Ben found Madison helping Father Bugnolio and Francine look after the children. The pair seemed to have formed a strong attachment. 'All the children are safe and well,' the priest said, crossing himself. 'Thanks be to the Lord above.'

Ben would be happy to thank him afterwards. In the meantime, the problem was how they were going to get out of Afghanistan with no vehicles. The smouldering Humvee was never going anywhere again, and as suspected, Ben found that the truck's engine compartment had been irreparably shredded by machine-gun fire. Which effectively meant they were stranded here, unless they could find a very good alternative, and soon.

When Ben put the problem to Khan Zada, the warlord grasped his arm with a pincer-like grip and replied, 'Let it never be said that Khan Zada is not generous to his friends and allies. I can offer horses and men, and a safe passage through the mountains to wherever you must cross the border.'

'Khan Zada is indeed kind,' Ben said, shaking his head. 'But wherever my friends and I go, these children have to go as well. It's my intention to carry them out of Afghanistan and help find them a safer home elsewhere.'

'All of them?'

'Yes. All of them.'

The commander scratched his beard. 'I do not have that many horses. And many of these children, I think, are too small to ride even a pony. Also you must think about water, provisions. It will be a long and difficult journey through the mountains. On foot, impossible.'

'Then we still have a teeny weeny bit of a problem, don't we?' said Wolf, when Ben went back to report the news. Madison walked over to join them as they talked. 'You can spoil a good thing by over-thinking it,' she said optimistically. 'That's what Dad always used to say, anyhow.'

'Good advice,' Ben said. Then a thought came to him. He walked back towards the barricade, stepping over bodies, peering down at the ground around him.

'What are you doing?' Madison asked, trotting after him.

'Looking for something I dropped.' He spotted the familiar blue cigarette pack lying squashed and flattened among the rocks where he'd tossed it earlier. Bending to pick it up, he took out the crumpled business card. No name, just an anonymous mobile number.

'Whose number is that?' she asked.

'Someone you wouldn't want to know,' he replied. 'But he might just come in useful.'

The tribesmen were finishing up the task of gathering their dead when Ben returned to speak again with their leader. 'Khan, can you lend me a few of your men?'

'Certainly. Of what purpose can they be to you?'

'We need to dig our way back into that cave,' Ben said, pointing.

'Then you shall have the biggest and strongest.' Khan Zada called them over. 'Azim! Hamed! Kawkab! Maalik! Jaafar! My brother Benedict Hope has a task for you.'

They stepped forward. The one called Jaafar was one of the most enormous hulks of a human being Ben had ever seen, with hands like the buckets on a mechanical digger and eyes set so far apart in his head that it was impossible to look at both at once. He was also mute, but one of Khan's most loyal warriors.

Ben and his helpers spent the next hour shifting rocks, until he was able to squeeze through the tight space into the cave. To his relief, once inside he found the tunnels were still intact. Hunting through the dark grotto he found where Liebowitz had left the repaired sat phone.

It worked.

'Good man, Doug,' Ben murmured, with a pang that the man was dead.

Back outside, Ben soon found a spot not too far off where he was able to get satellite hook-up, and dialled the number from the business card.

Four thousand miles away, Gordon Carstairs answered the phone on the second ring. He sounded weary and morose, as might have been expected from a man charged with a vitally important assignment that had utterly failed, marking not just the lowest point of his career but a disaster for the nation.

'Hello, Colonel.'

Carstairs' voice filled with a mixture of relief and bewilderment at the sound of Ben's voice. 'Benedict! I thought you were—'

'Dead,' Ben said. 'Funny, I thought that myself. As I'm sure you must know by now, the operation was a washout. The others aren't coming home.'

'But . . . you are?'

'Apparently so,' Ben replied. 'And I won't be alone. I have Spartan.'

Carstairs was incredulous, quite speechless, and it took him a long moment to get over his shock. 'W-where is he?'

'Standing here right next to me,' Ben said. 'You want to speak to him, to verify that I'm not bullshitting you?'

Richard took the phone. 'This is me. Yes, yes, it's really me and for Christ's sake stop calling me Your Highness,' he said irritably after listening for a moment. 'I'm just Richard, okay? Now I'm going to hand this call back over to Ben, because frankly I don't want to talk to you people.'

Ben took the phone. For a dried-out, implacable old vulture of a man, Carstairs was able to produce an outpouring of joy and gratitude that sounded almost human. 'All right, Carstairs,' Ben said when he'd heard enough of his waffle. 'Here's the deal. If you want him, you're going to have to come and get him at this location, along with sixty-four orphaned children and their guardian for whom I require safe transport out of the country, together with two Afghan citizens, several foreign nationals including a US citizen and a wounded SAS veteran, and a number of our dead who have to be returned to their families.'

'I can't possibly manage all that,' Carstairs blurted, wasting no time in reverting back to his officious manner. 'You're going to have to get to the same drop zone near the eastern border. That's the only way I can hope to get the authority for a pick-up. Have you any idea what kind of major international incident we risk sparking off otherwise, flying deep over Taliban airspace?'

'I thought you already had a major international incident on your hands,' Ben told him. 'Don't fuss over details, Colonel. You can spoil a good thing by over-thinking it.'

Madison smiled.

'It's my job to think,' Carstairs said defensively.

'Are you thinking now?' Ben asked him.

'Of course I bloody am.'

'Then think about how else I'm supposed to transport sixty young kids all the way back beyond Kabul, with no motor vehicles and troops all over the place. And trust me, after today they're going to be fairly well stirred up.'

'Forget the children,' Carstairs snapped, digging in. 'That's completely out of the question. Are you out of your mind?'

Richard held out his hand for the phone. 'Let me talk to him again.' He took the phone from Ben, and without giving Carstairs a chance to speak, he said, 'Now listen to me, you horrible little dirtbag. If you don't shift your fucking arse to do exactly what my friend Ben tells you to do, then you can forget about me, because I'm not coming back at all. And I mean it.'

Carstairs blustered as best he could, but the prince was leaving him no choice. Defeated, he sighed, 'Let me call you back.'

'Well done, Princey,' Wolf said, clapping Richard on the back. 'Maybe you won't make such a shitty king after all, when your time comes.'

Carstairs called back very soon afterwards. A lot had happened during those few minutes. Sounding as he didn't quite know whether to laugh or cry, he informed Ben that it had been arranged for a Chinook with RAF fighter support to come and pick them up at their chosen location within the next few hours. Apparently, some things were worth risking a major international incident over.

'Amazing what you can get done with the right connections,' Wolf commented. 'Now what?'

'Now we wait,' Ben said. 'And hope the soldiers don't come back.'

Chapter 52

Hours passed. The setting sun made a spectacular blaze in the east that lit up the whole landscape in a final brilliant, incandescent flourish before nightfall, but nobody was watching. They bided their time with the unpleasant task of seeing to the bodies of Holt, Baldacci, Nielsen, Liebowitz, Schultz and the fallen Pathfinders.

The soldiers didn't come back.

By the time evening had fallen and the mountain chill was setting in, the tribesmen had long ago mounted their horses and melted away into the hills. Two more hours dragged by before Ben and the others finally heard the distant thud of the Chinook in the night sky, its sound growing and growing until eventually the vast dark shape of the twin-prop helicopter was coming in to touch down on the gentler slopes near the orphanage, lights blinking, engines roaring, whipping up a dust storm from its huge rotors.

'Now there's a sight for sore eyes,' said Nobby Scraggs, in a voice weak with pain and blood loss.

They said goodbye to their base camp and made their way down the dark hillside to meet the idling helicopter. Some of the children were terrified of the enormous machine while others, with the resilience of youth, were jumping with excitement even after the horrors of the day. As the fighter jets circled overhead on the lookout for potential trouble, RAF personnel helped load the children aboard the Chinook's huge passenger bay. Scraggs was placed on a stretcher and given paramedic care, while the bodies of the dead were stowed in the cargo area with as much ceremony as time allowed – considering that they were intruding on forbidden territory and risking sparking off a serious international flap just by their presence here.

The last items to be loaded aboard were Madison's treasure casket and the bundle containing the Greek soldier's armour, both of which drew a lot of curious looks from the Chinook crew. Thankfully, Ben had drawn the line at bringing the Greek's skeletal remains along for the ride as well, much to Madison's disappointment.

'Well, that's your retirement fund sorted, anyhow,' Wolf said to her, as they lashed her valuables securely in the cargo hold.

'Nothing of the kind,' she retorted. 'This stuff is going straight to a museum.'

'Right,' Wolf said knowingly. 'That's how your dad got so rich.'

'I resent that accusation. I wouldn't dream of keeping any of it for myself.' Then a sly smile slowly spread on her lips. 'Except *maybe* just a couple of tiny trinkets that they'll never miss.'

'Keepsakes of your Afghan holiday,' Wolf said.

'I'd suggest a nice Mediterranean cruise next time,' said Ben.

'Except then you won't come and rescue me.'

'I don't know about that,' he replied. 'I could do with a holiday.'

'Hey,' she said. 'There's always San Diego.'

Ben was last to board the Chinook as it prepared for take-off. Halfway up the tailgate ramp he turned and looked to the west, to see the distant lone figure of the horse and rider perched on the crest of the escarpment, a billion glittering stars in the background.

Ben didn't know if Khan Zada could see him from so far away, but he raised a hand in a wave. As though in reply, the stallion reared up on its hind legs, magnificently silhouetted against the night sky. Then the warlord wheeled his horse around and was gone.

Some hours later they landed in Abu Dhabi, where an envoy from the US Embassy had been dispatched to collect the bodies from the aircraft and arrange for their journey home. For what it was worth, Ben had already decided to write to each of the families in person, expressing his condolences and telling them how their loved ones had died bravely doing the right thing. Would that make their loss any easier to bear? He didn't know.

Meanwhile, Nobby Scraggs was taken to hospital for his wounds, promised the best medical care in the world. And needless to say, the expected men in suits, six of them toting submachine guns, were waiting eagerly to receive the prince and stuff his precious person into a bullet-proof limousine. 'Wait,' he told them, sounding quite authoritative. The suits milled uncomfortably around as Richard came to shake hands with Ben, Wolf and Madison, and thank them once again for what they'd done for him. 'I won't forget it.'

'You mean we have friends in high places now?' Wolf chuckled. 'That's a first.'

'So long, honey bunny,' Madison said, giving the prince a goodbye peck on the cheek. No doubt the first time in history that a British royal personage had ever been publicly addressed as honey bunny, and probably the last.

Early next morning, the children were taken under special escort to their new temporary home in a comfortable humanitarian camp, along with Francine and Father Bugnolio, who were already discussing plans to set up a new Christian mission somewhere safer than Afghanistan. There were emotional scenes as they said goodbye. The last thing Ben, Wolf and Madison saw of them was little Gulnaz waving from the window of the minibus as they drove off.

From Abu, duly cleaned up, rested and fed with a few stitches and dressings for their minor wounds, Ben and Wolf in crisp new western clothing and Madison wearing a black T-shirt and jeans, the remaining trio departed for England on an RAF cargo jet. They were met at the military airfield by Carstairs and a team of secret service men.

Carstairs was all smiles, and delivered a very long and very dull spiel that droned on until its concluding words, 'And on behalf of HM Government, allow me once again to express our sincerest gratitude for your services to your country.'

Ben and Wolf looked at one another. Wolf said, 'With all due respect, Colonel, you have my permission to shove that where monkeys shove their nuts. Now if you'll kindly get me on a private jet to Spain asap, I'll be on my way.'

'Till next time, Jaden,' Ben said as they parted ways a little while later. 'Try and stay out of trouble, eh?'

'That'll be the day,' Wolf replied. Then with a last flash of a golden grin, he turned and walked away.

'I suppose I'll be off home myself pretty soon,' Ben said when he and Madison were alone again, or as alone as they could be with a bunch of secret service suits still hanging shiftily about in the background.

'Aren't you forgetting something?' she asked, arching one eyebrow. 'You owe me a cold beer.'

Ben made a big deal out of looking at his watch. 'Oh, I think I might just about have time to squeeze that in. As long as you're quick.'

'Asshole,' she said in the sweetest way, beaming at him.

A luxurious government car – black of course – sped them into London, where they quickly managed to escape from the suits and made their way to an upmarket bar in the heart of Soho. Madison got her promised beer in a tall frosted glass. Ben ordered a triple Laphroaig, fifteen years old, no ice, no water, the way it was meant to be drunk. They sat at a corner table, relaxing for the very first time in a long while, and Ben lit up a cigarette from his new pack. Let the management come and throw him out, if they dared.

'A little different from Afghanistan,' she said, gazing around her at the glitzy decor and the bustling traffic outside.

'Missing it already, are you?'

She smiled. 'Oh, you never know, one day I might go back there to rediscover what we found.'

'If there's anything left of it.'

'But in the meantime, there's so much else out there waiting for us,' she said. 'No more war zones, I swear.'

He paused with his glass halfway to his lips. 'Who's us?'

Madison shrugged. 'I figured you might like a change of scene. Be fun to have you along. Partners. Fifty-fifty.'

Ben shook his head. 'I already have a job, thanks. All this travelling around wears me out. And I miss my dog.'

She laughed. 'You always were the boring stay-at-home type.'

'Yup. That's me all over.'

'You'll change your mind.'

'I doubt that.'

'Still,' she said, raising her glass. 'A girl can always live in hope.' They clinked.

'Cheers, Ben.'

'Cheers, Madison.'

Acknowledgements

The author wishes to thank 'Soldier X', a.k.a 'Bawbag' for the military weapons and tactical advice that proved invaluable in writing this book. Your generous help made Ben's adventure feel all the more real to me, and, I hope, to the readers too.

Special thanks also to my wonderful editor Genevieve Pegg and the rest of the team at HarperNorth, where the Ben Hope series has found its happy new home.